38

2^{00}

FIC
2/17

WEDDING CAKES, RATS *and* RODEO QUEENS

WEDDING CAKES, RATS *and* RODEO QUEENS

ANNE CAMERON

HarperCollins*PublishersLtd*

First Edition

Canadian Cataloguing in Publication Data

Cameron, Anne, 1938-
Wedding cakes, rats and rodeo queens

ISBN 0-00-224001-7

I. Title.

PS8555.A5187W44 1994   C813'.54   C93-095384-3
PR9199.3.C35W44 1994

94 95 96 97 98 99 ❖ FP 10 9 8 7 6 5 4 3 2 1

Printed in Canada

For Liz, who knows Mz Kitty is alive and well;

for Constance, who looked me in the eye and opened a door which has allowed me to deal patiently (well, maybe not patiently!) with a whole bunch of stuff;

and most especially for Eleanor, who provided the title, the best lines and the happiest times of my life.

WEDDING CAKES,
RATS *and*
RODEO QUEENS

The flashing lights were all over the bridge and the abutment leading to the busy street. The burning sportscar was reduced to a melted hunk of plastic and metal, with emergency crews spraying foam on it from one side, water from another. The driver of the truck was on his knees, retching violently, while an ambulance attendant tried to give him a shot of something.

The kid sat on Kitty's hip, his legs locked around her body, his arms clutching tight around her neck. The jacket covered him from the neck down; it kept the winter rain from soaking him, and it ought to have kept him warm, but he was shivering so hard she wondered if the gristle in his joints would come loose and he'd collapse like a little bag of sticks.

She moved toward a cop who stood in an ankle-length slicker, waving traffic past with the help of a flashlight. The slicker was glittery with rain, bright with the reflection of the headlights. She saw pale faces like balloons staring from car windows, the mouths round Os, the eyes wide, eating up the sight of the burning gasoline, the flaming, melting plastic.

The cop turned his head, barely glanced at her. "Move along, lady," he said, sounding bored.

"Officer...," she started.

"Come on, lady, gimme a break here, will you?" His boredom was replaced by impatience.

"This little guy...."

"Lady! This is no place for a kid! Come on, please, don't push me on this. Get him away from here, please."

And the JimmySpook was suddenly dancing on the cop's hat, cavorting and pointing at her, mocking her, telling her she was barking up the wrong tree, this wasn't what she was supposed to be doing.

The cop watched her and something in the line of his jaw, the waiting expression in his eyes, told her he knew more, far more, than there was any sane reason to expect him to know. She almost tried one more time, but then the kid whimpered.

It wasn't much as decisions go. It wasn't well considered, it wasn't carefully thought out, it wasn't much of anything except maybe a buh-zillion memories. She didn't say anything, but the tense and waiting look went from the cop's eyes and was replaced by something she was pretty sure was approval.

She turned from the cop, retraced her steps and went around the edge of the bridge to the beaten footpath leading down the steep, slippery slope. The kid clung to her; at least the gut-deep grunts of fear had eased; he was breathing with deep, shuddering gasps, but his teeth had stopped chattering.

"Easy on, old guy," she said. "Easy on there, we'll figure something out." He buried his face against her neck and held on for dear life, held on the way a baby monkey might hang on, or a possum, maybe. They didn't belong here, but they'd begun to appear, either forced out of their natural habitat by housing developments or, more likely, because for a while they'd been *the* pet-of-the-week for the bored and overprivileged, who'd all too quickly lost interest and probably thought they were doing a kind thing by taking Pete and Polly Possum for a ride in the car, then letting them out in the brush along a seldom-used side road or skidder trail. Now people with chickens not only needed raccoon traps, they needed possum traps. When they caught the old lady possum the babies would cling to her even after she was dead, and cold, and stiff.

She'd carried Victor like a football that awful night so long ago, her arm under his back, his little baby head cupped in her hand, but later on, much later, after that awful nightmare time, during a summer vacation that just seemed to flow on forever, golden and soft, he'd sat on her hip like this kid and gripped her around the neck and trusted her even when she said, Vic, we're going to jump now, off this bank and into the creek. So plug your nose, Bubba, because *here we go!* He'd been scared just about shitless but he hung on, and when they came up out of the water he even managed a laugh. It was shaky, it was thin, it wouldn't have convinced anybody, but he did it all the same. So she laughed and wiped the long hair from his eyes and asked, Want to do'er again, Bubba? He didn't, but he nodded and they did'er again, then again, until all the scared feelings were replaced by the thrill of jumping and splashing. By the time Jimmy showed up with the fried chicken and potato salad, Vic was able to stand on the rock, nod, then jump into the pool, where Kitty was standing ready to scoop him up the instant he hit the water.

He sat next to her on the grass, the sun warming his creek-chilled body, packing away food, his shivering becoming less and his dark hair drying and springing out from his head in all directions. Lucy offered him the bowl of chicken and he smiled widely, took a piece, then made a little joke about how Lucy was his great-aunt, and a great great-aunt to have.

And the next day he went cannonballing off the bank as if there had never been one minute of his life when he'd been afraid. YaHOO, he yelled, last one in's the cow's tail!

Except this Bubba wasn't going to find much thrill in repeating anything like this. Small wonder! Only a total goof would want to repeat it!

She made her way to the dry area under the bridge and hunkered with her back against one of the concrete support pillars. Then she pried the kid from around her neck and held him tight against her chest, making those soft sounds that say nothing but mean everything. And the JimmySpook was hauling at the pocket of the expensive jacket, dragging at it. "Well, all *right*, then, christ, don't get your sticks in a knot."

Stuffed inside was a small purse, a woman's small purse. There was an identification card, one of those cheap printed name, address, phone number things, and marked in the spaces, in blobby ballpoint, printed awkwardly as if a kid in grade six had done it, some information. In the bottom of the little purse, in with eye glup and lipstick and tobacco dust and assorted useless crap, was a house key.

The JimmySpook somersaulted and waved his silly fist, made some idiotic faces and was gone. "Okay, Bubba." She stood and adjusted the five-year-old's weight. "Okay, Bubba, in for a dime, in for a dollar," and she headed back up the same stupid footpath to where she knew she could probably, with just a bit of help from the fright-mask only she could see, manage to flag down a cab.

The driver didn't seem to notice anything the least bit odd in a woman holding a kid wrapped in some guy's jacket. Maybe when you wrap a kid in something that cost at least six hundred dollars, the world pulls in its horns and overlooks other things, like the fact the kid is terrified, or that the legs sticking out from under the jacket are naked and goose-pimpled and have marks on them obviously left by a belt. The world is so goddamned good at minding its own business. Thousands of people have died because the nice people of the world were busy minding what they had decided was their own little-bitty bit of business. Other things, things you'd think were nobody's damned business but your own, the voting public of high renown would turn itself inside out to pick over, snoop into, remark upon and judge. You can live under a bridge unnoticed and unmourned, but don't try to teach school if you're like Glen's friends. Now wasn't that something. There they were, same family and all, and there was Glen and then there was Kitty. So was it the genes, the chromosomes, or just the only piece of really good luck you were ever given? Scrawled graffiti on the wall of the women's washroom in the bus depot in Vancouver: "My mother made me a les-bian." And under it someone else had written, "Wow, if I buy her the wool will she make me one, too?" Then under *that*, "Is your mom inter-ested in a franchise?" and "Will she take on an apprentice?" followed by "Do you suppose there's a retraining grant for those willing to learn the trade?" Kitty had snickered and imagined an entire softball team com-ing back from a tournament, lining up with their indelible markers, making their statements and laughing like happy loons. She wished she could meet the one who had the bright red marker and had written, "The nicest thing about being a dyke is being a dyke."

She didn't try to have a conversation with the cabby, and he seemed totally uninterested in starting one. She just sat holding the kid on her lap, her arms firm, his body pressed tight, his head under her chin, his face soft against her throat. He trembled, his hands clutching her sleeve, but the whimpering noises had stopped.

The apartment wasn't one at all, it was a basement suite. A couple of cement-floored, cement-bricked rooms. One of them was supposed to be a combo, kitchen/dining room/living room. The other was a bedroom just about big enough to swing a kitten, never a cat. The air smelled old and stale; too many cigarettes had been smoked in here, too many beer tops had been popped, and there wasn't enough hot water and Murphy's oil soap to scrub the place clean, make it smell like somewhere you'd want to spend your time. Lord God, there wasn't even a dizzy-lizzy plant, not even a dying-of-thirst cactus. If anything at all was growing, it was probably growing in the fridge, but Kitty didn't check to see if it was green glup or gray goo.

The way the kid swung willingly to the floor and moved confidently to the fridge told her that this was what passed for home. "Jesus, boy, looks to me like you ought to fire the hired help, the housekeeper hasn't shown up for a long time." He just looked at her, then reached into the fridge and hauled out a can of Coke. He pulled the tab and guzzled thirstily, then moved to the ratty sofa and sat up on it, the long sleeves of the jacket getting in his way. But he was too cold to take it off, and simply kept pushing the sleeves up his arms; as soon as he moved his hands the sleeves slid down again, and he'd push them up so they could slide down some more.

Kitty looked through the place. Nothing to write home about. Not enough food to feed PatsyRatsy. Some clothes, but hardly any of them fit the kid, and what did was so ratty he was better off in the damned jacket. The smell of dirty clothes and stale urine filled the place. And the JimmySpook was glaring at her as if she had rocks where her brains ought to be. Not only no plants, no books, either. You'd think maybe what Gran had called Diddycoys had lived here. Leave at a moment's notice.

She sat on the sofa, with no idea at all what to do, and the kid crawled on her lap. She put her arms around him and gave him a squeeze. That's when she felt the lump in the jacket. She opened it and from the inside breast pocket pulled out a wallet. There was still something in the pocket, and she dug for it. A key.

"Jesus, and aren't we the ones, two in one day, I guess that's what they'd call a co-inky-dinky."

"Parlee voo," he replied.

She stared, then hugged him so tightly his breath whooshed from his throat. "Right on, guy. Inky dinky parlez-vous. Let's go."

The second cab took the last of her money, save for a few coins in her jeans pocket. Well, wasn't she supposed to come with nothing? Okay, so here she was.

The key opened the front door of the building. Now how in hell did they manage that? Each individual apartment had its own lock and key but each individual key could also open the main lock? Fuck, what'd they think of next? Maybe it was some Star Trek kind of deal where there was a mark or something on the tip of the key, or maybe it was magnetic or non-magnetic and all it had to do was touch something else. What the hell difference did it make HOW it worked, it worked. Kept the lowlifes, the trash and the unwanted out on the street, with only the washed and rewashed allowed inside.

Well, fine, and now we're in and what good does that do us, there's no number on the key. The kid pointed to the elevator, so she walked to it and pressed the call button. When the door slid open she stepped inside and JimmySpook was already there, grinning sarcastically. Or maybe not sarcastically, who knew what in hell *his* damned expression meant? He pushed a button on the panel and the doors slid shut. She didn't bother trying to talk to him, she just shifted the kid's weight on her hip and concentrated on handing over control, she didn't want any, she didn't need any, she probably wouldn't be able to handle any. Let the JimmySpook have it.

When the elevator stopped and the door slid open, she stepped out into the hallway. The kid pointed. He'd been here before, obviously. Well, okay, go in the direction indicated. Maybe someone knows what's going on around here. Be nice if somebody did.

And there was the JimmySpook again—how did he do that, stay in the elevator, then get to the door ahead of you? Leaning on the door, waiting. Just waiting.

This wasn't a basement suite smelling of old clothes and stale urine. This wasn't too trashy at all. A person could get used to a place like this. Fish in a big tank, carpet on the floor, one of those entertainment console things where you could sit in a chair and aim a gizmo and have just about anything you wanted from radio to television.

Bathroom alone was bigger than the place the kid had lived. Tanning light set into the ceiling. The kid wasn't easy in this place, however, and clung to her, his body stiff.

"Considering where you came from and considering where I came from, there are two people in this place who don't belong."

The JimmySpook moved to the fridge, opened the door, then slammed the palm of his hand on the freezer compartment. And vanished. The fridge door started to shut. Kitty moved quickly, grabbed the door, stopped its swing and opened the freezer. She pulled some fast-food dinners from inside and dropped them on the counter. "Don't know what you had for supper, Bubba, but I think I forgot to indulge myself."

She microwaved the stuff, then sat across the imitation marble-topped table in the nook. The food was hot and probably still had a vitamin or two trapped in it somewhere. The kid wolfed his, but didn't finish it all. His eyes drooped, he looked around helplessly, then got off his chair and moved to stand beside her, looking hopeless, vulnerable and achingly too much like a couple of little guys he had never even heard of.

She put him to bed, and sat beside him until he closed his eyes and his breathing deepened. She wondered if he expected everyone to become sexual with him. Maybe he thought that was affection. Maybe that was why he looked at her as if he expected...something. Or maybe she imagined that look of guarded preparedness. Maybe what she felt tightening in her gut was coming only from her. Maybe she was just as sick as all shit. Maybe...what? But she had to admit, if only to herself, that for a moment there, looking at him, seeing that look on his face, that weary Oh Well look in his eyes, she had felt...something...and she didn't know for sure what it was but she knew she was shocked. It was so similar to what she had felt when she was trying to figure things out, trying to find answers to questions she couldn't even put into words, questions that had started bubbling when Mike had, well, never mind what.

She had wanted to find out why. And what. If she could figure out the what, she might know the why. What was it he felt that was so nice for him that it didn't matter that she cried with pain? What was so good that you could listen to the weeping and not feel anything? If she could feel whatever it was that must feel so good, maybe she'd know why he didn't care when she said, Please, no, don't do it again, Mike, it hurts. Maybe if she could find out the what she'd know the why, and understand why even blood didn't matter, not hers, anyway.

Except she didn't want to. She just did not want to. There couldn't be anything so good it was worth hurting something that small and uncomprehending. She didn't want to because she'd hate herself and then need to do it again just to feel good in spite of the hating. She didn't want to because, if she hated herself, how could Christie possibly continue to love her? Even if Christie never *knew*, she'd sense a change, a difference, a rottenness, and Christie wouldn't love any touch of anything like that. And even if there was no Christie, Kitty didn't want to because it wasn't what she wanted to do or be or become, or pass on to the kid himself.

She rolled a cigarette, smoked half of it and then went through the woman's little purse again. Behind the buckshee hand-lettered identification paper was a small plastic card, not quite the same as a credit card, but about that size and shape. "Well, weren't you a nice Christmas Eve present for somebody?" She patted the sleeping child. "If I had a kid born on Christmas Eve, I'd probably call him Noel, too. I'd probably have passed on the Mark, though, it's no fun trying to make your way in the playground with kids calling you Easy Mark, Dumb Mark, or writing Xs on your forehead and yelling Marked This One."

He stirred in his sleep. His arm moved, his hand found its way to his face. He almost put his thumb in his mouth—his lips opened to accept the thumb but his hand went slack and fell back on the pillow. His eyelids fluttered, his lashes long and thick. Spiderlegs, the Old Biddy called them. Close your eyes and let me see your spiderlegs.

The feeling in her gut altered. The tightness became another kind of tension. She brushed the hair off his face and thought of the twig-legged foals, how hard it was to just stand there and wait while they struggled to get upright, their hoofs still soft. Time and again they fell. Time and again it was an exercise in self-restraint not to rush in and try to help them. Time and again only the sure knowledge that if anyone helped, the foal was ruined for life. It might never get up without help, it might be such a fraidy it wouldn't leave its own stall, it might wind up fit for nothing but the goddamn dogfood can, all because it got a boost instead of learning it could do things itself. Weird, that one.

She heard a crackling sound, like winter brush rubbing against itself in a strong wind. It was the JimmySpook, prowling, snooping, working himself into some kind of rage again. And couldn't YOU get just a tad tiresome!

She followed the JimmySpook from room to room. There was more money hanging in the clothes closet than she saw in a full year. Nothing but the best labels. In a top drawer she found credit cards, keys and a leather box holding enough gold chains, rings and expensive watches to set up your own store. Somebody was living high off the hog. And that poor little bruised bugger on the bed probably paid for every bauble in the box. For which he got nothing, not even a thank-you. Life is truly wonderful, if you can overlook a few basic inherent flaws.

She pulled off her boots, stubbed out her cigarette and lay on the bed beside the kid. The last thing she intended to do was go to sleep, but the next thing she knew it was early morning and the JimmySpook was cavorting around the place, grinning his fright-mask grin. He pointed at the door and gave her the "do it" glare. She looked toward the still-sleeping child but JimmySpook was shaking his head. So far nothing he'd done had made her life any worse than it would have been without him, so she got up, pulled on her boots and followed him.

He didn't go four blocks down the street before he was pointing and making faces, shoving something into the pocket of her jacket. When she pulled it out, it was cash, lots of cash. She stared at it, then went where the stick person was insisting she go. Wasn't that a trip—walking through the store, waiting to be told what to choose, and nobody else could see the one doing the choosing.

When she walked out ten minutes later she had a shopping bag, and in it the things the JimmySpook had insisted she get.

Breakfast was just about ready when Noel wakened. He sat up, looked around, scared stiff until he saw her.

"Hey, Noel, it's okay," she lied. He got out of bed and headed to the bathroom. She heard the sound of him peeing, heard the toilet flush, heard water run in the basin, and then he was coming to the table, obviously ready to eat until he burst.

She cleaned up after them. Did the dishes, put them away, straightened the bed, the whole domestic routine. And then she took the price tags off the clothes, and dressed the kid. Everything fit, even the sneakers. Noel stroked his clothes, looked at her and smiled. "Thanks," he said shyly. She wanted to tell him it wasn't her, but instead she just smiled and said, "You look terrific." She lifted him to the dressertop, let him stand there seeing himself in the big mirror. "See the monkey?" she teased. He looked at her and nodded, but didn't grin. Instead, he sat down and began to look through the collection of booty. He tried a watch, but it was far too big for his skinny wrist and fell off; he picked it up and grabbed for Kitty's arm.

"Hey, guy," she protested. The kid just shook his head, Shut up I say, and tugged the expansion bracelet over her hand. Then he delved into the collection of chains and started slipping them over his head. "Didn't anyone tell you?" Kitty reached for her rollings. "One or two of'em's nice, but too many are tacky. And we must avoid at all costs anything close to tacky." What did he care, he just kept draping himself, looking up and admiring his reflection. "Don't be vain," she chanted, "you'll make it rain."

Mz Kitty laughed and left the villains for Matt and Chester to deal with. Why do it yourself when there are drones available? She had other fish to fry, a whole kettle of fish. Let the posse round up the guys in black hats, Mz Kitty was rounding up the remuda. Did you ever wonder what happened to all those friggin' horses in all those friggin' movies? All those bad guys shot and falling from the saddle, and the pintos, appaloosas, blue roans and buckskins just vanish from the screen, run right off the left-hand edge and are never seen again. The friggin' badlands must have been knee-deep in them, bloodstained saddles slowly rotting away, reins snapped off and dangling. Hope to god the bridles rotted enough the poor beast could spit out the bit.

And the wagon trains, too. All those rivers to cross, and in every movie they have to unload the cherished furniture, Oh no, the woman mourns, not my grandmother's chiffonier, she brought it all the way from Wherever and gave it to me when I got married. Oh no, not my great-grandmother's four-poster bed, we were all born in it, my children were born in it, Sorry says the wagonmaster, we'll never make it over the river if we try to take it.

Didn't anyone just tag along behind with a whole pile of empty wagons and pick up the discards? You could leave anywhere Back East without a pot to pee in or a window to throw it out of, and head Westward Ho collecting discards, then arrive in Pleasant Valley or Bountiful or Over the Rainbow with a fine collection of grandmothers' treasures.

Well, you could bet your last hope for salvation that Mz Kitty wasn't going to let any of that slide past *her*! No, by god, she'd do what the kid did, find the gold lockets or whatever and very calmly and wisely slip them into her pocket. Never look a gift horse in the mouth, it might snap your nose off your silly face.

JimmySpook jumped up and down, danced, ricocheting off the walls and laughing soundlessly as he led her all the way down to the underground carpark, then sat on the hood of a near-new, display-lot shiny four-by-four. She put the keys in the door lock and they worked, the door opened and Noel bounced inside. Kitty crossed behind the truck to the driver's side. JimmySpook was stuffing something into the back of the four-by. She looked, shook her head; it was a small satchel and she knew that inside it was probably everything that was worth anything at all. He put the satchel on top of a medium-sized suitcase, how in hell had *that* got in there? Taking it seemed wrong, it seemed sick, it seemed like something nobody would do, but she wasn't going to argue. And really, wasn't that part of it? You didn't just raid your enemy, you raided him and then insulted the shit out of him by taking something he prized. And anyone who would sell baby flesh to diseased minds probably prized his gold chains and Cartier watches more than life, as long as it wasn't his own, of course. How did they manage that? How did they manage to talk endless hours of drivel about Jenny Craig or Weight Watchers or Diet Center or whatever and not feel a bit odd about the fact that they were paying something like thirty-four dollars a pound to lose the weight they'd put on by stuffing themselves with the best of food while fifteen million kids a year starved to death? How could they wallow in too much of everything and still sit watching some TV show about life on the garbage dumps of the third world? Why was *their* life so frigging all-important and everyone else's wasn't? How did they manage that one?

The four-by started easily, and she let it sit warming up while she fastened the seatbelt for the kid, then did up her own. The JimmySpook had decided to ride on the hood, right in front of the passenger's seat where Noel was perched, looking around eagerly. For a minute she thought maybe...and then the kid grinned and nodded, and not in her direction. The JimmySpook wrinkled his nose, stuck out his tongue, and Noel laughed. Then the boy wrinkled his own nose and stuck out his tongue and she knew she wasn't the only nutcase who could see what nobody would notice as they drove through the heavy morning traffic.

"So, what do you think?" she said easily. "You think everything's going to be tickety-boo?"

"Yup," Noel wriggled in his seat, settled himself comfortably.

Kitty backed out of the parking space and drove toward the exit. The JimmySpook had a flute in his hands; it looked suspiciously like the one she'd seen in a glass case the day before, at the museum. He lifted the flute to his lips and began to play a song she only heard in the marrow of her bones.

"Guess we'll go get Christie and the dog," she said companionably, checking the street before pulling out into traffic. "Then, well, I guess we'll see what we see. Maybe take time off for a while. There's this school I could go to, teaches you how to be a rodeo clown without gettin' yourself killed. Might think about that. No damn need to smash every bone in my body, right? Maybe we'll go see Savannah and Seely and catch up on some of those reruns." She took her hand off the wheel long enough to pat Noel on the knee. "You ever watch 'Gunsmoke'?"

"Yup," he nodded.

"You know Mz Kitty?" she asked.

"Uh-huh." He was pulling faces at the JimmySpook again.

"You think she and Matt are lovebirds?"

"Naw," Noel shook his head. "Gimme a break, eh?"

PART
ONE

1

Nobody had come home. Seely woke up first, and the noise she made rummaging around and looking for something that could pass in a pinch for breakfast woke the others.

"How come you have to make so much noise?" Kitty snapped. "Can't you open and close cupboard doors without slammin' em?"

"Oh shut up, who asked you?"

"Talk to me like that and you'll have knuckles for breakfast."

"Oh shut up, yourself!" Savannah wailed. "Just shut up, okay?"

They found some oatmeal in a bag but it had creepies in it. So that was that, even though they all made jokes about free protein and meat-without-feet. The last bit of bread had blue furze growing on it but they cut off the crusts and wiped off the slices; it tasted funny, but wasn't too bad if you kind of toasted it on top of the old woodstove. Except the woodbox was almost empty and they couldn't get a hot enough fire to really toast the bread.

The boys were mad when they found out the girls had eaten all the bread. Glen gave Savannah a punch in the head, and if it had been either of the others he might even have been rewarded with tears, but Savannah just called him a fuckin' jerkoff asshole. He went at her to give her another good punch but Jimmy shoved him out of the way. "Smarten up," Jimmy yelled. "Just smarten up, okay?"

"Fine'en," Glen said sullenly, "be that way."

There were a few teabags, but the stove wasn't hot enough to get the water going to make tea. Finally, even though they knew they were going to catch hell for it, they jimmied open the window. It wasn't easy. Fred had done a real job on the windows, not because he was afraid someone would break in and steal something, there was bugger-all worth bothering about in the entire house, but because the last time someone had gone out the window and over to Gran's place to tell her there was no food, Gran had pulled out most of the stops and raised absolute hell about it. Mom had cried and howled so much Fred had a gutful of it all and he took little pieces of lathing and nailed them in the slots where the windows were supposed to slide up and open, effectively sealing the windows.

Jimmy had to find a screwdriver and break away pieces of the lath until he could get the hammer prongs in and start reaming out the rest. Then the window went further up on one side than on the other, and jammed that way. But there was enough space there that Seely, who was the youngest, the smallest and the skinniest, could squirm through; except she got scared because the drop to the ground suddenly looked ten times as high as it really was.

She was hanging from the outside of the windowsill—sobbing and snottering and saying how scared she was and what if she got hurt or maybe broke her ankle and anyway what if Gran wasn't home or— when Glen smashed his fists on her fingers. Seely yelped, lost her grip and fell into the brambles. Wailing and scratched in a zillion places, she hightailed it toward Gran's.

"You bastard!" Jimmy yelled, and started pounding on Glen. Nobody cared, because Glen was such a pain in the ass at the best of times that they all kind of felt he had it coming. Except that he'd pay them back later. Glen always paid you back later. In spades and aces, Glen paid you back. But not Jimmy, he never tried to pay Jimmy back, because everybody knew Jimmy was kind of crazy.

Seely went up the front steps and through Gran's front door into the kitchen. She was still snottering and wailing. Just what Gran needed to kick off her day.

"Stop it." She heaved herself from her chair and grabbed Seely by the shoulders. "Stop it or I'll put you outside again."

So Seely stopped goobering and wiped her nose on her sleeve and told about the creepy-crawlies in the oatmeal and the blue stuff on the last of the bread and no wood, and Gran just nodded and went for the ax.

It took the old woman about two minutes maximum and there wasn't enough left of the front door to keep anyone in or out. "Come on," she said, and they did. She held the ax handle just below the metal head, and went back down the tip-tilty steps as if she was the drum major and the rest of them were the parade.

They knew there would be hell to pay, but not right now. Right now there would be something to eat. Supper hadn't been anything to waste time remembering, some macaroni with the last of the margarine pretending to be sauce. Lunch had been the same thing only there was more margarine then.

Gran put them to work. Jimmy went for wood, Glen had to slice up the pork jowl, Seely was told to wash the snot off her face, Kitty cracked eggs and Savannah sliced bread. Gran did the cooking. She even hauled out a big bowl of cold boiled potatoes she had probably put aside for her supper, and sliced them into the hot fat once the jowl was crisp and draining on a piece of newspaper.

They ate. They sat at the kitchen table with their elbows on the red-and-white-checked oilcloth cover and they ate enough to make up for the three days since the welfare check had arrived and Mom and Fred had gone on a toot. There was even dill pickle. Sometimes nothing else in the world would do it for you but a big garlicky dill pickle. You could eat sixteen loaves of bread and still feel hungry, but if you had just one big dill pickle you were fine.

And after they'd eaten as much as they could eat, Gran told them to start lining up for the bathtub. "There's nothing wrong with being poor," she scolded, "but no reason to be dirty."

While they were doing that, Gran went over to the house and stepped through what was left of the door. She looked for clean clothes for them but of course there weren't any, so she got the least dirty ones and took them back with her. By then Jimmy and Glen were out of the tub and scrubbed clean. "Go bring the washing," she ordered, and off they went, back to the house.

The washing machine was on the back porch with a piece of orange tarp over it, to keep the wind-driven rain from getting at the motor and rusting it so bad it wouldn't work any more. The first couple of loads had to be done in cold water because the hot-water tank was working overtime making bath water, but by the time the jeans, overalls and shirts were out on the line everyone was finished bathing and there was hot water for the underwear and white stuff, none of which had actually been white in a long, long time.

Part of the price of calling Gran in was that she never seemed to know when to stop. It wasn't enough that the door was smashed and the kids fed and bathed, it wasn't enough that everything they owned was flapping on the lines, no, back they all had to go and into the bedrooms and turn the mattresses and sweep dustbuggers out from under the bed and put this away put that away put something else away and when that's done get started in the kitchen. Except for the sharded door, the place looked better than it had looked since two months ago, when she'd made them all do the same thing.

Lunch would have been nice but she didn't give them any. They just worked, because there was no saying no to Gran. Fill the woodbox, then go to her place and split wood and fill her woodbox too. Feed the chickens. Pick beans in the garden. Take the scissors out and cut the tops off the beets. Do this do that do the next and don't sass back or you'll catch it on the side of the jaw.

But then she went into her kitchen and they knew she was getting a start on supper. That made them all work like hell, because if you slacked off or lipped back or something like that she'd just say, Well, if you don't do it you don't eat, and somehow they were all hungrier once their bellies had been filled than they had been before they sent SeelySnotFace out the gap in the window they couldn't get shut no matter how hard they tried.

For supper there was what Gran called stew-dee-roo: anything you could lay your hands on went into the big black cast-iron pot and simmered until it was done, then it got thickened into a sort of gravy and poured over mountains of mashed potatoes. She'd started this one with a rabbit, cooked it until the meat came off the bones; then, she said, she just stood on the other side of the kitchen and chucked everything she could lay a hand on, and what landed in the pot got cooked.

When it was safely packed inside them and the dishes were done, they all got so sleepy they could have slept in a heap of crumpled tin cans. Gran got three sleeping bags, laid two of them on the floor in her living room and put the third over the top with the quilt from her bed. No pillows—she said it gave you curvature of the spine.

Mom and Fred didn't get home until noon the next day. By then everyone had a good night's sleep and a huge breakfast, and had pulled every weed out of Gran's garden and stacked the end of the porch from floor to roof with split firewood.

Even before they saw the shattered door they knew Gran knew, because Gran was heading across the grassy space like a cavalry charge. Mom started to cry. Fred got all set to argue.

"If those little buggers have been bothering you, I'll whip ass," he blustered.

Gran never even looked at him. She just hauled off and hit Mom a whack on the jaw that set her on her ass on the side of the highway. Dust billowed up and Mom's crying got louder.

"Here, you, you better stop that shit," Fred yelled. He reached down to help Mom to her feet and Gran kicked him right where it hurt the most. He puked. Some of it landed on Mom, who wailed as if the world had been pulled out from under her feet.

"Trash!" the old lady roared. "No-good low-rent Irish filthy trash!" and she hit them both as hard as she could as often as she wanted.

Which only meant Fred was going to take it out on anyone he could. But not yet.

Gran grabbed Mom's purse, and just to be sure she hauled Fred's wallet out of his pocket too. She took them both home with her and emptied them onto the table. Fred didn't have anything much in his wallet, seven dollars was all. Mom had about a third of the welfare money left in her purse. Gran took it all and headed for the highway, yelling at the kids to come with her, and to hurry up, the goddamned bus would be there soon.

The bus driver made sure he didn't even look at them. He knew what he'd get if he did. He'd get the sharp side of Gran's Royal Scottish Tongue, is what he'd get.

They lined themselves side-by-each from tallest to smallest along the seat at the back of the bus, Gran by the one window and Seely by the other. Not a word was said on the twenty-minute trip into town. When Gran grunted, they stood up and filed down the aisle between the other seats, and when the bus stopped by Grainger's Superette they all trooped off like chicks following the broody hen.

Grainger's didn't say a word about the fact that there was a bill to be paid in the book. They could tell by the look on Gran's face and the fact she had the kids that the wigs were about to get tossed on the green and any outsiders who involved themselves were apt to wind up sorry they'd bothered. You just didn't piss around with the old lady, and that was that.

She bought in bulk, and she didn't get one single solitary pre-made thing. Not a cupcake, not a butter tart, not even a loaf of sliced bread. She didn't even get potatoes. She only got things that either weren't in her garden or had to have something else done with them before you could eat them, like oatmeal and cornmeal and yeast and lard and stuff like that. Macaroni and elbow spaghetti and those thick twisty-spiral noodles and a couple of great big packages of dried lentils, what-ever they were, and margarine and enough cheese to sink a barge.

And Grainger's rang it all up, packed it in boxes, and took the money and made change. It wasn't much. Gran looked at it and then looked at the kids. "Give them each a stick of hard candy," she said quietly, "and put what's left over on the tab."

Each of them got something to carry back to the bus stop. But once they were there, they were allowed to suck on the stick of hard candy. "No biting, no chewing," she warned, "you'll bust your teeth." So they sucked. That made it all last longer.

Finally, the bus arrived and they got on it and rode quietly back out the highway. Then they followed the old woman off the bus, waited for it to pull away, checked both ways for traffic, crossed the highway and headed through the afternoon heat to the house, where Fred was already bashing and banging away, trying to fix the door.

And then it was all done. The clothes had been brought back, dry, and more or less folded or crumpled together and sorted into piles, the food had been put away, the house was clean, and Mom was in her bedroom with the door shut, still sniveling and sobbing. Gran went home, her face like something carved out of stone.

Fred ignored them. He glared vicious promise at each of the kids but didn't dare do anything except keep trying to make some kind of door. That was fine. Maybe they'd get lucky and he'd ignore them for the rest of their lives.

Gran showed up once more, about long enough to put a box of garden stuff on the counter by the sink, and then she was gone again. Kitty figured she was being hard because what she really wanted was to take them all home and keep them there, except that would only end up with Mom wailing on the porch and Fred nagging at the back door, and in the end what could Gran do? They didn't belong to her directly, they only belonged to her indirectly, when the ones they really belonged to weren't at home.

Kitty and Savannah made supper, with the garden stuff and some sliced and fried-up baloney. As far as they were concerned Fred could starve to death in the ditch, but they knew he'd only go to the table and take someone else's food out from under their chin, so they made enough for him too. And Mom, of course, even though they knew she was going to sit and pick and poke and say how greasy the tube steak was and how she hated, just *hated*, boiled potatoes that hadn't been mashed and creamed and fixed up to seem as if they were anything except what they really were. While of course smoking one cigarette after another and twitching because there wasn't a drop to drink within a half-mile and she knew without asking that Gran had taken every cent she could find for no other reason than to make sure none of it wound up going on booze.

Jimmy and Glen left as soon as their bellies were full. "Hey!" Savannah yelled, "What about the dishes?" but they were off the way they always were. So Savannah and Kitty had to do dishes, too. Seely was falling asleep at the table.

They sent her to bed, and that was her for the night. Her ankle was still kind of blue and puffy and she had circles under her eyes. It was hard on Seely, and it was funny how she could manage things while they were coming down on her head but once the worst was over, she just sort of caved in at the middle, folded in on herself and let go, more easily than she'd let go of the windowsill. All Seel really wanted was a normal life, just an ordinary old everyday life like the kind other people got to live, with stairs that didn't tip'n'tilt and some kind of orderly routine.

2

Debbie Hawkins was worried sick about her sixteen-year-old son. He'd been acting as if he had a secret for the last two or three days, and when Chad acted that way chances were he *had* a secret, and when it surfaced the shit would hit the fan.

Finally, she couldn't keep it to herself another minute. She finished the last bottles of tomatoes, wiped her hands on a tea towel and went out to where Lucy was splitting wood and stacking it in the shed in anticipation of the next ice age. Lucy had enough wood put away already to keep half the nation's capital warm, but she couldn't stand to waste a stick of it. There'd been five acres of good second growth on the place but Donovan had logged it before he put the place up for sale; what he'd left behind in slash and trash was enough to rebuild downtown Vancouver, and Lucy had decided as much of it as possible was going to be firewood before the guy came with the excavator to stack it, burn it and give them another section of pasture.

Debbie told Lucy why she was fretting. Lucy just stood listening. Once in a while she nodded. It was like pulling teeth to talk to her but at least she didn't interrupt.

"And I think probably he's hanging around with the Jacobs boys, and drinking."

"Well, if they're drinking they have to get something to drink," Lucy pulled out her wallet, checked and even managed a grin. "Want to go for a beer or two?"

Deb went back into the house to change her shirt, because the one she had on was smeared with tomato. When she came back out again, the fan was just starting to whir into action.

The first of the breeze came in the form of about twenty-five riders who trotted down the driveway as if *they* had been the ones to buy the sixty acres when Donovan went tits up. Some of them had on funny pants and those velvet-covered tin baseball cap things that were enough to give you the pip. They rode straight to the water trough, dismounted and turned on the big tap. Deb looked at Lucy, Lucy looked at Deb, then Lucy walked over and spoke to the woman who seemed to be giving most of the orders.

The woman made the mistake of looking through Lucy as if she didn't really exist. "I'm sure," she said haughtily, "if you check with the owner, you will find this has all been arranged."

"Lady," Lucy said, dangerously quiet, "I *am* the owner."

"There has to be some mistake." The woman got, if possible, snottier than ever. "I made all the arrangements."

"Not with me, you didn't. What do you think you arranged?"

"Why, we're hunt-riding here." The woman sounded as if there wasn't a single thing a person would think of doing with the place other than ride all over it pretending to be chasing foxes.

The problem was made more acute by the fact that Lucy had never learned the least little thing about being assertive. Lucy went from being passive to having her teeth sunk in your throat. All or nothing. And that was when the phone rang and Debbie made the tactical error of going inside to answer it.

"What the *hell* is going on?" was the opening line. She recognized the voice. Her ex-husband. And was *he* steamed.

"Calm down," Debbie said automatically. How had she managed to go from one frying pan to another? Now, wouldn't ACOA have fun with this—live fourteen years with one skyrocketing temper, and then take up with another one, different gender, same dysfunction.

"Calm down? Me? You want I should calm down when...."

"*Shut up!*" She almost screamed it. "Tell me WHY you're bursting a blood vessel."

"Chad is here."

"Well, that's enough to make anyone burst a blood vessel, all right," she agreed.

"He says he hates it out there."

"He probably does. He doesn't fit in very well."

"He says he won't go back."

"Well, there you have it."

"Well *Jesus Christ Debbie how can anyone expect me to pick up on this one I hardly have enough time now to wipe my own butt I don't have time to look after this kid.*"

"Tell you what." She felt absolutely weary. She'd been hearing one version of this or another for too long. The almighty career. The harried, upwardly mobile workaholic. "You sit down with your son and figure out what it is he's acting out this time. Then the two of you go looking for someone who cares a bit more than I do." And she hung up.

Not fast enough, though. She got outside in time to see Lucy shouting into the face of the SnotSister. It all had to do with who would and who would not get on her blooded thoroughbred and get the helland-gone off the property about three times as fast as she had got onto it.

"But we *paid!*" the woman screeched.

"Not *me*, you didn't!"

And that was when the rest of it hit the fan. Over the woman's shoulder Lucy saw something in the twenty-acre hay field. Something big, something bulky, something fast and something with many heads. At the same time another several-headed something was streaking away from the side-pasture fence. Looked as if whatever it was had four heads, maybe five, and either sixteen or twenty legs.

Lucy headed for the pickup and Debbie was right behind her. Within seconds the pickup was going like hell, spewing gravel and small stones at the horses, which were shying in all directions, scaring the devil out of the horsy folk. The several heads split up and each rider went off in a slightly different direction, but Lucy knew where she was going. Or seemed to, which is sometimes just as good.

She'd have got there first if she'd been able to go cross-country, but the roads weren't built that way and the pickup wasn't a four-by, it couldn't leave the road. And no use asking her what was going on; when she was in this mood the best thing you could do was not get in her way. "Mesatchie" was what they called it at home.

The blue roan was still slick with sweat and lathered up when the pickup skidded to a halt and slewed almost sideways in the dirt in front of Carl Dakins' place. A skinny, sunburn-faced seventeen-year-old was trying his best to get the shed door open so he could disappear through the hole it would make. Lucy had the door open and her foot on the ground at the same time as her right hand grabbed the .303 from the good-ol'-boy rifle rack above the rear window.

"Oh *shit*, Lucy!" Deb managed.

And then the gun fired. The skinny sunburned kid froze, half in and half out of the doorway. Lucy grabbed him by one shoulder, spun him around and slammed him against the door, closing it tightly.

"Okay, idiot, what the hell is going on?"

"Nothing. Watch what you're doing or my dad'll make you sorry!" he tried to bluster.

"Nothing my backside!" She was past fury by now, she was ready to drink blood.

"Somethin' wrong?" A man just an inch too tall to be called Shorty came around the side of the shed. He looked at the half-insane Lucy and his mild blue eyes crinkled at the corners, but not with humor.

"Tell him," Lucy invited the boy.

"Go to hell!" The kid was nearly crying.

"Someone tell me," the man with the soft blue eyes asked. "Or I'm apt to jump into this without knowing which side I'm on."

"You his dad?" Lucy shouted.

"No, but I'm here."

"You get off our place!" The kid was shaking so bad his legs wanted to fold on him. And then Lucy put the barrel of the rifle right under his nose and the kid nearly barfed. "Tell him what's going on, little boy," she repeated.

"It was just a joke!"

"Am I laughing?"

"We didn't mean nothin'!"

"Tell him." Lucy was shaking nearly as badly as the kid was.

"We turned some cows into their field is all," he wept. "It was just a joke."

"Twenty acres of prime hay's worth of har har har!" Lucy yelled.

Debbie looked over at the man with the eyes, and the gun went off again. For one mad second she thought Lucy had killed the brat. But Lucy still had a hold on at least a few threads of sanity; she had moved the barrel of the gun. The slug had ripped a hole in the wall of the shed and Debbie could only pray there was nothing of any importance on the other side, like maybe the grandma of the place parked in her wheel-chair, or the baby bouncing in a Jolly-Jumper. The kid's knees gave out, he sat on his butt in the dirt and began to sob that he was sorry, it was just a joke, it wasn't his idea, the other guys made him do it.

"I'll take care of this," the quiet man with the blue eyes promised. Lucy looked at him as if she had no intention of believing him. They just stared at each other. Then he took out a small plastic pouch, opened it, pulled out his papers, got some tobacco and started to roll a smoke. He held the pouch out, wordless, and Lucy took it, nodding her thanks. Debbie could see tears burning in Lucy's eyes. Twenty acres of hay might not be much to Carl Dakins but it was make or break for them. "I'll take care of it," he repeated. Then, finally, he looked at the kid, really looked at him. "He'll tell me who the others are. He won't give me any trouble, he'll tell. And I'll see to it their fathers take care of it too. Kids," he finished, as if that explained it all.

Lucy went to the truck and put the damned rifle back in the good-ol'-boys rack, but she didn't get behind the wheel and drive away. She handed the keys to Debbie, then she went over to where the blue roan was still standing, nervous and dancing her feet. Debbie watched as Lucy checked the saddle, then swung herself up and touched heels to the horse. It started to walk away and the kid jumped to his feet, yelling, "My horse! What you doing with my horse?"

"She'll never get those cows out of the hay with a pickup truck," the blue-eyed man said quietly.

Debbie didn't believe that was why Lucy was taking the horse.

Debbie didn't ream the engine out of the truck on the way home the way Lucy had on her way there, she just drove normally and tried to figure out why she had spent her life praying for quiet and never get-ting it. Any time she heard anyone else moan about life being boring, Debbie was hit with such a rush of envy she could hardly hold herself together. She wished boring was something you could buy at the Superette, along with soda pop in big plastic torpedo-shaped bottles or bars of imported chocolate. But they didn't have it there, nor did they have it at the Drug Mart. She'd spent a lifetime looking for boring and hadn't found even a speck of it.

And with Chad at his father's place there was less chance of boring than there ever had been. The phone was going to ring off the hook—Chad phoning to yell and shout and complain, then his dad phoning to do more of the same. Probably a girlfriend or two would get in on it. Maybe the supervisor of the building where they lived. A schoolteacher or two, without doubt, and who knows, maybe she'd get another two-in-the-morning call from the local constabulary, although she doubted Bill would ever again leave his keys where Chad could find them and steal the BMW. And to think she and Bill had once talked about having three or four kids!

She parked the truck and went over to turn the water off at the trough. The horsy set was gone, and as near as she knew the only thing they'd done to pay back Lucy was leave the tap running. The area around the trough was mud; a few chickens pecked in it, cleaning up the drowned worms.

She looked over at the hay field but all she could see was cows moving around, flattening what they didn't eat, probably shitting all over what was supposed to have been the winter's hay. Their own cattle were still in the rough pasture, just staring at the newcomers. Wait long enough and they'd try to head into the hay field too.

She turned off the electric fence and shut the gate to the rough pasture, keeping their own herd out of the picture, then walked through the grazing pasture to open the gate. Maybe the bastards would come through on their own, maybe they'd see the ten Pinzgauers and decide they wanted to visit. Except it was never that easy with beef. What you wanted was the very last thing the damned cattle would do.

Then she saw Lucy at the outside fence, opening the gate. Well, who knew, maybe nobody would get trampled, crippled or killed. You could always hope.

At least Lucy knew how to ride. Funny the things you've been told but don't know about a person. Well, she realized Lucy knew how to sit on a horse, you'd never rodeo if you couldn't sit tight on something, but she hadn't realized Lucy could ride this way, or this well. Or that she knew how to use a horse to herd cows. From this distance Lucy looked as if she was part of the animal, as if she had spent her life cowpunching, or maybe made her money wrangling for the movies. She made it look so easy! Or maybe it was the roan who actually did the work; if it was one of Dakins' horses it probably got used for this kind of thing, had probably been sent to a professional trainer—god, there'd be hell to pay over Lucy just climbing up on it and riding off as if it were her own animal.

Lucy moved the cattle from the hay field to the pasture and Debbie closed the gate again, then went back to turn on the electric fence. They had five strands of barbed wire but that wouldn't keep a cow from going where she wanted to go. They just put their heads between the strands and leaned until the wire snapped. As for the barbs, how much are they going to bother an animal whose hide gets used to make workboots? What's a little jab or scratch to something that size? But one thin strand of electric wire and the field is safe— until a pack of kids wallowing in testosterone overdose decide to give the local queers a rough time.

She went over to the loading corral and opened the gate. Lucy moved the cows forward and when they were in the corral she dismounted and helped Debbie shut the cedar bars. She stared at the dozen animals for long moments, then grinned, and the next thing Debbie knew, Lucy was on the fence and moving. "Would you open the gate when I yell?" she called.

Not two minutes later there were ten animals in the corral and two bulls in the grazing pasture. And a minute after that the two bulls were in the rough pasture with the cows. And Lucy was grinning from ear to ear.

"They'll realize in a few days they're a couple short. And they'll come back, polite as hell, to ask about them and collect them. But until they do...," and she laughed, "we've got them. And with even a smidgin of luck we'll wind up with some damned fine calves...those are Martin Conroy's animals." She realized from the look on Debbie's face that she didn't know what was so smile-inducing about Martin Conroy's goddamned bulls. "He's got registered Limousins," Lucy said, as if that explained everything. "We couldn't even afford the semen for AI." And she laughed bitterly.

She filled the trough in the loading corral and even carried over a bale of hay, cut the twine and tossed the flakes into the pen. Then she turned to the blue roan mare and stripped off the saddle. She rubbed the animal dry, checked her feet as if she knew what she was doing and took off the bridle. Next she turned the mare loose in the grazing pasture. It was when she carried the saddle and bridle into the barn that Debbie started to get worried. "Shouldn't you take the horse back over to Dakins' place?"

"They'll be over here sooner or later," Lucy answered casually.

They arrived the next day. All of them. A couple of pickup trucks, their beds piled with first-grade timothy, a jeepy-looking thing and a stock truck. The fathers got out and moved to the loading pen, the youths sat in the vehicles not looking at each other. Then one of the dads, an enraged-looking burly man with a Cat Diesel baseball cap on his head, turned and yelled, "Get your ass in gear!" and the boys were out of the trucks and moving. "Where do you want it?" the burly one asked.

Lucy moved to where the hay conveyor was lying under the overhang roof beside the barn. "They'll do'er!" the burly one roared. So the boys had to set it up, then they had to take the timothy from the pickups and the back of the stock truck, send it a bale at a time up the conveyor and stack it where Lucy pointed.

"They'll be working their asses off all summer payin' for this hay," Dakins' blue-eyed foreman promised. "And they'll be here crack a' dawn the day you decide you're bringing in what's left out there. And you don't pay'em a cent for the work they're going to do for you!"

"I don't know what to say," Lucy stammered. "I don't know what I expected but...I didn't expect this."

"Oh, we're not so bad once you get to know us," he grinned. "Don't judge us by those snotnoses." He pulled out his makings and made himself a cigarette, and lit it, squinting against the smoke. "Not enough good hard work for them," he decided. "If the little buggers were draggin' ass after twelve hours in a saddle on rough ground, stuff like this wouldn't happen. But we all of us did such a good job of makin' their lives better'n ours were, we turned out a bunch that'd be more at home in a Townie apartment than they are out here. Couple a' good kicks up the arse might do some good."

When the stock truck was empty and the hay was stacked in the loft, they backed the rig up to the loading chute and leaned on the fence, watching as the sweating teenagers sent the cattle from the corral to the bed of the truck. "Looks to me," a skinny man with a big nose said quietly, "as if we all contributed a couple of animals each." He looked over at the rough pasture and laughed softly. "I'll pick up my Limousins any time you phone and say you don't want'em around any more," he offered. Lucy nodded, and then she laughed, not even caring that she'd been caught out. Martin Conroy looked over at the blue roan mare, then looked at Dakins' foreman, who just shrugged and reached for his tobacco and papers.

"Seems to me like they were all in it together," Conroy said quietly. "So it ought to cost'em each the same."

"Oh, I think the use of two purebred bulls for a couple of months ought to about square you," the foreman answered. "Don't know what the others will do or think, but it seems fair to me."

Debbie wished she knew what people meant when they talked. More than three-quarters of the time everyone seemed to speak in riddles, as if what was between the lines counted for more than what got said. The biggest puzzle was that Lucy seemed to understand the silences better than she understood the words. She heard the blue-eyed foreman, she saw Conroy nod, and she took a deep breath and leaned on the cedar rails of the loading corral, the stiffness in her back relaxing. Debbie wanted to ask what was going on but she didn't want them to know how ignorant she was, so she kept quiet. Maybe they could read her silence and know without her having to talk.

When the cows were loaded, the corral was empty, and the big doors at the back of the stock truck were closed, the neighbors got in their vehicles and drove off, not saying goodbye, not saying much of anything, just nodding, grim-faced and obviously still burning with shame. The blue roan mare stayed and so did the saddle, blanket and bridle. The teenaged boys who had kicked it all off stared at the horse as if some very bad news was written on her side. One of them didn't even seem to care that there were tears dripping down his face.

Supper was finished and the dishes were done when the stock truck drove back down the long driveway. Debbie went out on the porch, thinking Conroy had come for his bulls. The truck backed up to the gate into the grazing pasture and two of the boys got out and moved to open the doors at the back and let down the loading ramp. The other boys were in the back with the horses they'd been riding when they opened the gate and turned their father's cattle into the hay field.

"What...?" Debbie moved to the steps, then stopped. "It seems a bit much," she objected mildly, understanding what hadn't been put into words. But Lucy just shrugged.

The boys turned their horses into the grazing pasture with the blue roan mare, then they replaced the loading ramp, closed the door, and crowded into the truck, and it drove off quickly, kicking up dust, the empty back end rattling.

"That seems a bit unfair," Debbie said. "And it sure won't make them feel any less hostile toward us."

"I don't care how hostile they feel," Lucy answered. "They'll think twice before they *do* anything about it again."

Bill phoned back on Wednesday, after supper, to ask Debbie when he could expect a child-maintenance check. "Oh, just about thirty days after you've caught up on your own back payments," she answered.

"Jesus, Deb, are you going to start in on that? This kid has no clothes at all."

"That kid has a closet full of clothes, I'll send them to you by the boxload."

"He says they're all gorky."

"You might suggest to him that if he wants designer underwear he should get a job and buy his own."

"Would you be willing to come into the city to go to family therapy sessions?"

"Would you be willing to come out here for some?"

"It's a five-hour trip, for chrissakes!"

"Is it? That's funny, you make it sound like it's only ten minutes."

"I've got a *job*, Deb! What in hell else have you got to do?"

"I've got a job too, Bill."

She half turned to sit on the edge of the counter in the kitchen, and down the hallway she could see Lucy sitting on the ten-year-old sofa with the jigger on the wide padded arm. The jigger was a battery-operated thing supposed to do something-or-other to ease back pain. You put a special kind of jelly on the little rubber paddles, then put the paddles above and below the area of agony and held them in place with tape. Then you turned on the machine and adjusted the volume, or whatever, and tried to pretend it wasn't, at the very best merely annoying, at worst hurtful. The batteries discharged little zaps of electricity which were supposed to go from one set of paddles to the other. Or whatever. Improve circulation, ease cramps, reduce tension, rah rah rah. Be nice if it worked. Well, it did for some people, but it didn't seem to be doing much for Lucy.

"Deb?" Bill's voice recalled her.

"Yes?"

"Well?"

"Well, what?"

"Were you listening or just holding the damned phone?"

"Don't I get a chance to *think* about things? Do I have to be able to come up with answers, solutions, whatever, at the drop of a hat or a hint?" she evaded expertly. "You've had some time to *think* about it. Take me through it step by step, give me a chance here, please."

"I took him to his old high school to enroll him again; they won't let him back unless we agree he goes into a special class and gets therapy."

"Uh-huh?" Lucy looked white-faced and the extra-strength Tylenol bottle was on the coffee table. It was going to be one of those nights when the best thing a person could do was find something else to do, muck out the barn, maybe.

"Well?"

"Well *what?* What do you want me to say? What *can* I say? If those are the terms under which they'll let him back, then those are the terms, and either he goes back under them or...."

"He's furious."

"Tough, eh?"

"They don't just have a teacher for that bunch, they have a shrink too."

"He needs one."

"So you think I should say he has to do it?"

"*You* aren't saying it, *they* are. Tell him that, Billy, let him know it isn't just you and me find his behavior shitty, the rest of the world is really unimpressed too."

"You think so?" He sounded more uncertain than she could remember him sounding in years. "He says he doesn't want to go back there. He wants to go to some damned private thing as a day student."

"So you go see them without having him along. Tell *them* why this chronic under-achiever suddenly has this burning desire to go to a school that caters to the upper crust and the scholarship set. Let *them* tell him if he can go a full year without involving the police in everyone's life, and if he can haul his marks up within sight of a passing mark, they might consider him, but that on the whole they aren't at all interested in some bad-news gomer who thinks the Gaza Strip is...."

"A topless dancehall, right?" and he laughed as easily as they had both laughed all those years ago. "Jesus, Deb, it all makes me feel crappy. I mean, he's our kid, right, and he's the only one either of us is likely to have and it's as if he *hates* us." If he had said Chad was *his* kid her reaction would have been different, she knew she'd have closed down and said exactly the wrong thing in the wrong tone of voice. But he had said our kid.

"Ah, Billy, don't let him do it to you. That's exactly how you're supposed to react. He's a manipulator. He wants everyone to feel sorry for him. And when you do, he has contempt for you because he knows he *made* you feel that way. He's almost seventeen. In all that time nobody's beaten him up, nobody's starved him, nobody's left him alone in the low-rent end of town with druggies and hypes breaking into the apartment to steal the silverware. Nobody's been shooting at him or dropping bombs on him, he hasn't had to survive pestilence, drought, famine or civil war." She could hear Bill laughing. "What in *hell* does he have to complain about? Things aren't the way he thinks he wants them? Oh gee, eh?" and she was laughing too. "Are they the way *you* want them? Are they the way *I* want them? Right now Lucy is nose to nose with the possibility she may have to have another operation on her back; you think that's the way *she* wants things? My boss is so goddam dumb I'm sure someone has to do up the Velcro straps on his underwear, does *his* boss do anything about it? I mean, you'd fire the fool. Actually, you'd never have hired him—he's got bad posture, a huge belly, he's flat-footed and he has dandruff specks on his shoulders, you'd have passed him without a glance. Let the kid find out there are things you just put up with, is all."

"What's wrong with her back this time?"

"Same thing. That's why our son and heir left for your place, probably. The mammoth Chad, the Hulk, the Incredible Growing Boy who eats ten pounds of potatoes at a sitting did exactly that, and sat, while the one with the eighteen-inch scar on her back did the thing with the hay bales. I'd come home from work and she'd be up to her ears in chores and *he'd* be watching 'Romper Room Playhouse' or something!"

"Yeah, I've noticed. Guess who does the dishes? I told him if he didn't do dishes he didn't get his allowance. Know what he said?"

"He probably said if he didn't get his allowance he'd rob banks."

"Something like that. So you think I should just kick his ass for him?"

"Hire the bikers, Billy, he's bigger than both of us."

When she went into the living room Lucy was putting the lid back on the pain-pill bottle. "Three-pill night or four?"

"Four. Might make'er to six, the rate we're going."

"You should get that bumper sticker that says, If I'd known I was gonna live this long I'd'a took better care of myself."

"The Old Biddy would say, Well, it's the price you pay for the fun you insisted on having."

"You must have had one *helluva* lot of fun."

"Whoopee-ding, eh? She used to sing this song, If I had the wings of an angel, or even the wings of a crow, I'd fly to the top of the flag-pole, and shit on the people below…but she didn't need wings or a flagpole, that one."

3

Seely was alone in the house, sprawled on the rumpled mess of her bed, coloring with the stubs of her wax crayons, when Glen came back from wherever he'd been on his rusty rattletrap bike. He made himself a sandwich in the kitchen, and slammed around the house in a bad mood, thinking himself alone, bored and burning with anger about something.

"Whyn't you let me know you were here?" he snarled from the doorway. "Why you just lollin' around here like some kind of sneak?"

"I'm no sneak," Seely answered, not even looking over her shoulder at him, "I didn't have anything to say to you is all."

"Don't get snotty with me or you'll wish you hadn't."

"Oh, sure," she scoffed. "Big tough guy, I guess."

"You shut up or I'll show you."

"Yeah?" She poked in the tobacco can of stubs, looking for a particular color. "And what are you gonna show me? Maybe what a jerk you are?"

He moved into the room and took a swat at her. Seely rolled out of the way and laughed. So he grabbed her and hit her two or three times; then, when she didn't cry, he lost it, and really hit her hard. Instead of crying she kicked at him, and the next thing she knew he was hurting her real bad.

"I'm gonna tell!" she sobbed, dabbing at the blood.

"You do and I'll break your stinkin' little neck," he promised.

"One word at the wrong time and you'll be even sorrier than you are now." And he left the room, his boots clomping. She lay on her bed and cried herself to sleep. When she woke up there were little dents in the skin of one arm where she'd lain on the stubs of wax crayon. She blamed him for that, too.

Kitty asked her if she was feeling okay.

"You didn't hardly eat any supper, and you look like you've been crying."

"I didn't eat supper because I wasn't hungry," Seely snapped. "And the rest of it is none of *your* beeswax."

"Fine'en. Be that way. See if I care." Kitty shrugged and flung some clothes around until she found her softball glove. "You comin' to practice?"

"Why should I? They never let me play."

"Maybe tonight you'll get lucky."

Seely didn't think for one minute there was any chance she'd get lucky—the only kind of luck she ever got was either bad or worse. But she wasn't staying in the house by herself. What if they came home from beerin' early, and what if Mike was in a bad mood or something and started takin' swats at people and everything? Maybe so far Mike hadn't done anything like that, but *Fred* always did. And Mom just sitting there yowling, You stop that, now, you just stop it, you hear, doing nothing about any of it except makin' him madder so's he hit harder. Mike had been hanging around a fair while now, longer than most of them. Not long ago Mom had come out of their bedroom with a phony-sweet smile on her face, her hair brushed and nice, same as when they went beerin', and in a false-face little-kid-type voice had suggested maybe it was time they started to call Mike "Dad".

Seely hadn't known what to say. She just stood, about as smart, Kitty would have said, as a cup of warm goat piss. Probably, if it had only been up to Seely to decide, she'd have gone along with the dumbtit idea, what difference did it make, what difference would it make, after all, it wasn't as if she had a real dad of her own, like some of the others.

"Call him what?" Savannah turned real slow and she had that look on her face, the one that made hard lumps form in Seely's belly.

When Savannah looked like that, boy, you'd better be ready to find a good place to hide.

"Well, after all...." Mom smiled and her voice took on a tone that made it seem, somehow, as if Savannah was being real dumb. Not a good move—it only made Savannah insulted as well as proddy. "Mike *does* fill the place of a dad around here. Goes to work, brings home his pay check, stuff like that."

"Goes to work when he's sober and not too hung over. Brings home that little bit of pay check he didn't leave in a bar somewhere. Eats the stuff Gran grows in her garden and never does a lick of the work. No more a dad than...than...," and Savannah just quit talking and shook her head.

"Now don't you *be* like that." Mom looked as if she was going to either cry or start hitting. "Maybe I should make it clear, Miss Priss, I am not asking, I am telling."

"Don't tell if you can't back it up." And it was out in the open, whatever it was.

"Why *won't* you?" Mom was going to cry. Probably because she knew if she took a swat at Savannah she might wind up bum-first to the linoleum.

"For the same reason I don't call a dog a cat. Or an elephant a cricket. You call things what they *are*, for chrissakes. Why bother having a language if you're going to call things what they aren't? Could call you 'lady' but it wouldn't make it so. Hell, could call you 'sober' and what a lie that would be!"

"Here, you!" Mike came from the bedroom then, already unbuckling his belt and getting ready to haul it from his pants loops and cut loose. "You're getting a bit too big for your britches, young lady."

"Don't even think of it." Savannah gave him a look Seely hadn't seen before, a different kind of you'll-be-sorry look than the one everybody was used to. "You'll be in jail so fast nobody'll even have time to bake you a cake with a hacksaw. Just do up your buckle and simmer down before someone rattles your chain."

She sat with the bat bag and watched Kitty. How come some people moved as if it was nothing new to them, as if they'd been moving like this forever, doing these things that were so complicated, so hard to do; other people, Seely included, had to try and try and try, and then

if ever they got it right even one time, had to remember how that
happened and practice until it all got boring and you almost didn't
care any more if you ever learned how. Some people, lucky people,
Kitty especially, just did it, as if everything they had, muscles and
bones and everything, had come already broken in and skilled.

Kitty hadn't hardly played any real ball before last year, no more
than Seely had, probably. Some pickup, some five-hundred-yer-up,
maybe some auntie-eye-over, but then she cashed in all the bottles
she'd collected and hid until there was a wheelbarrow load, more
even than that, and she got Gran to help her talk Fred into borrow-
ing a car and they put the bottles in the trunk. Even paying Fred for
the gas and a bit extra as a thank-you for his time, there was enough
money to walk into the sporting-goods store and start looking. Seely
would have got a trapper's mitt, but Kitty said no, she wasn't doing
that. "I want to learn how to catch, not how to stuff a goddam mitt in
front of the ball."

So she got a glove, not a mitt. And she practiced with it until the
stiffness was gone out of it and a pocket was formed, which she kept
tight by putting a belt around it at night, with a softball nestled
inside, like an egg in a nest. Not even the boys dared touch that
glove. "You do," Kitty promised them, "and I won't get mad, I won't
even get even; I'll get ahead, you understand?"

"Oh, big tough you," Glen blustered.

"You just touch it, mung-mouth. Just *think* about touchin' it,
okay?"

Glen glared but he didn't go near the glove. He'd been mad as
hell at Kitty for a long long time, but no matter how mad he got he
didn't do much about it, not to Kitty, anyway. Sometimes he'd take it
out on someone else, like the time he got mad at Kitty so he gave
Savannah a shove and she banged herself against the edge of the big
black stove, but he'd walked soft around Kitty ever since the time he
got hurt.

Neither he nor Kitty talked much about it. "Ask me no questions, I'll
tell you no lies," was all Kitty ever said. All Seely knew was, most of
them had been at Gran's, helping can fish, and then Glen, who had
ducked out the back way because he hated work of any kind but hated
it even worse if it had something to do with fish, came streaking for

the house yelling as if he was only a year old, holding his left hand at the wrist, blood pouring, the scissors stuck in him, not quite all the way through but close enough you could see the bumps, turned purple under his skin.

"Sweet christ in heaven," was all Gran said. And she made him lie on his belly on the kitchen floor with his arm stretched out, the back of his hand as flat as he could make it, the scissors sticking up and glittering. Then Gran stepped on his wrist with one foot and on his fingers with the other. "Start yelling," she said. "Loud as you can, and don't stop until I put a cold cloth on your face." He yelled. Because on the word "stop," without any change in her voice or any change on her face, Gran yanked and the scissors came out, but not easily. On the word "cold" Glen quit making any noise and his eyes just rolled back, his eyelids closed and he sort of gurgled. Gran kept on talking, though, then handed the scissors to Savannah and said, "Better wash'em off and put them away somewhere."

She poured turpentine on the cuts. That woke Glen up, all right, he came awake yodeling and sobbing. "There's a good wee boy," Gran said, and she wrapped his hand, then cuddled him, washed his face with a cold cloth and stroked his forehead. "Ah, laddie, laddie." She sounded so sad you'd have thought the scissors had been in his throat and he'd died. "Ah, laddie, ye poor thing."

And Glen let her do it. He sobbed and cried and said his hand hurt, and it took a long time for his fingers to not be stiff and swollen. It was funny how he let Gran fuss over him like that. But only at that time, not after, and he went back to being tough—hard as nails, some people said.

Gran had looked around—counting noses, she called it. "And where's our Kitty, then?" she'd asked.

Kitty was at the house. Savannah went and got her and took her over to Gran's place and Gran made her sit on a chair until she was finished with Glen. Then she just stared at Kit and said, "Come in my bedroom, miss," and Kitty, who never did anything if you got bossy with her like that, got up and went into the bedroom, and it was a good half-hour before she came back out again, and then Glen had to go in, and everyone knew it was Kitty put the scissors through Glen's hand. But neither of them ever said why.

And when Kitty said, Don't touch my ball glove or else, nobody touched it, because obviously Kitty was one of those people where maybe there's somebody home but nobody turned on the lights.

She was that way at school, too. Donald Gregor was a real bad tease, not a funny one or a friendly one—the kind of teasing he did made a person feel angry and somehow beat down at the same time. Instead of just giving a shove, Donald would shove and trip you at the same time, so you fell all the way to the floor; or instead of a pinch he'd grab your booby or something. And he walked past Kitty and ran his hand over her butt, his thumb following the crack in her ass. "Nice stuff," he said. Kitty whirled, fast as flash, and her looseleaf binder went right into his face, the spine of it cracking against his nose and making it gush blood all over his face and down his shirt.
    "Hands to yourself, peasant," was all she said.
    "I was just *jokin'*," Donald wailed.
    "I know that. I'm jokin' too," Kitty answered.

And she wouldn't go on the track team. The gym teacher wanted her on, the principal wanted her on, but Kitty wouldn't go on or even go for the tryouts. "Why should I run my legs ragged just so's people who wouldn't say hello to me any other time of the year can jump up and down and yell, Go Kitty go? Why should I go sweat like that? They don't like me, I don't like them and I really don't care if the school gets the trophy or not."
    They even sent her to the school counselor. Kitty went and Kitty listened and Kitty didn't join the track team. "No skin off my ass if they win or lose," she shrugged.
    But she was the first one at softball practice every night they had it. She didn't have spikes, she didn't have cleats, she didn't have anything but her old softball and her new glove. She wasn't the best on the team, not yet, because she was way lots younger than the others, but she was already better than she had been when she started. She didn't even care that the kids at school laughed at her for it. "Did you hear what crazy Kitty said to the gym teacher? She said softball was like something more than just a game, it was like a math question, too."
    "Did you *really* say that?" Seely asked.

"Sure I did."

"Didn't she get mad?"

"So what? Askin' me dumb questions as if she had every right in the world to know everything she wanted to know just because she wanted to know it."

"Didn't she give you a detention?"

"Yeah."

"So?"

"So what? She can give me detentions until her teeth fall out, that doesn't mean I have to go sit in her sweaty-socks smelly office. If she wants to go to the principal with it, fine, we'll go, and we'll just see what he says about people asking other people questions that aren't any of their damn business."

But nobody went to the principal and Kitty just kept going to gym class as if nothing had happened. The gym teacher obviously hated her, and just as obviously, Kitty didn't give a toot.

Other people liked her, though. The ball team seemed to think she was just about the best thing since sliced white. "How come you always seem to know what to do? Someone steps up to the plate and you know before they swing the bat where the ball's gonna go. How do you know that?" Seely puzzled. "I never know until it's too late which way I should move."

"You know those dumb questions like, if a hen and a half lays an egg and a half in a day and a half how far is it to New York? If A is to B what B is to C and C is to D what a bone is to a dog...well, it's like that, only more real. If there's a runner on second and two out, and if the one coming to bat hits to left field, and if she can usually get a two-bagger and has lots of home runs...what's she going to do?"

"Well, what is she going to do?"

"If it was me, I'd bunt. Unless I saw the shortstop leaning forward, or the second-baser getting ready to cover to short or something, that would tell me they were expecting me to bunt. Then I'd shift my feet so I maybe could get it to go to right field, because they're expecting it in left...."

"Jesus," Savannah hated softball. "You'd think it was bloody important or something."

"Oh, go fuck somebody else, will you? I mean, you haven't managed to get fucked by the entire town, yet."

"I don't get fucked," Savannah laughed, "I do the fucking. There's a difference."

Well, if there was, Seely didn't know what it was. Didn't want to find out, either. Savannah and her goddamn boyfriends. What a stink that had been.

"My own *daughter!*" Mom yelled and screeched and hit at Fred, and Savannah just laughed. And laughed and laughed and then laughed some more. And Fred grabbed his stuff and rammed it into bags and boxes and then turned at the door and yelled at Savannah, "Well, come on!"

"You have got to be kidding," Savannah laughed even louder. "Me? Head off into the wide cold world with *you?*"

Boy but he got mad then. He got as far as "But I thought..." and Savannah blew her cool. "Thought? You? With what? Jesus Christ, you're going bald, you've got a pot belly, you're drunk more than you're sober, you won't keep your hands to yourself and can't take no for an answer and you *thought?*" And when Jimmy figured out what it was Savannah wasn't quite saying, he blew up and went after Fred and chased him until he caught him. Well, good for him. But since then Savannah had hardly slowed down to take a breath.

"Lose your reputation," Mom warned.

"Oh, get real, will you? You lost it for us before we even started grade one."

So Mom cried. Then Savannah and Kitty had a fight about Savannah making Mom cry.

Seely didn't want to be the town bicycle, everyone entitled to ride if they wanted, the way Savannah was, but she didn't think she was going to wind up the kind of ball-player Kitty was. It was funny, really, Kitty could hardly even hold a pencil, let alone make it *do* anything, but she could move across the grass like there was no weight to her, she could go back after a ball and make it look like she was dancing. Seely would fall flat on her face in a cow-pie, probably, but she could grab a pencil and an old brown paper bag and draw a picture that everyone wanted. She even made some spare money making signs for Grainger's. Special This Week or !!SALE!!—but the ones she liked best were when she could take watercolors and do maybe Easter bunnies across the big front window, or reindeer and a sleigh, making it look as if they were coming down to land on the display counter just the other side of the glass. And she'd made forty dollars when Grainger decided he was going to have one of those deals where you sign your name to your grocery slip and put it in a big box and the one who gets pulled out wins something. "Could you make us some bit of artwork, then?" Grainger asked. Seely said she'd think about it, and she did. Even talked to Jimmy about it. He went into the box under his bed and brought out his pieces of wood and picked one he'd been saving for something special. And then he showed her how you soaked it in water and used a sharp sharp knife, and how you could peel each strip back and bend it with a piece of round metal pipe so it sort of curved, and if it got stiff you just soaked it again, and by the time you were finished there was a bird with what looked like layers of individual feathers. Grainger really liked it. Said he liked it too much to give to just any fool whose slip got pulled, would she sign her name to it and he'd keep that himself and give the winner some groceries, instead.

Funny the things people liked. The teacher had showed them splatter-painting, and it was fun. Even better, it was something you could do that didn't cost an arm and a leg. Just an old toothbrush and some watercolors and a piece of paper. And then she had this idea that if she took some of the mesh out of the old screen door that nobody ever bothered to shut anyway, because it had a big hole in it where Jimmy had pushed Glen and he'd gone halfway through, and rigged it up between the toothbrush and the paper, the splatters might look better. She practiced lots, with old bags and old newspapers, and then swiped some of the good paper from school and got it home without making any creases in it. She looked for a couple of days until she found just about the exact perfect cedar branch, and she cut more of it than she was going to need, to be sure, and set herself all up. For a minute she was scared. It had taken so long to get it all ready, and if the least little thing went wrong it wouldn't work, and then the being scared went and she just did it. And there it was, on the paper, out-lined in splatters, and she'd been able to make herself wait until it was dry before she lifted it off, so there were no smears or anything.

Grainger liked the bird, maybe he'd like this. He just stared at it for a minute and then grinned and said it was real good. She handed it to him because there was no use doing anything with it herself, it would only get messed up, and anyway it wouldn't look right with thumbtacks holding it in place. "It's yours," she said, "happy birthday or something." The next time she saw it she hardly recognized it. He'd taken it to the framers and there it was on the wall, and you could see where he'd had her sign her name to it, and the year.

But she couldn't seem to get everything together to throw the god-damned ball!

"Seely, *listen* to me," Kitty said patiently. "You don't just sort of flop it with your wrist and elbow. *Throw* it. Put your shoulder into it. Look, like this, see, and there's a line all the way down, even your waist and your hip, even your leg...YOU throw the ball, not just your hand."

She tried. She could get it from second to first or second to third, she could even get it from second to home, but she couldn't get it there fast, and she couldn't get it there from out in the field. The best she could do was field it and get it to a base, then let the base-person huck it where it was supposed to be. And somehow she couldn't fig-ure out if the runner was going to leave second, clear third and head for home or haul up and wait at third. So even if Seely got the ball and even if she threw the damned thing, she never quite managed to put anyone out.

"Oh, what do you care?" Savannah yawned. "Jesus, what a waste of time! I don't know what's worse, her wasting time trying to teach you or you wasting time trying to learn."

Seely was pretty good at bats, though. So after the practice was over, when some of them headed off home but others stayed to just goof around for a while, they let her play with them. It was rota-tion—you started in left field, moved to center, then to right, then to short, then to third, then to second, then to first, and on like that until you'd done chucker and catch, then it was your turn to bats. And there wasn't really a team—there were three at bat, sometimes four, taking turns, depending on how many stayed behind, and when someone got put out, that someone went to center and everyone else moved up one; unless you caught a flyball, and then you went straight to bats. Nobody really got to win, but everybody got to play, and that was fun.

"Listen, kid, don't feel bad because you're not as good as your sister," someone told her. "You're as good as most people and better than a lot, it's just that Kitty is going to be one *helluva* ball-player, that's all."

"She plays like she's done it forever and she never seems to have to practice," Seely mourned. "Me, I always feel...slow."

"Yeah, well, still, don't judge yourself against Kit, give yourself a break here, okay?"

They walked home together, following the highway, padding in the soft silky dust at the side of the road. "Where'd you learn to play so good?" she asked.

Kitty shrugged. "I dream about it. Sometimes at night it's like I'm doing it, and doing it and doing it and doing it, and when I wake up I can do it the same as if I practiced for hours. Daytimes too, when I'm not asleep, it's still like a dream. Like tonight, you saw how the catcher just scooped that tip ball? Just reached out with her arm, didn't even turn her head, nothing, just whap, she had her hand where the ball was going to be. Well, I can't do that. If it happened to me tonight I'd miss. But if I sit and dream about it enough it'll be like I practiced and practiced. And I'll be able to do it. It's scary sometimes," she admitted.

"I don't know what you're talking about."

"I don't either. But it works."

Sometimes, talking to Kitty was just about the most interesting and satisfying thing in Seely's life. Other times, and you never knew for sure when one of those times was on her, talking to Kitty was a good way to wind up feeling all mixed up and confused.

"Why does she want us to call Mike 'Dad'?"

"To keep him around, goof. She's not as good-lookin' as she used to think she was. I mean, look at her."

"Yeah, but Mike's lots better lookin' and all than *Fred* was. It's not like she, you know, went down from Fred or something."

"Mike is damned near old enough to be her father! He might be in real good shape and all, considering, but he's *old*."

"He's not, neither! How can you say that? Just 'cause of his hair, I suppose."

"Oh shut the hell *up*, Seely! You don't want to talk, you just want to argue. I'm tellin' you he's almost as old as *Gran*!"

"What a thing to say! Well, he is not!"

But probably he was. He had lots of lines in his face, and his throat was getting kind of poochy, especially under his chin. Mom didn't seem to notice, or maybe she noticed and didn't care.

It was odd, though. Inside, when she tried to think about it, she got this funny empty feeling. If Mike was old enough to be Mom's father, then what was Seely's own father doing, whoever he was? Was he with someone young enough to be *his* daughter? Well, how could that be? She wanted to talk to someone about it, but no use trying to talk with Kitty, she was obviously in a mood to bite off ears and noses. No use asking Savannah, she'd just say, Oh shut up, twerp, you wouldn't understand even if I told you. Jimmy might talk about it, but she didn't want to ask him, it wasn't a boy-thing, probably. It felt like it wasn't a boy-thing, anyway. And she wasn't going within ten miles of Glen if she didn't have to, you could bet on that one.

4

Grainger gave the splatter-paint cedar branch to his wife for her
birthday. Sandra Grainger said it was obvious to her Seely was an old
soul. "See," she smiled, "she's even got light-colored eyes," and she
asked Seely about her drawing stuff. "Do you have a little table all
for yourself?"

"No."

"A corner of your own?" she persisted. Seely laughed.

Sandra Grainger took her down to the basement and showed her
this room next to the steps. "I've got an old kitchen table," she said
firmly, "and I'll move it in here with some chairs. We'll put your stuff
on the table, and there's a radio I don't use, it's stored on a shelf down
here somewhere, we'll get that in here. A lamp or two and there
you'll be, with your own work area."

"Why?" Seely felt terrified. Gran had warned her, everyone has
their own idea of what's written on the price tag.

"Because," Sandra Grainger said firmly. "Just because. Maybe it's,
oh, who knows, a happy birthday or something."

Seely waited until Gran was alone and went over to talk to her about
it. "You do it," Gran nodded.

"Why?"

"Because I told you to."

"Why does she want to do this?"

"Doesn't matter why she wants it. You do it. There won't be any trouble, and if there is I'll take care of it. You do it, Celia Mary."

"But...what you said about the price tag...." She was nearly crying, and Gran stopped what she was doing and sat on a chair, then patted her lap. "Whatever the price tag is, it'll be worth it. And sometimes the price tag on things isn't a bad one. Sometimes the price tag is that the people *want* to do it, and all you have to do is let them do what they want and it's good for you, real good, and good for them because they feel good. It's a very complicated thing." And Gran grinned. When she grinned that grin she looked so much like Jimmy that Seely had to grin herself. "You just do it because it'll be good for you, and you'll get to practice what you do best without anybody muckin' about with your stuff. Hey," and she winked, "trust me. After all, I'm not tryin' to sell you a used car."

Seely liked being near Gran, and she wished lots of times that Gran was her real Gran. Most of the time the other kids just went on with things as if Gran *was* hers, same as theirs, but sometimes, if one of them had something up their nose—and it was easy for Glen to get something up his nose—she'd get reminded. For a long time the reminders made her cry helplessly, but not any more, because Gran handled it and now Seely could just shrug and say, Oh, go mind your own beeswax.

There was something about Gran that wasn't like other kids' moms or grans. Even when she was dressed up, with her teeth in her mouth and everything, even when she had her hair done in town, permed into little curls all over her head, all she had to do was move and there it was, something different. Maybe it was because even if you didn't know her at all, the way she moved told you this was a woman who hardly ever had to hire anyone to do things for her. She built the new woodshed all by herself, cutting the support posts and cross-poles in the bit of woodlot out behind the house. She even split the shakes for the roof, and how many other grans would think of doing a thing like that?

Seely knew there were lots of people looked down on her, on all of them, even looked down their noses at Gran, and said things. But no matter how low their opinion of everyone was, it was on top of the mountain compared to what Gran thought of *them*! Two-faced, she said, no better than you'd expect, she said. And once she had words with someone in Grainger's store, some woman all dressed up who said something Seely didn't hear, but Gran laughed loud enough for everyone in the store to hear and then said clearly, Oh for heaven's sake, Aggie, they tried to make a silk purse out of a sow's ear with you and all they got was a horse's ass.

Mr. Grainger started coughing so badly he had to go to the candy counter and get some Zubes for his throat.

And if Gran said it was okay to go to Grainger's place and use the pencils, crayons and nice paper Sandra Grainger put on the table, then it was okay, and Seely would do it without worrying about any old price tags. Maybe Gran wasn't her real Gran, but she was a friend, and a good one.

Kitty seemed okay about it but it stuck sideways in the throats of the others. Savannah was so teed she spent days in an anger so deep her skin almost vibrated with the effort of holding it all inside. "I can do stuff like that better than you can!" she finally exploded. "You couldn't draw a straight line with a ruler! Why'd *you* get all this? Because of some dumb splatter-paint silly-kid stuff? If you start practicing now, maybe by the time you're seventy-six you'll be as good as I am already, without practice. I could do lots better'n that, too. I just don't want to!" And more. She stomped from room to room, yelling and letting the tears pour from her eyes, not even trying to wipe them away, and nobody got in her way, not even Jimmy. "Fat lot of good it'll do you once summer's finished!" she screeched triumphantly. "You might be able to bop over there now and use all that good stuff, but once school's in and it gets dark by suppertime, just *see* if you get to go," and she started to laugh, finally finding something to use against Seely. "All that good stuff'll be over there and you'll be over here, miles and miles and *miles* away. Serves you right, SmartyArty, serves you right for thinking you're so great. You're not so great. You're not great at all. As far as real things go, you're not so Muckin' Fuch, and that's for sure!"

But Seely could go over at lunchtime, and she did, almost every day. That still gave her almost three-quarters of an hour by herself, in a clean, warm, dry place that was her own, or almost as good as her own. Sometimes she could hear Sandra Grainger playing the piano.

The music carried all the way to the street. Seely didn't want to press the buzzer and interrupt but Sandra would see her coming and stop playing anyway, long enough to open the door. Then she just patted Seely on the head and smiled, as if her mind was somewhere else. Seely smiled, even whispered, "Thanks," and went down the steps to sit at the little table, just touching things and feeling safe. The music started up again, as if there'd been no interruption. Seely let herself out when it was time, smiling her goodbye over her shoulder and wiggling her fingers instead of waving her hand.

She knew full well why the Graingers hadn't given her a key. That would have been stupid. What if she lost it? What if Glen or Savannah took it away from her and used it to break into the Graingers' place and steal everything that wasn't nailed down and half of what had been until they swiped the nails? You don't take any chances when you've got nice stuff. Someone always wants it without the bother of having to work for the money to buy it.

"Nyah-nyah, SmartyPants, forgot about 'cha, didn't they?" Savannah mocked those times Seely knocked on the door and there was no answer. "Har-de-har-har, little PetsyWetsy, invited ya over and then forgot, didn't they?"

Who knows how long Savannah might have kept this up or how far she might have gone if Kitty hadn't got fed up and chucked a rock that got her between the shoulder blades. "Why'n't ya leave her alone?" Kitty shrieked. "Just 'cause nobody'd ever want *you* in their house don't mean *she's* like that!" Savannah went at her and they had a fight in the playground until a couple of teachers came out and dragged them apart. The teachers looked at each other over the cursing sisters and did this thing with their eyes, half rolled them back and blinked rapidly, and that told Seely too much about what they were thinking and what their opinion of the whole family was.

It wasn't anything you could talk about with Gran, either. Gran's opinion of the family was so low you'd have to go down into the basement just to get a peek at it. Gran loved the kids, they all knew that, but she had few hopes and fewer aspirations for their future. "What's bred in the blood," she sighed, "will come out in the bone."

Gran's opinion of teachers was about as low as her opinion of her absent son's children. "You can tell what grade they teach by the way they talk and behave," she snorted. "The ones that teach grade one or two are always flapping their hands and jumping up and down and talking in little birdy voices. The ones in high school giggle and bat their eyes, and the men stuff their hands in their pockets and sneer a lot. Instead of the kids aspiring to grow up to be like the teachers, the teachers have held the line at some age where they were enjoying life the most—they aspire to go back down and stay with the kids."

And Gran couldn't stand Mike. She didn't care if he *did* have a sometimes job driving a chipper truck from the sawmill where the logs were sliced into planks and the sawdust and chips sprayed out into little mountains of reddy-colored stuff that got sucked up by big vacuum-hose things and spewed into enormous metal boxes mounted on wheels, then driven fifteen miles to where the pulp mill sat in its own purple stink. "What *is* so wonderful about a man having a job?" Gran scoffed. "There are some circles where it's so ordinary, so happen-all-the-time, that people never mention it. Some people have *two* jobs. Many, in fact. There's nothing earth-shattering about a man—or a woman for that matter—actually making a regular practice of earning his own keep. Or hers."

She hadn't had much of an opinion of any of the others, either. Every couple of months she'd get a letter in the mail, and the day after she'd stomp over to the house and announce that, come the weekend, she and the kids were going into town. Then she'd stomp back home again. All the land belonged to Gran, and she was the one paid the taxes on it; she could have booted them all off, too, because the big house they lived in was hers. And Seely knew that Gran's son, who everyone pretended was Seely's dad but he wasn't any such thing, had built the smaller house when he and Mom first got married, but then after Jimmy and Glen were born, when Mom was waiting for Savannah to come, they'd switched because the little house was getting too little and Gran was rattling in the big one like the last bean in the jar.

On the weekend they had to get up just as early as if it was a school day. Then they'd go over to Gran's and she'd check to make sure they were clean. There'd be a big breakfast of pancakes with syrup, and then it was out to the highway to flag down the bus. She never gave a cent to Mom, and she never bought Mom a single thing, not a hanky, not a pair of socks, nothing. "My taxes feed her," she snapped angrily, "and she's living on my land in my house drinking water from my well and that's about all *I'm* doing for her. Let her own look after her if she's too useless to look after herself."

The letter Gran got had a money order in it, and Gran would use the money for things like winter gumboots or warm jackets. Never toys or anything, although one time she did use some of it to pay for a bike at the second-hand store so Jimmy could do his paper route faster; but Jimmy had to pay back the money when he got his pay. Except that soon after he paid it back Gran showed up with a nice warm sweater for him, and everyone sort of knew she'd got it with that bike money.

Seely knew from things other people had said that there was some question about who her father was, but no question about Kitty's dad. Kitty's dad, they said, was the bartender at the Westwind, where Mom went to pass the time when Gran's son was in camp. The bartender was married and his wife wasn't about to throw out the pay check or those tips that made it home in his pocket. And once Mom was really big with Kitty he stopped smiling at her. When Mom got drunk she'd sometimes sit in a chair maundering on about how she'd had her heart broken through no fault of her own. "Talk the potatoes out of the ground," she'd blether, "and the birds out of their nests."

But there wasn't really any proof. It might have been Gran's son—you can't always be sure, even when you're positive. There were fights and lots of yelling, and he went away, but then he came back. Except the next time, when it was Seely, he'd been in camp too much and there wasn't any doubt at all and he didn't even wait to see her— he just stuffed his clothes in a couple of shopping bags, slung his caulk boots over his shoulder and took it all to his pickup truck, got in behind the wheel and that was all he wrote. From what the other kids had told her, usually when they were mad at her and blaming her for everything that went wrong in their lives, her own real dad was probably half the bums in town.

There'd been so many others since then that they'd become like one, and now it was Mike and he was sober half the time, or sober enough to function, except for days off, when he was as sodden as anyone could be.

"She's not *your* gran," Savannah said more times than she said hello. "She's just bein' nice to you so's you won't feel as bad as you look, you ugly little freak!"

"She is too my gran!"

"She is not. You got no gran. You don't even have a dad! You're like one of those mutt puppies at the pound!"

Gran sat Seely on her knee and wiped the snotters off her face and patted her leg and said, "Now you listen to me, Celia Mary, and listen good. If you let the things people say hurt you, people will go out of their way to say hurting things. If you can learn to shrug it off they'll stop doing it. And if you can't shrug it off, learn to pretend you can, and that'll be almost as good. At least it'll get their fangs out of your throat."

"She said you're not my gran."

"I'm not." Gran gave it to her honestly. "Not in the ways that people take notice of. But I *am* your gran if you want me to be and I want to be. And I do want to be. So if you want me for a Gran...," and she winked, "that's it, kiddo."

"She is *so* my Gran!" Seely screeched. "We chose each other, see! You she just got *stuck* with!" And she knew she'd won that one, because Savannah and Glen got so mad they ganged up on her and pounded her until Jimmy heard her shrieking and came in from outside to punch them off her.

"Leave her alone," Jimmy yelled. "For christ's sake, she's just little!"

"Jimmy's pet, Jimmy's pet," they chanted. "Jimmy's sucky little pet."

"You hit her, you've hit me, you hear? You make her cry and you'll wish you hadn't, okay?"

Gran didn't really think a lot more of her absent son than she thought of Mom. "Loggers," she snorted contemptuously. "They're the scruffy pups of the coast. Most families've got one but few brag about it."

Mom wasn't the only ex in Gran's son's life. He had another ex and two kids in Coombs, and an ex with a kid in Cowichan. There was an ex with some kids up coast, but they weren't *his* kids, so she didn't really count.

"It's easy for him," Gran snapped. "All he has to do is go into camp and send money. Easy come easy go. Someone to do the cookin', someone to make his bed, someone to make sure there's hot coffee and warm pie when he wants it, and he can go out and lay everything flat with his saw for as long as he wants, just roarsy roarsy har-har-bloody-har, and they pay him big money for actin' like a kid in a sandbox." So it seemed he sent one pay check for Mom's kids and split the next one between himself and the two kids in Coombs. Their mother was living full time with a guy who worked as a butcher in the Overwaitea store, a guy who was home for supper every night of the week, didn't go mesatchie on weekends and could be counted on to be there just about any time you looked up to see where he was.

"Am I dirty Irish trash?" Kitty asked once, almost glaring at Gran.

Gran looked at Kitty and started to laugh, reached out and pulled the stiff-with-insult skinny body against her own. "Oh, darlin', darlin'," she crooned, still laughing, "all a person has to do is look at you and they can see that, whatever else you might be, Irish isn't really high on the list."

"And Seely?" Kitty's voice was shaking, as if she was trying hard not to break down and cry. "Is Seely dirty Irish trash?"

"No, she's not. And neither are the rest of you."

"Then who is?"

"Anybody who acts like it. Anybody who chooses to be."

"Are you Irish?"

"Dear Lord, no!" Gran laughed again. "I'm a heather-hopper, not a bog-trotter. And the difference is that where my people come from, every time a person proves themselves too stupid to be trusted with easy things like feeding the cat or shoveling the mire from around the barn, we ship 'em off to Ireland, and there they make teachers and mayors out of them and build statues in the streets to them or call them great writers and poets and get all excited." And she laughed until Kitty started laughing too.

PART
TWO

1

The postman didn't just stuff the mail in the tin box and climb back in his little truck with the big round orange-red Rural Mail marker on the roof; he drove all the way up to the front steps, got out and came to knock at the door.

He had a piece of mail for Mom, and she had to sign in the book for it. Then he drove off and she stood in the doorway watching him leave, the tires of his truck splashing the water from the puddles in a gray-brown spray.

She sighed as if the weight of the North American continent was sitting on her shoulders, then she went to the table, sat down and ripped open the envelope. She read the papers inside and started shaking her head as if it was all beyond belief. The way she tossed them aside, you'd have thought she didn't give a hoot one way or the other about anything—but when she sat staring out the window smoking one after the other until she'd gone through three cigarettes, you knew she was chewing over something and not liking the taste of it very much.

Finally she got up and went into the bathroom. They heard the water running into the tub, and looked at each other. The balloon was about to go up.

Mom headed off to catch the bus and go into town. Kitty picked up the envelope and the papers that had been in it, and went over to

Gran's. Gran read everything, then she sighed even louder than Mom had. "I suppose he's found himself someone who understands the economics of it all," she said tiredly. "Nobody who can get milk free is going to buy a cow, and only a fool buys a dog and then does his own barking. Someone has given him a taste of cream, I suppose, then told him how much a quart it's going to cost." She dropped the papers on her table and Kitty swooped them up, stuffed them in her pocket.

"So what's it about?"

"What it's about is, he's divorcing her so he can get married again."

"What does she care? She hasn't even seen him since Christ was carrying his cross."

"Well, who knows why? Who but her would understand it? And likely she doesn't understand it herself. But that's what it's all about."

Kitty came home with the news and they all sat listening to the rain drumming on the roof, asking each other what difference any of it made. "Any excuse'll do," Savannah shouted. "You guys are so dumb! You think there has to be a reason for things? There's no reasons. Just excuses."

"Is that why you're what you are?" Jimmy roared. "Jesus Christ, you think nobody's talking? Well, they are, and what they're saying is, it's been used so many times a guy has to strap a two-by-four across his ass sideways just to keep from falling in!"

"You fuckin' faggot!" Savannah went at him and Glen got into it too, and they might have beat Jimmy up but Kitty started whaling away at them from behind, and when Glen turned to throw a punch at her Jimmy slammed him on the back of the neck and dropped him to the floor. Kitty kicked Glen on the side of the head and he started to cry and that was all Savannah needed, she turned and ran to the bedroom and locked the door. She knew Jimmy wouldn't go after her, he never did; as long as you left him alone he'd call it quits.

Seely cried a bit. It wasn't just that the kids were fighting, the fight was the straw too many. She didn't understand what was so awful about the papers or why Mom wanted the excuse, but she knew Mike was going to be mad if he got home and Mom was gone. He'd probably go looking for her, and by the time he'd checked the bars and caught up to her he'd have packed away enough that he'd sit with her, drinking shooters and probably getting so drunk he'd be too hung over to go to work the next day, and if he didn't go to work he'd head for the bar to work off the hangover.

Mom wouldn't have much money, though, that was a good thing. She got her welfare check once a month. Gran got money too, because she told the welfare she charged rent for the house. She didn't, but what they didn't know wouldn't hurt them; and the money didn't go to Mom, it went directly to Gran, because even the welfare knew that what Mom got, Mom had a way of spending in the wrong places. Gran kept one of the rent checks for herself, to pay the differ-ence in income tax the declared rent made, but the rest she used to make sure the kids were dressed and fed and had things like shampoo and stuff that Mom never quite got around to. Gran gave them their allowance money out of it, too. And that was why Gran was the one who got the money her absent son sent—because everyone knew that if he'd sent it to Mom it would have just done the water-into-wine trick, and the one it wasn't for would have got it while the ones it was for would have done without. He didn't send money for Seely, but Gran included her all the same. "Not *her* fault!" she muttered often. "Not her fault at all."

And the welfare check wasn't due for almost five days. With any luck at all Mom would be too hung over to do more than sign it and hand it to Jimmy, to give to Gran so they could go grocery shopping.

All in all, what with the welfare and the rent and the money from Gran's absent son, they probably ought to have done at least as well as kids who had normal parents. But it never seemed to work out that way. There was always something. Like bringing who knows how many others home from the bar and someone deciding to do bacon and eggs, only somehow there were never enough eggs or there wasn't enough bacon or something, and the next thing you knew anything in the house became fair game and they sat around stuffing their faces and gorping down all the groceries. Or they'd play poker and wind up forking over the money that should have gone for the Hydro bill or the fuel company instead.

They wouldn't even have a television if Gran hadn't won some money at the bingo and gone to the Sally Ann and had a talk with the lady who looked after the donated stuff. Some of the TVs were real clunkers, not worth taking home, but the one they wound up with was in pretty good shape, at least where it counted. Maybe the

outside casing was frapped and ugly, but the screen was only a little
bit scratched and it gave a good picture, as long as you didn't bother
yourself with the fact the colors were always a bit off. And when
Gran plugged it in she made sure she let Mom know that it was
Gran's television, and if it wound up pawned she'd have the cops out
to the house. Mom was great at pawning stuff. Not great about
redeeming it but, as Savannah said, you can't have everything, and at
least there was *something* mom could do. Pity it wasn't something like
hang onto money for groceries.

Kitty worried about stuff like that and so did Glen, but Jimmy just
shrugged it off, and Savannah seemed to have decided she was never
going to worry about anything again as long as she lived; she'd just
laugh it off, or find something to take her mind off things.

Jimmy had found a way to make money for himself. Over and above
the paper route, he had a surefire way of making money. He was the
one they'd joked about having a great future as a shoplifter, but he
quit doing that all of a sudden, said he just didn't feel it was safe any
more. Before he quit, however, he managed to lift quite a few things
from Nash Hardware. He sold a socket set to Mike, and a bunch of
other stuff, but a lot of it he kept for himself—especially the smaller
electric things, drills and such-like. He lifted an entire set of made-in-
Germany wood chisels, and then said it didn't feel safe and quit stealing stuff from Nash's. He stole from other places, but not the way he'd
swiped stuff from the hardware store. It was as if, once he had what he
needed to do his trip, he no longer wanted to run any risks.

The first fifty or sixty things he made wound up fuel; Jimmy said
they weren't good enough. He'd spend every evening for a week
working and then sit staring at it and criticizing it and saying this was
wrong and he should have done that, and then he'd burn it.

"Well, *I'd*'a liked to have had it!" Kitty raged. "I thought it was
good."

"Shut up," he answered, "it was *mine*, I can burn it if I want, see."

He burned a lot of little boats and canoes, and a bunch of little
figures like bearded old men sitting with their legs crossed. He didn't
burn the doll-babies he made, he gave them to Seely, and he didn't
burn the set of wooden spoons, he gave them to Gran, but there were
more truck-things and car-things went into the stove than you would

have thought a person could find the time to make. A bowl, a perfectly good bowl, as good as anything you'd find in a store, and what did Jimmy do but toss it in the stove. Off kilter, he said. A bowl? How could a bowl be off kilter, Jesus, if it held salad and didn't leak the dressing onto the table what did kilter matter?

Then he did a totem pole, and when it was done he stared at it and stared at it and stared at it and he nodded. He didn't paint it all up, he just took some oxblood shoe polish and rubbed it in carefully, changing the colour of the wood, making it darker and richer. He sat with an old nylon of Mom's and he rubbed and rubbed until the whole thing gleamed. It was about eighteen inches tall, and he hadn't done the bird with the wings outstretched, he said as far as he was concerned that looked dorky, and anyway, either you wasted a lot of good wood carving the thing out of a big block or you wound up doing the wings separately and they never wanted to stay straight, there was always one end lower than the other, as if the damned bird was drunk. His bird had its wings folded down. He took it to Spindrift, the books and curio store. Lied in his teeth and convinced the guy the thing was authentic, and left it to be sold to some gorpy tourist. It sold and the guy at the store took his fifteen percent, and said he'd take any others Jimmy could bring him, no questions asked.

So Jimmy sat at the arborite-topped chrome-legged table at night and pretended he was an Indian. "That's lying," Savannah snapped, "and I'm apt to tell."

"You're apt to be believed, too," Jimmy laughed. "Streetwalking little slut like you is sure to be considered the art expert of all time."

"Art? That piece of shit? Art my ass!"

"Yeah, well you'd know, wouldn't you?"

"Someone finds out and you're in trouble. Fraud, for a start. You're no Indian."

"Neither are the people who live in Japan, but the stores are full of stuff done by that old tribal carver Jay A. Pan."

"Can't put all of Japan in reform school." Savannah's eyes glittered with tears. "You'll go crazy in Juvie and you know it. And they're just waitin' for the chance to scoop you and send you off for a little stay behind walls."

"Fuck'em," Jimmy whispered.

He didn't just do totem poles and plaques, and he didn't just do Indian stuff, even though it did sell better; he also made little wagons and trucks with wooden wheels, and once he made a baby's rocking cradle. He didn't make it to sell, not at first. Everyone thought Mom was going to have a baby and Jimmy made the rocking cradle for it, but when it turned out that the pot belly wasn't a baby, but only beer and something she had to go to hospital to get them to take out of her, Jimmy shrugged and took the cradle into town and left it with the woman at Bunnikins. She sold it inside of two days for more than Jimmy had expected. She said she'd take more but he didn't do any more of them, he said it was too much fritzing around for the money you made on them. Kitty didn't see that it took any more time than frigging around with that soaking and shaving thing Jimmy was teaching Seely to do, and she didn't see that it took any more time than the eyes and beaks of the birds he did when he was pretending to be an Indian, but Jimmy told her to just shut her damned mouth, see, and he said if she wanted the goddam Bunnikins store to have baby cradles she could damn well make'em herself.

Not Kitty, thank you. She wasn't going to slash into her finger or, worse, stab into her thigh, and have blood pouring all over the place. After Gran had come running over and made what she called a butterfly with adhesive tape, and pulled the cut shut and got the bleeding stopped and all, after they'd washed up the mess and put a pillow behind Jimmy's head because he looked so white in the face, then they had to wash the floor—but the damned spots were still in the wood. Probably be there until the end of time and Kitty wasn't interested, thank you.

Gran humphed and mumphed about that, and then she phoned someone she knew who worked on the green chain at the sawmill, and she used some of the rent money to get two of the leather apronthings the green-chain guys had to wear. "At least you don't have to stob yourself in the leg or cut off something you can ill afford to lose," she grumbled, and she made Seely promise she'd wear the other one any time she was cutting at wood. But Seely didn't care for the wood carving, she liked the other things better, probably because she could always manage to get to the Graingers' place for a few hours a week and not be around home much. Besides, she still had little hands, and her wrists weren't anywhere near strong enough for carving.

Jimmy wore his, though. He could sit and do his carving while still keeping one eye on the television. "Don't have to *see* it," he laughed, "you can just *listen* and you know what's going on." The nights they made popcorn and sat side-by-each on the sofa like crows on a telephone wire, and there was no arguing over what they'd watch or wouldn't because they were all primed for their favorite old program, Jimmy would put his stuff aside and sit with them. And he'd watch as well as listen. Sometimes he'd grin and nudge Kitty and say, "Here you come, better stop chewin' so's you can talk without mumbling." He didn't even tell her to take a hike or jump in the air and bite herself on the ass if she put her head on his shoulder. Of course, she didn't leave it there long; you never dared go too far with Jimmy. He was unpredictable sometimes. Maybe not just sometimes.

"How much of this do you think is true?" Kitty asked.

"It's a friggin' *story*, Kit! *None* of it is true."

"Not *that* part, dim-bulb. I mean the other stuff...like the clothes, say. You think they really dressed like that? Did everybody have a couple of horses? What about saddles and stuff, did everyone have them like nowadays everyone has, oh, I don't know, hell, running water or something?"

"How would I know? Must have been *some* poor people! Not everybody has a car these days, do they? And even people who have cars don't all have new ones, or even good ones. Prob'ly some people had old wore-out plugs. You think people only got poor last year?"

"You think they ate like we do? I don't! Prob'ly had real horrible food. No fresh stuff all winter. No cans of stuff, just dried crap like beans and peas and all that."

"Yeah, can't you just see ol' Doc whippin' somethin' out of the microwave?"

"How could he be a doctor with no hospital? No X-rays or blood tests? Probably just guessed at a whole bunchstuff. Prob'ly most of the stuff in these stories is just bumph, right?"

"What do you care?" Savannah laughed. "Most of the stuff in the whole world is just bumph."

"Costs lots to make these shows, I guess, huh?"

"Why, you gonna make your own?"

"Lot of money to make bumph. Why not make something...real?"

"Who'd watch? Who wants to watch *real?* Wake up, Kit, will you?"

"So you think people got drunk and got to fighting and...you know, even back then?"

"Yeah. No good old days, Kitzer. Never was. Never will be."

"Bummer."

Mom didn't come home the night of the registered letter. Mike came in and found her gone and didn't even change his clothes, he just spun on the heel of his steeltoed workboot and headed back out the door, but he wasn't mad, just anxious to catch up to her before she latched onto someone else.

Seely put eggs on to hard-boil, Savannah made a salad, Jimmy set the table and Kitty cooked up Kraft Dinner. Seely peeled the eggs and cut them into eight pieces and dropped them in with the macaroni and powdered cheese stuff. She wanted Kitty to put a can of mushroom soup in, too, but Kitty said no, it made it too salty. "If you want it that way," she bossed, "then *you* cook the Kraft Dinner, but when I cook it I get it the way I like, so there."

"Shut up," Savannah yelled. "Just sit down and eat, okay?"

"Yeah, and Glen can do the dishes because he never helped with the supper."

"Kiss my ass," Glen answered.

"Take it off your shoulders so I can get at it and maybe I will."

"Yeah, if he washes it," Jimmy laughed.

But Glen didn't do the dishes. The girls did them, and Jimmy brought in a couple of armloads of wood, and told Glen if he didn't bring in his share Jimmy was going to beat his head in, so Glen went out and got some and dumped it in the woodbox. Then Glen went out and split a pile of kindling without being asked or told, and came in and sat on the couch that folded out to make a bed and grinned and grinned and grinned, and Kitty knew he'd done something to bug Jimmy. She guessed it was probably something real mean, like taking a good piece of dried cedar from the stuff Jimmy used when he was pretending to be an Indian and splitting it into kindling. If he had, when Jimmy found out about it there was going to be an awful fight. But Kitty wasn't going to let the cat out of the bag, because then Glen would just wait and get her alone, and the satisfaction of seeing him get thumped wouldn't be anywhere near enough to make up for what he'd do to her.

The rain got worse and the wind started to blow, and then Fred showed up and he had a three-quarters-grown German shepherd with him. "Where's your mom?" he said with a grin, just walking in the house without knocking or anything, as if he still lived there.

"She's out beering. What you doing here?"

"Came to visit, is all."

"Well, you'd better go visit someone else because if you're here when she gets back she'll have a fit."

"Oh, don't be silly, she won't be like that."

"No? Mike will be."

"Think I'm afraid of him? That'll be the day. That'll be the frosty Friday when I'm afraid of Mike."

"It was frosty last Friday." Kitty blew through her lips and made the horselaugh sound. "You better go," she repeated, and after a while he left and took his damned dog with him.

Just before breakfast-time Mike came home. He was sober, and that seemed like a not-good sign, but nobody got up out of bed to talk to him. He made coffee and cooked up some eggs and ate them, muttering to himself, then headed off to drive his big truck again.

They put themselves off to school and when they got home Mom was there and so was Fred, and even if they were sitting at the table playing crib and sipping beer you could tell they'd spent most of the day in bed together. The dog lay on a bit of blanket near the stove and just wagged its great big tail.

Mom even got up from the table and started to make supper. She frizzled some hamburger in the frying pan, then poured mushroom soup on it and added water and called it all gravy. They had it on a huge mound of mashed potatoes and everyone went back for seconds. Mike didn't come home from work for supper. Who cared, it just meant more frizzle for the rest of them.

Everyone felt tight inside because of Mike not coming home, but they were all tired from the night before, staying up late and Fred showing up and then Mike coming in and waking them up early, so they went to bed. About three in the morning they were all awake again, and the dog was barking, and Mike and Fred were swinging at each other while Mom stood with one shoulder pressing against the wall, not quite leaning, watching the fight as if none of it had anything to do with her.

Then Mike threw Fred out the door and slammed it shut and locked it. The dog growled, but when Mike threw a kick at it the dumb mutt had at least sense enough to tuck its big tail between its legs and run into the boys' room and hide under the bed. Then Mike jawed away at Mom for a while and she jawed back at him, and then the cops came.

Mike yelled at the cops and Mom yelled at the cops, and Fred yelled from the other side of the porch, and the cops told the kids to bring the damned dog outside, so Glen got it by the collar and led it out of the kitchen. Mike slammed the door and Glen yelled that *he* hadn't done anything, why did he have to sleep in the friggin' rain, so Mike opened the door to let him back in again.

"Nobody stole his damned dog," he yelled, "The bugger shoulda took it with him when he left!"

Things calmed down enough they could go back to bed, but they didn't get to sleep because Mike kept arguing. "No, I am *not* going to goddam work!" he roared. "If you think I'm goin' to work to make money for you to spend while some other guy sits in *my* chair drinkin' *my* coffee, you're nuts." But he went off to work when it was time. And sure enough, there was Fred coming in the door, with a grin on his face and the dog following him.

The next day, Friday, they went to school, and when they came home there were circus tickets on the table, but no sign of Fred or Mike or Mom. The dog was there, so Glen took it for a walk so it could do its stuff outside. It wasn't a bad dog, and it seemed to know about Come and Sit and Lie Down and No. It wouldn't do to get too used to it, though, or to start thinking how nice it would be to have one of your own, because that was just not going to happen, and all you got for hoping was disappointment. The circus tickets weren't the only thing someone had left, there was a five-pound bag of dogfood too, so they could at least feed it. Maybe the tickets were for babysitting the mutt. Who would know, there was nobody to ask. They hurried with supper, then ran to the highway to flag down the bus.

Seely had some money, enough for popcorn. Kitty had money for popcorn and a cotton candy each for her and Seely. Savannah saw some guys she knew and went to sit with them; they bought her anything she wanted.

Glen and Jimmy had plenty of money. Nobody knew where Glen got his but he always had some. Maybe not as much as Jimmy, but Glen didn't seem to *do* anything for his, he just always had ten dollars when he needed it.

They had fun. There weren't any tigers, but there were lions and people on a trapeze and some clowns, and the horses came in with a woman in spangles jumping on and off them and standing on their backs and doing a somersault, and then there were more clowns. At intermission they went out to look at the lions, back in their cages and already asleep. Jimmy glared and said they probably gave the poor things sleeping pills as soon as the show was finished, he said they kept them goofed up most of the time. They didn't look bad, though, no wore-off-fur places, no patches of mange or anything, and they all seemed shiny. It was just that they were sound asleep, even with the music playing and people standing not six feet from them and talking. The elephants looked dusty, and had big metal rings around their ankles, and hunks of chain strong enough to be boom chain, fastened to the big transports. One of them just rocked from one set of feet to the other, side to side, her eyes more closed than open, rocking, rocking, and Jimmy said she was bored almost crazy from being kept either in the truck or chained to it. Kitty didn't mind the sleeping lions so much but the elephants made her feel sad; something that big, you could tell looking at them they needed lots and lots of room and instead here they were rocking, rocking, with no room at all, not even enough to lie down. Then they went back inside for the second half, and a guy on an ordinary-looking bicycle was doing tricks and stunts that just about made you want to say it wasn't real, and yet there he was doing them, and no mirrors or trick cameras or anything. By the time it was over, their heads were so full of images they could have spent a week just remembering.

There was a midway, too, and Jimmy gave Seely and Kitty some tickets to go on the rides. Savannah was set up for rides, the guys were practically spitting in each other's eyes for the chance to get into the salt and pepper shakers with her, or onto the Ferris wheel, where they could sit with one hand on the seat and Savannah sitting on the other, her skirt hiding whatever it was they were doing.

Glen used some of his money to go into the hootchy-kootchy
tent. Jimmy just shook his head and said things like Jesus Christ,
Glen, but Glen laughed and said he wanted to see some of it up real
close. They had to wait for him and then they had to run like stink to
catch the last bus home. Glen looked like the cat who had swallowed
the canary, and all he said was, Yeah, well, don't believe anyone when
they tell you free stuff is better.

By the next Wednesday, Glen wasn't laughing any more. He looked
as if it was exam time and he cared about passing. Finally he asked
Mike if he could come outside for a few minutes.

"What's the matter?" Mike grumbled. "Why can't you talk about
it here where it's at least dry?"

"Gotta show you something," Glen muttered, his face red. "Come
on, please."

"Must be the end of the world, shithead said please." But Mike
went outside with Glen, and not five minutes later Mike came in
again, so mad he wouldn't speak to anyone; he just grabbed his jacket
and his truck keys and headed back outside. They watched through
the rain-wet window as Glen got in the truck and Mike peeled off,
spraying mud and puddle-water everywhere.

When they came back it was past ten at night, and Glen was very
very quiet. Mike grabbed Jimmy by the arm and hauled him out on
the porch for a few minutes, then they came in again and Jimmy was
laughing like hell. "Save the moldy cheese," he mocked, "there's
someone can use the penicillin," but he wouldn't explain more than
that. Savannah didn't need any explanation, but neither Seely nor
Kitty really understood what was such a big joke.

"Sure got *your* money's worth, eh, guy? Just hand over your cash
and I'll give you something you've never had before, she said, and
boy, was she tellin' the truth!" And Jimmy laughed and laughed and
laughed but Glen didn't even get mad, he just sat on the chair looking as if he felt too miserable to even bother crying.

Thursday morning Mike told Glen to get in the pickup, and they
drove out to the Circus grounds and asked a few questions, then hammered on the door of the trailer where the manager was still sleeping.

"What the hell do *you* want?" the guy snarled.

"You got germs in your hootchy-kootchy show," Mike said flatly. "This here kid just wound up getting his ass peppered with antibiotic shots. So you'd better shut'er down."

"Go piss up a rope, buddy," the manager sneered. "Where your kid dips his wick is no concern of mine, and what he catches when he tries to pretend he's a man isn't my business either." And he shut the door.

"You'll wish you hadn't done that," Mike vowed.

That evening Mike climbed up into his big chipper truck and, instead of taking the umpteen tons of sawdust to the pulp mill, drove in the other direction, out to the circus grounds. It was between seven-thirty and quarter to and the show was due to start at eight; most people were in the Big Top waiting for the clown car to appear. Mike hit the airhorn to warn them, and then drove the chipper truck right through the snow fence. Circus people were yelling and other people were screeching and everyone was running away from the loaded chipper truck, but Mike just laughed and laughed and laughed, and blew his airhorn. The first thing he hit was the manager's trailer. He nosed up to one end of'er and kept on going, right down in bull low, and the trailer bounced and hopped across the vacant field like a flat stone going over the still surface of a pond. One of the circus guys fired both barrels of a shotgun, but all that did was punch some little holes in the chipper box and allow sawdust to sift down like salt out of a shaker.

Mike and the big truck pushed the travel-sized single-wide right into the boggy area where the bulrushes grew thick; then he backed up a bit, swung her around and headed back, airhorn still bellowing. This time he took out the hootchy-kootchy tent. All the painted canvas panels with the gorgeous Marilyn Monroe-type girlies in feather bathing suits went tumbling into the mud; the picture of the black woman with the big snake coiled around her leg caught on the bulldog on the hood of the truck. The women who came rushing out the back of the tent in bathing suits covered with tarnished sequins, yelling and slipping in their rundown high-heeled shoes, didn't look much like the paintings in the mud—they looked like just about anyone you might see at the beach, except lots paler and with gobs of makeup smeared on their faces.

Mike drove the chipper truck right through the kootch tent, then whipped'er around and drove'er back through what little was still standing. What had been on the mud wound up ground into the mud, and the flimsy little collapsible bleachers broke into a thousand pieces.

On his way back out again Mike clipped the edge of the counter where the crown-and-anchor game was set up. Everything tipped and spilled and went flying, and the guy running it got tangled in the ropes holding up the awning. Before he got himself untangled, the money he'd taken from the fools had gone into the pockets of the kids who swarmed like rats, snatching and grabbing. Hitting the crown-and-anchor game had been an accident, but it seemed like such a good idea that Mike took out the ring-over-the-peg game too. Reaching out his arm as he went by, he snared three enormous panda bears and dragged them into the cab, and kept on going, scattering money and rings and teddies and grinning stuffed dogs and big pink panthers, all of which were snatched up before they had time to get wet; a few never hit the mud at all, they were caught in midair and raced off across the lot by laughing young guys in jean jackets.

Mike took out the rest of the snow fence and clipped his tail on the ticket booth. It was empty, the guy running it had taken off like a greased pig when he saw the truck coming his way. The tail of the truck tipped the fancy outhouse-shaped booth and sent it onto its side, the door flying open and the roof smashing. By the time the cops got there, all that was left was some splintered wood and a couple of rolls of tickets lying in the mud. The money was gone, little tin box and all.

Mike drove the truck all the way out to the pulp mill and even got his load half dumped before the cops caught up to him. The cops coming clued in the millworkers, and Mike told them what he'd done. The cops were busy trying to take notes, but later on the judge said they couldn't use any of that as evidence because Mike hadn't been questioned or arrested or read his rights, and anyway Mike took the Canada Evidence Act, and nothing he said could be used against him.

The judge gave him three months—then suspended the sentence. Mike lost his job, of course, but he didn't seem to care. "Hell, I was lookin' for a job when I walked up to the place, I can look for another job when I walk away from it," he laughed.

From the way Glen acted, you'd have thought catching a dose was something to be proud of. And from the way the other boys at school behaved, you'd have thought they agreed with him.

"Oh, shut the fuck up, will you?" Jimmy shook his head as if he couldn't believe any of it. "It's not as if it took brains or talent, you know."

"Oh yeah?" Glen sneered. "And what do *you* do that takes brains or talent? Play with yourself, I suppose."

"You stop that!" Kitty snapped. "You wanna yap, go somewheres else to do it, okay? We're watching our program, okay?" She fluffed her panda and sat it on her knee as if it was alive. "Okay," she confided, holding its stiff little arms in her grubby hands. "Now you watch. And don't be scared. There might be some shooting or fighting or something, but it isn't for real. It's pretend. And Matt *never* gets killed. Not ever."

"He gets hurt, though," Seely warned, tucking her panda in the crook of her arm and rocking it gently. "He gets hurt. Mostly shoulders and ribs. That way they get to bring Doc out and have him *do* something. Bandages. Strips from tore-up sheets, usually."

"I don't have to tell *my* bear all that silly stuff." Even Savannah was getting into it. She sat her bear on her knees and jiggled, giving it a horsy-back ride, comfortable again with some sidetrip back into babyhood. "My bear is the smart one."

"Your bear has a cockeye," Kitty said sharply. "Someone sewed her button on crooked."

"Yeah? Well, it doesn't bother her one little bit, she can see the TV just fine." Savannah wasn't about to be sucked into some argument that might wind up with her bear proved deficient. "And it doesn't stop her from being the smartest one, either."

"Prob'ly has to wear glasses." Kitty wasn't going to let go of it. "She likely has big round Ollie-Owl type uglies, too, like a bookworm or teacher's pet."

"She does *not* have Ollie-Owl glasses!" Savannah winked. "Just look at her. She's a bear, isn't she? So she's got bare eyes, all right?"

"Bear feet, too." Kitty pulled on the socks she had fitted over her own bear's little stub feet. "Some mother *you* are, your bear is naked."

"Shut up, it's starting," Seely shouted. "Jesus, just shut up, okay?" and she slapped Savannah's leg with her bear.

"Some bearbysitter *you* are," Savannah scolded, "using the poor thing as if it was a club or something."

"Good!" Jimmy grabbed a handful of popcorn. "Chester's in this one. I like it best when Chester's in the show."

"He's a gimp. Old Crip himself," Kitty snarled.

"Shut up, Kitty, or I'll shave off your hair."

"I bet," but she dug into the popcorn and held her hand under her panda's nose, as if she really believed the thing would open its mouth and take a bite or two.

2

Savannah saw the damned thing first. She was just out of the bath, her hair still damp, and she was getting dressed to go out on the town. She opened the closet door and shrieked—several times. Savannah shrieking wasn't unusual, but Savannah unable to do anything *but* shriek was enough out of the ordinary they all raced to help.

"It went under the bed!" she insisted, but even when they shone the flashlight under and poked with brooms and all, there was no sign of it. So they pulled the furniture away from the wall and found a pile of little dried ratshit pellets behind the dresser. In the back of the closet, behind the shoes and stuff, they found a hole, and they set a trap there, with peanut butter for bait.

In the morning there was a rat leg in the trap, but no rat—just some blood sprayed around. Jimmy said the spring-loaded trap bar had probably broke the rat's leg and the busted bone went through the meat and skin so the rat chewed off the rest and hopped away. "Bugger's in the wall," he roared, "with a Band-aid on his stump, gnawin' a kindlin' stick with his teeth, tryin' to make hisself a pair a' crutches!"

"That's not funny!" Savannah yelled. "There's nothing funny about ratshit in the bedroom!"

They found more of it in the bathroom, in the back of the cupboard under the sink where the sanitary pads and shampoo bottles were kept. They found it under the sink in the kitchen, too, and when they checked the yellow package where the scouring pads were kept there were holes chewed in the steel wool and most of the blue soap stuff was sucked off what was left. The candles in the drawer were gnawed at and there was a hole in the wood where the rat had chewed his way in, and more lozenge-shaped pellets in the pull-out drawer in the stove where the roasting pan was kept.

But worst of all was what they found when they pulled the flour bag away from the wall: a big hole in the bag and baby rats squirming in the flour that had spilled out.

"Jesus Christ!" Jimmy quit laughing then and looked as if he was going to puke. "And we used that goddam flour to make bannock!" He got the dustpan from behind the stove and used the broom to sweep the dozen or so pink squirmy things onto it. Then he lifted the lid off the stove and dumped the whole lot of them into the fire. Seely started screeching, but nobody paid any attention. "There!" Jimmy shouted, his face pulled tight in a grimace of total grossed-out disgust. "Dead rats don't shit!"

They saved the lids off all the cans they opened, washed them off and nailed them over the rat holes they found behind the furniture and up in the attic. But they kept finding pellets in the oddest damned places.

They set traps and checked them, sometimes finding dead rats, sometimes finding rats still alive and trying to get away, leaping as far as they could with the trap attached to a leg or a tail. One of the buggers had the trap right across the spine, its back legs paralyzed, and still it managed to jump four feet in the air just using its front legs. It was crazy with pain and fear and kept trying to bite at them, and finally Jimmy grabbed the broom and swung it like a softball bat, but he missed and knocked over a chair. The noise scared the crippled rat even worse and it leapfrogged toward the girls' bedroom.

Kitty was the prize-winner that time. She did just the same as Jimmy had done, but she didn't use a broom, she grabbed her aluminum ball bat, and if she'd been on the diamond instead of in the bedroom, with a softball instead of a crippled rat, it would have been a home run.

"Well, smart-ass," Savannah screamed, "now YOU can clean up the bloody mess!" and she ran into the bathroom and puked.

"Me?" Kitty raged, "Me clean it up? Jesus, do I have to do *every-thing* around here? Let *Glen* clean it up."

"Clean your clock, you mean," Glen growled, his face white. He tried to tough it out but wound up kneeling beside the porcelain altar ralphing right along with Savannah.

Jimmy and Kitty cleaned up the gore and Seely tried to pretend nothing had happened. "Just don't do it again, see," she threatened. "Just don't do it any more *ever*, you fool."

Jimmy bought rat poison and went all around the basement and the attic, leaving little jar lids of the stuff and muttering over them like a witch doctor leaving a trail of curses in the jungle. The amount of little oval pellets diminished rapidly, but Gran's cat must have caught some of the dying rats and ate them because he wound up dead too. "It would *have* to be a dying rat if *that* cat caught it," Kitty decided. "Tomcats don't catch rats. They couldn't catch *fleas* most of the time."

"Oh, and what do *you* know about it?"

"Probably more than *you* do, Savannah, because I use my brains, not my twat, okay?"

Much as they fought all the time, and much as Kitty obviously detested Savannah, she stuck up for her any time anyone outside the family had anything to say. She stuck up for Seely even more, because people teased Seely about being a pound puppy and about how it was like some kind of lottery as to who held the winning ticket to be her dad.

Martha Hollett picked on Seely because Seely was easy to pick on, she was the youngest and she was the skinniest, too. And Seely was so used to being tail-of-the-cow that lots of times she wouldn't even stick up for herself.

"Yah," Martha Hollett screeched, "and your stupid sister Savannah likes doing it with guys so much she even convinced your dumb brother Glen that getting it instead of giving it was fun!"

"What a dumb thing to say," Seely marveled. "It doesn't make any sense at all."

"Oh no? If you weren't such a dumb bunny of a baby you'd know what it meant. Cornhole is what it means, Seely, bum-numb is what it means. Gearbox is what it means, idiothead."

That's when Kitty swung her roundhouse right. She got Martha right bang on the jaw, halfway between the chin and the place where the bottom jaw connects with the skull. And all of a sudden Martha's mouth was twisted further over on one side than on the other, and she was howling and wailing like crazy. Mrs. Chouinnard grabbed Kitty by the arm and marched her into the principal's office. Old Cabbageguts—that was what the kids who took French called Mrs. Chouinnard—who decided she wouldn't wait for the principal to get back from taking Martha to the hospital, she'd just go ahead and give Kitty the strap herself.

"You will like hell," Kitty declared.

"Don't make it worse for yourself," Old Cabbageguts lectured. "You've got yourself in quite enough trouble as it is."

"You try, grumbleguts, you just try and you'll eat that goddam thing, handle-end first."

Kitty backed away until she got the principal's desk between her and Cabbageguts, and then she just chucked stuff. The *Oxford English Dictionary*, *Bartlett's Quotations*, a big brass paperweight made to look like the British bulldog. She aimed them for Cabbageguts' head, but she couldn't have been really trying to hit her because she just lobbed them, so Cabbageguts could duck. If Kitty had zinged them she'd have taken hunks out of Cabbageguts' ugly face.

Mr. Marpole, the maths and sciences teacher, came running in because of the uproar Cabbageguts was making.

"Here, here, here!" he shouted, stepping in front of Cabbageguts and glaring at Kitty. "What are you *doing*?" he demanded. "Trying to put yourself in reform school?"

"She's not giving me no strap," Kitty answered, shaking with rage—and probably fear. "Not her or anyone. That damned Martha Hollett was picking on Seely and Cabbageguts didn't even try to stop it. She didn't do anything at all until that damned Martha, that fat pig with the big bazoom tits, got exactly what she had coming to her."

"She broke Martha Hollett's jaw!" Cabbageguts accused. "She punched her and broke her jaw."

"Well, maybe that'll shut her up for a while," Kitty yelled, "and make her think twice about the things she says and the lies she tells." And Kitty said right out loud what it was Martha Hollett had said about Savannah and Glen. Mr. Marpole swallowed two or three times, and then suggested they all calm down until the principal got back and then maybe they could talk about it.

But Cabbageguts wasn't going to back down. She rushed forward and grabbed Kitty by the arm again. Kitty yelped and squirmed, then

bit Cabbageguts on the hand and ducked underneath the desk, coming out through the hole in the middle where your legs are supposed
to fit. She dodged past Mr. Marpole, who made no move to stop her,
and streaked off down the hallway and out the front door. She didn't
even wait to get her jacket, but ran across the playground, past the
swings, to the smaller gate at the back of the schoolyard. It was usually locked, but it was lower than the crusader wire fence and she
jumped up, caught the top of the gate, pulled herself over and
streaked through Pelter's cowfield. Seely figured Kitty was likely
heading home to get her side of the story told to Gran before the balloon went up and the police arrived or something.

Nothing much happened. After all that, and the biting and
Bartlett's Quotations and everything, nothing much happened. Mr. and
Mrs. Hollett had to take Martha down to the principal's office. She
couldn't say much—she had wire things attached to her teeth and to
each other to hold her jaw in place while it healed, and she was losing weight, which she could well afford to lose, because all she could
do was drink Tigers Milk and Moose Milk and stuff like the
weightlifters used. No more fish'n'chips for her for a while.

Then Seely had to go in and tell about her hair getting pulled,
and she showed the big bruise on her arm where Martha had pinched
her. Then Glen got called in, and all he said was that he knew nothing about any of it, he hadn't even been on that side of the playground. Jimmy said just about the same thing, except for promising
Martha Hollett if she didn't keep her tongue to herself he'd do more
than break her fuckin' jaw. Mr. Hollett said Here, here, little man,
and Jimmy gave him a look that shut his mouth in a rush and said,
You can eat shit too, daddy-oh. Mr. Marpole went in and talked for a
while, told them all they had to do was check Glen's report card and
they'd see that whatever it was Martha had thought she was talking
about, it was obvious Glen got good marks in both maths and sciences, and while it was true he didn't do as well in English, especially
the grammar part of it, he was basically as good a student as could be
expected, all things considered, whereas he, Mr. Marpole, could say
without fear of contradiction that Martha had never done much
about extending herself or making a real effort. He said more, too; he
said Martha was known to pick on younger kids and had often made
Seely's life miserable, and that while he didn't agree with hitting and

punching and breaking jaws, he could understand why Kitty had felt she'd been pushed too far. He also said he thought it could all have been much better handled from the get-go, and that grabbing Kit by the arm and all had been almost guaranteed to have her feeling she had to defend herself physically.

Mr. and Mrs. Hollett both said they were going to sue for medical expenses. Mr. Marpole said he was quite sure they had medical insurance so they probably weren't out any of their own money, and anyway did they really think the court was going to take welfare money away from a woman with five children, it would be the same as taking food out of the mouths of the children, and he pointed out that there was the matter of the bruise, and of Seely being so much younger and smaller, and he doubted the judge would blame Kitty, who was merely defending her little sister and who had, after all, only swung one punch.

Kitty refused to apologize to anybody for any of it. She didn't even have to apologize for calling Mrs. Chouinnard "cabbageguts". Seely said she didn't see what *she* had to apologize for, she was the one who'd been teased and pinched and shoved and told lies to by Martha, but if they needed someone to apologize for something she'd apologize for everything whether it was her fault or not. "None of it makes no never-mind to me" she shrugged. "I don't even know what in hell she was talking about, pardon my French."

What she was talking about, she being Martha Hollett, had to do with Glen and the money he always had when he needed it. Glen and Jimmy had a great big shouting match about it, and then Mike got into it and Glen told him to go fuffle up a gum tree and mind his own beeswax. Mike said there wasn't enough room in the house for him and a goddam gearbox and Glen said, Well who gave a shit, it wasn't Mike's house for one thing, and nobody had invited him for another.

Mom went on a ten-day bender over it, and decided it was all Savannah's fault. "If you didn't have a reputation like you've got," she yelled, "nobody would say things like that about your brother, and nobody would pick on your sister."

"Sister? Seely? Hey, she's no sister of *mine*!" Savannah raged. "As for reputation, what in hell would *you* know about reputation, the only one you ever had was a bad one, you had nothing to LOSE for cryin'

out loud!" And she was so mad and so disgusted she just quit school
and stuffed her things into a shopping bag and moved in with three
construction workers who were part of a crew widening the highway.

She couldn't have been too mad, though, because she went round
by way of the school at lunchtime and waved for Kitty to come over
to the fence. "I didn't take all my stuff," she said, smiling easily. "You
can have it. There's some okay sweaters and stuff will fit you. Some of
it's not all that great, but...it's yours, such as it is."

"When you coming home?"

"I *am* home, now," Savannah said, still smiling. "I'm not going
back to that loony bin ever again, Kit. Who needs it? And if you...or
you and Seel, for that matter...ever decide *you've* had a gutful
too...come join me."

"Well, Mom's already sorry. She didn't mean...."

"She's really got nothin' to do with any of it. I mean, it's not *her*.
It's the whole thing, it's just...." She shrugged. "Listen, there's a whole
bunch other stuff I'd rather talk about, okay? You all right?"

A couple of weeks later she was waiting after school with a couple
of shopping bags. "One nice thing about not bein' in school," she
laughed, "is you can get down to the Sally Ann before everything's all
picked over and the good stuff is gone. This ought to fit someone."

It fit as if it had been carefully chosen. Except for a few things like
maybe a missing button or a bit of a rip at one corner of a pocket, the
stuff was almost as good as new. Better, maybe; it didn't have that
stiffness that screams Look At Me. Gran fixed the bit that needed it,
and gave Kitty a big square of fruitcake to take with her to school and
give to Savannah. "You might," Gran hinted, frowning, "take the
time to go by the motel and visit. She *is*, after all, your sister."

So Kitty took the fruitcake with her and skipped afternoon classes in
favor of going by the motel. The three construction workers were on
the job and Savannah had been busy as a bee all morning cleaning
cabins, changing the sheets, taking stuff to the laundry room and
such. "I get paid," she said happily, "same as if it was a real job. And
the lady says she'll give me a good reference when we move on, so
maybe I can get lucky again next place we go."

"Go?" Kitty echoed, feeling as if someone was pulling the chair
out from under her. "Go where?"

"It's a wide wide world," Savannah laughed. "And construction work takes you all over it, too. Oh," she said hurriedly, "we'll be here a while longer, and you can stay over any time you want. We'll be here *lots* longer," she lied, "it's not as if I'm going to China or something. And it's not as if it's going to be *forever*."

Savannah looked lots better than when she was living at home and mad all the time. There was a softness to her, as if she didn't need her hard edge any more, so had put it aside. Probably she still had it, she wasn't one to throw away anything she might need again, but it was carefully packed away somewhere. She smiled lots more, and when she laughed it sounded more as if she meant it.

She must have done a good job for the motel lady because the lady started letting Savannah look after the whole thing in the afternoons. Of course, there wasn't much to *do* that time of day—the cabins, or units, or whatever they called them, were all cleaned, linen changed, stuff like that, and anyone who was going to check out was usually gone by eleven in the morning; after all, they'd have to pay for another night if they stayed past that. The ones who were going to check in usually didn't start to show up until after supper, but still, there was the phone to answer and reservations to take and stuff. And she *could* have swiped them blind, but she never did.

Of course, job or no job, the whole damned town knew Savannah wasn't just working there, they must have had a great old time talking and making jokes about the three construction workers. Only one kid at school said anything out loud, though. Bobby Barton walked up to Jimmy in the playground and asked, "You figure one of them holds the flashlight, one does the aiming and the third...," and that was as far as he got. Jimmy moved so fast even Kitty was amazed, and his hands had Bobby Barton by the hair, hauling his face down to meet the knee coming up. It was pretty gross.

"Jesus, Jimmy," Kitty whispered, "you don't think maybe you went a bit far?"

Mr. Barton came to the school without Bobby, who was still up in Emergency getting his top lip stitched and his nose packed and straightened. He went into the principal's office and talked for a bit, then Jimmy went in, looking white in the face but not really scared. They talked for quite a while but nobody had any idea what all got

said. Mr. Barton was upset, of course, although the dentist said the
loose teeth would set themselves firm again and they wouldn't need
to do much with them. But he didn't really seem mad as much as he
was sad. Well, maybe he figured Bobby got what he deserved, talking
when he ought to have been listening, and all.

"What happened?" Seely asked, so scared for Jimmy she was set to
start crying.

"Never you mind." Jimmy tried to glare but he was too relieved to
be able to get the frown set firm on his face. "It's okay, Seel," he
added, probably feeling sorry for her because she was such a little
fraidy most of the time.

Nobody else said anything to them directly, but Kitty knew there
were lots of things got said where they couldn't hear. Well, who
cared—if they were talking about her and her family, they weren't
talking about her friends. Not that she had any.

It was odd about those construction guys, though. They just sort of
smiled a lot. Well, no wonder, they hardly had enough of the language
between them to order french fries and gravy. And maybe Bobby Barton had been on to something. What *did* they all do? Flip a coin? One
after the other? Turn about, maybe, two nights each and Sunday for
going to church? But you didn't dare ask Savannah stuff like that or
she might really get mad. And nobody wanted her mad. Not because
of the stuff from the Salvation Army store, not even because she
sometimes handed over a bag of groceries. She just seemed so much
more like the sister they'd known all along, and less and less like whoever it was had been so mad all the time. She invited them for supper,
and they went. Without Mom or Mike, though, because Savannah
said she wouldn't give house room to either of them.

The three construction workers smiled a lot and nodded a lot and
helped set stuff out on the little table. There weren't enough chairs,
so the boys sat on the floor and left the table to the big bowls of food
and the chairs to Savannah, Kitty and Seely.

"You cooked all this stuff your*self?*" Glen gaped.

"Yeah," Savannah nodded, and you could tell she was pretty
pleased with herself. "You like it?"

"You cook as good as Gran does," Jimmy said. That really made
Savannah happy so it didn't matter that it wasn't altogether true;

after all, the dessert was a bought cake with ice cream, and most of what Gran gave them was made from scratch.

When supper was finished the three construction workers just up and started to clear the table. Jimmy wasn't going to be shown up by any friggin' foreigners, so he moved fast to help, and gave Glen such a jab in the ribs with his elbow that Glen pitched in too, which was almost enough to make a person think the Last Trump had sounded. When they were getting ready to go home Savannah cut a great big piece of the bought cake and wrapped it carefully, then handed it to Jimmy. "For Gran." She sounded almost fraidy herself. "She used to talk about Black Forest cake, remember? So that's what I told them I wanted. Except I think they used canned cherries instead of the kind you're supposed to use, with brandy."

Gran looked at the piece of cake and then she smiled as if there wasn't anything the least bit odd about Savannah living with three strangers at once. "Why, you tell your sister this will do just fine, canned cherries or not. And tell her not to be such a stranger, there's a bus passes in front of the place half a dozen times a day."

And Gran *took* that bus, too. Didn't say a word to anyone about it, but they found out when Savannah told them she and Gran had sat together on the big front porch of the motel office and had sandwiches and little pastries, and talked about stuff without ever once mentioning what a load of crap was coming down at home, with Mom half cut all the time and starting to get the shakes, and all like that. Gran gave Savannah some recipes and wrote down some of the ones Savannah had learned from the big cookbook she'd borrowed from the library. Savannah said they had a real nice visit. She even came out to Gran's little house and visited, then helped make supper. But that didn't go so well because Mom came storming over to know why *she* hadn't been invited. Mike came after her but that only made it worse, because the Old Biddy went up his face and pointed at the big ramshackle house and told him he might think he had the right to come and go as he pleased, but not in her yard or her house. "And you"—she took Mom by the shoulders and spun her around—"you just waddle your way back to where you came from, I'm under no obligation to invite *you* into my house just because my grandchildren are having dinner with me." She pronounced it obleegation, so they knew she was really angry; she didn't start to talk broad unless she was either real sad or real mad.

"Guess I should'a stayed went." Savannah tried to make a joke of it but you could tell she felt hurt. And before much longer that's what she did. Went.

3

Mom's sister Phyllis came to stay with them. She and her old man had split up and she couldn't see staying in the same town as him, just asking for more trouble, so she emptied the bank account, bought an old International Harvester Travelall, packed some stuff in it and another bunch of stuff on it and drove her two kids to the big house because, she said, "blood is thicker than water."

"If you're going to be there more than a week," Gran said, "you'll pay rent too."

"I'll pay half *her* rent," Aunt Phyllis snapped. She and Gran hated each other, probably because they were close to being two of a kind.

"You will not, because *she* don't pay rent, the whoofare does. And the whoofare is going to keep paying the same amount but *you* are going to pay rent too, because you're using the place, your kids are wearing out the steps with their inning and outing, you're drinking water from *my* well and you'd pay rent anywhere else you parked your carcass."

"What a stingy old bitch you are."

"Me stingy? You're the one wants a free ride!"

"Taking money from your own family!"

"You're no family of *mine*!" Gran spoke quietly and coldly but it made Phyllis' eyes slit and her mouth tighten. She glared, but didn't say anything.

Phyllis paid her rent. No flies on Phyllis. She paid six months in advance. "Might as well while I've got the money," she laughed. "I know that mad bastard isn't going to be sending anything, he'd see his kids starve on the side a' the highway before he'd let s'much as one nickel cross *my* palm. He is," she laughed, "about as crazy as they come."

Aunt Phyllis had tattoos. The first one she got when she was still married to her first husband. He got sick and tired of her never being at home and he lost his temper. "You're not married to *me*," he yelled, "you're married to the goddamned booze."

The idea pleased Phyllis so much she wove her way off to the tattoo parlor and had the biker who ran the place do what looked like a wedding ring, only right on the top of her third finger, left hand, the wedding ring turned into a bottle with three Xs across the label. She liked it so much and got so many remarks on it in the bar that she got a sort of bracelet thing tattooed around each wrist. "Nobody's gonna steal *my* family jewels," she brayed, laughing until she choked on her own cigarette smoke.

So many tattoos look muddy—the lines spread over time, the colors fade or blend together, the designs become obscured, a person can't tell if it's Death before Dishonor or Born to Boogie—but Phyllis' tattoos were something else. The blue lines marking the outline were thin, crisp and clean, the colors of the flowers were bright like the vegetable dye colors you mix in little cups or bowls to color Easter eggs. Jimmy was fascinated by them, and asked time and again if Phyllis would explain the process to him. "You gonna be a tattoo artist when you grow up?" she teased.

"Naw." He almost blushed. "I'd have to touch people and I don't like to do that."

"Then what's the big attraction?"

"Skin"—he seemed nervous—"and what it is, and what it does. It's like magic, sort of. Bones too. We never even think about them, but they fit together just right."

"Yeah." Phyllis nodded but she had a look on her face for a moment that was almost like she was worried about him. Later on, when they were alone, she told Mom Jimmy was a deep one. "You gotta worry about the deep ones," she warned, "their thinking so much can sometimes bend'em outta shape."

Donald and Mervin were even younger than Seely, and for a month or so, because their last name was different, nobody really knew they were cousins. In that month the two boys had time to find out for themselves who was tough and who only thought he was tough, so when the crap started about being more of the Trash Team, they knew who to lip back and who to pretend to ignore.

Seely didn't like either of them. Donald told lies and Mervin tattle-taled. The only good part was, Aunt Phyllis ignored them both, so it didn't matter who said what, true or false, they might as well have said it to thin air. Seely admired the way they stuck together, though, so if anyone started to pick on one he found he was fighting off both of them, and of course, since they were her cousins, she had to jump in to help or someone would listen for *sure*, when they told that one at home. "Stick with your family," Mom maundered often. "If you haven't got family, you've got nothing."

Savannah didn't move back home, not even after the construction crew followed the road and wound up with such a drive back and forth to work that they packed their stuff and moved into a motel down where they were working. "Not me," she vowed, "I'd rather go live in a rented box on the side of an unpaved highway than move back in with this gang of screwballs." She was pregnant and about half the size of a freightliner truck, but she said she'd never felt better. She'd quit smoking and drinking beer, or coffee, although she still had her cups of tea. "Take every vitamin they hand out at prenatal, what the hell, it's free, right?" When Mom asked her if she had her names picked out, Savannah looked her in the eye and with a perfectly straight face said, "Well, I think if it's a boy I'll call him Jesus, and if it's a girl, maybe Jessie or Jesusette. After all, its father is three wise men, each of which is hung like a camel." Mom just gaped. Aunt Phyllis started laughing, and kept it up until she had to get off her chair and hurry to the bathroom, walking funny, sort of sideways, because she had to keep her legs crossed.

"That's not very funny." Mom was insulted and angry. "It's blasphemy."

"Oh poof." Savannah didn't care, and she started laughing, not so much at her own joke as at the look on Mom's face and the tone of her voice.

Savannah moved on with the three guys she insisted were called Larry, Shemp and Moe, but of course they weren't, not really. "I probably wouldn't mind so much," Mom lied, "but they're obviously rug-riders and I can't get used to the idea of having a Buddha-eyed grandchild."

"Don't you worry about it," Savannah snapped. "You won't have a Buddha-eyed grandchild because this one isn't *yours*."

"How can you say something so stupid! *Of course* it's my grandchild!"

"If Gran is Seely's grandma because she and Seely agreed she would be, then you *won't* be because you don't want to be and I don't want you to be so we agree on that much, at least," Savannah raged. "You probably won't see anything more than a birth announcement card with one of them stupid little pictures where all you see is the blanket and a pair of clenched baby fists. Because for sure if you're gonna call its fathers rug-riders and call it Buddha-eyed, I'm not bringin' it around *here*, where it's all so tacky the ratshit piles up in the corners and the cats drop dead in the yard!"

She moved on with the three construction guys and didn't even come back to have the baby in her hometown hospital. "That dump?" she laughed to Kitty through the phone. "Give yourself a rest. Take a break from it. We checked into a place so posh it could be a bloody hotel, and we did just fine with no help from anybody."

"So is it a boy or a girl?"

"Can't tell yet, it's too young to grow whiskers," she teased.

"Well, didn't you check?"

"What do you think I am, a pervert? You think I go around pulling the underpants off little kids? It's a boy. Nine pounds eight ounces. And no, he's not the least bit Buddha-eyed. Just a bit darkish, but that's okay, we'll tell the world he's Black Irish."

"What's his name?"

"I thought I'd call him Abdul Ali Singh-Song."

"You *stop* that!"

"Maybe Hajii Baba?"

"If you were here I'd slap you."

"Ever stop to think that might be why I'm *not* there? Anyway, I'll send you a picture and keep in touch."

But nothing would do but Mom get herself sober and climb onto the bus and take herself off down the highway to check on Savannah and the kid. They were out of hospital and back at the motel, and even if the three guys were nice, it was more than Mom could handle. She called them hear no evil, see no evil, speak no evil, and insisted she couldn't tell one from the other. She also insisted they just sat on the sofa, one beside the other, holding the baby and passing him back and forth, back and forth, back and forth, as if he was the most incredible wonder they had ever seen. If any of them had any doubt about paternity, he kept it to himself. Each was convinced his sperm had won the race, each was positive the child was his own, and all Savannah had to do was sit around and make milk, like some kind of two-legged arbutus-bark-colored-haired Jersey cow.

"Ah," she sighed, lighting up a cigarette. "Boy, I have to tell you that tastes *good!*" One of them said something to her in a sort of singsongy voice and she shrugged. "Fuck you." She smiled widely. "I gave'em up while he was still in the oven, but now that he's baked and out, I'll be who I am, and the one who don't like it can hit the road." He smiled at her and shrugged, and reached for the baby. Mom said she wasn't sure he'd understood the words but he seemed to grasp the concepts.

The three wise men cooked supper, the three wise men did the dishes, and two of the three went off to the laundromat to do the washing. "What do you do?" Mom glared at Savannah. "Other than sit there like a cat fed on nothing but cream?"

"I keep'em willing to trot their little feet off looking after things," she answered. "You oughtta try it sometime. It's called being *nice* to people!"

Mom only stayed a few days, and then came home, with enough snapshots of the still unnamed baby to bore everyone to tears. "He looks like every other newborn I ever saw," Aunt Phyllis decided.

"*Three* dads?" Seely marveled. "How did they manage *that?*"

Glen got arrested. The police showed up at the house about eleven or twelve at night to tell Jimmy his brother was in the cells and could be bailed out in the morning. "Where's your mother?" one of them asked.

"She's working late at the hospital," Jimmy answered quietly. "She's busy doing brain surgery. Trying to put one *into* the chief of police."

"You want to sit in the cell with your faggot brother?"

"You want to get your ass in a sling for running off at the mouth?"

"Don't get smart with me, boy."

"Go fuck a dog, I always did want a police-dog puppy. Lay a hand on me or take one step into the house and you'll wish you'd got chickenpox and called in sick instead of coming to work. You're already in it up to your ears, because Glen isn't old enough for you to hold him in cells unless you call out a social worker." And he closed the door, almost cutting off the cop's nose.

They didn't have to post bail, the cops just let Glen out in the morning and he never had to go into real court about it, just go see the probation officer. Mom was supposed to go with him but Aunt Phyllis went instead. She said she didn't think it would do his case much good if Mom went down as drunk as she was and either lipped off the PO or puked on his desk.

"As near as I can tell," she said quietly, making sure the probation officer got an eyeful of her bracelet tattoos, "the kid wasn't doing anything but riding in a car with a fully licensed adult driver. Right? He wasn't drunk or even drinking, he had no grass or hash or what they call pro-hibited substances, he wasn't mooning the world out the window...so what's the big uproar?"

"They'd been parked on a side road for almost an hour."

"What? Side roads are suddenly out of bounds? Side roads have been declared vital to national security?"

"The lights were out, the car was in darkness."

"Is *that* the crime? We have to run down our batteries to stay out of jail? Listen, I have to tell you, either I'm overreacting here or democracy has taken a shit-kicking without me noticing it."

"We've had our eye on your nephew for some time now."

"That makes sense. I'd keep an eye on him too. I really would. I mean, what with turning out the lights and going up back roads and leaving his breadcrusts on the table or, worse, feeding them to the dog."

"We've also had his friend under observation."

"Yeah? Official observation? Like color photos and tape recordings and taps on the phone and all? Or just sort of observation, like listening at keyholes and trying to see what's going on in the darkness?"

"We have reason to believe they had been engaging in sexual practices."

"So? You going to arrest all the fuckers in the world? They just passed a law against carnal knowledge or they put a tax on it and he forgot to pay? Jesus Christ, he's sixteen years old! Of *course* he's humping everything he can catch up to, warm or not! You going to sit there and try to convince me that *you* weren't doing it when you were sixteen? Or at least praying to God you *could* if you could only find someone to do it with?"

"The driver of the car is a thirty-five-year-old male." The probation officer glared. Aunt Phyllis leaned forward and smiled that gorgeous smile that had kicked off more than one barroom brawl.

"Listen, let me tell you a little secret. Thirty-five-year-old males are about the cream of the crop. Believe me, I've tried'em all, from eighteen to eighty, and I'll take a thirty-five-year-old any time."

They couldn't even charge Mr. Marpole with contributing to the delinquency of a juvenile, because Aunt Phyllis lied through her teeth and said she had asked the man to tutor Glen in calculus.

"You need that," she said confidentially to the enraged probation officer, "if you're going to go on to college or university. But thank you for caring, and"—she winked—"anything I can do for you...just let me know."

Of course, that wasn't the end of it. There was a whole lot of yelling and hoo-rahing, Mom crying, Aunt Phyllis stamping around the house smoking cigarettes one after the other and warning about varicose veins of the anus and saying things like, "Boy, you'll be sorry if you wind up with trenchmouth of the asshole, boy."

"You mind your business, I'll mind mine." Glen had taken as much of it as he could put up with. "It's *my* life. You've ruined your life your way, I'll ruin my life my way, okay?"

"I'm not having any fuckin' faggot living in my house," Mom wailed. "How will I sleep nights worrying about the little boys?"

"Oh for crying out loud!" Glen was shaking with fury. "I never laid a hand on a little boy! I'm not turned on by little boys! *Men*, mother, *men*, just the same as you! Men with jobs and money and nice clothes and cars. And something you'd know nothin' about...men who can *talk to me*!"

The next day he left the house, so angry he was almost crying. At suppertime he walked in with Mr. Marpole, looking pale but determined. Mom yelled at Greg Marpole and Aunt Phyllis said some sarcastic and probably very hurtful things, and Greg stood there and ate every bit of it. Then Glen came back from the bedroom with all his stuff heaped in a sheet, the four corners knotted together. "I'll return your goddam sheet," he sobbed, "and don't worry, Mother dear, I'll *boil* the bastard before I bring it back."

"You aren't going anywhere!" She tried to grab him. But you can't keep someone if they don't want to stay, you can't have authority over someone who refuses to grant you that authority, and Glen left with Greg Marpole.

Half the town believed the story about the shack-up, the other half refused to listen to a word of it. "A fine Christian thing he's doing, someone should give those children some kind of decent, normal upbringing. And the boy has never looked better. He's well dressed, well fed, and his marks have improved. As for the rest, well, I'll believe it when I *see* it and not a minute sooner."

Jimmy was so disgusted with all the maundering and oh-how-could-he and where-did-he-go-wrong that was coming down around the house that he took his fury out on the rodent population. He went down into the basement to try to find a quiet place where he could set up his stuff and do some work without having to pry the little kids off his back all the time. He shoved some things around and made himself a sort of table with a piece of plywood and a couple of wooden sawhorses, then started taking his tools and gear there. He thought it might even be nice to take some milk crates and set them on end, stacked maybe three high, and put his tools there, next to his right hand, where he could just reach out and take what he needed. To do that he had to move an old wood and tin steamer trunk. He grabbed one corner of it and heaved. It moved, one end pressing tight against the wall, the other moving five or six inches away from it. Jimmy shifted his weight, grabbed the other end and heaved. It came away from the wall but the first corner skittered backwards again. There was a loud squeal, a high-pitched wail, and nine half-grown rats streaked from between the pulled-out corner and the wall. Jimmy jumped so high he nearly cracked his cranium on the overhead beam.

The wailing and indrawn sobbing sounds were still squeaking from behind the trunk. Practically shaking with revulsion, Jimmy grabbed the handle and reefed the trunk away from the wall. Momma rat was lying in a little half-circle, her front paws clutching her belly. She had obviously zigged when she should have zagged and got the corner of the trunk as it slammed against the wall again. Blood dribbled from her nose and mouth. But it wasn't momma rat who was doing the wailing and howling, it was the runt of the litter, sitting on her haunches, her front feet tucked under her chin, her mouth open, yellow front teeth showing. She had her head back, her ears accordioned on each other and pressed against her head, and she was wailing from so deep it was a wonder her tail hadn't turned inside out.

"Jesus God!" Jimmy spun, looking for something to use to stop the noise and put an end to the dying.

"Who got hurt?" Seely came down the steps, all set to cry.

"Get outta here, Seel."

"Who's making that awful...oh, Jimmy! What did you *do?*" And she ran the last few steps and headed for the bereaved runt.

"Get away from there, if she bites you the next thing you know you'll swell up and go green!" He grabbed at Seely, and missed.

Seely-the-fool made a swoop, grabbed the runt in her hand and held her pressed against her chest. "Christ Almighty, Seely, if that thing bites you there's no telling *what* you'll get."

"She's not going to bite. There there there," Seely crooned, "it's okay, Jimmy didn't mean to hurt your mommy." Without looking up or changing the loving tone of her voice, Seely continued, "Jimmy, kill that damned thing and put it out of its misery, it's bleeding all over the floor."

"Kill *that* one too, Seel," Jimmy pleaded.

"Don't be silly." Seely started back up the stairs. "They've got'em in the pet store not half as nice as this one and they want ten bucks each for'em."

Once, years before, either Savannah or Kitty had bought a hamster and a cage for it, one of those Habitrail things where you can keep buying bits and pieces of plastic tube to connect with the pieces you already have so the Habitrail grows and the rodent's exercise yard expands. Conceivably you could turn the entire house into a maze of plastic tubing, and the rat could run in endless circles while being fed the finest of balanced diets. Four-fifths of the world's population are homeless, fifteen million children under the age of ten starve to death every year, but the pet rats have miles of courtyard to make them think they aren't confined, and you can buy packages of vitamin-enriched, nutritionally balanced processed food to keep them fat, sleek and healthy.

Of course, Seely couldn't put her hands on the Habitrail right away, nobody could ever find anything quickly in the house because the house took things, hid things, sometimes gave them back but usually ate them. The rat lived for most of one week in a big old mayonnaise jar someone had found out behind the Merry Widow hamburger joint.

Then the house took pity on the runty rat and gave back the Habitrail; it was found in the back of the closet in the boys' bedroom. Seely installed her runt in the plastic cage and made sure the water bulb and food dish were full. She fed the rat the same things she ate herself, and that included Pepsi, Mountain Dew, corn chips and doughballs. She didn't get the doughballs at home, of course—neither Mom nor Aunt Phyllis baked bread—but Gran always saved just a little smidgin of dough for Seely and handed it over with the warning, "One of these days you're going to get worms eating this stuff raw."

Jimmy said Gran was right. "Of *course* you can get worms eating raw dough," he told Seely. "Everyone knows that. You can put flour in a jar with a lid on it and six times out of ten, if you keep it in a warm place, it'll start crawling with worms. *Weevils*, Seely, *weevils*."

"They must be in the flour, then. They can't crawl in if they can't crawl *out*, Jimmy. So prob'ly *that* means every time you eat bread you're eating weevils that just didn't hatch yet! So what's the diff? Anyway, they won't live in your guts and breed, you'd digest'em same as if they were any other food." Jimmy stared at her, then turned away, so defeated by blind logic that it was days before he could make himself gag down a sandwich.

The rat didn't care about weevils, she ate bits of bread dough too. She stayed in the Habitrail when Seely was at school and came out when her person came back home again. "You might think that rat is your pet," Kitty shook her head disapprovingly, "but that rat thinks *you're* the one who's the pet."

"She isn't 'that rat'. She's PatsyRatsy."

"Yeah? Well, in that case she's Little Orphan PatsyRatsy, because Jimmy's wiped out every other rat for a mile and a half."

He hadn't, not really, but he'd tried. He put little packages of war-farin with Brolin in the attic, in the basement and even in the space between the inner and outer walls. He took a screwdriver to the elec-trical fixtures and pulled them from their holes, then stuffed paper twists of rat poison in there. He put poison in the woodshed and got six squirrels with it, he put poison in the unused barn and wiped out a family of raccoons living in the patient hope someone would get more chickens one day. He put poison in Gran's basement, he put poison in Gran's woodshed, he put poison in little plastic bags and walked along the ditch dropping them into everything that in any way resembled a tunnel mouth or a lair hole.

But he didn't dare do anything to PatsyRatsy. Seely was small, and physically Seely was tough, but that wasn't why Jimmy didn't dare off her rat. It was because Seely was just about ready to go over the edge and everyone knew it. Jimmy didn't want to be the one to tip her over by killing her rat. There was something frail in Seely. Inside, where it wasn't immediately obvious. As tough as she was, as wiry as she was, as ready as she was to try anything the other kids tried, Seely was delicate. Even Mom knew that. "Don't you do anything to her PatsyRatsy," she warned, "or you'll have me to contend with."

"For crying out loud, why is everyone convinced I'm stayin' awake at night tryin' to think up ways to kill Seely's rat?"

"Because you got a thing for rats, Jimmy."

"I don't have a thing for rats! Jesus, I don't spend my life prowling around looking for rats to kill. If the bastards stay away from me I'm willing to live and let live. It's when they shit in the cereal boxes that I get more than a bit bent out of shape, okay?"

"Rats are smart. Some say they're as smart as people."

"If that was only how smart they were they'd'a died out long ago," Jimmy growled. "There's people in this country never even saw a live one, and we gotta have'em making cities in suitcases in the basement and setting up states and republics in the attic. It's like tryin' to keep track of those goddam new countries in Africa! Every time we walk into socials class the map is different! I don't know what we'll do if the Soviets ever lose their grip and all those old-timey damn places get their own names and borders back again!"

"What are you talking about?"

"*Rats!*" he yelled. "I thought we were talking about rats and how I wasn't going to do anything to Seely's damned house-mouse!"

"You better not," Seely shrieked from her bedroom. "You just better not, Jimmy, or you'll be real sorry."

"I'm *not*, Seely, okay? I said I wouldn't and I won't."

"You just better not, Jimmy."

"Better not what?" Kitty asked.

"Kill my rat."

"Jimmy, you leave Seely's rat alone, you hear?"

"I *can't stand it!*" He whirled, frustrated, and headed for the basement.

"I don't care if you can stand it or not, you leave it *be!*" Kitty went into orbit. "It's not even yours, you don't have to stand anything, *I'm* the one has to sleep in the same room."

"I *said* I wouldn't!"

"You better not, see," but the words just kind of hung in the air. Jimmy had gone down the steps to the basement, where he hoped to find some quiet.

"Jesus, I have to tell you." Aunt Phyllis poured herself a big juice-glass full of plonk and lit yet another cigarette. "That boy's nerves is about shot, you ought to go see a doctor with him."

"You think so? Maybe I will." Mom took the glass of plonk, and Phyllis just rolled her eyes and got up to pour another one for herself.

Mervin had been told and told again to stay away from other people's stuff, but nobody ever really expected him to do what he was told so he wasn't about to start now. He went down into the basement when Jimmy wasn't there and started messing around with Jimmy's tools. He took the edge off two knives and put a big chip in Jimmy's best chisel by dropping it onto the cement floor. When he bent to pick it up he bumped the yellow plastic milk crates and Jimmy's wooden-handled knife fell. Mervin reached out to catch it.

The sound of his screams woke both Aunt Phyllis and Mom, who leaped out of bed and followed the noise to its source. Mom grabbed Mervin and started to cry right along with him, and Phyllis had to race out and fire up the Travelall herself, then do the driving all the way to the hospital. "Boy, are you going to get your ass warmed," she promised the still howling kid. "Providin' you don't bleed to death before we get you to the doctor."

The thought he might bleed to death scared Mervin so bad he peed himself, and his auntie, too. "Jesus, Merv, you want to get out and walk?" she said mildly. "Look what you done now. Not enough you're bleeding through my best towel, you got to piss on me as well?"

"You reach down with your good hand, mister, and you pinch the end of that thing and make sure you don't do it again or the least of your worries is gonna be that you've about cut off your damned hand!" Phyllis roared. "Christ Jesus in heaven, can't you do anything right?"

"I think he's gonna faint."

"I hope he does, it'll make the trip easier and quieter."

Phyllis felt a little more maternal when she found out they weren't dealing with just one or two stitches. The doctor on duty looked at Mervin's hand and shook his head, then started barking orders. Two nurses took over with the hand, two more started stripping off the clothes Mervin had been wearing for the better part of three days and an orderly took one look and went for a big basin of hot soapy water.

He scrubbed Merv at least halfways clean while the others did everything they had to do to get him ready for the operating room. They called in the lab technician, they called in the anesthetist, they called in the surgical assistant and the head nurse, then wheeled the now quiet Merv down the hallway.

"Looks awful little," Phyllis worried. "He looks so *puny* on that big gurney."

"How long's he gonna be?"

"I don't know. But it better be long enough for me to get me some courage, I have to tell you."

Mom had on her nightgown and dressing gown, her sloppy fuzzy slippers that had once been pink, and a lot of Merv's blood. Phyllis was wearing pajamas and rubber thong sandals, and she had her share of Merv's blood too. But they went into the bar all the same.

The guy working the early shift was the same one who was Seely's dad, but only he, Mom and a few others knew about that. He grinned and said hi, and Mom nodded. "You look like you had a bad night," he teased.

"Naw, one of the kids damn near cut off a hand."

"Celia?" he said quickly, frowning with worry.

"Her? No, one of *her* kids." Mom pointed at Aunt Phyllis. "My kids don't cut their hands to hamburger."

"Right, *your* kids are more apt to use a knife on someone else."

Pajamas or not, nightgown or not, blood or not, money is money and Seely's dad served them two or three stiff ones, including one on the house. They went back to the hospital with the edge taken off, and found Merv was out of surgery but sound asleep and would stay that way for most of the day.

Phyllis drove them home, and they got cleaned up but forgot to do anything about the mess down in Jimmy's carving spot. He came home from school with the other kids and about five minutes later the tantrum started. "I wish he'd cut his goddamned scrawny *throat!*" he screeched at Phyllis. "I'm sick of this. I'm just fuckin' *sick* of this. People comin' and people goin', people to'in and people fro'in and none of them anything to me! And *you*"—he pointed his finger in her face—"you with your goddam artwork on your body and your smartass mouth and two kids who aren't as well behaved as that fuckin' rat of Seely's! Those goddam kids of yours are a total pain in the ass. *Nobody* wants to be around them. Not me, not Kitty, not Seely, not even *you*. Because all you've done is sit and drink and sit and smoke and sit and talk and sit and grin and let'em run around like something worse than fuckin' animals. What did I ever do to you that you'd have kids, turn'em into what they are and then turn'em loose on *me!*"

He stormed out of the house and went over to Gran's and continued his tantrum over there. Gran listened. She didn't say Now now, and she didn't say Calm down, and she sure didn't say They're young, they'll learn better. She just listened.

Jimmy had supper with her, then he did the dishes while Gran sat on the big old maroon sofa and watched television. When the dishes were done and the kitchen tidied, he went into the living room and joined her. After a while Gran got up and went into the kitchen. She made a pot of tea and brought out the cookie tin with its bright red-and-gold Chinesey pictures painted all over it. They drank tea and ate peanut-butter cookies and said very little to each other. There was a western movie on the tube, and they both enjoyed cowboy-type movies.

Jimmy didn't go home that night. He slept at Gran's place, in the bed that had been used by his on-the-road aunt, the one nobody ever

heard from, the one off doing some odd thing. And in the morning
Jimmy went to school from there.

Mom and Phyllis were at the hospital again when the kids got
home from school. Seely got PatsyRatsy and took her down to the
creek so she could get some exercise and have her bath. PatsyRatsy
didn't like bathing in the sink or basin, and no matter how cold it
was, given even half a chance, she'd race into the stream, dive and
roll and twist and splash, then come zipping back out again to sit
on her haunches and smooth her fur dry. Kitty had better things to
do than watch a rat swimming in a cold creek. She grabbed her ball
glove and headed off on her bike to see if she could scare up a game
of keep-away or something. Jimmy went to his room and started
packing up his stuff.

"But someone has to *stay* with me," Donald pouted. "You can't
leave little kids alone."

"Go eat something poisonous, Donald Dimwit," Jimmy invited.
"Go eat some rat poison or something. Lie down on the track, the
four-thirty-four is due soon. Sit on the yellow line and wait for a
freight truck. Anything, as long as you're not pestering me."

He took his clothes and stuff over to Gran's, then went down in
the basement and packed up all his carving stuff. The whole time
Donald whined and sniveled and grizzled and insisted *someone* had to
look after him. "See, that's what you get for being such a jerk." Jimmy
said quietly. "Even your own goddam mother don't want to be here
when you come home. We *all* of us effed off rather than be around
you. Because you"—he pointed his finger almost into Donald's eye—
"are a pain in the ass."

Donald followed Jimmy over to Gran's place and walked into the
house howling about being left alone. "You get OUT of here!" Gran
snapped. She picked him up by the scruff of the neck and put him
back outside the door. "*You* are nothing to me. See that big old house
over there?" She pointed. "*That* is where your mother pays rent. Not
here. See that fence? Well, there's a hole in it to let my grandchildren
come over here...but that hole isn't for *you*. You go back where you
belong. If you *ever* come over here again I'll have the policeman take
you away and put you in a steel cell. But before he comes, I'll beat the
living daylights out of you. Go!"

He went. He went howling, he went wailing, he went bawling his guts out, but he went.

When Mom and Phyllis came home Donald was sitting on the floor in the kitchen, still crying. "Nobody likes me," he sobbed. "Nobody will play with me."

"Well, there you have it," Phyllis agreed. "You got the message. Didn't I tell you if you were a pain in the ass people wouldn't want to be around you?"

"But Gran said...."

"She's not your Gran." Phyllis slapped his face. "Didn't I *tell* you not to go over there? Didn't I?" She slapped his face again, harder. "Well, there you *have* it, Donald. People tell you and you don't listen. People give you the word and you just do any fuckin' thing you take it into your head to do. If you'd'a done what you were told you wouldn't have gone over there and she wouldn't have chased you away. Stop gettin' up people's noses, chrissake."

"But I only went over with Jimmy."

"He probably didn't want you either. Nobody wants you around. Now eff off, Don. Leave me alone, I don't want you hangin' off me either. You aren't very fuckin' pleasant, if the truth be known."

He went off wailing and bawling and then they found out Jimmy had moved out lock, stock and barrel. Mom headed over to Gran's place and banged on the door.

"I want my kid," she said when Gran answered.

"Well, you better come in and settle it with him."

"You got no right!"

"Hey, don't you start in on me! If that boy doesn't want to live with you, don't give *me* static. Figure out why he doesn't. Clean up your act, don't get on MY case!"

"Jimmy, you just march yourself home."

"I *am* home," he said. He didn't yell, he didn't pitch a fit, he just stood there, and he even smiled. "And if you try anything at all, I'm going to slit your bitchin' throat."

"He's crazy," Mom told Aunt Phyllis.

"Yeah, well, who ain't, y'know?"

"You wait until *your* kid runs away from home. See how *that* feels."

"Fuck, I can hardly wait, I tell you."

They sat on the sofa, side-by-each, with the big jug of plonk on the floor between them. After a while Kitty started to scrub potatoes and Seely washed and cut a cabbage. "I don' like cabbage," Donald whined. "I won't eat any."

"Tell someone who gives a shit," Kitty answered.

"I want steak."

"Find one and cook it yourself, then."

"I don't *want* that for supper!"

"Then don't eat it."

Donald didn't really care what he had for supper as long as he had something—what he wanted was some attention, any kind of attention. Everyone was focused on someone else, Merv and his hand or Jimmy moving to Gran's, and nobody seemed to care if Donald came or went. He squirmed and wriggled, trying to see what Kitty was doing, getting in her way, even teasing her. He sat up on the drainboard pestering and she ignored him, so he swung his foot just a bit too far and kicked her, not hard. She swung her arm, hard, and knocked him off the drainboard to the floor. He howled until Seely snapped: she dropped the cabbage leaves into the sink, grabbed Donald by one arm, dragged him to the back door, pushed him outside, then locked the door.

"I can't stand him," she whispered, suddenly shaking.

"Ah, Seel." Kitty stopped fritzing with the spuds and gave Seely a good long hug. They both ignored the noise of Donald howling and kicking at the door.

"Sometimes I just want to *hurt* him."

"Yeah. I know. Me too."

"He's *awful!*"

"They both are." Kitty smiled. "Jesus, you could start walking right here and now and keep going for six months, knocking on doors as you pass them, and you wouldn't find another who came even halfways close to those two bastards. I wish the whoofare would take'em, I really do."

"Probably couldn't *pay* people enough to keep them!"

"You got'er, Seel."

"Boy, if I was Aunt Phyllis and I was walkin' out on some idiot who liked to beat me up, I'd *leave* those two monsters with the idiot! Pay him back and be shet of them!"

"You got'er. Damn straight!"

Phyllis and Mom after a while noticed the noise. Phyllis stomped through the kitchen, unlocked the door, swung it open and glared down at Donald.

"They locked me out," he whined.

"You stupid bastard!" She hit him, hard. "Walk around to the *other* door, dim-bulb! You're just makin' all this noise so someone'll feel sorry for you and fuss over you. About time you learned all you get when you act like a goober is treated like a goober." She hit him again, then closed the door. Before she locked it she whipped it open once more and yelled, "And if you kick it again, or if you start yowling again, I'll use a belt on you until you can't move or make noise. And that, you little asshole, is a promise!"

She slammed and locked the door, then turned to go back to the living room. She took a swat at Seely, but Seel ducked. Phyllis wound up to take another swat, but before she let it go Kitty cleared her throat, and Phyllis turned.

"You hit her and I'll plant this in your back," Kitty promised.

"Is every single soul in this house totally lunatic?" Aunt Phyllis asked, so scared you could see it.

"Yes. Probably so. But you aren't treating Seely the way you treat your own kids."

"Well, why'n hell did she beat him up and lock him out, then?"

"She didn't beat him up. He's *your* kid, *you* look after him. We"— she didn't lower the butcher knife, and the hand holding it didn't tremble—"hate the little bastard totally."

"Alla you's nuts. So help me."

Phyllis went back to the sofa, sat down and told Mom about Kitty and the butcher knife. "You oughtta do somethin' about her."

"Me? She'd cut me as quick as cut you. Just stay out of her way, is all. Left alone she's okay."

"Well, I don't blame them for not wanting Donald in there with them. He *is* a pest."

"They both are. Hell, they *all* are." And the two sisters started to laugh, as if they were watching a funny show on TV.

Donald came in the other door and sat watching them, his big eyes damp with anger, frustration and tears. He stared, hoping to guilt them. They ignored him. After a while he started looking around for something to do that would call attention to himself. Just as he found it and started to get off the chair, Aunt Phyllis tossed a cushion his way. "You do," she said softly, "and I'll whip you until you bleed." He settled back on the chair, consumed with the unfairness of it all.

4

Merv got out of hospital with his hand in a bandage as big as a grape-fruit. It even went halfway up his arm toward his elbow. He expected to be fussed over, the way he'd been treated in the hospital. "Hey, get it straight," Phyllis told him, "those people get *paid* to get you a drink; here, you get it yourself."

"But my *hand*...," he whined.

"Oh, fuck your hand, it's your own fault, if you'd'a done what you were told to do you wouldn't have a sore hand and Jimmy wouldn't'a moved out." She gave him a whack on the ear. "You want a drink, go get it, Merv."

"You hurt my hand!" he screeched.

"I never touched your hand, but if you *want* me to...." She lunged, he darted out of the way, terrified. He'd learned what the word "hurt" meant and he didn't ever want to get another lesson. "So get your own drink and clean up your act, you hear? Because if you don't start doing what you're told, I'm going to hurt you worse than you can even imagine."

"You're gonna be sorry," he muttered. "I'll show you."

He waited until they were asleep, then got out of bed and crept down to the kitchen to use the phone. It rang and rang and rang and he was almost ready to give up when finally it was answered.

"This better be worth gettin' me outta bed," a voice growled.

"Dad?" Merv said quietly.

"Who's that?"

"It's Merv."

"Good boy! That's my kid! Where'd she hide you?"

"I got a bill here. The 'lectricity bill. The front of it says...," and he, who could barely read, got enough of the address read off that his father, who could read only slightly better, managed to figure out where to go looking.

He came into the house Saturday morning, his eyes red from driving all night. Everybody was asleep, but they woke up in a hurry when the Lee-Enfield .303 went off and blew a hole in the wall between the living room and the kitchen. "Wakey *wakey*!" big Merv roared. "Wakey fuckin' wakey. Tea and cakey. It's daylight in the swamp and the natives is *restless*!"

"Sweet Jesus Christ!" Phyllis didn't hesitate; she grabbed the window, shoved it up and open and went over the sill.

"What's going *on*?" Seely demanded, from the top of the steps.

"Where's your Aunt Phyllis?" big Merv shouted.

"Prob'ly in bed." Seely started down the stairs. Big Merv pointed the gun at her. "Don't move," he said, "there's a rat on your head, chrissakes."

"Don't worry, Uncle Merv," she said calmly, "she won't bother you." She'd never seen big Mervin before in her life, but who else could he be, waving a gun and roaring about Phyllis? "You want coffee or something?"

"I want that bitch Phyllis."

"Well, I can't do anything about *that*. But I can make coffee."

"What in *hell* you doin' with a rat on your head?" He stared, fascinated.

"You'll have to talk louder," Seely laughed, "I can't hear you with this rat on my head," and Mervin burst out laughing.

"I heard a banana in my ear," he agreed. "Which is Phyllis' bedroom?"

"Same as Mom's," and she pointed.

When big Merv arrived, the bedroom was empty. The window was open, the curtains blowing in the breeze, but not a sign of either woman. The other kids were awake and standing in a small group, wide-eyed and obviously frightened. With nothing else to do with his time, Merv went into the kitchen and used up all the bacon making breakfast for himself and the rest of the litter.

"Nobody likes me," little Merv whined. "They won't play with me." He pointed at Seely and Kitty. "They run off all the time and they ditch me."

"Then leave'em alone. Take the hint, for chrissakes."

"Their gran said she didn' have to put up with me. She said...."

"Shut up, will you?"

"And Mom said...." That's when big Merv gave little Merv a solid crack on the side of the head, driving out any thought of sulking or whining. "Didn't I tell you to shut up?"

"Uncle Merv, he doesn't *ever* do what he's told. It's like he's deaf or something. But he can't be deaf because he can hear us from clear across the house if we're like unwrapping a candy or something." Kitty moved her plate to the empty space next to Merv and sat beside him. "And he's not lying when he says we ditch him. We do. If we can. He's not lying when he says we don't want to play with him. We don't. Mostly because he tells lies."

"Really." Big Merv pushed most of a piece of toast into his mouth and chewed, mouth open. "What kinda lies?"

"Oh, he says his mom said he was to have the bike, or his mom said we had to let him have his way, or his mom said...and when we tell him she never did, he runs back to the house and he tells Aunt Phyllis that *we* said something we didn't say, or that we're doing something we aren't supposed to. I'd rather go to school than play with him."

Big Merv slapped across the table and got little Merv on the other side of the head, almost knocking him off the chair. "See?" he shouted. "*See?* You're the one makin' it hard on yourself. Smarten up, will you?"

"And the *other* one," Seely contributed, "is even more of a pain in the face. Because he's the baby or something, and he gets petted for it. I hate'em both."

"Shut up, Seely," big Merv said pleasantly. Seely just nodded and shut right up, which was fine by big Merv. He figured he probably wouldn't do any better job of civilizing either of his sons than his wife had done, and he didn't really want to have them around any more than necessary, but he knew it would drive Phyllis up the wall if he took them. Not because *she* wanted them, but just because he'd come and got them.

He looked around the big old house and knew as much as anyone could about life in it. The furniture was old, and hadn't been taken care of since it had been hauled inside. The counter, cupboards and drainboard were plywood, on which had been epoxied some cheap, bright yellow arborite. It was chipped and gouged, and entire hunks had parted company with the rest, leaving ugly blackish patches. The linoleum had been laid on top of other linoleum so that the holes worn in each layer exposed other layers underneath, and in front of the stove the floorboards showed grimy black. Well, if the dumb slut wanted to live in a place like this, where the kids thought rats were pets, fine, let her live here. He'd thought he wanted her back, and maybe he still did, but not right now. He could get more fun out of driving her up the wall by swiping the kids than he'd get out of forcing her to go back with him. So he loaded them both in his pickup truck and headed back home.

The kids thought it was too bad he didn't get six miles before the cops pulled him over, scooped them up and brought them back home to their mother, who'd run over to Gran's and phoned to report a kidnapping in progress.

"Hey," big Merv said mildly, "my kid phoned me, eh? Said he wanted me to come and get him. That's not kidnapping. She's got no court order, nothing."

"She's their mother. She wants them back." The cop shrugged

"I'm their father. I want them back." Merv made himself sound calm and logical. But the cops hadn't fallen with last week's rain, they knew everything about him they needed to know, had seen it in his eyes when they pulled over his car. One of the cops was almost convinced that, if Merv's gun had been in the front seat and ready, instead of zipped shut in its case, he'd have popped them both off as he got out of the pickup.

They gave Merv a warning. He swallowed his anger and waited until they'd done their paperwork and let him go, then he hit the bar and put in a few hours of dedicated and determined drinking. One or two people tried to talk to him—the Westwind is a friendly place—but Merv's responses were so downright owly that the regulars decided nobody had even the beginning of a hint as to what was festering in *his* ugly head, to hell with him, let'im sit there like a bump on a log.

He sat there until he got hungry, then he left and went across the street to Barb's Bar-BQ and put away a big plate of ribs, extra-hot sauce, heavy on the chili seeds. He paid his bill, then, burping and belching, headed out to his rusting Chev. He stopped at the liquor store just before it closed and bought a half-gallon of Catawba, and drove back out to the big old house.

He knew only the kids were at home because the Travelall wasn't parked where it had been. There was a light on in Gran's place but he knew better than to go over there—the Old Biddy would just give him a mouthful of sass and call the constabulary, and he'd already seen more of them than he had any appetite for at the best of times, and this wasn't shaping up like the best of times.

He drove down the road a ways and pulled off on an old skidder trail, then sat in the gathering gloom drinking Catawba and reciting to himself the litany of woe that was his life.

Have him pulled over, would she? Have him marched into the local crowbar hotel and held like he'd done something wrong? She's their mother, they said. Big deal. So what? Wasn't he their damn father? Next thing you knew she'd be showin' up with a lawyer or some damn thing and layin' claim to half of everything. Well, let her try. He'd chainsaw the table right down the center, by god, let's see what she could do with two legs and half of a top. If she thought for one minute he was going to work until sweat ran down his back and into the crack of his ass, she had another think coming. Some nights, especially in the summertime, the crack of his ass was raw and there were bloodspots on his gaunch from all that sweat and salt rubbing and rubbing, like a baby with diaper rash or something. He'd lower himself into the bathtub and the water would sting. And when he was out of the tub and dry, before he got dressed, he'd smear Vaseline on his crack, then some unscented talc. Sometimes he had to go so far as to use zinc oxide ointment. And she thought he'd go through that in order to give *her* money for sittin' on her ass in a bingo hall while his kids ran around like feral animals, sharp-faced and weaselly and so friggin' unpleasant their own cousins preferred the company of a rat? Well, no, madam, actually, after due consideration of all the facts, I regret to inform you that you can kiss my ass. Your story has touched my heart, never before in the history of human endeavor have I met anyone so badly treated by unkind fate. The depth of your misery, the height of your frustration, the breadth of your thwarted ambition is such that my heart pumps piss. Verily.

Seely and Kitty were mad because they got stuck babysitting the two brats. Nobody ever paid them to babysit, either; they just got stuck and if they complained all they got was "Somebody did it for *you*." Maybe somebody *had*, but it hadn't been *their* idea! No use saying that, though—Kitty had tried it one time and collected a fat lip for her trouble. People say the dumbest things, and sometimes it's a joke—like the time Mike, with his belly packed with beer, suddenly stood up and pointed at the doorway as if there were folks standing there. "You're a fine pair, you three, if ever there was one," he roared, and people started to snicker. "Coming in at this hour a' the night, three o'clock in the morning, well, if you think you're gonna live here you'd better find another place!" That was a joke, and safe to laugh at. Not safe *not* to laugh at a joke. But when Aunt Phyllis said something dumb it wasn't safe to laugh, because probably she wasn't joking. Jimmy clued them in, though; told them most of Aunt Phyllis' jokes had to do with either private parts or toilet bowls.

"What's funny about toilets?" Seely asked Gran. The old woman coughed a few times and had to go to the sink to get a drink of water, and she coughed some more before she answered.

"I don't know"—she didn't even smile—"but the damn English seem to find it all highly amusing. That and men wearing women's bras."

"So what's funny about *that?*" Seel wouldn't have got a joke if you'd had it special-delivered to her.

"Nothing." Gran patted Seely's skinny shoulder and smiled at her. "Nothing at all, except to the English, and *we* don't pay any attention to them, none at all, not even to be bothered killing them."

"How come my mom's what you call shanty Irish and Aunt Phyllis is damned English?" Kitty puzzled.

"The one of them's luckier than the other," Gran answered, laughing easily.

It didn't do any good trying to tell either of the damned boys anything, they did what they wanted. And it didn't do any good telling anyone about it when and if they finally came home, because all *they* did was yell, "Didn't I tell you little buggers to do what the girls said? Well, didn't I? You watch out, fella, or next time you're going to wish you had." And so the boys just laughed.

The girls were supposed to watch the boys until Mom and Aunt Phyllis got home, but the boys wouldn't go to bed and the girls were tired. When Kitty tried to make them go they ran away from her, laughing and taunting, making so much noise it was impossible to even hear the TV. Kitty knew she could catch one of them easily and haul him to bed, but when she went after the other the first one would be out, and she wasn't interested in spending the whole night chasing them. Times like this she wished Jimmy was still home, he'd have handled them. She almost went over to Gran's to get him, but didn't want an argument with him too. In the end the girls went to bed. "And if they burn the house down, who cares?" Kitty yawned. "Either we'll wake up or we won't. If we wake up, fine, no harm done. If we don't wake up we'll be dead and it won't matter anyway."

Seely didn't really think the logic of that was defendable, but she was tired. "You burn it down and kill us," she promised, "and I'll come back as a ghost and haunt you."

With nobody to tell them what not to do, the boys got bored, and not long after that they fell asleep on the sofa with the TV still blaring. When Phyllis and Mom came home they saw the boys sleeping and had a good laugh. Not much of a one, though, because big Merv had seen the car come home and he wasn't long behind it.

He came in through the front door waving his .303 and promising to increase the number of angels in heaven if things didn't go the way he wanted. Mom screamed, Phyllis screamed, the boys woke up and started screaming and upstairs Kitty jerked awake, jumped out of bed and headed for the window and the fire-escape rope Gran had made Jimmy install after watching a National Fire Alert program one winter night.

Kitty streaked for Gran's place barefoot, cutting herself on a piece of rusty barbed wire, so by the time she made it to the kitchen she was streaked with blood. Gran heard her coming up the steps and was out of bed and heading for the kitchen, a fire ax in her hand. "He's got a gun, he's got a gun," Kitty kept repeating, "he's got a gun, he's got a gun."

"Who?" Gran yelled, giving Kitty a shake.

"Big Merv." Kitty wept.

Gran phoned the police and for the second time in twenty-four hours they headed out to the big old house.

The boys wouldn't go with him. Young Merv remembered all too well the whaps on the head he'd collected only a few hours ago. That wasn't what he'd had in mind when he phoned. The medication the doctor had given him for his hand had worn off, he should have had another pill hours before but he'd been too busy driving the girls crazy to take it when they told him to, and now he was paying the price for being stubborn. And Donald had seen the whap Merv got, sore hand and all, and wasn't about to go anywhere with anyone who hit that fast or that hard. Anyway, he was tired. So he started to cry. That seemed like such a good idea that Merv joined him.

Seely sure wasn't going back down there. Not with all the yelling and cursing and banging and thumping and screaming. She did what PatsyRatsy did, except Seely could only make it as far as the closet, she couldn't go through the little hole and into the space between the walls.

When the police arrived, both Aunt Phyllis and Mom were black and blue. Merv had more than his share of lumps, though, including a big slash where one or the other of them had used a paring knife on him. The police put cuffs on his hands and took him off to jail.

"Take me to the hospital," Phyllis managed. "I need a doctor."

"*He* needs the doctor," the cop answered, obviously disgusted by the stupidity and squalor, and left both women behind. Neither of them was in any shape to drive the car, and Gran refused to do it, so Jimmy took them in the Travelall. But he refused to go inside with them; he didn't want anyone thinking he was in any way related to two bash-faced drunks.

The hospital fixed them up and sent them home again. Aunt Phyllis had three stitches in her eyebrow but no bandage over top of it, and Mom's lip looked like the ones in the pictures of those natives who store their plates in their mouths. They woke up Jimmy, who was sleeping in the back, and he took them to the big old house, and no sooner did he park the car than he was out of it and heading back down the hill to Gran's place. "My own son!" Mom said bitterly. "I don't even get a lift up the stairs."

"Kick your ass and give you a lift," he threatened.

Kitty didn't go home until noon; she fell asleep at Gran's place and Gran just let her sleep. Seely came out of the closet once the police had left but she didn't go downstairs, she'd had enough of it all, she crawled back into bed and cried until PatsyRatsy, emboldened by the quiet, scurried from the wall and darted under the covers. The runt rat snuggled tight against Seely's warm body and made little comforting squeaking sounds until they both fell asleep.

The boys wailed and howled for a while because Jimmy had refused to let them go to the hospital and wouldn't let either of them in the Travelall, but they were tired too, and went to bed.

The police kept big Merv in jail for three days, then he went up in front of the judge and was given a chance to have his say-so, after which a date was set for a trial and he was released on his own recognizance. They wouldn't give him back his gun, though. "You better give me a re-seat," he threatened, "I know my rights."

He drove home madder than he'd been when he'd headed off to bring back his kids. The more he thought about it, the madder he got. She'd had no damn business taking off in the first place. And now look at the trouble she'd caused.

Things hadn't even quietened down when Savannah came for a visit with little Victor. "It means winner, right, and he's a winner. Aren't you, bubba?"

"He sure is cute." Kitty moved closer, smiling at the baby.

"Where'd he get curly hair?" Seely asked.

"Two of his daddies have curly hair."

"He really can't *have* more than one daddy, Savannah."

"Shows what you know."

She hadn't come home for good, just for a visit. The three wise men were tired of living in a motel, they didn't think it was any place for their son to be raised, so they'd put their money together and were buying a house. A big house, because they were pretty sure there would be a pack of kids growing up in it. The house was on a double-sized lot so there'd be plenty of room for the kids to play, but it needed some work done to it; the last people had broken it up into apartments and now some of the walls had to have doors put back in so they could use the space. Not all of it, though; they were going to rent out the second- and third-floor apartments and let the rent cover the mortgage payments. "What about when the road crew moves on?" Phyllis asked.

"Oh, they're not going with it," Savannah answered easily. "They're starting their own house construction business."

"What do *they* know about that?"

"Hell, what's to know? You hire carpenters and plumbers and stuff like that and *they* do the damn work, don't they?"

Mom and Aunt Phyllis would have just walked out the door and bipped off into the night, assuming, assuming, assuming, but Savannah amazed Kitty and Seely by actually *asking* if they would mind keeping an eye on Vic. They were so surprised they just stared at her, one of them shaking her head, the other nodding. "He's pretty good," Savannah assured them. "Usually, as long as his bum is dry and his belly is full, he sleeps. If he does start to fuss, and he's clean, dry and fed, then he's maybe bored. So what I do when he's like that is just snuggle him and, like, play with his feet or talk to him or something." She grinned. "A half-hour of that and he's as wiped out as if he'd played a two-hour football game."

It could have been a real fun night, except both Donald and Merv had to get in on it. When Savannah had first arrived she'd given each of them a beanbag. "Just don't get it wet," she'd warned, "or you won't even *believe* how awful things will get."

She shouldn't have said anything. It was like an invitation, or a dare. Merv dropped his in the sink and waited to see if it would explode in the dribble coming constantly from the worn-out tap. When nothing happened he decided Savannah had been lying to him. Donald went further than that: he dumped his in the toilet, where there was lots of water. Nothing happened. After a while he fished it out, then whined because it wasn't any fun playing with it any more. "I told you," Savannah shrugged. "Told you it would ruin it. Too bad for you, dope."

Donald was so angry he tossed the beanbag behind the woodbox and left it there. He had a lot of fun the next three or four days; he just kept stealing Merv's bean bag. That sent Merv into a fury, and there wasn't much in the world more fun than watching Merv Junior have a tantrum. Merv's tantrums usually earned him a good swat or two, and there was *nothing* Donald liked better than to see Merv get a straightening out.

But now Merv had found a good hiding-place for his beanbag. Donald looked everywhere he could think of and still couldn't find it.

After a while he went behind the woodbox to get his own; maybe he could throw it at Merv and get something started that way.

He came out screeching. Kitty thought he'd maybe seen a rat in there or something, and she went to check. She came out laughing, holding up the beanbag, ugly bits of beansprout growing through the fabric. "It came from *outer space!*" she screeched. "And it came to get *you!*" She flourished the still sodden bag with the pallid sprouts wavering and almost hit him in the face with it.

"*Stop it!*" he screamed.

"Gonna *git* ya!" Kitty teased. Donald raced out of the kitchen and up the stairs, into the bedroom he shared with Merv, and locked the door behind him. Nobody cared that the door was locked. Nobody wanted to be within six feet of Donald at the best of times.

"And if you come out," Kitty promised, "it'll gitcha for sure."

Gran wasn't sure what was wrong with Jimmy. He looked awful. And he acted as if he was about ready for a nervous breakdown. "Are you all right, laddieboy?" she asked. He looked at her, his eyes huge, and he shook his head.

"Somethin' awful's gonna happen," he whispered.

"Something awful? What?" She felt chills race up and down her spine.

"I don't know," he admitted. "I just feel...."

"Ah, laddie, you're probably coming down with a flu or something. There's nothing going to happen any worse than what we've all already lived through several times. You're just feeling sad and low because of that bad throat you've had." He looked at her, hopeful for a moment, then shook his head and almost said something, but didn't.

"Tell you what." Gran gave him a quick hug. "The bizzums are gone, so why don't you just hop on over and see for yourself that everything's as good as it ever gets."

Jimmy nodded and headed for the front door. Gran settled herself on the sofa with her knitting. Poor boy, he worried himself so about the younger ones. No youngster should have that much responsibility laid on him.

Jimmy almost felt better when he saw the girls sitting with Victor on the couch between them. Jimmy liked Victor. He joined the girls and played with the baby, tickling his feet, making juicy slurpy noises against the little guy's pot belly. Victor laughed and waved his legs, and Merv nearly puked with jealousy. He tried everything he could to get their attention, but they'd seen every dumb stunt he could pull, and ignored him. They didn't even tell him to be quiet, or to stop bothering them, until Kitty got fed up with his jackassing and told him to go to bed.

"Won't!" he screamed. "Can't make me!" And he cavorted around, pulling faces and taunting them.

They ignored him. He tried again and still they ignored him. So he got their attention all right—he darted in and flicked Vic on the sole of the foot, hard. The baby's face crumpled, he wailed in pain and Seely moved as fast as PatsyRatsy. She had Merv by the throat, choking him and shaking him, and both Jimmy and Kitty just fussed over the baby, calming him down, letting her shake Merv until his head threatened to leave his shoulders.

Merv had never been quite so scared in his life. He'd been hurt lots of times, and he'd been scared lots of times, but this just went on and on and on and on until his knees buckled and he wasn't standing up any more, he was kneeling and his hips were trying to give out too. Jimmy moved then, took Seely's wrists in his tanned scarred hands and said her name over and over until she heard him. She let go of Merv, then grabbed him by the front of the shirt and hauled him to his feet. "Don't you *ever* hurt Victor again," she said quietly. "If you ever hurt him again, you are going to be so goddamned sorry you won't believe it."

Donald had come from his bedroom to watch, he liked to see Merv get what was coming to him. He started to laugh and Jimmy just pointed his finger at him and Donald shut up. He'd heard his mom say Jimmy was crazy as a coot.

Victor stopped crying and the girls told both Donald and Merv to go to bed, but neither of them went. Seely didn't really care by then, she was scared stiff by how angry she had been. "I could have *killed* him," she whispered. "I didn't even care if I did!"

"But you didn't." Jimmy gave her a hug. "Don't let them get to you so much." But he knew the little farts got to him too. "Want me to drag them to their bedrooms and lock them in for you?"

"They'll just howl and screech and kick the door and then when the others come home they'll tell lies and we'll catch heck."

"Jesus, I wish they'd move," Jimmy sighed. "If you're sure you're gonna be all right, I'll head back home."

"We'll be fine, Jimmy. And thank you." He looked surprised, then grinned widely.

"You"—he bowed—"are welcome, oh fair maiden."

When Savannah came home she gave the girls a big triple-sized bag of chips, a can of Orange Crush each, and two dollars apiece. "Thank you," she said, and gave each of them a little kiss on the cheek. "It's nice to be able to go out and know the little guy is havin' as much fun at home as I'm havin' watching *those* two parade their wares. Boy"—she pulled a funny face—"what a performance." She plopped herself on the sofa between them, put an arm around each and gave a quick squeeze. "Just about time for the reruns." She grinned. "I'm not missin' the reruns!"

"Just a minute or two," Kitty agreed, "and then *I'm* on the tube."

"You," Seely scoffed. "That isn't you or anything like you, just because the name's the same." She dug into the bag of chips, brought out a handful and started chewing happily. "Thanks, Savannah." Seely blinked rapidly, as though she was going to bubble over and spill down her face over a few deep-fried slices of potato. "It's real nice of you."

"What about *me*?" Donald whined. "Don't I get none?"

"Don't I get *any*, you mean," Savannah corrected, "and no, you don't, if you were in bed asleep like you're supposed to be you wouldn't even know there *were* any. Bugger off with you, who wants you hanging around?"

"They got *money*."

"They earned the money. They looked after my kid for me. What did *you* do except get in their way and be a pest? You're not getting any money. You can't even get your ass in bed when it's bedtime."

"They got money and chips and everything," he screamed. His screams usually got him what he wanted. Any time nagging failed, he'd open his mouth and let rip with such an awful noise that, before you knew it, his mother caved in and gave him the very thing she'd said he'd never get.

"Oh, don't be so cheap," Phyllis sighed, "give the kid some chips."

"I'll burn'em in the stove before I give them to him. I got these for Seely and Kitty because they babysat my kid. If you wanted *your* rotten brats to have some, you coulda opened your purse and let out a few moths."

"Christ, what's the big deal?" Phyllis might have said more, but Donald upped the volume. She winced and leaned over to take a handful of chips from the bag, for Donald. Savannah's hand came up, wrapped around Phyllis' hand and squeezed, turning the chips to salty dust. Phyllis stared, unable to believe what had happened.

"I don't think you care how *awful* those kids are." Savannah spoke very quietly and calmly. "I don't think you care that they just about drive these two nuts when they're left alone. Well, I do. And what's going on is none of your business."

"They're my kids!"

"Then *you* look after them. *You* clean up after them. *You* cook for them. And leave *my* sisters alone!" She turned her head and spoke to Donald: "Get outta here or I'll hit you so hard your crazy damned father'll feel it." Coming off the sofa, Savannah grabbed him by one arm, scooted him upstairs and gave him a whap on the bum that sounded as if it really hurt. "You too, you little worm, get!" She glared and Merv was gone like a flash.

"They don't listen to *me*," Aunt Phyllis laughed nervously.

"Why should they, you never DO anything," Savannah agreed. "It's easier to crack open another beer than pay attention to their bull."

"Now, don't you start," Mom warned.

"Who? Me? All I'm doin' is getting set to watch the rerun of 'Gunsmoke', crackin' open a beer and eating potato chips with the niggers."

"What an awful word to use!" Mom took a slap at Savannah, but missed.

"What's awful about it? They cooked supper for you, and those useless brats upstairs didn't help with the dishes, and we went out and these two got stuck with everything, and Aunt Phyllis never pays them, and you don't think any of *that* is awful, so why kick up dust over the word nigger? Boy, you got some weird ways about you."

"Pay them? For what?"

"Jesus, Phyllis, if you were any cheaper you'd fall apart," Savannah argued.

"What's that supposed to mean?" Phyllis had the look on her face that meant she was about to get shirty. Well, she'd better be careful how shirty she got with Savannah, because there'd been some real changes there, not all of them having to do with Victor. Savannah squirmed down between Seely and Kitty and wiggled, but she wasn't really wiggling, it was almost like a cuddle thing, rubbing against first this one, then the other. She winked so they knew she wasn't upset, she was just doing a thing like sparring or play wrestling, yet she meant every word and was fighting for them.

"What do you mean, so cheap I'd fall apart?"

"Like a two-dollar watch or those cheap blouses that give out in the seams when you wash them, that's what I mean." Savannah sipped her beer, then passed it to Kitty so she could have a taste. "You never even say thank you when these two cook your meal and clean up your mess, you don't even make sure those ugly bastard kids of yours help around the place. They don't bring in wood, they don't clear the table, they just march around here as if they were some kind of somebodies instead of bein' nobody at all. You don't give these kids a thank-you, and you sure as hell don't give them the occasional dollar or go out of your way to buy them some new socks or anything. Just take take take take take. Cheap. Now shut your face, will you, because we're going to watch 'Gunsmoke'."

"You've got no right to talk to me like that. I pay my way. I pay my share of the groceries and...."

"Shut the fuck up, we're watchin' 'Gunsmoke'," Savannah shouted. "Put a sock in it, will you?"

Savannah had lots of money. She took them into town, Jimmy too, and they all had supper together, and not at the hamburger shack, either. They went to the Dining Room and had supper with a white tablecloth and real napkins instead of paper ones. The radishes looked like little roses, and when the dessert came even the ice-cream had been fancied up to look like flowers.

"That's what I'm gonna do," Seely decided. "I could do that if I had the thing to do it with. I bet it's like one of those icing-tube things."

"Tell you what"—Savannah smiled—"you finish school and find out where it is you go to learn how to do that, and I'll see to it you got the money to go."

"Where *you* going to get money like that?"

"The three wise men, of course."

"You'll be split up by then."

"I bet I won't." She laughed. "You think I don't know a good thing when I see it? Listen, I've got my own room; well, I don't got it yet but it's picked out and everything. All to myself. I've got clothes any time I want them. I just look at something and say "nice" and it's mine. They sent me to cooking school," she said proudly. "They did! More than one time, too. I can do their kind of cooking and Chinese kind and I'm going to learn the kind they do in New Orleans. And about all I got to do that I think is dumb is that I can't drink more than one or two beer when any of *them* three are around. I can smoke in my room, though, any time I want. Well," she amended, "with the window open, right, but that's only fair."

"What if they get another girlfriend?" Jimmy asked. "What will *you* do?"

"I'll be so bloody nice to her she'll think she just got herself a brand-new sister!"

"Savannah"—Jimmy smiled the way people do when they hear another fish story—"you were the hardest of anybody to get along with. You never had a nice word for anyone at all. And you want me to believe all that?"

"You might as well," she said calmly. "You'll see."

After supper they went over to see Glen, who was still living with Mr. Marpole. They were supposed to call him Greg but only Savannah could manage that. She'd invited Glen for supper too but it turned out he had other plans already. The other plans were supper at home with two other couples.

Jimmy was uncomfortable, but Savannah said it was no skin off her nose one way or the other, as long as it fit and didn't keep the neighbors awake. "Who am I," she laughed, "to say anything about how someone else lives?"

"Cast no stones," one of the faggots agreed.

"Or aspersions," another added. Glen and the faggots all laughed at that, but it went right over Seely's and Kitty's heads. Savannah seemed to understand it, and grinned. It was pretty surprising how well she seemed to get along with the gearboxes, all things considered.

They had more dessert and visited for a while, then they had to leave to catch the bus back. "I could drive you," Greg offered, but

Savannah shook her head and patted his face gently. "You visit with your friends, Greg. And thanks. For bein' so nice to Glenny. He seems a whole lot better."

"I love him," Greg said quietly.

"Well, he's not easy to love," Savannah warned. "He can do some real ugly things at times."

"Can't we all," Greg laughed. "From what I hear, you were almost legendary."

"What do you mean, 'almost'?" She gave him a little shove and Seely realized for the first time that Savannah was more than just pretty, she was enough to make anyone stop on the street, turn and stare. That was hard to believe, hard to realize. Savannah had been big sister for so long Seely hadn't thought of her as a person. But she was. She'd grown into someone so beautiful you knew you'd never, no matter how many courses you took, be able to draw or paint or take a picture of something even a little bit as nice. She looked better than any of the ones on TV, because you knew looking at them they'd had to call out the entire makeup and special-effects crews to do the hair, and another crew to get the stuff on the face. But Savannah just *was*, and with no more help than some shampoo and conditioner for the rebellious mop of arbutus-bark hair, and some on-sale face cream once in a while.

They walked from the bus to Gran's house to drop off Jimmy and pick up Victor. And to give Gran the plant they'd bought her in town, the pot of it covered in green and gold tinfoil. "Oh, Savannah!" Gran breathed. "It's *lovely*."

"You shoulda got more and better than this a long time ago, Gran." Savannah smiled, hoisting Victor to her shoulder and rubbing his back to make him burp.

"He's a good baby." Gran's voice was soft and for a change so was her face. "You must take really good care of him for him to be so pleasant."

"He's my bubba." Savannah grinned. "And he's easy, so easy you *want* to do good for him. But boy, if I thought for a minute he'd turn out like those two barbarians up at the house, I'd drop him on his lovely little head."

"No chance of that if you keep on treating him as nicely as he's obviously been treated." Gran kissed Savannah on the cheek. "You're a good mom to him, and a good granddaughter to me," she said gently.

They tiptoed into the house and took Victor upstairs with them. He'd spent most of the time they were gone on Gran's knee, having his feet pedaled as if he was riding a bike, having his arms moved while Gran played time-in-the-gym with him. He'd been tickled until he laughed, he'd been bounced horsy-back on her knee, and now that his belly was full he was ready to just close his big black eyes and go to sleep. They put him in the bed and made sure there were pillows to keep him from slithering off, then Seely and Kitty got into one bed and Savannah got in the other with Victor.

Big Merv came busting in just as they were falling asleep. The noise of the gun going off downstairs jarred them wide awake. "Out the window!" Kitty yelled, and she grabbed Victor as she raced past the other bed. They could hear the boys screeching and yelling for their mom. The sound of heavy boots clumping came to them clearly.

"Jesus, he's headin' up the stairs!" Savannah grabbed Seely and got her over the sill and onto the fire-escape rope, then swung herself over and started down too. Her head had just disappeared past the bottom sill when the bedroom door swung open and Big Merv fired into the room. He missed the window but got the gyproc below the sill. The bullet punched a hole in the wall not a foot from Seely's face. It scared her so badly she lost control of her bladder and peed on Kitty's head.

"Fuck!" Kitty hissed, "he wants to shoot me, you want to drown me! Take it easy, I've got the baby!"

The next bullet blew the window glass to bits and it showered down on them like snow. "Jesus Christ," Savannah breathed, "run!" She scooped Seely under the arm, lifting her from where she'd fallen on the ground. "Come on, Seel, he ain't kiddin'!"

The lights were on in Gran's house and they headed there, Kitty in front with the baby. Jimmy came out on the porch but dove back into the house when a bullet smashed the window beside him.

"Come on!" Gran shouted before she turned out the light. "Into the house!"

"Never mind the house, he's coming this way with a gun!"

"Into the house," Gran insisted.

They went in the front door and Gran reached around the corner and turned on the light in the hallway upstairs. But she didn't go upstairs or let them go either; she took them downstairs, into the basement, and she locked the basement door from their side. "Hold hands," she hissed, "and be quiet."

She led them through the dark to the little doorway where the wood for the furnace could be brought in, then she opened that door a crack and peeked before she went into the side yard. Big Merv was in the kitchen, yelling for them to show their goddamn selves so's he could teach them all a thing or two.

Gran took them across the grass to the barn, and they huddled there, half leaning against the wall, trying hard not to breathe loudly but just about gagging with the need to fill their lungs. They looked to Gran for some sign of what to do next, because sure as hell they couldn't just stand near the door to the cow stall, sooner or later Big Asshole would find them. Gran looked as if she was staring eye to eye with ghosts; her skin was the color of old cottage cheese and someone had cut lines criss-cross and zigzag on her face, someone had added a thousand years to her age. It was Jimmy who led them away from the barn to where the drainage ditch cut across the field. He didn't exactly look like Jimmy, though, and he didn't exactly *move* like Jimmy—he moved stiffly, as if his arms and legs were made out of sticks. The skin on his face was stretched tight over the cheek and jaw bones, but sunk in deep in the soft places. It looked almost as if someone had decided to take an old hunk of tide-bleached driftwood and carve a mask that looked like Jimmy. But then they were at the culvert ditch and he took a deep breath and was more like himself once he thought he was safe. They crawled into the big cement culvert and cowered. Victor was making little snuffly noises as if he was going to cry, but then they stopped.

"How is he?" Gran whispered.

"He's fine," Savannah answered. After a minute they could hear Victor sucking and slurping.

They heard the sirens coming from a long way off, and out the end of the culvert they could see down the highway, see the headlights and the bright revolving red and blue lights on the police cars and the ambulance.

"I hope they shoot the son of a bitch," Jimmy sobbed.

They heard big Merv yelling and shouting. Jimmy crawled out of the culvert and lay on the wet grass of the field, watching things and whispering back reports. He saw big Merv come out of Gran's house and run, yelling and raging, back to the big old house. "He's gone." Jimmy sagged with relief. The others came out of the culvert, Victor asleep again at his mother's breast. They could hear big Merv raging and hollering for Donald, hollering for little Merv to get in the goddamn car right now you hear you little bastards. Then they heard him yelling at Aunt Phyllis for being every kind of useless bitch as ever lived and stealing his kids and calling the goddamn police. It's all your fault, Phyllis, the whole dirty mess. There were more shots then, and the windshield on one of the cop cars exploded. The cops scattered, surrounding the house. The guy with the bullhorn was yelling for big Merv to calm down, take it easy, let's talk this thing out, no need for any of this.

They heard the big gun go off one more time. Then all they heard was sirens and police yelling at other police to surround the house, bring out the dogs, get the loudhailer. The police surrounded the house and waited for two hours, and then threw stun grenades through the downstairs windows. Once that had settled down, they went inside.

Gran led them from the field to her house. "I gotta know," Savannah sobbed, "I gotta know!"

"You'll know soon enough. Wait here." And it was Gran who stomped across to the other house to talk to the police.

Phyllis and Mom hadn't even made it out of bed—they were both sprawled in their own thickening blood, and it isn't possible to be more dead than they were. Donald was halfway under his bed. Little Merv was in the hallway, his injured hand thrown forward, his good hand pinned under his body, his face turned to one side. The police figured big Merv had come in quietly, done in the two women, then gone after the kids upstairs, and only blown his own kids away when he realized they weren't going to get in the car and drive off with him. With them dead, he turned the gun on himself. "Son of a bitch shoulda done that first," Savannah said, rocking Vic and staring over his head at nothing anyone else could see. "They were rotten stinking lousy awful kids but they didn't have that coming to them. *Why*"— she began to sob—"*why* don't those dickheads ever shoot themselves *first*? Their whole lives it's been me first, me first, me first, and then, when it counts the most, it's not like that at all, no, they get gallant or some damned thing and it's the old Women and Children First."

PatsyRatsy was fine, hidden in the walls, and didn't come out until two days later, when Seely went over to get her.

Gran didn't even say, Get that rat out of my house, she just nodded and patted the table in the living room. Seely put the Habitrail house down but kept PatsyRatsy cuddled against her body. She sat on the sofa next to Gran and stared straight ahead, petting her rat, blinking once in a while.

The day after the cremations and memorial service, Savannah packed up her stuff and took Victor back to his fathers. "They can stay with me," she said. "We'll be fine with them."

"We'll see," Gran said, already dead tired from having so many kids in her house. They all knew she'd try to do it. And they all knew she wouldn't be able to.

And then the Graingers drove out in their big car and parked in front of Gran's house. They went inside, and when Seely saw them she started to cry and Sandra Grainger just knelt down and folded her in her arms, rat and all, and stroked her back and said, There there, my darling, there there there.

Mr. Grainger looked over at Gran and, before he had to say one word, she nodded. And an hour later Seely, with all her things in bags and boxes, went to live with the Graingers, in a big house in town where she could have PatsyRatsy in her bedroom, Habitrail and all, and have her own room in the basement to keep all her drawing stuff in.

Jimmy stayed with Gran, and for a while Kitty did too. But when school let out for the summer, Kitty and all her stuff went on the bus to stay with Gran's absent daughter, the one who hardly ever even phoned to say hi, let alone wrote a letter.

When the bus pulled away, Gran went back to her own house just long enough to get the blue-painted half-gallon can of lamp oil. "What you going to do with that?" Jimmy asked. Gran just pointed. Jimmy nodded and took the can from her. "I'll carry it," he said.

Together they walked over to the big old house and, working overtime to not look at the big stains of dried blood, pinching their noses against the smell from the gore-stiffened mattresses and blankets, they spread the lamp oil on the floor. When the can was empty they tossed it into what had been a kitchen for all those years, then Jimmy helped Gran down the steps. He let go of her arm and went back up the steps, and stood in the front doorway with a piece of paper and a Bic lighter. He lit the corner of the paper and tossed it into the house, then jumped down the steps and took Gran by the arm, and they walked back to her house.

"We'll be fine, Gran," he said. "We'll be fine."

PART
THREE

1

Kitty didn't see the old house burn. She didn't even look back. She slumped down in her seat and stared dry-eyed out the side window. She had no idea where in hell she was going, and she didn't much care. She had two brand-new pocket books, she had ten Oh Henry! chocolate bars and two packages of Juicy Fruit gum, she had a bag of sandwiches in case she got hungry, which she knew she would, and she had two cans of Pepsi. She had money, too, so if she needed more to eat or drink she could get it. Gran had told her she never again needed to worry about money. "There's this thing called the Victims of Crime fund, darling, so you kids will be fine until you can support yourselves. And if you're smart you won't do that in a hurry!"

"Bastards," Jimmy agreed, his voice half dead, "they should'a never let the crazy bugger outta jail."

"Happens all the time," Gran sighed. "We're just lucky, is all."

Funny, Kitty didn't feel very lucky. And yet every time she thought that, about not feeling lucky, she remembered how she just left the bed as if she was going after a high fly ball, she remembered how her feet had known exactly where to come down, missing all kinds of stuff she could have tripped over or slipped on or something. Her hands, without her having to look or think or fumble or anything, just reached and Victor was in them, and she was over the windowsill with Vic under her left arm, like a guy running for a touchdown with the football gripped tight and safe. Her right hand had that rope and she couldn't even *see* it. And down she went. So what's to feel not lucky about? She didn't drop Vic, she didn't squish him, she didn't even make him cry, she just was up and out of bed and scooping and going and over the sill and then Seely peed on her head.

For all how awful it was, every time she thought about Seely peeing she got the giggles. Even at the undertaker parlor or whatever they called it, everyone all sad and crying and she looked over at Seely and remembered the warm on her own head and she giggled. And afterward, as she was getting ready to leave for the bus, Savannah suddenly started to laugh out loud and she pointed her finger at Kitty and said, "And there she is with my kid in her arm, going down a rope with some lunatic coming after us with a gun, and she makes a *joke!*" Savannah had moved then, and grabbed Kitty and squeezed her hard and said, "Thank you, darling, thank you. Even before you got yourself safe you had Vic on his way out of there. Any time, Kitty, *anything*, you just name it," and for a minute it was as if Savannah was going to cry but then she laughed instead and said, "One of 'em's tryin' to shoot me and the other's tryin' to drown me." And that felt good. To be safe like that, and alive like that, and laughing with your own sister. Kitty tried to remember why it was that for so many years she had disliked Savannah. She tried to remember what it felt like being PO'ed with her because the way she behaved made people call her Round Heels and Hooer. And all that was gone. So gone even the memory of it had gone, burned with the dead, burned with all of them, so many of them, gone, all gone. All she could feel was a big golden warm thing, not hot like the sun but gentler and kinder, more like a great big peach, a great big fuzzy-skinned peach filling her inside when she thought of Savannah. And so how come Savannah was a hooer and that was so awful and the guys she went with were... what? Not awful. So how come Glen was awful and the guys who clambered around Savannah like hungry puppies weren't? And didn't those people have anything else to do with their lives but get all hung up on other people's doings? Savannah was alive. Jesus, didn't anybody know how wonderful *that* was?

Kitty didn't know how to say any of that so she just snugged up close to Savannah and wrapped her arms around her and pressed close and tight. She sobbed once, but not because she was sad. She sobbed because there was just so much inside her that she couldn't hold it all easily, but she didn't want to lose even one tiny drop of it, so she sobbed to hold it in.

It would be real different not having Seely around all the time. Gran's absent daughter had said she'd take them both but Gran said no, Seely was just fine where she was, safe with people she knew, safe in a place she was already comfortable in, going to the same school, do her more harm than good to shift her now. They love her, she said, and that's the most important thing.

Well, Gran's absent daughter didn't love Kitty. Never even set eyes on her. That would take some getting used to. But still, nice of her to make room.

Gran's absent son, Kitty's possible father, had said she could go stay with him and his new wife, but Gran put the nix on that. "Take a week," she grumbled, "and there'd be someone else out firing guns at people! And you'd be on the old lonesome trail again. You can't mix a daughter you don't know with a wife you hardly know and expect to have them get along." And that was probably true. Nice of him to offer, though. And he'd promised to send money, some to Gran for Jimmy, some to the Graingers for Seely and some for Kitty. Well, Jimmy had told him to keep his lousy money, but Jimmy held grudges. And anyway, Jimmy was making money himself, and would make more now that he wasn't going to waste any more time sitting in school. He was just going to carve stuff all the time, he said.

Didn't seem possible. Not all the time. You'd get bored sick doing one stupid bird after another. What did a person even *think* about, sitting there with a knife or something turning perfectly good wood into ducks? And who'd buy a wooden duck when for a lot less money they could have a real one, complete with quack?

Seely, well, what she did was different. What she did was sometimes real weird. But she was happy. Mrs. Grainger had this kind of bag in the kitchen, and you put icing in it and pushed and the icing came squidging out the bottom, like when they gave you a shot in the arm. Seely could do that and put little things like Maple Bud chocolates, only they were icing, all over the top of a cake. When Kitty tried she got a big glob. Seely said all she had to do was practice a bit, but who'd want to be bothered, and how much icing would you have to waste before the globs became like Maple Bud chocolates? Only Seely had gone far beyond those little things. She could make roses out of icing, each individual petal just so. Pink ones, pale yellow, you name it. And leaves.

But God in heaven, how many of them could you make before you started to go a little bit strange? Surely you couldn't just sit there smearing icing and thinking about the cake, the whole cake and nothing but the crumby cake!

But there you had it. And Mrs. Grainger had already sold more cakes than you could shake a stick at, and not because people felt sorry for Seely, either. She even did a wedding cake, with the little plastic bride and groom standing under this archway thing with lace stuff on it.

"You going to add a little rifle in there?" Kitty asked. "Just in case the little doll groom decides to blow up the doll bride, and prob'ly the cake too?"

"Oh, you *stop* it!"

"Maybe you could make a little icing hand grenade and put it on the side in the middle of the flowers—you could disguise it, maybe, like a pineapple; then if the doll groom gets out of hand the doll bride can grab the grenade and just...," and Seely got the giggles and had to stop before she smeared something.

She didn't know one single solitary soul on the bus. She had all those chocolate bars and no appetite. Well, what do you expect, Kitty, you damned fool. You should'a stole PatsyRatsy and brought her along, she'd have eaten the stuff for you. And gave the other passengers a real exciting ride. They'd be eeking and shrieking like hell, tumbling out the windows, hitting the emergency stop, popping the panic exits, and every one of them nothing but a walking compost heap, if the truth be known. The science teacher had told them all about the little mites that live on everybody's skin, not just one or two but zub-zillions of them. More of them in your eyebrows than there are people living in Paris. And intestinal worms. And, as they say, others too numerous to mention. But one little rat and my good God in heaven, let us all flip our wigs.

Sandra Grainger didn't feel quite right about having a rat living in the house. One part of her head said, Why not, people have cats and dogs, gerbils and hamsters, boa constrictors and turtles, goldfish and canaries, why not a rat? An ordinary goat sells for maybe eighty dollars, but one with a cracked chromosome which causes it to fall on its side and lie

stiff and unblinking for several seconds before getting to its feet and
walking off as if nothing had happened can sell for as much as five hundred dollars. *Oh*, they say, *we use them to protect the herd; if the predators come the goats will all run for home, the fainting goat will go
ka-bang to the ground, the hungry beasts will go munchy-munchy and
our herd will be safe.* Why not just bust a leg on some of the forty-dollar
goats and let them hobble and hop with the herd? Some people have
tigers and chimpanzees, some people have drapes shredded to
hell'n'gone by monkeys swinging on them, other people have lop-eared
rabbits hopping down the hallway, what's so odd about a rat?

It was just that PatsyRatsy wasn't white. She hadn't been inbred
to albinism, she wasn't like those poor things they called dancing
mice and sold for five dollars each, which were the product of an
inbred genetic flaw similar to cerebral palsy—not dancing at all,
merely unable to control their twitching muscles and minor epileptic
seizures. If you could give houseroom to a misbred mouse as apt as not
to fling itself into the air and come down in your cup of tea, why not
a shiny, bright-eyed and friendly rat who was probably twice as smart
as any poodle who ever pranced on the end of a leash? But all you had
to do was look at PatsyRatsy and every horror story you'd ever heard
leaped up on stage and started to tap dance. PatsyRatsy wasn't exotic,
she was *Rattus rattus*.

Bob Grainger liked her. Not at first, it took a day or two, but one
night, after the store was closed and swept out and he was back home
with his shoes off, sitting in front of the television with a nice cold
beer and a stack of chocolate-chip cookies, PatsyRatsy climbed up the
side of his cloth-covered big chair and sat on the back, only an inch
or two from his shoulder. Just sat, watching the television. It was an
accident or a coincidence or something, but when the program went
off so the commercial could come on, PatsyRatsy squeaked. She sat
on her back legs and rubbed at her nose with her front paws. "Right,
Patsy," poor tired Bob agreed, "commercials stink." And co-inky-
dinky number two, the rat squeaked again. "Rattus Ordinaryus, eh?"
Bob yawned. "You'd think if an Ordinaryus knows that much, people,
who think they're the top of the creation pyramid, would catch on
too. You're okay, Patsy. Have a chocolate chip."

Some people would gag at the thought of eating cookies while
drinking beer. Wait until they found out that some nights, when he

was so tired and so bummed out by the impoliteness and loftiness of the voting public that it was all he could do to focus his eyes, Bob Grainger ate chocolate bars with his beer. Of course, that's not couth. What *is* couth is eating snails.

Seely wasn't any more trouble than the rat. Sort of made you wonder just what was and was not a bad environment. She helped without being asked to help, if she saw something needed doing she just went over and did it. She never got up from the supper table and sauntered off; she asked to be excused, got up, took her plate, cutlery, glass and such to the sink, rinsed everything under the tap, and stacked it all neatly in the dishwasher. When the others were finished, Seely came back and cleared the rest of the table, and no moaning or griping about it. "I can't believe this machine," she said. "All you have to do is put the stuff in and turn it on and it does the dishes. What'll they think of next?"

Sometimes he wondered how smart Seely was. He was never sure if she was as simple, as uncomplicated and child-like, as she appeared, or if she was expertly wearing the role of innocent in some movie unwinding in her head. There was...something...in the way she said, What'll they think of next? that made him almost suspect something else was going on. But how could that be, and why? She was just a kid, a kid who'd survived some real crap.

And she knew about people needing time to themselves. She visited with them after supper, then went down to her little room and gave them time to slide back into what they'd known every evening since they'd started living together.

That "just me'n'you, babe" hadn't been enough, but that didn't mean you wanted to throw it away overnight. The first few years they hadn't worried, they weren't in a rush for a family, there were other things they needed first, but then they started to wonder why and finally they had the testing and after that it was the old thermometer-in-the-morning sex-on-demand thing, and none of it worked. For a while Sandra thought about fertility drugs and in vitro fertilization, but it seemed as if everyone who did that had three or four or five, and all she wanted was a kid, not a litter, and anyway, you wondered what it did to the kids themselves. What if they were short some stuff? Humans maybe only had enough of some kind of hormone juice or something for one, and if it got divided up, well, what happened? They said most twins were like that, as if there was one soul or something that got divided and one of them was a bit more than the other, one smart, the other just a bit slow, one nice, the other leaving a lot to be desired. And look at the Dionne Quints—one pitched fits, one was a religious nut, none of them was stable, and how many were good-looking?

They considered adoption and even put their name in but you could grow old waiting on *that* list. It was real easy to slide down to the bottom and have to work your way back up again. Just say no thank you to the idea of fostering someone else's kid for a while and that was it, you didn't have a lot going for you alongside of someone on the list who had said yes and then spent a day a week in juvenile court with the foster kid.

It was nice before the shootings, when Seely would come at lunchtime for a quick visit. And god knows Sandra would never say she was glad what happened had happened, but it was nice now, and good for all of them.

Bob Grainger worried, at first, that Seely would go into a depression or start hanging around with a tough crowd or change from a kid he really liked to the kind he saw coming into the store with their parents and nagging or whining. Bob Grainger worried about a lot of things. Life was made up of worries. But he was starting to think maybe Seely wouldn't be a worry at all. She wasn't running around craven and saying thank you thank you thank you, not at all, she was very matter-of-fact about some things. She knew they'd driven out to that awful place because they wanted her. She knew they knew she'd gone to pack her few miserable possessions and gone with them because she wanted them. Fair deal on both sides. No need for thank you. Would you like to, yes I'd like to, then let's do it.

Thank god she wasn't a teacher's kid. He saw those ones. Enrichment didn't seem to be good for kids if you judged its effect by the children of teachers. Whining, self-centered, spoiled little tyrants with vastly inflated opinions of their own worth and importance. Smug. Never saw a teacher's kid who wasn't insufferably smug. Gimme, gimme, gimme, I want I want I want so gimme. And by god, if you want to know about shoplifting, watch a teacher's kid. Then when you caught them it was a lofty Oh don't be so cheap, my dad'll pay for it. As if *you'd* done something not quite socially acceptable, my dear, by catching them swiping stuff.

Seely's brother Jimmy, now, there was a shoplifter a shopkeeper could admire. Slick? Bob *knew* Jimmy had lifted stuff. He knew it the way he knew there'd be water when he turned on the tap. But he'd never had even a hint of when or how Jimmy stole things. Old man Nash insisted the kid had nearly bled him dry for a few months, but he never once caught him at it.

And Seely didn't just dump her family in the ditch. She went out on the bus every Saturday to see her Gran, and took her things, maybe a cake she'd decorated up herself, maybe a picture or something she'd made. Poor old biddy. Some people get a rough row to hoe and no two ways about that one. But at the same time don't you wonder what in hell *they* were up to while it was all starting to form itself in their kids' personalities? What was going on and what was the old lady's role in it that the daughter hi-de-ho'd off and got herself involved in some bizarre damned thing, and the son married, unmarried, remarried, re-unmarried like a bee sipping flowers or a golden barnyard fly going from cowpat to horse bun? Has to be *something* wrong when nobody visits.

Glen worried. He was scared stiff now that everyone was shot to hell or scattered around living with other people; scared the welfare would show up and say they'd found some kind of shirt-tail uncle or aunt or something and he had to go live with them. He was happy just where he was. Greg made him go to school, but what else can you expect from a teacher? They think the answer to everything is in a school-book. World peace in fifteen minutes if you can just get the president's men into the right class with the right teacher. So Glen went to school, and he did his homework at the same table where Greg marked papers.

Why would anyone want to be a teacher? Christ, Greg worked all day at school, and how much fun could that be, then came home and had homework, same as if he was still in school himself.

But Glen had nice clothes, he had a proper haircut, the place was clean and the furniture was top of the line. Greg was a real good cook and was teaching Glen, and the people who came over for supper and drinks after were great. Funny as hell, some of them, and never treated him like he was a baby, or a freak, or some kind of slimy thing Greg had picked up out of the gutter and wiped dry but not quite managed to make presentable.

If they came and said he had to go live with some goddamned workie with rough hands and a rougher tongue, he'd just hit the goddamned road. He wasn't living with people who'd always see him as a freak, a faggot, a queer, a gearbox who needed to be hypnotized or psychoanalyzed or some damn thing. Whose damned business was it anyway? And how normal were *they*?

2

There was only one passenger got off the bus, so they knew it had to be Kitty. The driver got off, moved to open the luggage bay. The kid looked around, her face carefully pleasant. Lucy moved forward, unsmiling. "You Kitty?" she asked.

"Yes, I am. Are you my Aunt Lucy?"

"Lucy'll do." She turned and held out her hand. Debbie took it and stepped forward. "This is Debbie."

"Hello," Kitty smiled and nodded.

"Hello, Kitty. How was your trip?"

"Long. I didn't think it would take so long."

"It's not quite over yet, I'm afraid, but we'll be home in less than an hour, and you can rest."

"Oh, it wasn't *that* kind of tiring. My bones are fine," she grinned. "It's just inside my head. They've got these No Smoking signs up and a notice in the can in the back about how they're worried about the air people breathe and the healthy environment, and you can't get your window open no matter *what* you do. Not one of them in the whole bus will open. So the only time there's any fresh air is when someone gets on or off. We all sit there breathing in what everyone else has just breathed out, and how healthy can *that* be?"

The kid didn't have much. If what she was wearing was her best, she didn't have much at all. Well, she could wear some of what Chad

had left behind when he took off, it would be fine until they could get her something of her own.

"There's a parcel for you from Gran in with the stuff in that black plastic garbage bag." Kitty pointed. "You want it now?"

"Later." Lucy picked up the bag and the apple box with the tops folded over and under, then taped shut. "Truck's over this way."

"You talk like Gran does," Kitty told her. "You walk like her too, only you're taller. You don't much look like her, though."

"Is that so?"

"Does my dad look like you or like her? I don't really remember him much. Jimmy does, and Savannah does, and Glen a little bit, but I don't and Seely, she hardly even *saw* him."

"Hmmm," Lucy nodded.

"Well?" Kitty looked up. "Does he look like you or Gran?"

"Like her, I guess."

"You sure don't talk much. You don't have to do this, you know. If it would work out better for everyone, I've got the money to get a ticket right back there again."

"It'll work out fine." Lucy put the stuff in the back of the truck, then made herself turn and look the kid in the eye. "I don't do well with conversation," she understated. "I don't want you to feel unwelcome. I don't mean to do that. I just...." She shrugged.

"Yeah, Seely's like that sometimes, too." Kitty nodded again. "Once she knows you she can talk your ears off; Gran said she could talk the ears off five acres of corn." She laughed softly. "But if she doesn't know you she's like a damned clam."

"Lucy's like a clam even when she *does* know you." Debbie stepped into it. "There are times I think she's mad about something and she isn't. Sometimes I even thought she was mad at me and it turned out she was just off in the clouds somewhere. She thinks a lot." She confided this in a tone meant to suggest there was something drastically wrong with someone who did that.

"Oh. Thinking." Kitty nodded yet again. "Yeah, I've heard about that. But she might be the first person I ever met who actually *did* it."

The ride back wasn't uncomfortable but it wasn't the nuclear family on tour, either. Lucy drove and smoked, her window rolled down. The smoke was supposed to go out that window, and it probably eventually did, but not until everyone else had had a dose of it.

"Aunt Phyllis smoked all the time, too," Kitty observed. "Did you know my Aunt Phyllis?"

"Never met her."

"Never *met* her?" Kitty seemed amazed. "Did you know my mom?"

"Met her once."

"And that's all? Wow, I'm almost afraid to ask if you know my dad."

"Met him a couple of times." Lucy grinned slightly. "Didn't much care for him."

"And Gran?"

"Oh, she's okay. A bit bossy. A bit rigid. Critical."

"Yeah? Never criticized me, much. You should go and visit her." Kitty just barged in and damn the consequences. "She's getting real old. And I think she's lonely. She never says, but I think that's why she wanted Jimmy to stay with her. She never said he *had* to, but when he said he wanted to she was glad, anybody could tell that. Maybe if you can't take time off to go there, you could have her come here for a visit or something."

"Oh, I don't think she'd agree to that. I invited her a couple of times before but she always had some excuse."

"Yeah, but that was before." Kitty rolled her window down and put her elbow on the door. "She couldn't leave then because she never knew when we were going to wind up going to her place because things were going nutsy again." She sounded so matter-of-fact Debbie almost gasped. "She feels real bad about all this mess because she detested my mom and had no use at all for Aunt Phyllis, and now...she told Jimmy she felt real bad because she wouldn't let Donald and little Merv hang out at her place with the rest of us. Jimmy said it was just as well because we all had more of them than we wanted, and she said, Yes but all the same it wouldn't have cost me much. But they'd have driven her nuts. They were awful little kids. I mean, like, they were *really* awful. Savannah said if she thought Victor was going to turn out like them she'd shoot him now, herself."

"My god!" Debbie blurted.

"Oh, you have to get used to Savannah. She says the things other people only think in their heads and then say to themselves, Stop that! But Savannah says them and doesn't feel bad at all." She slid a look at Lucy. "Gran says Savannah's a lot like you."

"Hmmm."

"Sure is *dry* around here, eh?" She looked out the window and chewed her bottom lip, wishing Lucy would squirt WD-40 down her throat and see if she could loosen up some words.

The country looked like something out of an old cowboy movie. Kitty wasn't sure if she was going to get used to all that dry grass. Just the start of summer and already it looked as if someone had baked it.

"It's all lots greener at home," she mourned.

"Yes," Lucy agreed, "I miss that. Sometimes I look at all this and I think, Shit, no wonder land is one-tenth the price here it is on the coast! You only get the use of it after it's blown off the place to your right and before it blows on to the one on your left. I don't know why we pay any property tax, what with the damned dirt being in mid-air most of the time."

"I guess it's awful in wintertime, eh?"

"Winter is a bitch."

"Yeah. Figured."

3

When Kitty sat down and figured it out on paper it made nothing but no sense at all. She paid five dollars each for twenty-week-old pullets, all of them due to lay "soon". Then waited while they made up their minds whether they'd condescend to drop the occasional egg into the nest. She fed them laying pellets at six-something a fifty-pound sack. She made sure they had water, she made sure their floor was clean and free of lice, she made sure they had fresh hay in their nesting boxes and she picked them armloads of weeds, wheelbarrow-loads of weeds, absolute bloody *mounds* of weeds. She made sure they had grit, she got them oyster shell, she kept the eggshells and dried them in the oven and smashed them up and fed them back so the next eggs would have good shells. She gathered the eggs and washed them and then she sold her eggs for two dollars a dozen. Which meant she paid for the laying pellets, grit, oyster shell and electricity and maybe took a penny a month off the original cost of the chickens. *So* any eggs they ate at home were "free" if you worked on the supposition her birds would live long enough to pay for themselves, and her own work wasn't worth anything.

And it said in the book that each laying hen produced a hundred and twenty pounds of chicken manure a year.

So how much education did you need before the government would give you a job gathering up and weighing the shit from a laying hen? Because it obviously paid better than what she was doing.

It was nice on the farm, though. Ranch. Whatever. Debbie had told her the story about the jerkoffs and the cows and the hay and the horses, and every time she looked at the blue roan mare and her gorgeous baby, Kitty had to smirk. Lucy had traded three geldings and some money for one registered quarterhorse stud and then set about getting more stock. Every night she read the "Livestock" section of the classified. For Sale, eighteen-year-old thoroughbred mare, fully trained, gentle disposition, must sell, seven hundred dollars. Lucy would phone and say right off the bat, "I'll give you five hundred. If you get the seven hundred you're asking, fine, no hard feelings, but if you don't, phone me back and I'll arrange to have her shipped up." Lots of times you never heard a word back, but Lucy said that by October or November, with feed costs staring them in the face and the horses needing something more than a vacant field with grass in it, and the cost of a stall in a stable and all the other costs, the phone would start to ring.

She said that was how she got the appaloosa. "For Sale, fourteen-year-old appaloosa mare, jumping potential, professionally trained, easy to trailer, needs experienced rider. One thousand dollars." But by November the appaloosa was coming out of the rented trailer and it hadn't cost Lucy any thousand dollars. And she put her in with the quarterhorse stud and now they were waiting for the baby.

Funny how excited people got about some things, and how it was fine for the horse but not for Savannah. She'd said as much one night and both Debbie and Lucy looked as if some kind of strange idea had been put forth. Then finally Lucy had shook her head and said, Careful, Kitty, they hear you saying things like that they're going to think you're not normal.

"Well, I mean, like, so it's different, but if they treat her good and they're all happy and nobody's jealous, whose business is it? I mean, Vic is a great little guy. I bet if you saw him you'd fall in love. I mean it. And now she's going to have another one and even the bloody welfare is involved. They should *never* have bought that damned house. When they were on roadwork and moving all the time, living in auto courts or whatever, who gave a toot? Now they have neighbors and you'd think crimes were being committed."

"Oh, they are, my dear, they are." Debbie said. "Vile and dastardly crimes are being committed every day. So vile and so dastardly they frighten people. So those crimes get ignored, and the snivel servants pester your sister."

There were other things she really liked here. Nobody butted in. You wanted to lie in bed reading a book until one-thirty in the morning, you lay in bed and did it. Gran was great for just showing up at the door and switching off the light. Not a word, just Let there not be light saith the lord, and shit, you couldn't see the page. It didn't seem to matter to Gran that for most of Kitty's life "bedtime" was a word seldom uttered and never applicable; when the cuckoo jumped from its cage inside Gran's head, lights were turned out, doors shut and silence fell. But Lucy and Debbie seemed to feel that if she wanted to read until dawn it was up to her, after all, she'd be the one who was tired next day.

Kitty could barely remember her first week at the place. All this brand-new stuff coming at her, and her with all she could do to try to remember it all. Cows, for crying out loud. Cows. Not to milk, and not too friendly, either. Great big reddish-brown things with white tails, white stripe, and their own ideas about how things should happen. "Shift it," Lucy said, almost casually giving a shove to a stubborn thing with an equally stubborn small one pressing close to it.

"Won't it...kick or something?" Kitty hung back, nervous.

"Might do," she replied. "You learn which ones will and which won't, and you learn how to tell before they do it, and even so every now and again you get dumped on your butt."

"I hope you make buckets of money," she told Debbie as they restacked the bales in the barn loft.

"Nobody makes buckets of money farming. You don't even make cups of money."

"You telling me you could have a nice job in an air-conditioned office instead?"

"And make probably twice the money."

"Then why do this?"

"I really don't know." Debbie dropped the bale and wiped sweat from her face with her arm. "It sort of crept up in the dark, sank its teeth into my ankle and held on tight."

Lucy was at the bottom of the conveyor, loading bales. She grinned up at them, hay and chaff caught in her hair. "Ah, g'wan," she teased, "you love it."

"I love *you*," Debbie said calmly, "that doesn't mean I love this. Just think"—she looked around the barn loft, the hay stacked five bales high along one side—"now we've got room to bring in the second cutting and we get to do this all over again. And with even a little tiny bit of luck, we'll get a third chance, too."

They hired teenaged boys to help with the haying. First Deb and Lucy took turns driving the tractor around and around and around and around in the field, cutting the long grass. Then they brought the tractor back to the machinery barn, disconnected the mower, and wasn't *that* fun, and connected another thing they called a tether or a tedder or something. And went out to drive around and around and around and around the field, turning the hay so it dried evenly.

That gave them the chance to come back, unhitch the thing and hitch up the rake. Even more fun and games. And then around and around and so it goes, raking hay into lines. And finally, off with the rake and on with the baler and around and around we go again. When the hay was baled the big switcheroo happened one more time, off with the baler and on with the big wagon.

About then the boys arrived. Some of them looked at Lucy as if she had two heads, and one of them obviously hated her guts, but out they went and it was time to lift the bales from the field, throw them on the wagon and go get another bale, with two guys on the wagon stacking.

Two loads into the horror of it all, Debbie motioned for Kitty to go up to the house with her. Kitty had never been so happy in her life to head for a house!

"Jesus," she almost wept, "I have *never*...." She didn't finish the sentence.

"I know," Debbie agreed. "And did you notice how *dedicated* they are? I mean, you'd think at least *some* of this could be done at normal speed, but no, my God, we're all at a dead run out there."

They hauled the lemonade, ginger ale and iced tea out of the fridge, grabbed the packages of entire loaves of bread made into sandwiches, took that and two pies back out and got to the barn just as the last of the bales were going into the loft.

They all sat on the wagon with the sweat drying on their bellies, gulping glasses of juice, munching sandwiches and sighing deeply. The boy who seemed to hate Lucy looked at Kitty, then reached out with one finger and touched the inside of her arms, scratched and itching. "Short sleeves'll do that to you," he said quietly.

"Thanks." She rolled down her sleeves and buttoned the cuffs closed. "You do this a lot?"

"Did our place yesterday, do his place tomorrow." He pointed at one of the other boys.

"I'll be dead tomorrow," she mourned.

"Yeah, well, you've got to use your legs more and your back as little as possible." He reached for another sandwich. "One day," he promised, "I'm going to walk away from this and never even look back."

The hay wagon went back out into the field and Kitty took things back into the house, washed the glasses and plates and helped Debbie with the next meal. They basted the turkey, checked the chili, then got their leather gloves and headed out to the barn to wait for the next load. While they were waiting they went up on the stack and settled the hay, checking there were no wobbles or tilts waiting to happen.

They put twenty-five acres of hay into the barn and sold five acres of it in the field. The trucks arrived at five-thirty and drove behind the tractor and wagon, the boys sitting with their legs dangling over the end, staring at the ground, saying little to each other. They filled the trucks first, waved tiredly as they drove off, then went back to filling the wagon.

Before they got the wagon back to the barn and unloaded, two more trucks were driving out into the field and Lucy sold some more hay. The boys loaded the trucks, and then grinned at each other. "Just about there," they sighed.

They had almost finished unloading the wagon when the first two trucks came back. The drivers sat waiting, and the boys practically ruptured themselves trying to show the men that twelve hours of steady hard work was nothing to them.

After the last bales were stacked, loaded and driven off the place, the crew headed for the house, their hair wet with sweat, their faces drawn with fatigue. They looked as if they wouldn't be able to lift their hands to their faces, but once they'd taken the broom to each others' clothes and scrubbed up they were ready to put their feet under the table and pack away so much food Kitty worried there wouldn't be enough.

"That was good," they each sighed. "Thank you."

"Thank *you*," Lucy smiled, handing each of them an envelope. They didn't even check the money inside, just tucked it in their shirt pockets.

"Well," one of them said wearily, "off we go. And just think, we get to do'er all again in the morning."

The phone dragged them out of a sound sleep at two in the morning. Lucy stumbled down the hall to answer it, and Kitty rolled over on her other ear. She had just got back to sleep when Lucy was touching her shoulder. "We have to go," she said quietly, "we're needed."

It was miserable. Kitty was tired when she got there; two hours later she could have lain down on a wet rock and slept. But she didn't. She kept stacking until her sore hands wouldn't close and her tired arms wouldn't lift, and then, since she wasn't any help with the heavy bales, she got behind the wheel of a pickup and drove bales back to the barn.

And when they had the hay out of those fields, they roared off down the road to do what they could for the next place. They lost that race. Two hours after they got there the rain started.

"Some days"—Lucy said what everybody else was thinking—"you can't win for losing."

"Come on," Debbie said firmly. "It's only the outside of the bales getting wet."

There was nothing they could do for the place after that. Just as well, for they were too tired to move. Kitty was asleep on a sofa in the living room, her fingers swollen.

"Some introduction to life on the farm," one of the boys laughed bitterly. "Look at her. That's how I feel." He sat down in a big chair, put his head back and was asleep in minutes.

"Appreciate the use of your equipment," the last lucky farmer said.

"Any time," Lucy answered, thanking all the gods and goddesses the rain hadn't caught her hay and knocked its value in half.

Kitty wasn't sure she wanted to learn how to ride a horse. But everybody for miles around had been riding since they were babies and, scared or not, it looked like something you were expected to know how to do.

"Don't worry," Debbie said. "I learned, you'll be able to learn, too."

"Looks awful *big*." And it did. She knew it wasn't the biggest horse in the world, it wasn't even the biggest horse on the place, it just looked too big for anyone to climb up on top of. But when Lucy had it saddled and bridled and was standing holding its head, Kitty put her foot in the stirrup and heaved herself into place. "Now what do I do?" she worried.

"Take the reins and sit there."

Lucy and Debbie swung up and headed off on their own horses. Kitty's horse stood, shaking its head and making noises that sounded as if it was getting ready to explode. "Just click with your tongue and very *very* lightly touch your heels to her sides," Lucy called back.

Kitty did what she was told, and the horse stepped out, following the other two.

They just walked that day, around the fence lines, checking the wire, cutting back the weeds and long grass, cutting away any vines or branches, shrubs or bushes, that might ground out the electric wire. Kitty was on and off her horse more times than she could remember, and by the end of the ride could mount up without worrying that she was going to fall or that the horse would take off without her—or, worse yet, that it would take off with her foot caught in the stirrup and her body bouncing on the hard ground.

It wasn't until she climbed into the bathtub at night that she discovered that her ass end, as far up as her tailbone, was raw and sore. She smeared herself liberally with cream, but it still hurt like hell. And the next day they went out again, and they trotted. By the time she got home her tail end was bleeding and her clit was sore.

"Is this some kind of initiation?" she asked. "You know, like Hell Week at college, or something?"

"You get used to it," Lucy promised.

"By the time I get used to it I won't have any parts of me left to get used to it! Isn't there something a person can *wear*? My snap is sore."

"You really do get used to it," Debbie smiled, and gave Kitty a quick hug. "You learn how to sit so you won't cripple yourself."

By summer's end Kitty was tanned almost as dark as her saddle, she could ride well enough to go off by herself, and she weighed ten pounds more than she had when she got off the bus—and not an ounce of it was fat. A bale of hay no longer jerked her arms out of their sockets, she could drive the tractor, and even if she wasn't old enough to get her driver's license she knew she could handle the pickup on the highway.

She was standing at the stove, stirring tomato sauce and keeping one eye on the bottles upside down in boiling water, when Bob Dakins rapped on the wooden frame around the screen door.

"Hi, c'mon in."

"Your aunt home?" he asked, his face brick red.

"She's around here somewhere. Just give a shout, she'll turn up."

"You shout," he muttered. "She knows your voice."

"Jesus, Bobby, she also knows her name, right?"

Lucy walked into the kitchen, saw Bob sitting at the table looking like he'd rather be anywhere else in the world, and nodded. "Like something cold to drink?"

"Thank you."

"So what can I do for you?"

"I wanted to know if I could buy back my horse." He looked at the tabletop and knotted his fingers together. "I wanted to try to buy'er back last year but I knew I didn't have the money."

"She's in foal." Lucy poured cold juice for three, took it to the table, nodded for Kitty to join them, and sat across from Bob. He waited. "I'd want that foal back when it was weaned."

"Couldn't I buy it?"

"You could, but it would cost. I took her to Princeton and left her with a registered quarterhorse stud."

"Expensive?"

"Eight-hundred-dollar stud fee."

"Jesus."

"Of course," Lucy pointed out, "there's always the one she brought packed inside her when she came."

"Got that from Bill's cow pony." Bob half grinned. "He was about all I could find around here at the time."

"Twelve hundred dollars," Lucy said, and even Kitty knew she wouldn't budge an inch on the price. "I get the quarterhorse foal back when it's weaned, and I get an explanation."

Bob looked as if he wanted to crawl under the linoleum. He nodded, hoping the nod would mean he could put things off to a future, much later, date, but the silence stretched. He licked his lips and looked at the wall, then at the table, then tried to look at Lucy and couldn't.

Debbie came in with another box of tomatoes, and smiled at them. "Hi," she said cheerily.

"Hi, yourself," Lucy answered. "We're horse-trading here. Bob wants his blue roan mare back."

"Oh."

"We'd get the baby when it was weaned."

"Oh."

Bob took a deep breath. "It was stupid," he said miserably. "It was just stupid. We'd been giving Chad a rough time all year, and that was stupid, too. New kid in school and all that, only it never quit on him. And he had a big fight with Ronnie Jepson. Chad won. Ron was mad. And I don't know who started it, someone said something about, well," he shifted uncomfortably, "you know, two women and all. And we just kind of talked ourselves into it." Finally he lifted his head and managed to meet Lucy's eyes. "It was stupid. It was worse than that, it was...shitty. We were just mad at you, is all. And mad at Chad. And"—he shrugged—"I don't know, it seemed like the idea just kind of had us, instead of us having it."

Two days later the foreman of the Dakins place drove Bob up in the pickup, and sat waiting while Bob unloaded his gear. The foreman grinned slightly and did a thing with his eyebrows that lifted his battered hat, then winked at Lucy and Debbie, waved and drove off. Looking as if every step hurt, Bob carried his gear to the gate and put it on the ground. He took an envelope from his shirt pocket and walked over to hand it to Lucy. "The money," he managed, "and a letter of agreement about the foal. And my dad says I have to leave the filly here." He looked at the ground. "He said to tell you it's one thing to be fair and another thing to let an asshole get away with something."

"I'll put the filly in the stall. Blue is used to being taken for rides without her baby, but she'll probably kick up hell when she doesn't get brought back here."

The baby kicked up hell. They kept her in the stall for a week, and she whickered, whinnied and neighed the whole time. "Poor little thing," Kitty mourned, "it's not fair, is it. It's not fair at all."

"Don't baby her too much," Lucy warned. "She's a horse, not a human. She has her own way of thinking, her own way of doing things. She needs a herd, Kit, and if you let her think *we* are her herd, she'll treat us the way she'd treat horses. And in a herd they have to know their place, it's like the friggin' chickens, peck peck peck all the time. She'd challenge you every chance she got and you'd wind up with a filly who bit or shoulder-shoved or something. She needs to be out with the others, with a mix of young ones and old ones, where she'll get put in her place and kept there. And we'll be the ones who come and boss the bosses; she'll see you catch up the lead mare, gear'er up and ride off giving the orders. When it's time to start training her, she'll already know a whole bunch of stuff that otherwise she'd have to learn the hard way."

"She misses her mommy."

"Sure she does. We all do." Lucy draped her arm around Kitty's shoulders, gave a slight hard hug. "Even people who never had a mommy miss her."

4

Sometimes Jimmy felt as if all he wanted to do was go into his little carving room, close the door, and do the best carving job he'd ever done in his life: on his wrists. Other times he knew he wasn't going to kill himself, but nobody else was safe.

He told the doctor at the emergency room that the blade on the knife had snapped and that was how he'd got the bone-deep slash up the palm of his hand and into his forearm. When he got sixteen stitches in his upper leg he had a different story. Most of his cuts didn't require any medical attention, he could do what needed doing himself. From his elbows to his wrists his inner arms were decorated with fine white lines of scar tissue.

"You might be good at carving wood," Gran sighed, "but you sure do manage to open your flesh a lot."

He didn't answer her. There were too many things waiting to leap out if he opened his mouth at the wrong time. He smiled. He smiled a lot. He nodded yes, he shook his head sideways for no, and he shrugged often.

Sometimes at night, when he was watching television, Gran would come into the living room with a great big slice of cake or a piece of pie, and she'd hand it to him with a glass of milk and then, when he smiled his thanks, she'd rumple his hair and say, "You're a good boy, Jimmy."

He knew lots of people thought that about him. He knew what they saw when they looked at him was a kid who worked hard at his craft, did fine work and never had any trouble finding a market for what he did. They knew he gave most of his money to Gran. When he quit school they all thought it was so he could spend more time developing his techniques, more time working, more time making saleable items.

Really it was because he could no longer sit for hours in a class and listen to some glorified jerk going with no end in sight, talk talk talking about things that meant absolutely nothing to anybody. Jimmy was afraid the day would come when the wrong thing was said at the wrong time and he'd explode.

Better to just stay away from them.

So he stayed home and worked in his room, turning red or yellow cedar into elegant shapes. Outside he might hurt someone. Here, if he absolutely had to hurt someone, he would only hurt himself. And he figured he had that coming to him.

Once in a while Glen would come out to visit. Jimmy didn't like to go in and visit with Glen because nine times out of ten Greg would be there, and Jimmy didn't want to be around Greg for even four minutes at a time. Greg made him uneasy. Greg made him feel as if he had to bite hard not to let the words come out—words that, once said, would never be forgotten or forgiven.

Glen had his own car now, and didn't have to rely on the damned bus. He didn't have much of a car, but he had one. Greg had got it for him. Greg got him his clothes, and his shoes, and whatever his little heart desired. Nothing was too good for Glen. And didn't Glen know it, too! Table manners like some picky-pokey who thought food was a game or a social event instead of something to keep you from starving to death. Talking about going off to university. Greg thinks I should try pre-med, Greg thinks this, Greg thinks that, Greg can jump over the moon.

Still, sometimes Jimmy felt bad about his reaction to Greg. The guy at least tried. You had to give him that much credit, he at least tried, which is more than could be said of the majority of the voting public out there in TVland. Offered to pick up the tab if Jimmy wanted to go down to Vancouver and enroll in the Emily Carr School of Fine Art. Nice of him to offer. Nicer of him to try to understand when Jimmy said no.

It wasn't safe down there. A person was hardly safe in his own basement, it was more than your life was worth to go strolling around in the city. Just pick up a copy of the *Sun* and you'd know all about it; an old lady found stabbed to death in an alley, a guy shot in the face coming out of a pub, half of Asia using tommy guns on the other half and kids dealing crack in the hallways at school. No thanks, Jimmy would just sit here and pretend to be a Siwash, turn out his carvings and sell them.

The first time he saw it he must have fainted or something. He was working on a big bowl shaped like a whale, with the back hollowed out except where the dorsal fin was, and he was humming to himself and feeling good about what he was doing. He put his tools aside and straightened at his work bench, pushing his right hand against the crick in his back, the one just above the hips. He had his right hand on his back, pushing, when he lifted his head and saw it sitting cross-legged in the middle of his work table.

And the next thing he knew, he was sitting with both hands folded in his lap, staring at the nearly finished feast bowl. He was so friggin' cold he thought he'd die. Had a hot bath to try to warm up but it didn't work. He was still cold as a clam when he went to bed. Still cold when he woke up and got something to eat. He wanted to tell about it, wanted to tell what happened, but couldn't.

The next time he saw it he was so scared the tears started to run down his face. He knew that it was going to point its stick at him, and that when it did he'd either pass out, turn to stone or die. And he almost hoped he'd just die and get it over with.

He didn't die. But when he came back from wherever he'd gone when the stick lifted, he knew he had to know. And he knew, too, that he had to make another stick. He didn't know how he knew that, or knew what kind of thing to look for to make the damned stick, but he went looking all the same, and knew he'd know when he found it. Two weeks' tramping around in the bush with a pruning saw hanging from his belt. Two weeks of walking through the toolies in gumboots, old jeans and a black and red checked wool jacket, and there it was, an arbutus tree leaning with the wind, one wrist-thick branch pulled toward the ground by a length of some kind of vine almost as thick as his thumb. He told the branch what it would be used for, he told the vine he was sorry but there was no choice. He knew to cut through the branch first, because if he cut the vine the branch might swing up and be a real bitch to get at. He knew to catch the branch before it touched the ground, and he knew to hold it while he cut through the vine. He even knew to leave four cigarettes for the tree. And four more for the vine.

He didn't cut himself once while he worked on it. Up at the thick end he smoothed and smoothed and smoothed with a rough rasp. Not much use trying to do anything to arbutus with a knife. The knob of knot he turned into the head of a snake, with the vine becoming the body.

When it was finished he didn't know what to do with it. He wanted to take it to someone who would know what it was for, but he didn't know where to find that person. You can't just walk into the pizza parlor and walk up to the first rez brother you see and say, Pardon me, but.... In all probability the guy would scream fuckin' murder and run away. If he even had a clue what you were talking about, because most probably wouldn't, now.

So he bought a yard of red ribbon, three-quarters of an inch wide, and he used that to hang the frigger from a wooden peg he put in the wall. And one day he looked up and it was fading. You could still see it, but just barely, as if, well, as if it was fading, is all. He knew the time would come when he'd look up and it would be gone. And he knew who would have taken it.

He supposed he'd gone nutsoh. Loonytoon. Nutbar. A few bricks short a load. Not playing with a full deck. Goofy as an outhouse rat. Probably the whack from the stick had done it. Turned his brain to kitten-fried rice. Over the fuckin' water.

But he wasn't afraid any more. He did, however, want to know who that skinny guy was!

He went to garage sales and looked through old *National Geographics*, buying any that featured aboriginal art. He went to the bookstore every month or so and took a boo through the new titles. Anything that had Indian designs, anything that had pictures of the stuff the government had taken and stored in the basement of the House of Commons, anything with pictures of the artwork of Bill Reid, Robert Davidson, Henry Hunt, Henry Green or any of them, Jimmy bought and took home.

He read everything he could find about the old stories they'd told their kids. And he carved. He tried to keep the shavings and mess in a big box, and when it was full he took the box up to the kitchen, where Gran could just grab a handful of waste and use it to start the fire. She teased him that one of these days the environmentalists would hear about him and come and picket the place because of all the trees he was turning to shavings.

The thing about Gran you could never be sure of was what was a joke and what wasn't. What did she know and how did she know it?

"You like old stories, right?" she said one night as they sat watching an old "Gunsmoke" rerun.

"Yeah, I guess so."

And then she told him this story, it sort of rambled on, about this woman who had bad luck and people never quite treated her right and finally she picked up a knife and sawed off her nose. "And that fixed them all," Gran finished.

Jimmy sat waiting for the end of the story. Finally he looked over and she was staring at him. "You might try that, son," she said softly. She reached out and touched the slash on his arm, hidden by a bandage. "It'd be a lot faster than this and people might have more reason to pay attention to it."

"What are you talking about?" he managed. "You aren't making any sense."

"Yes, I am. You get many more like that one and I'm going to take all your knives and chisels away from you. Only let you use them when you're sitting at the kitchen table with me across from you, just like when you were wee and I didn't want wax crayon all ground into my floor, remember?"

He remembered. He remembered sitting there with a Player's tobacco can loaded up with crayons, and every time you finished using one you had to put it back in the can, because somebody had dropped one and Gran had stepped on it; she was holding a kettle of hot water and nearly dumped it on herself when her foot slipped. And then there was a big purple streak on the floor, right into the shine, and it was there for a long time.

He wanted to say something but couldn't think of a single thing to say. She'd do it. And he could yell if he wanted—when she said she meant something she meant it, and you couldn't shift her with dynamite, the old biddy.

He just stared at the pattern in the carpet for a while, then nodded. She nodded too—enough said. "Guess you'd better make popcorn." She got up and headed for the bathroom. "Time for the family gathering."

Jimmy hurried to make a bowl of popcorn and laced it liberally with real butter. He liked margarine well enough, actually preferred it for sandwiches, but Gran insisted you couldn't have popcorn that tasted like popcorn unless you used butter. Clogged arteries or no clogged arteries, she wasn't paying all that money for glorified car wax. "I might'a used it when it was way cheaper," she fretted, "but now it costs just as much as the real thing and it's full of stuff I can't even pronounce."

The stream of commercials ended and they sat together watching and eating as the saloon doors swung wide and an exhausted Matt Dillon walked into the Longbranch. He bellied up to the bar and nodded. Didn't even have to name his poison, the barkeep knew what he wanted. And Miss Kitty walked in from whatever was off the saloon, was it her office or the bathroom, you never saw it, she just always came in by way of the same doorway, as if she'd been hanging on a hook in suspended animation, eyes like glass marbles, smile fixed and frozen, waiting for Matt Dillon to show up and breathe life into her.

Jimmy didn't really give a shit about any of them, but wherever they happened to be, they'd all be watching. Glen laughed about it and said Greg and his faggot friends had started making an observance of it, coming over with candy bars and soda pop, making popcorn and settling themselves. Said Greg had made a joke of it and some bumlover had said something about social history and someone else ran off at the mouth about semiology or some damned thing and now it was what their crowd was "into". Savannah would be watching too, puffed up about twice the size of a John Deere, maybe she'd have Victor sitting on what was left of her lap, maybe the Three Wise Men would be there, although Jimmy wasn't sure if hear no evil, see no evil and speak no evil would understand the first damned thing about it. Seely would watch, you could count on that, sometimes she phoned after the program was over and you knew she'd been crying a bit, but not about Matt or any of the others. He always made sure he told Seely he loved her, she seemed to really need to hear that. He gave Glen shit for not going over to see her more often but Glen just started to look mad and told him to butt out and mind his own damned business. Jimmy couldn't figure out for the life of him why Glen had a mean on for Seely. Of all of them, for God's sake, little Seely was the last one to hold a grudge. And Kitty, she'd be watching, for sure.

Just about the only argument he'd ever had with Kitty had happened because of this damned show. Before everything blew up, before
those two dead rugrats even showed, they'd been watching and Jimmy
had said something about how he couldn't remember a show that had
explained what Mz Kitty was *doing* at the Longbranch. "What is she?"
he'd asked. "One of the whores or something?" And Kitty had gone
into orbit. Man, had she ever! Little twerp yarded off her shoe and
flung it, got Jimmy on the side of the head, old Dead-eye Dora herself.
"She *owns* the fuckin' place, Jimmy, you moron! She doesn't work
there. She *owns* it, okay? It's *her* place! It wouldn't BE there without
her! They shouldn't have to *say* that, okay? If she was a man you'd
know, you jerkoff asshole, but because she's a woman you don't think
she can own her own saloon? Jesus Aitch, if she was a potbellied Irish
man in one of them dumb pisspot hats and just came strollin' in saying
Faith and begorra, bejabers and bejayzus, you'd *know* the saloonkeeper
had just arrived, but she's a woman so *you*, you dumb creepy shit, you
have to wonder what she's doin' there. It's *her place*, okay?"

He'd been so flabbergasted he just sat, with her dirty old shoe on
the floor in front of him, watching as she pitched a fit that ought to
have been filmed and saved for future generations. "Well, Jesus Christ,
Kitty, you don't have to have a hairy about it," was all he could say.

"Well, fuckin' *smarten up, Jimmy*! Don't keep your brain in your
bowels all your life, okay?"

Yeah, old Kitty would be watching. He smiled.

Gran watched Jimmy go wherever it was he went when he
watched this program. He sat with the popcorn bowl between his
legs, his body loose, relaxed against the back of the sofa, a small cushion under his head. His hands lay loose, his scarred fingers curved
around the bowl, the bandage on his arm whiter than white against
the deep tan of his skin. The old scars were white like spiderwebbing,
one beside the other, mostly on his left arm because he was right-
handed. One beside the other, top of his arm or underside, some of
them all the way around, a tracery of torment that made her feel sick
inside. He looked like a tired three-year-old, and she was filled with
such a feeling for him she could have broken down, scooped him onto
her lap and rocked him, saying over and over again, It's okay little
boy don't be scared, Gran is here, it's all right my darling don't be
frightened, you're safe, you'll be fine.

She didn't know what scared her the most; that she'd do it and he'd push her away and say, Hey, take it easy, or that she'd do it and he'd put his head on her shoulder and sob helplessly. They had the SPCA for dogs and cats. Why couldn't they have it for children too?

Savannah watched Mz Kitty, too. She sat nursing Elaine while Victor snuggled up against her, watching and, he thought, helping. Victor's role in the process was to gently stroke Elaine's tiny wrinkled feet. When the baby had guzzled all the milk she could hold and been well and properly burped, Savannah placed her on Victor's lap with her head on his small shoulder.

He could barely contain himself. He didn't care much one way or the other what happened on the TV, his attention was focused almost exclusively on his baby. *His* baby. His *good* baby.

She was careful with Elaine, even more careful than she'd been with Victor, and God knows she'd been careful with him, afraid she'd drop him, afraid she'd lose her grip on his slippery little body and he'd slither out of her hands and drown in his own bath before she managed to get him safe again. She'd been afraid to breastfeed him in case her milk wasn't strong enough, or in case something she'd ingested months before had made her milk bad, or sour, or contaminated, and yet she'd been afraid not to nurse him because of all the stuff you heard about chemicals in formula and too much salt in baby food and kids developing food allergies because of the crap put down their scrawny throats before they were three months old.

She wasn't afraid for Elaine that way. She knew her milk was rich, she knew that, except for a few stolen cigarette breaks, she'd been really good about what she took into herself, she knew she wasn't going to drown the kid in the bath or drop her at the top of the steps or any of the other things that had terrified her first time around. She was careful about those things, of course, but it was other things, new things, that kept her poised for action.

The welfare. No way one of those old battleaxes was going to show up at the door and just march in as if it was *her* place, and find dishes undone or the baby lying with next to nothing on, spread out on a blanket on the floor, with Victor playing beside her. The old snoop would probably say the child was endangered. Probably scold everyone because Victor might trip and fall on the baby, or someone might forget she was there and walk on her head—or get to yammering about germs on the floor or something.

She put Elaine on the floor. Savannah firmly believed a kid had to get used to things, and if she couldn't see the entire living room stretched out and beckoning she'd have little incentive to learn to crawl. It was good for her to squirm and wriggle. And Savannah was certain it was good for Victor to think he was playing with the baby—good, too, for the baby to see her brother and know he was there and she was safe. She just made sure Elaine was fully clothed all the time, and if there was a ring at the front doorbell Savannah scooped up the baby, blanket and all, and carried her in one arm when she went to answer. Didn't open the door until she'd peeked through the security hole and knew who was there. If she had to she'd talk through the intercom the Three Wise Men had installed.

"Could you explain your relationship with these men?" The old bitch had asked, looking as if she was getting a whiff from the compost heap.

"What do you mean?" When in doubt play dumb.

"Well, are you cohabiting with any or all of them?"

"I don't know what that means."

She stalled the snoop that time but knew she'd be back. You couldn't be *too* stupid or they might think you were a retard and decide Victor needed to be with sane and sensible people.

Before the old fart returned, Savannah talked to the Three Wise Men and they talked to a friend who referred them to a lawyer who spoke English better than Savannah did, and their own language, too. When the welfare worker came back, Savannah was ready. She just handed over a little white card with the lawyer's name on it and smiled ear to ear.

They had their story ready, too. Savannah was the housekeeper. "Well, sure I let him call them 'daddy'. A kid needs a daddy and they're about as close as he's going to get, all things considered."

"Don't you think that might confuse him?"

"Why would it? He thinks 'daddy' means 'nice man' or something like that. He's never had a dad, he doesn't know what a dad is, you could point at that chair and tell him it was a church and he'd believe you. If I told him you were a water buffalo, that's the word he'd use, but he wouldn't think of a water buffalo, he'd think of *you* when he heard the word. He doesn't seem confused to me. You saw the report from his daycare worker, he's doing fine."

The Three Wise Men left it all in the hands of the lawyer. It was just another example, to them, of how bizarre things were in this country. An entire government bureau set up to investigate the welfare of children who had more stuff at birth than half the population of the world would acquire in a lifetime. And to get to the beautiful big house from her office the social worker had to drive within a block of an area where eleven-year-olds lived in abandoned cars and sold their bodies for money to buy food to make it through until tomorrow, when they could do it all again.

It was simpler when Mz Kitty ran the Longbranch. Savannah figured she'd have done well in those days. She could have been the bartender in the place, and Kitty would have advertised her as The Only Female Bartender In The Wild West. Or maybe she'd have been the cook and general cleanup woman. Maybe any time something was about to break loose in the bar, and the bad guys were getting ready to draw a bead on Matt Dillon, Mz Kitty would do whatever she had to do, but do it knowing Savannah was in a doorway somewhere with a double-barrelled shotgun pointed at the leader of the crooks.

"Do you have plans for marriage?" the worker had asked. And Savannah couldn't continue to play the game. She knew she was supposed to act puzzled and more innocent than a kitten, just a good girl doing her best, working hard as a domestic so she could provide for her children. But she couldn't carry it off. She laughed. "Marriage?" she blurted. "Hey, I *saw* what that was, okay? My mom and dad were married. My aunt and uncle were married. I think I'll pass on that until they do what they do with cars, recall it and fix the flaw in the design, make it safe for the human race."

The lawyer had come up with some other suggestions, and while Savannah thought it was all too stupid for words, the Three Wise Men were going to follow even the most trivial hints. Nobody was moving in on *their* kids.

Savannah was supposed to work on the image, like a paint-by-numbers, and not only be the good girl, working hard as a domestic. She also had to appear to be planning and working for the future of her children. And that meant back to school.

Good job they had the "Gunsmoke" reruns on the weekend, because she'd have skipped class before she skipped even one episode. So what if you could practically predict who'd do what, who'd say what, wasn't life itself like that except for the occasional surprise that showed up after dark with a goddamn rifle in its ugly mitts?

It wasn't exactly the same as going to high school during the day. There was no gym, no sports teams, no spare periods, no library period, no pottery classes or any of that stuff. Just the basics. And more damned homework than you could shake a stick at, good job she had the house aced and organized and could just start at the beginning and go like stink until the whole thing was done.

She guessed she didn't mind, though. The guys were great about it. No problem with babysitters or anything like that, and no problem about the dishes and cleanup, either. It all got done. She'd rush home after classes, come pelting in at half past ten, and Victor would be asleep on someone's lap, with someone else keeping Elaine amused until her supper got its coat off and sat down to unbutton the taps.

They loved to watch her nurse the baby. One would pour her a cup of tea, another would bring it to her. What was all this crap about meaningful discussions, anyway? Wasn't it what you did that counted?

Besides, they were learning English. They could talk it if they wanted to. So she didn't go to their church. If they wanted to go, and if they wanted to take Victor, then let them take him. It wasn't as if they tortured him when they got him there. She supposed in time they'd take Elaine, too. Elaine the lovely, Elaine the fair, Elaine the lily maid of Astolat.

Of course Elaine wasn't fair, and the only lily she resembled was a chocolate lily, but leave us not pick nits on this, a name is a name is a name and it doesn't mean any more than what you make it mean.

Well, there you had it. Matt was flanked. Chester could stiff-leg it all he wanted, they'd been decoyed. And sure enough, here came Mz Kitty, overlooked by the burly boys because who'd take anyone seriously dressed in a riggins like that? And Mz Kitty was speaking softly and she was every inch a lady, but the gun looked as big as a cannon.

And Savannah stepped into view from the kitchen, a sawed-off shotgun in each hand. Her brown eyes glittered like ice. Her hands and arms, made strong by hours of hard work, held the weaponry easily. She didn't say a word, she just let her presence be felt, the guns

doing all the talking as she backed up her friend. There was something about Savannah that scared the hardcases more than even the
sight of the marshal and Chester. After all, the marshal and Chester
were outflanked, they were standing facing the Whozit Brothers and
their gang with their hands hanging limp and empty at their sides.
But Savannah's hands weren't limp or empty, and they knew she'd
just as soon shoot'em in the back as in the front. She'd done it before,
she'd do it again, and the knowledge sapped their spunk.

"Give'em shit, Mz Kitty," Savannah whispered. Victor paid no
attention to the glowing screen, he was whispering secrets to Elaine.
"Give'em shit all the way, Mz Kitty."

5

Kitty watched the last images flicker, then clenched her fist, pumped it in the air and breathed "Yeah!" Sometimes, most times in fact, Amanda Blake hardly got any air time at all, or if she did it was just to soothe Matt's hard-done-by soul or wipe his fevered brow, but every now and again, often enough to keep you coming back for more, Amanda-Kitty actually got to *do* something. And when she did, by god, she did'er all and did'er well. Maybe one of the screenwriters was a woman.

"I don't guess it was much like that, really," she sighed. "I wonder if a hundred years from now they'll be doing stuff about *our* lives, making it all seem...you know."

"Cars instead of horses and lawyers instead of guns?" Debbie laughed softly. "I suspect they'll still be doing things about the Old West, instead. Or else what they do will make it seem as if a few good and noble souls kept life on planet earth alive in spite of almost overwhelming odds...."

"What amazes me"—Lucy surprised them both by actually speaking—"is how they can have these shows and you *never* see anyone do any of the stuff that had to be done all the time. Matt or whoever goes into the livery stable to get his horse, right? And there's the horse, waiting. No sign of horse shit. No sign of five gallons of piss on the floor. No sign the guy *ever* picks mud, rocks, shit and sticks out of his horse's hoofs. No sign he ever brushes it or untangles its mane or does anything other than toss a handful of hay, a *little* handful of hay, in its direction. Once in a while they give the horse a drink out of their hat. Jesus. Any horse I ever knew would have drunk the water and then sucked on the hat! He just pats the horse on the neck and then they cut away so you see him riding off down the road, as if the friggin' horse saddled itself."

"And," Debbie added, "Mz Kitty might own that place but she never has to do any bookwork, never has to do much of anything except maybe check to be sure the bartender is keeping the glasses polished. I'd like that."

"When I own my own saloon," Kitty vowed, "I'm not bustin' my back, either."

"Well, at least whoever's writing Mz Kitty's stuff is a dyke," Lucy laughed, "because I don't think I've ever seen her smooching with Matt. They're good friends, yeah, and sometimes they make it look as if they love each other, but friends can love each other. And that's what they are, friends. Which is a thousand miles ahead of that other stuff."

For Lucy it was a marathon night. She'd said more in five minutes than she'd said all day. But the bugle called and Duty needed to be tended to, and she yawned, stretched and got off the sofa to go do the tending.

She padded sockfoot across the living room and down the hallway to the little room just inside the back door. The smaller freezer was stuffed in there, with the bootjack in front of it, and the boots sitting on a thick pad of newspaper. She stuffed her feet in her gumboots and headed outside to do the evening chores. Halfway to the barn she pulled her light blue earband from her pocket and pulled it over her head. The wind was enough to give you chronic earache this time of year. No wonder horses hated the wind. The sound of it whishing past their ears probably blocked out all other sounds, leaving them unprotected against a world full of predators. And it brought with it smells from everywhere, and no way to tell if the bear smell was from close or far away, if the wolves were in your own field or someone else's. Can't be easy living life as an animal that, all things considered, qualified for a classification of legally blind. They had to depend on smell and hearing, and the wind effectively ruined both.

The dowager thoroughbred was more than ready to come into the stall. She was butting the gate from the main barn with her head, rattling it, and making demanding little sounds. She lifted her head, looked at Lucy and pawed the cement floor of the barn with her unshod hoof. The message was pretty clear: Hey, Luce, you flat-faced bitch, do the trick that opens this, will you, it's colder'n a witch's tit out here. At least as smart as your average five-year-old kid, the dark bay darling had the running of the ranch just about figured out, though she'd spent most of her twenty-plus years in a style which hadn't even begun to accustom her to such basic and unfrilly life.

Lucy turned on the lights, opened the gate, and Molly moved, quicker than the pregnant cows, snorting loudly, warning them to get the hell out of her way and not get any ideas about stomping their cloven hoofs in her private suite.

"G'wan, y'old whore." Lucy swung the gate shut and pushed the metal bar through the slot. "Spoiled much, Molly? Oh, don't get your fancy blanket in a knot, nobody's going to trespass."

Helluva thing, really. How do you explain to her why life changed so totally? You can't sit down at the table and share a pot of tea and say, Look, Moll, I know you were born to something about ten rungs up the ladder from this. I know you had professional handlers and the best of everything. But tempus fugits, old girl, and the one who fussed you, raised you, trained you and took you into the show ring to accumulate more fuckin' ribbons than hell would hold just can't do'er any more. You can't muck out a stall in a wheelchair. And she didn't want you sent off to wind up in a dogfood can. So here you are. And there won't be any dogfood can for you, or any minkfood package either. It's the best she could set up for you.

But if you could, Molly would drink her tea and nod and try hard to handle it with grace and dignity. She'd wait until she was alone before she put her head down and sobbed. Not because she'd come down in the world, but because the one she'd known and loved for so long was being twisted out of shape by arthritis and would probably never again experience the total pleasure of riding.

She'd stood in the pasture, facing the direction of what she considered to be home, and waited. Day after day, week after week, the old mare stood, puzzled and waiting. "Christ for snotty!" Lucy bent to brush the mud from the huge belly. "There was nothing going for me but your training. If you hadn't been a good old girl with probably the equivalent of a university degree, you'd have ignored me altogether, eh, Moll?"

But she did what she was told. Obeyed her halter, her lead shank, the little pushes and shoves. Good manners don't fade. It was just that she was waiting for her person to show up so she didn't have to take guff from this shit-shoveling stablehand. Noblesse bloody oblige, Moll.

And so Lucy did what she could do to explain. Just as if she'd been talking to a person. God, the animal had spent her life in the company of humans, why wouldn't she understand some part of the language?

They knew. Knew a whole helluva lot more than we dared admit. There was that guy down by Gibsons' had an old Andalusian mare. The mare had a two-year-old son. And the mare also had cancer. So the guy phoned a neighbor with a backhoe to come and dig a good-sized hole in the pasture, then phoned the vet to come and do the number with the needles. The two-year-old stood quiet while the mare was led out to stand beside the hole, he was quiet enough while the needle number went down, even quiet when the mother lay on the ground, made sleepy by the first of the injections. He snorted a bit when the vet did the cut-down in the throat, opening the flesh and exposing the big vein so he could inject the last of the mercifully gentle overdose. The mare put her head flat on the grass and her heart quit beating—no thrashing, no kicking, no mess, no fuss—and the two-year-old sniffed her, sniffed and even made little kissy-things with his lips. No teeth, not little love bites, just nuzzles.

The vet used the stethoscope and said the old mare's heart had stopped, they rolled her in her grave and put her horseblanket over top of her. The guy who owned her turned aside then, sobbing. Funny how it's okay for a man to cry when his horse dies, but he has to stand like John fucking Wayne for anything else. Except maybe his dog.

It was when they started pushing the dirt in the hole that the two-year-old went nuts. Jesus, what a horror that was. They didn't know what to be most afraid of, that the colt would fling himself in the grave with his mother and break his damned front leg, or that he'd attack the tractor and break both his damned front legs. He screamed, he raced around the field, tail up, this awful sound coming from his throat, and time after time he charged them, skidding and veering at the last minute, not quite nuts enough to bash into people or smash into the tractor. Lucy felt as if she was going to puke.

They finished the grave, tamping in the dirt by raising the bucket and letting it drop, then they went back to the house. Nobody could quite talk to anybody and yet nobody wanted to leave the guy alone.

The pastures sloped down to a good deep year-round pool where the ducks and geese overwintered. And the next morning that's where they found the two-year-old. He'd bust through the board fence of his paddock, bust through the six-strand barbed-wire fence (one strand electrified) supposed to keep out bears, and was floating in the pond.

How in hell does a colt drown himself in a small pond unless he wants to? And what is that but suicide?

They got a rope around him and pulled him out with the tractor. The backhoe was busy digging another hole, right next to the one they'd used to bury the old mare. Lucy looked at the dead two-year-old and for a minute she felt as if she *knew* so much, as if some last little part of him was trying to explain something.

His front legs were raw from slamming against the board fence, his chest was ripped and gashed by the barbed wire, but what had killed him was water in his lungs. He must have made it through both fences, charged into the pond, stuck his head under the water and just sucked'er in, filling his lungs deliberately. It wouldn't have been that calm and peaceful, though; whatever his mind or heart wanted, his body would have fought. But that first deep lungful would have guaranteed he'd fall into the middle of the pond, and all the thrashing his body did wouldn't have changed anything.

It shook Lucy. Shook everything she thought she believed. Right up until then she had thought you lived, you died and that was it. Like mold on cheese or something. One two three you're finished. But looking down at that gorgeous two-year-old, looking at what he'd done to himself to finish his grief, changed her mind. It had to have been for something. There had to be something waiting. His mom for one thing. And she suddenly knew there had been, and maybe it was endless pastures of clover, all the gates wide open, no predators, plenty of room to run in the land of clover and apples-year-round, and not a halter to be seen. Because if it's possible for a horse to commit suicide, anything can be true.

"Fuck, and we put you guys in dogfood cans."

6

Kitty waited beside the highway for the school bus to arrive. She turned up the collar of her jacket, pulled the scarf tighter over her head and ears, tucked the ends of the scarf under her jacket for added warmth and pushed her hands in her pockets. She stamped her feet on the frozen ground and wished to Jesus she could find a way to get rich overnight. If she was rich one of the first things she'd do would be buy herself a car. Not necessarily a big one, not necessarily a fancy one, as long as it had a good heater. This was shit. This was ratshit. If she stayed in the house until she saw the bus, she couldn't get down the driveway fast enough, and the big yellow torpedo left her behind. Then she had to either miss an entire day of school, oh grief, oh sorrow, or hitch a ride, and she wasn't even going to think of doing that, not with the weirds of the world out cruising for another victim. Some mornings she only had a minute or two to wait, but some mornings the bus got held up—maybe the road was bad, it only took a difference of a couple of miles per hour for the damn thing to wind up ten minutes late, with her like a human Popsicle. And then she was so damned cold she didn't seem to thaw out all day. What did they do in the good old days, before heating oil and electricity and all that stuff? No wonder you looked at old pictures and saw faces that might have been chipped out of stone. Probably hadn't thawed out yet.

Lucy had told her this joke that, at first, she had thought was a real story, about a woman who'd been outside doing chores and when she tried to speak she couldn't. Oh, her mouth moved, and her throat vibrated, and she thought she was speaking, but she didn't hear anything. So she decided she'd been struck deaf. Felt dreadful about it. Sent off to an address in a magazine for one of those hearing-aid things that fit over your head like a pair of stereo headphones. Still couldn't hear bugger nothing. Until spring thaw, when all the words she'd said, shouted and yelled thawed out, and for three days the noise was so bad she thought she'd go insane.

By the time the bus arrived, Kitty was afraid the ice shards building up in her veins and arteries would move along with the rest of her blood and stab her in the heart. She hunched in her seat, shivering. The driver glared in the rearview when she opened her backpack and took out her thermos. The driver didn't like anyone to eat or drink on the bus. Kitty didn't care. The driver was fine, she had the heater blowing right on her, she hadn't been standing on the side of the highway with toes so stiff it hurt when she finally started to walk. Kitty poured half a cup of coffee, put the stopper back in the thermos, replaced it in the backpack carefully and sipped the coffee. They just won't get off your case, though. They're so used to being right, so used to being boss, so used to being big people and seeing you as a kid, a nothing, that they think they can poke their pointy little noses in every part of your life. The driver had complained about Kitty's coffee. So the girls' counselor had called her in and suggested coffee wasn't really appropriate. "Perhaps soup?" she added brightly.

"May I be excused, please, I'd like to get back to class."

"You haven't responded, Kitty dear," and the geek smiled.

"I have responded, ma'am. I have responded by asking to please be excused so I can get back to my French class. S'il vous plaît."

As if a thermos of coffee was going to ruin your life. As if a thermos of coffee was some huge threat to survival, as if it was anything compared to some bozo with a Lee-Enfield .303 coming through the bedroom door. Put the damn guidance counselor in the bedroom and see what her response would be. Probably nothing more constructive than eeeeek.

Bob Dakins got on the bus, looking as cold as Kitty felt. He moved down the aisle and slid into the seat beside her, shivering. She handed over the red plastic thermos cup. He tried to smile, nodded and took it, sipping gratefully. The bus driver glared again. "One of these days,"

Kitty promised, "I'm going to bring a *huge* thermos of cream of tomato soup and the first time she glares at me I'm going to stand up and fling soup all over everything. Give her something to glare about."

"Old douche bag," he agreed. "She's been driving this bus since before I even started school, and I bet she hasn't said four pleasant words in a row the whole time. Maybe all the rattling and bumping does something to her kiddley stones."

"You think she's got kiddley stones?"

"Got something." He handed back the cup. "You ask?"

"Yeah." She laughed softly. "Boy, the things you find out when someone tells you to check, eh?"

"It true?"

"Yeah," she said, trying to seem casual, as if it was every day of your life you found out your button-lip aunt had a trunk full of silver belt buckles, fancy spurs and solid silver saddle conchos, as if everyone in the entire world had an aunt who'd been with the women's rodeo circuit in the days when it was more than the Rodeo Queen and the barrel racing prize.

"Jeeee-zus," he laughed softly. "And I had to pick a fight with her, huh?"

"I guess you're lucky she didn't break both your arms at the elbow." Kitty unstoppered the thermos, refilled the cup and handed it to him. "Guess next time you'll know better."

"Fuck," he breathed softly, "that was so dumb. I mean, dumb-dumb-dumb!"

"Well, nobody's going to argue about *that*."

"So is it true she got disqualified at Madison Square Garden?"

"Yep." Kitty grinned widely. "She sure did! They said she couldn't ride broncs in jeans. Said she was a woman and had to wear a skirt."

"You're kidding. A skirtsy-wirtsy?"

"Oh, they were real white about it, said she could wear one of those split ones, like culottes, you know the kind. But she had to wear a skirt. So she shrugged, I guess, and she didn't say so but I bet she grinned and shook her head, and she walked off, and when next seen she had on one of these damned things. And then they called her number and just before she sat her ass down on the critter, she stepped out of that riggins and rode in her jeans. So they disqualified her."

"What did she do?"

"I asked her and she said, Nothin' I could do. But I bet she just laughed and laughed and said, Fuck you and the horses you ride. I mean, can't you just imagine it?"

Kitty could imagine it real well. Lucy would have stood there relaxed and easy, and the smile on her face would have said Fuck you clearer than any words ever could. The crowd would be raising holy old hell. They'd just seen one helluva ride, maybe the best they'd ever witnessed, and now the voice from the loudspeakers was saying that the rider was disqualified because she didn't wear a skirt. They'd be just about ready to rip the roof off Madison Square Garden, by god! And Lucy, she just grinned and let the potbellied baldheads hear the noise. Then she probably nodded and said, Thank you, gentlemen, and just sauntered off and went home. And never even argued about it. Just turned up the following year and went about her business, her very presence embarrassing the shit out of a whole bunch of dinosaurs.

Lucy didn't remember it quite that way. In fact, Lucy tried hard not to think about it. Not much more than an overgrown temper tantrum. Not very different from a kid grabbing up her ball and bat and yelling, That's not fair! and storming off home.

And what good did it do? No, it hadn't been fair, no two ways about that. Lucy didn't mind they'd separated the events into Men's and Ladies'. She would personally have preferred either Gentlemen and Ladies or Men and Women, but she didn't figure it was up to her to start giving lessons in the English language to a bunch of guys who could barely grunt their own names. There were some events women would probably never be able to do as well as men simply because they weren't as strong. Period. Oh, a really strong woman, like Lucy herself, might be just as strong as a small man, or even a medium-sized man who didn't have to spend hours every day with a Bull-worker. But overall, general average, men were stronger.

She didn't even mind that the money a guy could win was always, somehow, more than what a woman could win. You weren't really out there for the money. Well, some were maybe, the top of the line, but most were out there because that's what they did, and they might not be the very best, although some were, but they enjoyed it, they loved it, they would rather be ill paid doing that than well paid doing damn near anything else.

It was the damned stupid dress code that made it impossible for women's events to interest the crowd as much as men's events did. That and the fact they used the code as ammunition so they didn't have to let women compete in every event. Harumph harumph, can't really expect to do bulldogging in a skirt, now, can you, harumph harumph.

Those few extra strips of cloth made a difference. Maybe you didn't get tangled in them and fall to the ground in a knot, but when you were dealing in tenths of a second, it made a difference. And just the look of the goddamned things took away something important, diminished the competitor and the event.

Anyway, she was going for something more and bigger. She wanted to be champion all-round in her category. Best in the world. And she knew she wouldn't have as good a chance of setting a world record if she wore a skirt, with or without fucking fringes. And nobody said bugger nothing until she came nose to nose with the big one. Then the word came down from on high. And if she'd just kept that stupid riggins buttoned around her waist, she'd still have had the crowd up and screaming blue bloody murder. She'd have ridden the same critter, she'd have ridden as well, she'd have gone down in the books, and the galling part of it was that her accumulated points would still stand. But no. Not Lucy.

No, she had to tuck two sticks of Juicy Fruit in her mouth, gnaw and chew on the gum, then bite it in half and put a half between the molars on her left jaw and the other half between the molars of her right jaw so the jarring and slamming wouldn't crack her bloody teeth—and then drop her skirt and get herself disqualified.

To prove what? That she could cut off her nose and spite her face right along with the best of them?

You get the one big chance. Blow that one and you live the rest of your life knowing *you* did it, not the ones with the pencils, not the ones with the rule books, not anybody but you yourself. And at that point you can damn well sit back and decide, was it worth it or not?

One thing about it, you sure found out in a hurry who your friends were—and who they weren't! Right up until then, if anyone had asked her, she would have said she figured she got along fine with most people. But that winter she heard stuff that brought her brain to a dead halt. Some ten-cent reporter for the two-bit home-town newspaper had phoned for an interview. There was nothing in that for

Lucy; they didn't pay a cent for the two or three hours of your time they took so some semiliterate putz could do a poor job writing something they could sell. But she'd said yes because, somehow, they always managed to make you feel obligated to play their little game.

Halfway through the interview the soft-handed little doughboy-bodied mommy's precious darling had laughed as if he'd discovered oil in his own back yard. "You aren't anywhere near as hard to get along with as they warned me you'd be," he blurted, probably thinking his own charm was making all the difference.

"Me? Hard to get along with?" she laughed.

"They told me you were ornery," he confessed.

"Me? Ornery? Who told you that?"

"Oh, some of the people I phoned for background stuff."

He wouldn't tell her who "they" were, but he did tell her some of what he'd been warned. Not long after, she heard the same kind of stuff from someone else, and when she asked who'd warned him he named someone Lucy had never met in her life. "I don't even *know* that guy," she protested. "I never worked with him, I never even had a cup of coffee with him, I sure never had an argument. Not even a discussion!"

But it did no good. The ones who knew the least about her had the most to say. Revisionism seemed the order of the day. Jokes she'd pulled on her friends, even jokes her friends had pulled on her, suddenly got half told in a way that made it seem some deep-seated, hard-hearted spite was involved.

It was puzzling. It was also very upsetting. Seemed as if trying to set the record straight would only give them more of a chance to make it seem she was fighting with people.

So Lucy just buttoned her lip and went about her business. Hard to go about your business when your business is closed for the winter and you're back in a town where nobody's doing anything that interests you and what you do is positively irrelevant. If she'd made her money standing on a cold cement floor getting varicose veins by shucking oysters, she'd have had plenty to talk about over the occasional coffee at the Esquire Café. If she'd been married to some sawmill worker and keeping house while trying not to get pregnant again she'd have had plenty in common with the ones she'd gone to school with, but while lots of others had dropped out of school before grade twelve, she was the only one who'd left on the four-thirty bus and headed south with her tuition money in a cloth moneybelt around her waist.

"Rodeo school?" Even Kitty had seemed flabbergasted. "You mean there's a *school* to teach you how to *do* that?"

"Sure."

"Well, I wondered." The kid shook her head, amazed. "I mean, I didn't see how you'd'a managed to grow up on horseback livin' with *Gran*. But I never thought of a school. What'll they think of next, eh?"

She went back again in the spring, got her critters from the ranch where she'd paid to board them for shut-down, and just went back to what she'd been doing since she was eighteen. And she did well. Damn, but she did well.

And then it was like the daring young man on the flying trapeze, and she was flying through the air. That part didn't hurt. It was what else came down when she did. The hard-packed ground came up to meet her and she knew she was in more than just bullshit, she was in deep shit, and then she had company, but it's a proven scientific fact two bodies cannot occupy the same space at the same time, and the horse was heavier. The horse was also on top.

She'd never had much love for appaloosas anyway. Bastards have weird eyes. It does something to you when you look at them and they've got white eyeballs like a human. Jesus. A horse ought to have brown eyes. When you look at them you should see brown from top to bottom and side to side, and there's a damned appy looking at you and even if it's in a good mood, which might not be all that often, you think it's about to bite a hunk out of your ass because you can see this white, as if its eyes were spread wide wide and frantic.

And there has to be a reason the Indians used them for war horses. Out of all the kinds, types, sizes, and shapes available, the appies were reserved for battle. Well, as her old pal Bill, who might have been championship material except for his unfortunate thirst for booze, had said, by the time they ran the buggers down, caught them up and held them still long enough to climb on top, they were proba- bly so fuckin' mad they were ready to take on anybody.

The only break she got, other than the one that did it to her hip joint, was that she was home at the time and had her medical insurance card in her wallet. Jesus, if she'd got racked up in the States she'd have been bankrupt for time and all eternity. When Alice got busted up in

Nevada she even had to pay for the damned tissues to wipe her nose. Every glass of juice she drank was added to the tab, like in a low-rent bar. By the time Alice had her operation, spent a month in bed with her leg hanging from an overhead sling, had X-rays, got her cast changed and got out of bed with a pair of crutches tucked under her armpits, she'd spent every dime she had and was in debt for three years.

Lucy at least was north of the forty-ninth and had medical coverage. And thank the Old Biddy for nagging about that, too. So other than the minor inconvenience of being stuck between starched sheets and lifted on and off cold bedpans and hurting so bad she wanted to cry and knowing there wasn't much left of her chances and a few other suicide-inducing matters, things weren't too bad. Cost her more to rent her TV than to pay for her keep in the place.

And then that was behind her and all she had to do was get the leg to move again. Nothing to it! Jesus, even babies can walk. But it's easier to learn first time around than after something like that.

She could still ride. Hell, she could ride as good as the best of them around here. Of course, not one of them would even begin to qualify for the dinkiest damned rodeo on the circuit. That was over, done, finished, and she'd be better off if it was forgotten, but it wasn't.

She probably could have been a catch-up rider or a clown, and she'd have done it, too, but you don't change a little bit of your life without changing the whole thing, and oh-my-dear-denny-mcginty hadn't it all changed?

She'd thought it was all maybe a minor difference in levels of acceptance, or expectation, or maybe boredom. For a while, before she quit school, she thought it maybe had something to do with other people. When she got past that she decided it was just her, some part of her brain worked at a different rate or something.

It was like when she realized that no matter how hard she tried she was never going to satisfy The Biddy. Something just was not right or correct or acceptable or good enough or something. The Biddy always had something held in reserve.

Well, god knows what all the Biddy herself was trying to deal with. You never really know how to unravel *that* mystery. And odd how the things that make the dimes drop are such little things. No huge *bang* and you know something, just a little click will do.

She was working that summer, the summer after grade ten and before grade eleven. All you had to do was show up on time and wait at the side of the road, and the truck would slow down so you could jump in the back with the rest of the sunburned stiffs. Then out to the hay fields, and technology hadn't hit the place yet, it wasn't lifting bales, it was grabbing the old three-tined fork and pitching hay up to the wagon where two poor suffering bastards had to handle the stuff. Easy enough the first fifteen minutes, maybe, but then the load of hay on the wagon was so high you had to hold your fork up with your arm extended, and the slob on the wagon had to take the hay off with his fork and maybe even hand it up to yet another strong-armed fool.

Hour after hour, field after field, until your fingers looked and felt like sausages. Even with leather-palmed gloves your hands got slick-skinned and callused. Before that happened you bled a lot. Sat at night with your hands in a basin of water and vinegar, trying to toughen the skin.

At about mid-morning they brought out the cold Cokes and some sandwiches, then back to work again until noon. You got a meal then. Potato salad, cold roast chicken, sliced thick, and cold baked ham with spicy mustard. Pie, usually, because cake was kind of cloying and sticky in your mouth, too dry to be enjoyed with the sun burning holes in your head in spite of your hat.

Then back out again, wagonload after wagonload, field after field right up until it was getting too dark to see, and in the summertime that could be ten o'clock at night.

A good meal then, hot and plenty of it, and you rode back in the bed of the truck so sleepy you had to work overtime not to start snoring. Into bed and out like a light so you could get up in the morning and head off to do it all again. And all this for maybe a dollar fifty a day. Hip hip hooray.

And jeans, the very best jeans, which they don't make any more and why not, pray tell, Cowboy Queens, fifteen-ounce denim with a sort of bib-front fly, like navy pants, three brass-headed snaps on each side of the nine-inch flap, were seven dollars a pair. Work damn near a week for a pair of jeans. But she got them. They were twice the price of the other kind and lasted five or six times as long.

The problem was, the Biddy didn't want her in jeans. You couldn't wear them to school back then. God forbid! You wore what the principal and school board decided was appropriate, and jeans weren't on the list for girls. The Biddy wanted her to buy herself some clothes for school. Well, she did that. A couple of pleated plaid wool skirts, some blouses, even a couple of V-neck sweaters. But she got the Cowboy Queen jeans, too.

And even with a chainguard on your bike you had to roll up your jeans or you'd wind up tangled in your greasy chain, ass over appetite likely as not, the chain biting holes in the denim and, if you weren't lucky, your skin too.

Anyway, everybody folded up the cuffs of the jeans. It was how you showed you were wearing the fuzzy-topped ankle socks that were in fashion. But don't try to tell the Biddy about it.

The fight wasn't about the folded-up jeans cuffs anyway. Even at the time, Lucy knew lines had been drawn and sides chosen for some other kind of war. Something to do with having your own money and spending it on what you wanted instead of on what you'd been told to buy. Something about having your own ideas and opinions, about being your own person. Knowing that didn't make any of it any easier. It was too puzzling, too scary and too intense, and it frightened the shit right out of her. She walked in the house after softball practice and the Biddy went up like a hot-air balloon. "Just *look* at the mess of you!" was the opening line, and not a minute later "You look ridiculous," followed by "Enough to make us all ashamed of you."

It was the first time Lucy had been so upset she thought she'd cry. And she would go to hell in a handbasket before she'd give the Biddy the satisfaction of *that*! Instead, she fought back, her voice shaking. "What would *you* know about it?" she said coldly. "You don't have the first idea of what's really going on in the outside world."

That's when the Biddy took her swing, and that's when Lucy caught her by the wrist and blocked the swing. Muscles developed in the hay fields of the first cut and honed in the fields of the second cut tightened, and the Biddy's arm was held insultingly easily. "Don't do it," Lucy said quietly, "don't even try. You've hit me for the last time. You and everybody else has had their last bit of fun pounding on me!"

"I'll tell your father when he gets home!" the Biddy promised.

"Yeah, sure, whatever," Lucy shrugged. "When and *if* he bothers to come home, when and *if* he's ever sober enough to understand what you're saying, and when and *if* he ever bothers to listen to you. Sure you will." And she laughed. "But it'll take him and you both, and then the only thing you'll have proved is that the two of you together, ganging up on me, can do it. It won't make you *right*, you crazy old bat."

He came home, but not that night or the one after. And came home drunk, of course, what's new. Too drunk to talk to, so it was the next day, when he was hung over and feeling mean as hell, that the Biddy fulfilled her promise and told him Lucy was out of control, full of lip, and he should Do Something About It.

He didn't do anything until she'd come home from school, changed out of her skirt and blouse, and was heading outside in her jeans and teeshirt to start the chores. That's when he saw what the Biddy had been talking about. The jeans folded between ankle and knee.

She didn't even see it coming. Open-handed, against the side of her face, knocking her sideways into the wall. Her shoulder hit so hard it pushed a dent in the gyproc.

"You watch your mouth!" he roared.

She didn't say a word. That enraged him further. He came at her to give her a match-up welt on the other side of her face. But he was already two inches shorter than she was, he was as skinny as a rake and he wasn't in good shape. She dodged him. "You aren't hitting me any more," she promised.

"Any time I damn well feel like it," he answered.

"You have to go to sleep some time," she said quietly. "Sooner or later you'll close your bloodshot baby blues. And maybe never get to open them again."

"Are you threatening me?" But he didn't raise his fist.

"I'm promising you. And her too. I've eaten the last plate of shit I'm going to eat."

She left, went out to the woodpile and took some of her fury out on the big hunks in the heap. Then she loaded up the wheelbarrow, pushed it to the back steps and carried the first armload into the house. He was sitting at the kitchen table, glaring. She ignored him. She just emptied the load into the woodbox and went for the next armful.

Nobody talked about it. Not one word. They all went about their business the way they had always done, except there were no more slaps, no more sudden wallops, no more inexplicable shoves.

And nobody at school asked why one side of her face was bruised. Nobody asked about the black eye. Well, it wasn't as if there was anything new in either, she'd had them before and so had most other people she knew.

The Biddy didn't forgive her. It got worse. Sniffs of disapproval. Those looks that mean, Oh my God it's doing it again.

So she left. But not before she was ready, and not with her pockets empty, either. She didn't exactly know what it was she'd learned, she couldn't put it into words, but she'd learned it, and it had to do with making your own money and paying your own tab. And maybe even with being your own person.

She never gave the Biddy the satisfaction of being able to say Lucy had run away from home. She sent postcards regularly. She just didn't send a return address.

She didn't go home for three years. And then she made goddamn good and sure everybody in town knew she was back. Checked into the Seaside Motel, waited several hours, then got herself dressed for the occasion. Bright red cotton shirt, worn, well-fitting jeans and the ox-blood top-of-the-line tooled leather boots she'd won in Colorado. She took maybe three minutes to decide which of several ornate belt buckles she'd wear front and centre. Didn't bother with the hat. Didn't much like them when they were anything except battered all to hell.

Made sure half the insular town saw her, too. Into the Golden Dragon for the special, and only after they'd had a chance to fill their eyeballs did she head out to her brand new pickup truck and drive out to say hello to the folks at home.

Jesus, the satisfaction of it. They knew without having to ask that everything was paid for in full. Truck and all. And the look on their faces. The Biddy asked her what she was doing for a job of work, and when she told them they didn't know whether to cough or fart, shit or steal home plate.

"Rodeo?"

The word hung there like some kind of mini-UFO. She might as well have said test pilot or race car driver or gollywumpusitifier.

"Whatever made you do *that*?" the Biddy blurted.

"Whatever made you *not* do it?" Lucy laughed.

Well, you don't know what you don't know until you know it and realize you didn't used to know it. Or, as someone once put it, an option has to be perceivable to be an option.

She'd always known she wasn't just going to quit school, get married and settle into more of the same. She'd listened to the guidance counselor and felt nothing but total boredom for any of the ideas put before her; work for B.C. Telephone Company saying, Number please thank you, work for Eaton's, work for the town's law firm, take teacher training and stay in school forever, take nurses' training and be a glorified char, work for the Canadian Imperial Bank of Commerce and train zit-faced boys for promotions denied her simply because her body pumped estrogen, not testosterone. And she wasn't going to marry some nice guy and live her life secondhand, through him.

She'd experimented and enjoyed it. She and Bill had even been a bit of a hot thing for a while, but not hot enough for her to burn out her brain cells. And then, ninety-nine-clumping it to her physio session, there it was, practically put on a golden platter and shoved under her nose.

"You're looking much better."

"I'm feeling much better," she answered. The face was almost familiar, but not quite. And the person behind the face was laughing.

"You don't recognize me, do you? I was your night nurse the first couple of weeks after they brought you out of surgery."

"My god!" Lucy blurted. "Do you ever look different with clothes on!" And then they both laughed at the stupidity of the remark.

"Hey"—the golden platter floated down from heaven—"you haven't had a chance to see me with my clothes *off* yet."

So what do you do? There it is. You can say, Oh, sorry, what I meant was you look different out of uniform, and then she'll say, Yes, everyone says that when they see me in street clothes, and that's that, it was all just a joke and not even a particularly good one. Maybe you'll even see each other a couple more times, maybe go for coffee or something, but drift apart with nobody recognizing or identifying or acknowledging anything. Or you can wipe the grin off your foolish face and say, "That's right, I haven't. How do I get the chance?"

What you did was go to physio, let them put you on the rack and play Spanish Inquisition for a while, then go home, soak in a nice hot tub while the two pink pills took effect and the pain receded. And then, by god, you got ready to do something you knew full well was going to change your life forever, and you could only pray it would be for the better.

"Well, you didn't learn that around *here*."

That's for damn sure.

Still no hat. Not a red shirt, either. Pale blue, and as plain as they make them. Best underwear, though. The jeans fit like a second skin, the socks were practically brand-new and the boots, my dear, said it all. Oh yes they did, because if they'd been any plainer, any more tasteful, any more expensive, they'd have left home and gone on tour. And just because the shirt was plain and the boots were plain and her own face was pretty much plain, out came *the* belt buckle. Oh yes, I mean, really, silver is nice but there's no denying platinum is better, right? You don't buy these suckers. You only get these one way, and it's not the easy way.

When it was good it was very very good and when it was bad it was fucking intolerable. Pardon me, I've enjoyed just about as much of this as my mental health can stand. But by then the leg was as good as it was ever going to be, and she packed her clothes, filled the gas tank of her pickup and yo ho for the open road.

Didn't take long for other dimes to drop. Her *leg* was as strong as ever. The hip wasn't, and never would be again. And yes, she could ride, but no, she could not ride as well. And yes, there were pink pills for the deep driving ache, but no, they didn't stop it, they only made it retreat and gnash its sharp yellow fangs. And the pink pills did more—they got between the reflexes and the job at hand.

She was making money, and it was good money. But it wasn't top money. And you pay, one way or another. She wasn't afraid of getting hurt again. Hell, you could get hurt sitting at the kitchen table. Stab yourself in the eye with a fork loaded with spaghetti, maybe. But you know when you aren't as good as you once were. You know even if nobody else does. And it's not as if it was something with a long career at the best of times.

Her hand hurt, too. Not to mention it looked funny as hell with that great big bump on top where the strap had bust some bones as she went ass-over-the-moon off that goddamn leopard appaloosa. Parabola, that's what she'd done, a parabola. Crunch time. And what in *hell* was it about appies? Seemed like every time she wound up cracked, bent or broken there was a damn appie in the picture. Chief Joseph's fucking revenge!

Exp'd person to run equestrian center (25 stalls), accommodation provided.

Wanted immediately, experienced stablehand.

Manager required. Extensive experience with horses. Salary commensurate.

Riding school and boarding stable needs experienced manager.

The accommodation could just as easily have been used as another stall. For a small-sized Shetland pony, perhaps. The salary was commensurate, maybe, but she didn't figure out with what, or why she was obviously worth less than the spoiled Polish Arabians she was keeping alive, fit and trained.

And the fucking people! Dear god, this is me, Lucy, would you please send a couple of bolts of lightning, super grand-slam size? Beam them up, Scotty, for christ's sake.

The one old twat drove up in her let's-pretend-it's-a-car, never the same time two days in a row, and got out of it with her jaw going a mile a minute. You'd think her tongue was connected in the center and flapping at both ends. Ya ta ta tat, ta ta ta tat, rin tin tin. Yippety yappety and she knew it all, by the Lord Harry if she didn't.

She'd grab a couple of flakes of prime hay on her way past, then out into the paddock with it she'd go, spreading it around as if she was feeding grain to a hen. Then the quarterhorse-Arab cross could frisk around gnawing at it, ingesting dirt, dust, gravel and grit, because the very nature of a paddock is that there's seldom much in the way of grass, what the little bugger doesn't eat he tromps to death. Not only did it throw the balanced feeding program all to hell, there you were at two in the morning, usually on the worst night of the year, pouring mineral oil down his throat, walking him around, trying to get him to shit out the muck giving him colic.

Explain it to her? Oh, fall on your head. Same old fool would show up with a great big bag of apples, dump them in the dirt and stand there grinning like a jerk while her baby gorped out on them.

"Lady, please. For starters, one apple only, okay? And cut into four pieces, please, or he's apt to get it stuck in his throat."

"Oh, but he just *loves* them."

And there you are with your goddamn arm drenched in oil, going down his throat, trying to dislodge the apple and praying to god the speculum will hold, otherwise he might chomp you off at the shoulder.

And argue? Each and every one of them had a little war of some kind going with at least two or three others. Pity the people who own horses can't get along as well as the animals do. He said she said we said they said and it's just not *so*!

But at least her savings were racking up interest in the bank, she had a place to stay, supposedly and purportedly rent free, and she could make some extra on the side. "Yes, ma'am, part of my job is to see the horses are exercised. That doesn't mean I'm supposed to *train* them for you. Training is extra. Especially if what you want is *de*training."

"Well, that's a bit much!"

"You'd better talk to the boss about it, then, because it's not in *my* job description." They'd stalk off, insulted, but they'd be back. A little less lordly, too.

"It's not that he's BAD, or anything, it's just that, well, he's very high-spirited."

Yeah, sure. High-spirited as hell. And he knows full well that if he doesn't want to do something all he has to do is be an asshole. If that fails, just rear up and fall over backward. Who knows, he might be able to crush and kill the one he couldn't intimidate or dislodge.

Ah, but he hadn't come up against someone who'd learned from the bandylegged who'd grown up with animals tougher than this one even dreamed of being. He reared and overtipped himself on purpose, and Lucy had her feet out of the stirrips and was on her way off. Stupid son of a bitch hit the ground and Lucy sat on his head.

"Go on, you mad bastard!" She laughed, slapping him in the face with her hat. "Just fuckin' *try* to get up!" And she stayed on his head until he quit thrashing and heaving. When he was quiet, she allowed him to get to his four feet, and she climbed right back up.

He did it again. And so did she. And she kept on doing it until he let her get up there without pulling his little stunt. She rode him until he was just about ready to tip over sideways, then she took him to his stall, stripped his gear, and left him.

The next morning he was so goddamn sore she almost felt sorry for him. But not so sorry she let him rest up. The whole thing came down again.

When he finally caught on she took him for a good long ride, then groomed and fussed him and turned him loose with a mouthful of carrot. "Good boy," she said, giving him a few solid slaps on the neck. But no more fuss than that. Why teach him he was doing huge favors just being what he was supposed to be? Not as though he was the first friggin' spoiled brat to let a rider climb into a saddle.

And when she didn't have an evening jam packed with work, there were lots of things to do. Drive ten miles to the city and find out more about that stuff you didn't learn at home!

She didn't know anybody around here had put two and two together and come up with anything more than three. Wonder where Bob Dakins heard about it?

He had Kitty half thinking she was being taken. "Aunt Lucy?"

"Hmm?"

"Is it true what Bob Dakins says?"

"What's that?"

"He says you were a rodeo rider."

"He said that?"

"Were you?"

"Yes."

"Barrel races and such?"

Well, there you have it. They cut back and cut down and cut away until people thought barrel racing was all there'd ever been for women. Might get hurt, they said. Hell, more women got permanently crippled at their husbands ever-loving fists than got seriously hurt on a bareback bronc! More women died in childbirth than coming off the back of a bull, but they didn't outlaw having babies.

Lucy almost shrugged it off—almost brushed it aside like some hairbrained idea she'd tried out briefly when she was a teenager. But something in the depths of Kitty's eyes stopped her. Lucy looked away, to give herself time to pull it all together.

"You really want to know?"

"Yeah," and the kid swallowed, then nodded.

So Lucy took her down to the basement and got her to help haul out the old blue-painted metal trunk. And there it all was. Well, not *all* of it. But there it was. The twenty-five-hundred-dollar saddle, all the boots, carefully polished, stored away with shape-keepers stuck inside. Belts, belt buckles, spurs, conchos—the flim and the flam,

Rosie Benson used to call it. Bring out all the flim and all the flam, we're riding in the parade today!

"Ho-lee!" the kid breathed.

Lucy let the magazines do the talking. When she knew Kitty was well and truly sucked into the printed pages, she left the basement and went up to the kitchen. If Debbie had asked, "Are you all right?" Lucy would have nodded. But Debbie didn't ask. She just came over, wrapped her arms around Lucy's waist, tucked herself comfy up against her and said, "You are something else, woman."

"Oh yeah?" Lucy breathed. "Look who's talkin'."

And it was true. Look who's talkin'. You get one chance at the big one, one chance at the real one, and if it comes when you're too young and stupid to recognize it, you'll mess it up and never get another chance for anything more than second- or third-best. But she hadn't been young, although she was probably still more than a bit stupid, and she hadn't messed it up, which was probably due more to good luck than good management. She was grateful, and not merely grateful to God, if in fact She existed.

Chad moved back in with them. Lucy half expected all the pony poop to start up again, probably made worse by the fact there was now a teen-aged girl to be his audience. But Chad seemed to have learned a lot in the time he'd been living with his dad. Maybe everyone had learned a lot. Or maybe it was just that the stars in the sky had shifted and everyone's astrological wotzits were in harmony.

"I had no idea what'n hell to expect last time," he told Kitty. "I felt like I'd been put down on the moon or something."

"Yeah." She nodded. "The far side of the moon."

"Right." He seemed both surprised and grateful that she understood. "And I didn't know how to do a damned thing!"

"Hey, I know *that* one." She nodded again. "I mean, you see them do it and it looks as if anyone can, and then you try and...I *still* can't just grab one of those damned haybales, lift it up level with my own armpits and then huck it as if it was just an extra-big marshmallow! I stumble, I lurch, I look like all three of the stooges at once, and if my damned aunt tells me one more time that it isn't a matter of strong, it's a matter of co-ordinated, well, I might pick her up and chuck *her*!"

"Well," he laughed softly, "I have to admit you do make me look good."

"Then gimme a dime, dope! It ought to be worth at least that much. You think it's easy making *you* look good?"

He'd already been put through the New Kid In School hell, they didn't bother doing it again. They acted as if he belonged and had just been off on an extended vacation.

"And on top of that," Bob Dakins mourned, "on top of *all* that, we had to come up with the money to pay back the horsy-crowd!" And when Chad roared with laughter Bob didn't get angry, he just nodded and grinned ruefully. "Boy, never again, I tell you. That woman has *no* sense of humor!"

"She really stuffed a rifle up your nose?"

"Alongside my head. And pulled the trigger! Man, I thought I'd been deafened. Jesus, I was scared. I mean, man, I was *scared*, you know? She looked just about crazy, and I figured if I did one little thing wrong I'd be busy with the scoop shovel filling the furnaces with coal while the little pointy-tailed demons stuck me in the ass with their stickers. I *still* think she's half a step from being a public menace."

"Me, I just walk real soft when she's around," Chad admitted. "I won't even argue with my mom if Lucy's in the room."

"The whole family's like that." Kitty smiled sweetly. "So don't get proddy with me either, city-boy."

"You gonna let her call you city-boy?"

"I'll have to if all you're gonna do is stand and watch." A look passed between them; Bob Dakins nodded and they lunged; but Kitty was already moving, racing away from them yelling city-boy, city-boy, city-boy.

He was in that Alone place. He had to come to the Alone to get any work done. At first Alone had been terrifying, but he had been here so many times now, it was more home than home itself. All he had to do was start walking toward the door down to the basement, and it began to happen. Voices did not impinge on Alone, even a touch on the arm meant nothing when Alone was forming.

He would go down into the basement, move to his bench and sit picking up his tools, feeling the wooden handles, the metal shafts, the sharp chisel blades, the curved points. Sometimes he sat and felt the sandpaper, the graphite paper, the diamond-dust paper, barely touching it with his fingertips but feeling each grain, each fraction of a grain, each dust mote, feeling and thinking and entering Alone.

He might stay in Alone for minutes, hours, days or even weeks, deeper and deeper into the work, deeper and deeper into the Alone, deeper and more comfortable with the faces, with knowing there was no need to explain anything. He didn't know how to explain anyway. They would ask, Where did you get the idea for...and it wasn't an idea, it was just that you looked at the wood and the face was there, all you had to do was pare away the wood, pare away what was layered over the face, or the figure, or the form, or the design, peel it away bit by bit as the tree itself had grown, bit by bit by ring by ring, around and over and even into the face or the figure or the form or whatever was living in there, caught in there, asking gently to be released.

They went there to be alone, to pass time. You could do that when it was time to come back—instead of being a person or whatever else, you could go into a tree and stay there, looking out at the magic of the world, feeling the wind, feeling the rain, feeling the sun, dancing in the moving air, washed by showers and squalls, decorated by snow and ice, just stay there in the tree a hundred years, a thousand years, learning patience, learning calm and quiet and breathing through your skin and hair.

And when he was in Alone he could look at the murdered tree, look at the face, and just peel it away like the hard shell on a lichee fruit, peel it away slowly and carefully and there they were, individuals each, freed again.

But he had to go to Alone to do it. And Alone was, after all, alone, and it had been hard to learn to go there and get comfortable and not hear the teacher or the other kids talking or laughing or saying he was crazy, or feel them shaking him. The school doctor had come one time and forced him back from Alone, but that didn't last, you ignore them long enough and they'll go away. They wanted to take him to what they called a hospital and he knew was a loony bin but the old lady wouldn't go for that one, and they weren't about to tangle with her, by god.

He'd thought once, for a little while, that he'd found someone to come to Alone with him, but even though he was sure she'd been telling the truth when she said she understood, even though she knew Alone and knew that territory well, even so, when he knew how it really was, he knew he was still in Alone all by himself, she might be waiting when he came back but in Alone he was alone because that's where you went to do the work and nobody could go with you, Alone is what it says it is. And those who don't go have no idea. They might love like crazy and accept and not be scared but on some level be grateful they didn't have to go there, on some level think going there was just a little bit...just a tiny bit...just a weeny bit like being retarded...or nuts...or...afflicted....

and really, all he was doing was going to Alone and letting the faces and figures out of the wood. Be nice to know what happened after, but that didn't seem to be his business. Some of them zipped off, leaving nothing but the wooden mask, lifeless eyeholes staring; others slithered up out of the finished piece and moved around the work room, not quite transparent, more like an image projected from some screwy kind of camera, maybe one of those old jobbies they rolled into the classroom and set up on someone's desk, the kind that were always wibbling and wobbling the reel off the thingamajigs and everyone scrambling to grab'er before she fell to the floor.

The shadow-on-the-wall ones stayed a day or a week or however long, went away, came back, who knew where they went or what they did when they were gone, and sometimes it was like they came to look at other masks, other shadows, to reacquaint themselves or something.

Some evenings he almost felt he understood them. On those evenings when the old girl made popcorn and they sat watching Matt and Mz Kitty and Chester making the world safe, on those nights, even though there were only the two of them on the tatty old sagging sofa, he was somewhere else, not in Alone, and things were as they never had been, not for even one day, they were all there, even the gone and the long-gone, and he could almost smell Savannah's perfume. The old girl was good about it, too, she never once mentioned the tears he shed. Not a word. So he didn't mention the ones she shed, either. Turn about's fair play. He didn't know if she cried silently for the dead, the gone, the long-gone or the never-made-its, he didn't know if she cried for her reasons or his. Wasn't his business, anyhow.

Sometimes in Alone he'd look up and out over the huge distance and there'd be someone else looking up and out over the distance toward him. Someone else in Alone. Someone carving, maybe, or painting, someone writing or bringing music from an instrument, some other soul who knew and, more than knew, Knew. And they could nod and make eye contact and for a moment, a brief magic warm loving moment, neither of them was in Alone but connected in Together. But it didn't last, you can't work in Together, you can only take a break, and you're together briefly, then back to Alone

only sometimes, some twisting sad frightening and sorrowful times, he looked up and it was a little kid, not a boy, not a girl, just a kid, in the Alone for the first time, terrified, past terrified to something else, past that to the brink of a big deep dark hole of forever, alone and not knowing what to do, and he'd try as hard as he could to think to the kid, think because he couldn't go there physically and stoop down and hug and say, It's okay, kid, it's fine, it's going to be fun, it'll be great when you get used to it, look, we can paint, we can carve, we can write, we can sing, we can do what we need to do, and we come to Alone to do it, look, here, do this, I'll show you, come carve with me, draw with me, paint with me, come on, don't be scared, I'm here, but he couldn't do that, he could only scream inside his head, It's okay little kid it's okay it's okay don't be scared it's okay, and sometimes it worked and the kid looked up and saw him and that awful cold stiffness went from the small shoulders and a hand reached for a crayon or a pencil or something

but sometimes he knew the kid couldn't hear, couldn't feel, was too scared, had too much chasing after it, was too pained, too hurting, too lonely in Alone to find comfort there, and the kid would wind up falling in the black hole falling in the black hole falling in the black hole and then it was jail or the loony bin for sure. jail or the loony bin for sure. jail for sure loony bin for sure kid in black hole for sure send the fucking faces and still those who can't see won't see those who won't see can't see don't trust not even the faces they recognize so it's the loony bin for you kid, the jailhouse for you kid the dead in a ditch on the side of the road for you kid no use crying over spilt milk no use crying over spoilt chances no use crying over dead kids hurt kids scared kids terrified kids

just send the faces send the masks pick up the soft wooden-handled tools and snuggle into Alone and do the work so they don't dare say loony bin they have to say art gallery fuck ya fuck ya fuck-yasall. Don't say nutbar, say eccentric, don't say crazier'n a shithouse rat, say inspired, can't say off his rocker if you pay two weeks' salary for a mask, thou shalt not make unto thyself any graven images, fuck-yasall, everything has its own power and you go to Alone to find it, then turn it loose because what we need is more of the faces to help the lost find the abandoned.

PART
FOUR

1

Seely stood for long moments looking down at the four-tiered cake. It looked finished—finished and just fine. Still, she checked it, because it would be just awful if she overlooked something. Even if nobody else noticed, what if she suddenly realized, when it was too late to do anything, that she'd forgotten something? What if, for example, after the cake was paid for, picked up, taken away and out of her control, she noticed one too many little Doric columns on the work table? How would she feel? Worried sick that the missing column would mean the thing would tip or tilt or fall over or look goofy. All the columns were there, the braids were in place, the roses; the little bride stood half-facing the little groom, who was turned at a matching angle toward her. The archway was just fine, not higher or lower on one side or the other.

She smiled, then giggled, remembering that crazy crazy time and Kitty yelling, Where's the little hand grenade, don't forget the machine gun. Now when Seely put the archway in place she whispered to the little groom to just watch himself, see, because there's a warhead in here, and if you get out of line, fellow, she's got the detonator in her bouquet. Then she whispered to the little bride to remember, she didn't have to put up with him if he got owly, just stamp your foot and it's finished. It was just a silly game, of course, she didn't really believe people should kill people to prove to other people that killing people was wrong.

Well, it looked to her as if she'd done everything that needed to be done. She could start folding up the sides of the box. She wouldn't close the lid until the people had come and seen the cake. That was usually a big deal for the bride's mother—seeing the cake somehow made it all more real. A lot of them cried. Well, why not? They didn't know and Seely couldn't tell them about the warhead or the warning she put in the ear of the groom doll. And because they didn't know she was evening the odds, they could only worry.

Seely did everything she could to make it easier for people. She made each individual tier separately, and only when the covering of hard icing was totally dry did she start building the thing, like the leaning tower of pizza-pie, only pray god it wouldn't lean. First she got the carry-tray. Jimmy had made her any number of them, and the back of each had a number painted on; she had a book people had to sign when they took one away, and if they didn't bring the carry-tray back she charged them fifty dollars, which was probably way lots more than the tray was worth but there you go, bring it back and you don't have to pay anything, not even rental for the use of it. There were handles on the tray, like wheelbarrow handles only smaller and shorter, and it meant two people could carry the cake out to the car or van. Less worry about dropping it.

Once she had the carry-tray on the table, she put the box on the tray, in the middle, with all the flaps spread out flat. Then she got a bottomboard, and that fit the bottom of the box. It was covered with aluminum foil but nobody would really see that, because the bottom layer fit over top, pretty well hiding it. Once the bottom layer was in position she could start putting the columns in place. Not as easy as you'd think—you had to be sure the tops were level, you had to be sure the bottoms were securely set. Otherwise all it took was one of them tipping or tilting, or even sinking a bit, and it was too awful to think about.

The mother of the bride came on time, and saw the cake. She smiled and dabbed at her eyes with a Kleenex, and if you saw her out of context, if you saw her but didn't see all the wedding-cake stuff on the display shelves where people could choose icing patterns and designs and everything, you might think she was at a funeral or something. Dab dab the eyes and smile determinedly.

Two older men, probably the father of the bride and his brother, stood awkwardly, waiting, while the mother of the bride paid for the cake and all. Then they took the wheelbarrow handles and moved stiffly, carefully, through the door Seely held wide open, taking the cake to the station wagon.

Some people you didn't mind making their cake. Other people, even though they paid you and everything, you wished you could tell them to go make their own. Some people she'd turned down flat.

Well, why not? They hadn't passed a law yet!

Those people who used to be summers only but moved in full time after the kids went off to university and he took retirement, Yanks from Idaho or some place like that, showing up with their jaws flapping and saying how they'd never understood why all Seely's cakes were like English Christmas fruit cakes because they didn't want that, they wanted a sponge cake.

"Oh. Well, I'm afraid you'll have to find someone who does that," she said, and she was pleasant and even at first a bit regretful, because you do like to give people what they want.

"Someone else?" The mother looked amazed. Well, they don't like to be told they can't have what they want the minute they want it. "But we don't *want* someone else! You just make a sponge cake; I've got a recipe I'll give you. And decorate it up and...."

"No thank you."

"But there are *lots* of us who would...."

"No, I don't do that." And Seely smiled again. "You have to use a whole bunch of imitation things when you do it that way. And I don't use those things."

Well. One thing about them, they sure can argue. They might call it a discussion, but it's not, it's just High Noon in the bakery, and old wotzisname strolling off down the street, gotta do what he's gotta do, get his own way, individualism, by god, if you want a thing done you have to make sure the help does it your way. And finally, exasperated and almost angry, Seely explained as carefully as she could, lordy, a kid could figure it out.

"Sponge cake won't hold the weight of the other tiers. Sponge cake might sink at one corner and your top layer could wind up in your lap, or on the floor. Besides which, the cake gets made over a period of time, you don't just whip it up the night before, you know.

The icing has to get hard. *Hard,* because it has to hold the weight.
Sponge cake dries out. It goes stale. It doesn't taste nice. I use a very
rich fruitcake recipe because the older it is the better it is, and it stays
moist without being soggy. And I cover it with almond paste and...."

"Oh, we don't want *that*. That marzipan stuff...."

"Not marzipan—almond paste, it's different. Richer. I don't buy
it, I make it myself and...."

"Well, we don't want that, all we want is...."

"Then go home and do it yourself," she said bluntly. The woman
glared.

"If I go home and make it myself and bring it in, will you decorate it?"

"No."

"No? *No!*"

"No. I told you. It'll go dry, it won't taste nice, it won't hold the
weight of the top tiers, the little columns will tip, the bride and
groom will look drunk, and I won't do it because when people see the
stupid thing they'll think that's the kind of work I do, and when they
taste the stale old dry mess they'll decide to go somewhere else for
their cake, and anyway if I can't make the best one I know how to
make I won't make any."

"You *have* to...."

"No I don't."

You'd think they'd never had the chance to watch the program,
you'd think they'd never seen Mz Kitty just set a cold smile on her
face and hunker down to outwait them. You'd think they had no idea
some people had grown up with more going for them than what
showed to the outside world. She didn't just work in the damn saloon,
she *owned* it, see? The look on Jimmy's face when Kit blew her cool
that time! And the look on the faces of the Listers when Seely
refused to make a pretend-cake.

Mad? My god, it just went on and on. Eventually they left. Then
he came in to try to smooth it over. Must have been a real-estate
salesman, or insurance or brand-new cars or something. Slick. When
he smiled his teeth were so white and even you knew they were top-
of-the-line china clippers, the kind where the dentist filed the god-
given ones down to little stubs and then epoxied the pricy ones
overtop. Took about fifteen minutes for him to realize he wasn't but-
tering her up and getting her to make some kind of pretend-cake. So

he left. Then the bride-to-be came in, and she cried. Looked like the kind of sorority brat who'd been crying all her life. Whenever she wanted something, turn on the tap, go from Miss Moneybags to Princess Rain-in-the-Face in the blink of an eye. Gran used to say it was a physiological disorder, the bladder was too close to the eyes and she pissed out of her face.

Eventually Mommy came back, stiff with fury. "Oh, all *right!*" she snapped. "We'll do it your way!"

"Sorry." Seely knew she didn't sound the least bit sorry. "I'm booked right to the eyebrows and I couldn't have it ready in time."

"You *what?*"

"I'm sorry. Your wedding is next week and that isn't enough time, I've got six other wedding cakes on the go and...."

"We'll pay extra." The woman was about ready to explode.

"It isn't a case of paying extra. I'm not trying to blackmail you. I'm not trying to prove a point. I don't have the time, I'm booked solid."

"But, what are we supposed to do about a wedding cake?"

"I don't know." She wanted to say, You figure it out, you're the one who knows everything. But no need for that.

"Well, what if we came down to help you?"

"No."

"What about if you worked on it in the evenings?"

"I don't do that." Seely was getting angry. "I've got kids. That's what I do in the evening."

"I'll pay for a babysitter while you work on the cake."

"I don't want a babysitter. By the time supper is over, all I want to do is sit down with the kids. By the time supper is over, I'm tired." She knew it was no use, you can't explain something to people who refuse to listen. Still, she tried, because maybe one of them, one day, would clue in to something. "You aren't listening to me. You aren't paying any attention to what I say. You want your own way. Well, you'll just have to get on the old blower and start phoning around. Here's a list of places in the city, maybe someone will have an extra or something."

"*I don't want a commercial one! I want you to make it!*"

And that's when Seely lost it. "Oh, go fuck yourself."

Well, it was all over town before suppertime. Seely felt so miserable she thought she'd wind up the way she sometimes did, lying in a dark room with an icepack on her face, trying to get the pounding headache to subside. She was afraid she'd be sick to her stomach. Sometimes that went on for days at a time, the room spinning, her eyes hurting, her head bang bang bang banging and she didn't dare open her eyes because everything swam around as if it had lost whatever held the molecules together. Things that ought to be solid looked liquefied, other things looked as if they'd been done by a kid, with a solid line drawn around them, only a kid usually outlines things in black and this was different, as if it all had a greeny glow around the edges. And the worst part was that she had to get someone to come in and take care of Sandra, and that was just awful because Sandra hated to have anyone see how things were with her. Be all over town in no time, and everyone thinking, Oh poor thing, oh what a shame, oh my how dreadful, why the poor thing would be better off dead.

Except they don't let you get dead. They don't let you make yourself dead, they don't let those who love you help you get dead, they talk about prolonging life and all they're doing is prolonging death, with pills and the tube in the arm and the once-a-day nurse with her injections.

The phone started ringing before supper was finished. "Seely, you *didn't!* Did you?"

"Did I what?"

"Tell Lister-the-Blister to go fuck herself."

"Oh god. You heard?"

"I think it's great!"

People she didn't know phoned. Jimmy phoned the next day. She was in the bakery and the phone rang and she picked it up and Jimmy was laughing like some kind of candidate for the funny farm. "Ah go fuck yourself," he said, "why the fuck don't you fuckin' go and fuckin' fuck your fuckin' self."

"It's not funny, Jimmy," Seely whispered. "It's awful. I got *so* mad."

"No you didn't," he contradicted her, still laughing. "You got fuckin' mad, Seel."

"It's not funny," and she wept. Jimmy told her to stop crying and get back to work, and he hung up. That made her feel even worse.

But then he walked into the bakery and he gave her a big hug, looked around and said, "Okay, tell me what to do here."

"I'm way *way* behind," she sobbed. "She made me so mad I got a headache, and when I get a headache my hands shake and I can't do anything, and I *told* her I had too many cakes to do already, she'd waited too long, and now I'll be late with *everybody's* cake and it's just *awful.*"

"Yeah. Fuckin' bitch. Burn her fuckin' house around her fuckin' ears. Then she'll have to postpone the fuckin' wedding, and the problem'll be solved...do you know a gallon of gasoline has the explosive force of twenty-one sticks of dynamite? Do you know if you take nitrogen fertilizer and pour diesel fuel on it you've got nitroglycerine?" He was holding her as if they were wearing fancy-dress clothes, and he was dancing her around the basement room that was her bakery display, and he was talking about blowing up the courthouse too, and sending the cop shop sky-high, but he sounded as if he was singing and they were dancing. "We'll clamber around the supports of the bridge out of town, Seel, just you'n'me and Chester'n'Matt Dillon and Mz Kitty and, Jesus, maybe we can even get Spock to come with us as science officer, and we'll fly around like Peter fucking Pan, and put red plastic five-gallon jerricans of gasoline on the bridge, with a fuse from one to the other, and then we'll take some of that barbecue stuff, the white waxy cubes you set in the charcoal briquets, and we'll light it on fire and sit it on a second one and we'll put the both of them on the fuse and we'll get in the car and drive back to town and go to the cop shop and tell them some crazy story about a prowler, and while we're in the cop shop the barbecue stuff'll burn down to the fuse and the fuse'll burn to the jerrican and the thing'll go off like a stringa firecrackers and the whole fuckin' bridge will come apart and we'll have an alibi, we're talking to the fuckin' cops at the time!" The scars on his tanned arms gleamed like little white rivers and he smiled and talked and crooned and the headache went away and she felt safe for a little while.

"Now, tell me what to do, okay?"

And maybe he didn't know how to bake, and maybe he didn't know how to do a lot of things, but he knew straight when he saw it and he knew level when he saw it and he could copy just about anything you'd care to mention, so they stood together, and it was so nice it almost seemed like everyone in the family had come along and decided to make life a party.

They said he was crazy. Who were they to talk? Just because some idiot came up from the city to do an interview for TV and asked a bunch of dumb dumb questions, and Jimmy said the stuff he carved came to him out of the clear air. Said he'd just close his eyes and he could see how to do it. Said he never knew until it was finished what it was he was doing. And the drip didn't understand that, so he asked how sharp Jimmy's tools were and Jimmy said, "This sharp," and picked up a curved blade and cut his arm open right in front of the TV. "That's how I test the edge," he said, and you'd'a thought he was sincere. "If it doesn't cut so slick I can't feel it, it isn't sharp enough."
    Some academic egghead who probably needed help to pull his hat on over his swollen dome wrote a thing for the city paper saying Jimmy was obviously seriously disturbed. Well, of course he was. So what? What did that have to do with anything? He was no more disturbed than the dinkhead who wrote that awful thing. Practically said Jimboh ought to be locked in a room with mattresses on the walls. Paragraphs about some guy Jimmy said had cut off his ear, then more paragraphs about that awful night and the rugrats who got killed, and on about extreme mental trauma—as if he'd been there his own self and knew what he was yammering on about. Seely said, Get a lawyer, but Jimboh laughed and said, Hey, why give him the time and the energy? Worst that'll happen is all the co-llec-tors will go zippin' out to buy up stuff in case I off myself and the prices skyrocket. And sure enough, inside of a month there were orders like hell wouldn't hold. So who's crazy, really? And what *is* crazy, anyway?
    Well, that was water under the bridge. The bridges they'd burned behind them all had spilled milk flowing underneath. Mix a metaphor or two, slide'em in the cake. You might as well, don't cost any more or take any longer. They'd had fun in school with words and meanings. Called synonyms "cinnamons" and made the teacher laugh. Cinnamons and Auntie Mins.

She'd quit school early, but then Sandra got sick and it meant so much to her that Seely went to Upgrading in the evening. The whole town sniffing and pursing its withered lips because of the kids, one after the other, and Seely, big as a bus, had to sit at a card table with a chair because she couldn't get into the dumbnelly desk, but she went and got her Equivalency, for all the good it was ever going to be. Because it made Sandra feel better and there was no end to what Seely would do to make Sandra feel a bit better. Boy, some people sure wound up having a rough time of it. Didn't seem fair.

My god, look at the time. Darlene and Lizzy'll be racing up the walk soon, wanting a snack, needing to talk about all the stuff they've learned and heard and said and seen and done, and here she was and another hour or two had dropped into whatever hole swallowed time when she was working! The people would be here for their cake, too. Four-thirty, the woman said. Well, that was fine, the cake was ready. They'd save one layer for their first anniversary party, and one for the baptism of their first kid. Some people just took a slice off for every big occasion like that and kept the cake in the freezer for years. The ones who did it *right*, they took off all the icing when the wedding reception was finished, and they wrapped the rest of the cake in cloth and put it in an airtight can and every six months or so spilled some more brandy on it until it was preserved, and then they just opened up the can on Occasions and cut off a slice. It could last a lifetime that way. Like some Egyptian mummy stuffed with spices and wrapped in cloth and still staring from the museum wall a thousand years later.

My god, stop this. Better get upstairs. Sandra's sure to wake up soon and when she does she'll need to be taken to the can. Awful thing, that. Better to be dead than have your brain trapped in a useless body, kept prisoner in your own flesh. Sometimes it seemed to Seely that Sandra was probably going crazy in that cell of flesh, bone and blood, almost solitary confinement, except she got to see and hear people, she just couldn't talk to them or move around with them.

It was as bad as what happened to Gran before she died. One minute there she was playing with Lizzy, lying on the big braided rug in the living room, her arms up and folded under her head like a pillow. Laughing and singing with Lizzy who was marching around waving one of those long skinny balloons that are so hard to blow up, using it like a baton or something, and singing, Be-bop-a-lula, she's my baby, Be-bop-a-lula I don't mean maybe, just those two lines, over and over, be-bop-a-lula—and then Gran got this look on her face,

like a combination of surprise and total horror. She made a whimpering sound. Her eyes rolled back, then closed. Just...just closed, is all.

"Jimmy...something's wrong," Savannah gasped.

"Huh?" Jimmy looked at Savannah. "What's wrong, pork chop?"
He grinned, then he looked in the direction Savannah was looking
and for a minute there it was as if whatever had happened to Gran
was about to happen to him too.

"Get the *car!*" he yelled. Savannah just up and off her chair and
headed for the car. "Can you look after all the kids?" Jimmy was crying, his face shining with tears.

"Yeah," Seely managed. She couldn't move. She felt like she'd felt
the time she peed on Kitty's head and she could only squeeze her
muscles as tight as tight could be so she wouldn't do it all over the
chair and the floor too.

Jimmy picked Gran up as if she didn't weigh any more than Darlene, and he ran with her.

Savannah always drove like she was in charge of a firetruck or
something, and Jimmy said half the time the tires weren't even touching the blacktop. Said he was so scared he just sat in the back seat
holding Gran, and hoping that if they went off the road they'd all be
killed and not wind up locked in a life-support machine for fifty years.

Seely managed to round up a babysitter, promised to pay double
because of the tribe of kids. Gave them a big supper, stuffed them into
the tub, hauled them out, crammed them into pajamas, got them to
bed and even had most of them sound asleep before the sitter arrived.
Then she had the sitter take little glasses of milk to the ones still half
awake, and she made sure they heard her, Seely, singing in the bathroom, walking down the hall, shit like that.

"Are you the enforcer?" Victor asked.

"Enforcer?" The babysitter wasn't sure what to say.

"Babysitter." Vic grinned. "We call it the Enforcer because Mom
makes the rules and you have to see to it we follow them. Mom says
you're allowed to do whatever you have to do, except no hitting on
the head with a hockey stick because they cost nearly twenty dollars
and you're sure to break it on our thick skulls."

"Yeah," the babysitter said, "yeah. But I don't use a stick. I use a
great big heavy rock. That's what they mean when they say, 'Rock
them to sleep.'"

When they were easy with the sitter, Seely left and joined the others at the hospital. Even Glen was there, the sick-minded creepo crud. He stood around looking like some kind of advertisement for fancy clothes or something, mister dress-for-success, home to gloat over the losers. He thought.

Savannah was having trouble with Jimmy. He was talking funny by then. Talking about all these ghosts in the hallway of the hospital, and how every mask he'd ever carved had shown up. Kept saying they'd come because they knew he loved her, and he hoped Gran could see them too, because she'd understand. Sometimes he said things and it didn't even sound like words. Once he started to sing, and you could tell he thought he was singing real words but what came out of him sure wasn't anything that made sense. They wanted to give him a shot in the arm but he said if they tried he'd give them a shot all right, but not in the arm, so they backed off on that one.

He was better once Seely was there. Seemed like he could relax with her there. It wasn't Savannah's fault, it was just that she wasn't used to Jimmy, she spent most of her time with ordinary sane people, living an ordinary sane life. She loved him. Just wasn't used to it, was all.

Well, it was kind of hard to get used to. Really.

It wasn't fair in some ways. It meant that she and Savannah had to keep taking turns leaving the hospital and going back to look after the kids. Jimmy wouldn't leave and nobody expected him to, and you sure as hell wouldn't want old Glen near the kids! Nosirree, thank you. Mean bugger. Killed the damn kitten and everything. "It shit on the floor," he said. "I can't stand catshit."

"You eat worse than that," Seely told him. She knew he wanted to hit her but he didn't dare, she'd call the cops so fast his head would spin right off his Hawaii-suntanned shoulders. Creep.

What it was was, Savannah and Jimmy knew each other the longest, and for a long time they knew each other best, but they only saw each other sometimes now, and they both missed what they knew they'd once had. You couldn't say anything about Jimmy without Savannah squaring up her shoulders and getting all set to jump in your face, and you sure couldn't say one single word about Savannah without Jimmy's eyes squinching in the corners because as far as *he* was concerned she was fine, just fine, and never did a wrong thing in her life.

2

Kitty could tell by the feel of the sheets and the smell in the room that, wherever she was, she wasn't at home. It seemed to require more energy than she had to open her eyelids. She couldn't manage both so she concentrated on the one that didn't hurt quite as much.

"Easy," a familiar voice said softly. "Easy, hon."

"Christie?"

"Who else? Nobody else loves you enough to sit on this bum-breaking chair for hours on end. Hell, they won't even let me smoke."

"Do you smoke after sex?" Kitty tried for a joke.

"I don't know," Christie picked it up and whispered the answer. "Usually, I'm so tired afterward I can't sit up to look."

Kitty closed her eye. The light seemed godawful bright. She had a headache that wasn't going to stop for a long long time. Her face hurt. She couldn't breathe through her nose, and when she lifted her hand to her face, Christie caught her by the wrist, gently, and lowered her arm back down to the sheets. Kitty would have protested but it was all too much trouble.

She lay trying to pull herself back together. She knew she wasn't awake. But she wasn't asleep either. Somewhere in between the two, some nice, slow, soft, lazy place where everything was so warm and easy that maybe she'd just stay there for the rest of her life. Rest of her natural-born life. That's what Gran called it, natural born life.

But she fell out of that place into something heavier, and hours later, when she swam back up out of there, she heard Lucy's voice, and Debbie's, too. Jesus, she'd better get a wiggle on, get out of the old sack and put on coffee or something, funny, she didn't remember anybody telling her they were coming for a visit.

She raised her head, and gasped with the pain of it, and Christie was right there with another pillow. "That's better," Kitty tried to sniff; her nose felt plugged but it also felt as if it was leaking or something.

"They say"—Lucy's voice was not quite firm, a bit of a tremble in it as if she had been running hard—"a thing of beauty is a joy forever."

"Face only a mother could love," Debbie agreed. "Or in your case a not-quite-but-almost aunt. How you doing, sweetheart?"

"How? What, is more to the point."

The light wasn't as bright, she could open her eyes and as long as she squinted a bit, she could keep them open, even focus. "Jesus, you all look like you've been up all night in a high-stakes poker game."

"Up all night getting here, you mean."

She knew then that she was in hospital and she'd been hurt. "What happened?" She made her face grin. "Isn't that the standard question? Who'hoppen? I can't," she admitted, "seem to remember."

"Yeah, well, if I'd'a done what they say you did, I'd want to forget too."

"My face hurts. And my hand."

"Oh, your hand is sure to hurt. Dumb shit."

It all has to fit tight and it all has to fit smooth but sometimes that snug wrap can fuck itself up, no help from anybody. Maybe there's a hint of dampness in the air, maybe things are all just too dry, maybe the goddamn critter is sweating, maybe your hand is sweating, maybe the elves and pixies are pissed off, who knows? She remembered now. "Couldn't get the fucker loose," she sighed.

"Well, if it was easy," Christie reassured her.

"Everybody would be doing it," they said together. Kitty went back into that easy, soft, almost loving space.

Right. Everybody would do it if it took no effort, energy or expertise. So she'd got hung up. Hand felt as if the classic thing had happened.

Usually the wrist breaks first. Then all the bones along the back of the hand, the ones leading to the fingers. Unless you've got outstanding good luck your thumb will probably dislocate. Although, from what she'd been told, it wasn't as much a case of the thumb coming away from the hand as of the hand coming disconnected from the thumb. And all the while, of course, the critter is going in every direction, the broken ends of the bones are grinding and jabbing and the wrist—well, best not to think about that.

She got hung up and then, in trying to get herself free, wound up turned toward the ton of flailing muscle. That was probably why she couldn't open her eyes, why her nose felt so strange and her teeth ached.

"My teeth?"

"None missing. But that's some lip, lady."

"Don't give me none of your lip, kiddo, or I'll knock you into the middle of next week. That's what she said. Any more from you, you little yahoo, and it'll be knuckle sandwiches."

"Who?"

"Phyllis. Dumb twat."

Lucy laughed softly and said something about maybe she'd rattled some of it loose but she hadn't broke anything important. Made no sense. She'd broken a few things, obviously.

Well, at least with her nose all banged up she didn't have to smell those awful dirty smells that mean hospital, like when Gran was in there that time. Jesus. People going around swishing mops reeking of Dettol and Lysol and who knows What-all, the sharp bite of disinfectant lying over but never getting rid of the smell of piss and sweat and probably rotting stuff.

Smell. Yes. She remembered the smell of the critter, sweat and piss and fear. Big as he was, fear. He'd been doing what he was trained and encouraged to do for two or three years, he knew he was supposed to just keep twisting, bucking, leaping, hopping, starfishing and calvicating until the gate opened and the guys on horses choused him toward the exit. He knew he had to keep looking as if he was turning himself inside out, and that's what he did, but what in *hell* was this thing hanging down one side of him, the *thing* was supposed to land on the dirt and roll out of the way or run or something, but it was hanging and yelling bloody murder and he could smell her blood and Jesus he didn't want to hurt her, he didn't *want* to hurt her, they were just doin' their jobs, and then she was smelling him up closer than she'd ever wanted, his big sweat-slick glistening hide stretched tight over bulging muscle, and she didn't feel it but she knew she'd slammed face-first into that mountain of meat. Ker-thundering-pow.

And now, even with her nose packed and plugged and probably held on with Krazy Glue, it was as if she could smell the hospital— but not this one, the other one, when Gran had been there.

Lucy'd gone to the hospital with her. Savannah had phoned, she'd been on one of her extended visits, staying with Seely, and who knows, maybe she'd have told Kitty right off the bat, but it was Debbie answered the phone and Savannah didn't know her well enough to talk to her about it so she asked for Lucy. And Lucy turned from the phone after she'd hung it back up again and she had a strange look on her face. "You have to pack a bag and get ready for a kick in the gut, kid," she said. "The Old Biddy's had a stroke."

God, and hadn't she. Couldn't talk. Couldn't swallow. Couldn't manage much of anything. Three or four days into it all, Jimmy left and came back with all these little bottles out of the spice rack and he held them under her nose, one at a time, god knows why. She just looked at him and you could see, even though there was no change in the awful expression on her face, her poor old frozen face, you could see in her eyes she knew what he was trying to do for her. She blinked as fast as she could, and that wasn't fast at all.

It was because Jimmy'd had this big go-round with Savannah about smells. Savannah made supper one night and Jimmy had a fit about the spices. "And what the *fuck*," he yelled, "did you do to the rice?"

"Jesus, you going to spend your entire life stuffing your face with nothing but spuds?"

"There's nothing wrong with spuds!"

"Nothing wrong with rice, either."

"Rotten muck. Rotten *muck!*"

"I like it," they said Gran had said. "Something new. Nice to find something new."

"Rat meat, probably. PatsyRatsy's goddam granddaughter, done up in some kind of rugrider sauce." And he'd gone off on what Savannah called his Triple-K rant.

"The grand dragon speaks," she taunted. "*Sieg Heil*, Jimmy."

"Muck. Bloody rotten muck. Stink the whole house out for weeks!"

"Oh, give up on it. If you don't want it, don't eat it."

"Bloody right I won't eat it! I don't like stuff that's *different*, okay? I like stuff to be the *same*, okay? I'm no fuckin' camel driver! They got different enzymes, they got a whole other digestive system. Hundreds of generations of them have grown up eating *crap* and they can digest it, but I can't because we didn't grow up eating *crap*, okay, we maybe ate shit but not *crap!*" And on and on, until finally everyone yelled, *Shut up Jimmy.*

He made himself a couple of grilled cheese sandwiches and went down into his fury hole to cut what used to be trees into horror faces. They said all the kids ignored him, just sat packing it away, yum yum is there more and Savannah said sure, she'd made enough for everyone to have seconds and warm up the next day and Jimmy hadn't eaten any so there'd be *lots* for everyone. There was that night, sure enough, but in the morning the leftovers were significantly diminished, Jimmy'd come up from his hellhole and warmed up rice and sauce and eaten a big bowl of it before he went to bed. Nobody said anything to him about it, but halfway through his second cup of coffee he rolled himself a cigarette, lit it, then sat holding it under his nose, sniffing at the blue smoke rising from the ash-tip, and then, in a voice so small and quiet they said you could hardly hear him, he announced, "I don't like things to change, see. When something new comes, it usually means something old has to go to make room for it, and I don't want to lose anything." And Savannah nodded, then stood behind him, with her arms around him and his head resting back against her belly. "It's okay, my Jimmy," she wept softly. "You're not losing anything. Hell, look at the increase in population already." And she kissed his cheek and he nodded.

And who knew *what* it was he was telling the old lady, but she died with the smells in her nose, cumin and turmeric and curry and mace.

They were afraid Jimmy would go crazy—he was never far from crazy at the best of times. But he was no worse than usual.

He bought a new suit and a white shirt and a nice plain red tie, he got new shoes and socks and underwear and he even made sure his hair was tied back neat. Dumb bugger wouldn't cut it, though. No, he said over and over and over, I sure as hell will *not* cut my hair.

"Well, Jesus, you look like some kind of *wildman!*"

"Since you don't know fuck all about it, why don't you just zip your damn lip? I have my reasons and they are *my* reasons, and *she* would understand, so shut up and get outta my face or I'll stay home!"

But he wouldn't have stayed home. He'd made all the arrangements, said he knew exactly what she wanted because they'd talked about it lots. Probably not, probably just some idea he had but what the hell, if it meant that much let him do it. He looked as if his guts had been taken out of his body and put on ice for the duration, but he pulled it all together. Nothing bizarre. Told the mortician to forget about the preacher part. "She wouldn't spit on the fuckers when she was alive, they don't get a go at her when she's dead."

So they sat quietly, not even any music, because Jimboh told the guy if he didn't turn off the grisly grim noise he'd find some other place to do things the way the Old Biddy would have wanted. No music. No preacher. No flowers. Just some candles flickering. And they sat there and they just thought about her and about everything, and then that was that and it was over and nothing left but a little waxed cardboard box with maybe four pounds of grit, bits and ashes in it.

Rules and regulations said you could only dispose of the ashes in certain ways. Like pay through the nose to buy an entire cemetery plot for it. You couldn't scatter the ashes just any old where—what about the public-health risks? Jesus, they're dumping the most unnatural shit in the drinking water, filling the air with you don't even want to know what, but heaven forfend the ashes of the dead be given to the wind.

"Can't even bury your cat in your own back yard without breaking the law," Jimmy grumbled. "I guess if the old budgie bird goes you have to fork over twenty-five bucks for the vet to incinerate it. And then what? Where do they dump *those* ashes?"

Who cared where the budgie bird went? They were trying to figure out what to do with *Gran*, never mind a damn dead budgie. "She didn't *like* the damn cemetery," Jimmy said, trying hard not to cry. "She just *hated* the damn place. Said it was morbid."

"Well, you can't just stuff her in the linen closet between the towels and the facecloths. Get real, Jimmy, for chrissake."

"Yeah," Seely chimed, "what you gonna do, put her under the sink with the Brillo pads and sudsy ammonia? Store her in the garage with the lawnchairs and roto-tiller? Maybe set the friggin' box up on the shelf with the rose dust and plant food and lawn fertilizer? And *why* do you have all that stuff and this place looks like a hay field?"

"Fuck you with the hay-field crack. Nothing wrong with grass." And he sat with the damned box in his hands, holding it as if the nicest dreams of his life were inside it.

"Well, you can't just pack it around with you. It's too big to hang around your neck like a religious medal or something."

"Up yours, Savannah."

"It ain't goin' up mine, Jim, forget that idea."

"Well"—Seely sounded totally bored—"what in hell would *she* care? She's *dead,* for cryin' out loud! You could go over and step on the little pedal on the trash bucket and drop that dreary box in with the teabags and coffee grounds and put it out for garbage collection on Tuesday, and nobody would know, and Gran wouldn't care."

"Oh, shut up. You just say things like that for attention." But somehow Seely had done it, he no longer had the empty holes where his eyes were supposed to be. He almost grinned. "Fuck, they'd be mad, eh? I mean, it's the city is charging all that money for graves, and it's the city says you can't bury your cat in your yard, and it's the city says we're not supposed to bury Gran's ashes in the field, and it's the city got its hand in your pocket all the way, but it would be the damned *city* picked up the garbage with the ashes. And they'd do themselves out of the money they're trying to screw out of us."

In the end they sat in the field, same as if they were sitting on the sofa watching "Gunsmoke". Little kids running around nattering and nagging each other and the honeybees busy in the lilac flowers, and Jimmy took the lid off the wax-coated box and let the wind have what it wanted. When it was time for them to leave he just dug a little hole and put the big cinders or whatever in the hole and tamped them in good. Carried the stupid box back and burned it in the furnace. And that, as they say, was that.

He made a bench—Jesus, it looked like something you'd have to sell your car to buy from a furniture store. Put the bench out near the lilac bush. Went there on nice days to do his work. Said he was visiting with her. Said she gave him real good ideas.

Creepy. Even creepier, Seely acted as if what Jimmy was saying was absolutely rock-solid true. And Savannah, well, whatever else was going on with her, she was still undeniably Savannah. She just shrugged and said, "Hey, if it makes him feel better, why knock it? It doesn't seem to hurt him, and it sure doesn't hurt anyone else, so what's the big prob here?"

The next time Kitty floated up out of that place she was able to sit up a bit, although it sure did make her head ache. Felt like hammers going off. And then that stopped and it felt so good. Funny, maybe that's where they got the joke about bang your head with a rock, it'll feel so good when you stop.

She asked for a mirror. The nurse didn't want to give her one but Christie just pulled a Christie and brought one from home. Kitty looked at herself and didn't know quite what to say or what to do. "Jesus."

"Aitch," Christie agreed.

She couldn't see enough of her hand to get an idea of what it looked like. Whatever else they'd done, they seemed to have put pins or needles or wires or some damn thing into *something*; the tips of whatever it was showed through the ends of her fingers. "I bet that hurts." Christie's big brown eyes flooded.

"No." And it was true. Either the nerves had been killed off or the stuff they shoved into her butt every three hours or so was powerful goof. She hoped it was the stuff. Dead nerves seemed like serious business.

There were other contributions to the mess, too. She saw them when Christie helped her out of the fever-sweat-stinking pajama top and gave her a good wash with nice warm water and some pink fruit-and-flower soap she'd brought to replace that homemade lye soap the hospital was using. "Take that stuff back home with you," Lucy suggested. "Be great for killing sucking lice in the horse blankets."

"Dissolve the blanket, though."

Big reddish-brown bruises, some scabbing-over scrapes and the clear imprint of a hoof on her rump. "I'll have that bastard served up with Yorkshire pudding and gravy," she vowed.

"He's so tough you wouldn't get your fork in the gravy, let alone the damned meat. Besides, he was only doing his job."

She felt better with her own blood and sweat washed off her, and a clean pajama top. Christie even brushed her hair, taking it easy around the goose eggs and mourning the bald patch where they'd shaved around a big scalp cut that looked worse than it was. "Maybe that's where I got the headache," she yawned.

The doctor came in then and shone a light in her ears, in her eyes, then he changed the bulb thing on the end of his shiny flashlight and took another look in her eyes. They got busy then. The nurse had to go for a cart with something that looked like a mini milking machine, and the others had to leave the room. He didn't exactly kick them out, he just suggested the cafeteria was open and they all looked as if they needed a good bowl of soup and a bit of a break. "We'll keep her occupied for a while," he promised, and smiled. But the smile didn't go past his lips so even Lucy took the hint and effed off.

They pushed a needle in her upper arm and stood chatting to each other as if it was Sunday afternoon in the park. She was going to suggest they get the fuckin' lead out, but then whatever had been in the needle hit the bull's eye and she didn't care if she never spoke again.

This was a whole other place. This wasn't sleep, and it wasn't that soft warm place between sleep and waking, this was like floating in something not quite water. Drifting. Bobbing gently up and down. Knowing full well they were hauling literally yards of packing out of her nose, knowing it probably hurt like a son of a bitch, knowing she didn't feel a thing, not even the pressure or release of pressure as the Vaseline-soaked bloodstained mess was gently pulled free. It coiled in a basin like a long, skinny snake or a great big worm or something.

Nice of them to bring some of Jimmy's stuff to decorate the room. She didn't know Jimmy had gone beyond masks and started making entire figures; but she could see at least one. Just beyond the edge of the bed there was what had to be a sculpture, because if it wasn't a sculpture it was a fuckin' real live spook and that wasn't possible. She was all set to say something about it when they turned on the mini milking machine and started vacuum cleaning the inside of her christly head.

"Hey," she managed.

"You have a blood clot," the doctor said, as casually as if he was telling her she had a thumb or a toe or an anus. "This isn't pleasant, I know, but it'll be a lot less pleasant if this clot moves."

"In my brain?" Jesus aitch, isn't that the same thing as a stroke? Didn't they say that's probably what happened with Gran, a clot moved and lodged and good-night nurse, goodbye kids?

"Not yet," he said absently, intent on what he was doing. Whatever it was, it got past whatever they'd shoved in her arm. It was like a hot red wire being shoved into her eyeball. She figured she'd better tell him that, he might not know, it might be important.

"That hurts," she said. He stopped right away, took a step back, put the nozzle or whatever in a little kidney-shaped dish and the nurse poured some kind of clear crap on it. He said something and the nurse nodded, handed him what looked like one of those little spray bottles you get when you've got a cold and your nose is so stuffed you can't breathe. "This ought to fix it," he said, no smile on his face at all.

She heard the squirt. Felt nothing at all. Then the euphoria hit, and she just grinned, bruises, split lip, the whole shiterooni, so what, she grinned and knew she must look goofy. "What's that? You could get rich selling it on the street."

"That's an idea. Want to go into partnership? You handle the advertising, I'll supply the spray." And then he was sucking and sucking and sucking. Well, not him, but the bird beak he had in his hand.

Jimmy's carving moved closer, came up the other side of the bed, leaned across, elbows resting on the blankets, chin cupped in the palm of that dark brown hand. "You shouldn't do that," she said quietly, "the guy with the bird beak might not like it."

She heard the doctor chuckle and say something to the nurse about the effect of...she didn't hear what. The spook turned its head and stared at her with that big strange face. Round round eyes. She saw a seal diving into the waves, coming up again, turning, head above the water, staring. But it wasn't a seal, it was one of Jimmy's masks.

It reached out with a stick, a carved stick, looked as if something vine-like had grown so tightly around an arbutus branch that the vine and branch had grown together. Someone or something had taken the two-in-one and wrapped copper sheeting around one end, and from the strip of copper came what looked for all the world like either the tail of a horse or some young woman's long long *long* ponytail. Fastened to that, or in that, a big dark brown feather with a beaded shaft. The stick touched her chest and for a brief flash she felt as if she'd been slammed with something icy cold and about twice as heavy as the critter who'd won the last round.

The doctor was talking, sounding urgent, the nurse was answering, the vacuum cleaner was making an awful buzzing, but it wasn't that bird-beak mini milking machine vacuum cleaner, something else was making the buzzing sound and she felt her chest heave and fresh sea-scented breeze was filling her lungs. Ah, that was one helluva lot better than Dettol stink or Lysol stench or the nasty smell of whatever it was the nurse had poured on the end of the nozzle.

"Nah, nah," Gran said, her words thick with Scots. "Nah my precious one, not the now."

"Jimmy misses you," Kitty said clearly. "He cuts himself sometimes. Locks his door for days on end. Says it's nobody's business but his own."

"Aye, and he's right. Leave him be. Tell them all tae leave him be. He knows what he's about. He's nae dangerous. Except to his own sel'."

"Got it." The doctor breathed a sigh of relief.

"Tell the wee man thank you, Kitty."

"Thank you," Kitty said obediently to the doctor.

"Nae him!" Gran scolded, laughing.

"Thank you," Kitty said to the Jimmy's-mask man. He nodded and waved his stick, then moved away from the right side of the bed, moved to the left and watched over the doctor's shoulder, briefly. He nodded as if he was totally content with the state of the world and all its affairs. Then he danced stiffly, stiffly, shaking his stick, sending bright golden threads spinning from the end of it, coiling threads that drifted, but not aimlessly, and wrapped themselves around Kitty, chasing away the cold she hadn't realized was invading her limbs. "That's better," she said, and tried to smile.

The doctor was clinking stuff and rattling stuff in a *most* annoying way. She lifted her hand to give him a push and the nurse took it in her own and squeezed gently. "Just a bit more," she said softly. "Just put up with it a bit more."

"It fuckin' *hurts*, okay?" Kitty snapped. The nurse laughed. "I don't feel a thing and neither does he," she teased.

"I went to this friggin' dentist one time." Kitty felt as if her mouth had a mind of its own. "I told him what was wrong. No, he had to haul out the old X-ray machine and zap me with roentgens, as if they weren't the least bloody bit dangerous. Then he says, Listen, he says, I gotta do a root canal. Well, I said, I know how it is, good sense walks when bullshit talks, but you freeze that bugger stone solid and if I say it hurts you *do* something about it, okay? So he says okay and he starts with the damn needles and then he says, There, he says, that's got it. He drills this friggin' hole in my tooth and then he gets this thing looks for all the world like a cross between a crochet hook and a little screw or spring thing or something. Up it goes and down it comes and that's okay, and up it goes and down it comes and that's okay that time too, but about the fourth or fifth time I said, Hey, I said, that one hurt. No, he says, you only thought it did, it's frozen, he says, you didn't feel a thing, and he puts'er up and I tell you I damn near shit! I didn't mean for it to happen but he zinged me with that damn little thing and I yelped and my hand came up and just *zap* on the side of his cheeky face. Here here, he says. You're fuckin' right, here here, I said, right here in my face and all the way up through my eye into my head. Well, he says, that's impossible. And finally I said, Could you just maybe take a little step back and survey what you've got here in front of you? You are the one with the tool. I am the one with the *tooth*. Now when you use your tool on my tooth, *you* aren't apt to feel bugger nothing, but I'm sitting here with the tooth and I'm telling you it fuckin' hurts, and if you hurt me again I am going to beat the shit right out of you. So off he goes for more of his roentgens and he does another X-ray and he says, Oh, excuse me, this is very rare, he says. You can fuckin' bet, I say, if it's rare or weird or inconvenient or expensive, I'll be the lucky one who's got it. Well, he says, you have a double nerve in your tooth, see, he says, holding it up like it's something to be proud of, See, it makes like a Y and there's only one canal at the bottom but up near the top there's two and only ONE of them has taken the freezing. So he froze'er all up again and finished what he was doing, and then I had to go back the next day and he got all set to finish'er off and I said to him, Okay, dude, here's the word, I said. You go get a Q-Tip and you do your ears real good, because the minute I say ouch either you grab the freezing needle or you'll be grabbing your nuts." She knew she was babbling and she didn't care, she knew the nurse was laughing as much at her as with her and she didn't care about that either. "He did just fine. See, that one there,"—she pointed—"it got finished off with a gold cap, I figured it was as good as money in the bank, better because I could see it any time I took a mind to."

She felt pressure on the front of her face, and frowned.

"That hurt?" the doctor asked. Then he half-chuckled. "I don't want a fucking slap on the fucking side of my fucking face, right?"

"People," she said clearly, "who put a 'g' on the end of 'fuckin''' are swearing. Without the 'g' it's a description, like an adverb or an adjective. As soon as you whap that 'g' on the end, it's swearin'. It doesn't so much *hurt* as feel sore, if you know what I mean."

"Sniff," he suggested. She sniffed, and heard the squirt. "Whee," she gasped. The euphoria hit her again. Jimmy's spook was laughing, laughing, laughing, and she realized he wasn't wearing a mask at all, it was just what his face was. And she knew he was a he because she could see he was a he but she knew there were others pretty much like him and they weren't dangling a woody. He pointed his stick at her and the golden threads looped out, moved slowly, wrapped around Kitty, and she knew she was going somewhere.

When she came back the cart was gone, the mini milking machine was gone, the doctor was gone, but the nurse was there. She had a blood pressure riggins attached to Kitty's arm and was watching it carefully.

"Hey," Kitty managed. "Who do I have to fuck around here to get a cup of tea?"

"You try it with anybody but me," Christie said clearly, "and you'll think what you're like right now is just a preview."

"I," the nurse said clearly, "am never first in line. I don't think it's fair. But if you promise not to do what you did about three hours ago, I'll get you some tea."

"What did I do?"

"Scared the pants off us all." Christie came into view then, and Kitty saw with shock and a kind of deep sorrow that Christie had been crying. Not weeping, crying.

"Hey." Kitty held out her good hand. "Hey, Christie, it's okay."

"I thought you were going to die," Christie said, voice trembling.

"Nobody asked me." Kitty kissed Christie's hand. "You should'a asked me, darlin', I'd'a told you I'm not going to die."

"Could'a fooled me too," the nurse said flatly. "As for asking you and getting told the truth—you were too busy telling me about how you got that gold tooth. You didn't say one word to ME about not dying!"

She let Lucy and Debbie come in then. Lucy just looked at Kitty and she shook her head, and Kitty realized Lucy was long past what anybody would call young. "You!" Lucy's voice shook. "Boy, when you want attention you'll go to any lengths to get it. Don't you *ever* do this to me again, you hear?"

The tea was good. Just the way Kitty liked it. Not strong, god save us from that black bitter brew like Gran drank, she thought, sipping gratefully. Gran damn near boiled the stuff. Never understood how Kitty liked to make the tea so she could get her own cup out of the pot first, while the liquid was still light brown. "Pony pee," the old woman called it.

"Never drank pony pee," Kitty answered. Once. "You're ahead of me on that, I guess."

"You be careful," Gran answered. "Nobody likes a smartass."

Funny how Lucy had been when Gran was dying. All those years of calling her the Biddy or the Biddy-Bitch, years of hardly keeping in touch, of hardly ever writing or even phoning. And then she walked into that room as if there were no hard feelings at all. Moved to the side of the bed, reached out, touched her mother's face and said, "Hey, you. Not doing too well, I see."

The old woman wanted to say something. Anybody could have seen that. Tears coming from her eyes and Jimmy getting his shirt in a knot. And Lucy just said, "It's okay, Momma. Hell, we all get older and wiser. It amazes me how much smarter you are now than you were when I was sixteen." And everything between them was fine.

The headache was gone. That horrible dull thump thump thump had been chased away by the needle in the arm or the squirt up the nose or maybe the little suction dealy-job. But her hand was some sore. The tea didn't perk her up, she'd hoped it would. What it did was make her realize she needed to puke. She grabbed the kidney basin, turned her head to one side and just let'er rip. Four spews and it was over. "God, I feel better," she sighed.

"Glad you do," Debbie said, "but I have to tell you it just about wrote finish to *my* day."

Christie got a toothbrush from the drawer and smeared toothpaste on it, even got the basin so Kitty could spit, and some kind of horrible mouthwash stuff to rinse her mouth, although once she'd done that she wished she hadn't bothered—she'd rather have the taste of tooth-paste than that yellow foamy stuff.

She had half a second cup of tea and knew she'd done as much as she was able to for at least a few hours. "I'm sorry." She felt the cup slipping, then someone, Lucy probably, took it from her. "I don't think I can stay awake."

She didn't hear them leave. She went deep into somewhere, then came maybe a quarter of the way back out of it.

She was walking along an unpaved road, near but not alongside a wide river. Across the black strip of water, on the other side, the sky glowed with the lights of a city. There were lights on this side too, but not down here—they were up and beyond the bank that rose steeply to her right. Ahead of her the massive pilings of a bridge thrust up to a span which crossed the river. Cars were going across the bridge in both directions, she could hear the sound of their engines, a sound made faint by the swishing chatter of the oil-slicked, reeking river. The ground was littered with garbage; some of it defied description, some of it had once been simple stuff like newspapers and discarded juice containers. She knew she was going to go under the bridge. The road passed between two sets of supports, she supposed delivery vans came down here, avoiding traffic. She doubted, though, that the road was a real one or that you'd find it on a city map. She had no idea why she was going to walk under the bridge, no idea what she was doing on this ugly road, in this ugly smelly place. And then some-thing was coming at her head, something dark, something like a huge bat, one hell of a huge black heavy fucking *bat!* Wings fluttering, it swooped for her face and neck, swooped to rend her throat, drink her blood, cover her face with its lice-infested furry body and smother her, filling her eyes with its stinking fur....

And it was finished. She didn't know if the bat had grabbed her or not; the dream or nightmare or whatever in hell it was was over and she was watching herself lying in bed sound asleep. Sound asleep, but terrified.

3

When Lucy phoned to tell Jimmy that Kitty had been hurt, his first impulse was to phone Glen. He had the receiver in his hand when his second thought took over. So he phoned Savannah.

Victor answered the phone. In the background Jimmy could hear Elaine practicing on the five thousand dollars' worth of piano her fathers had bought when it became obvious the kid was good, the kid didn't mind practicing and the kid, given half a chance, could go far. Personally, Jimmy thought it was all very well and good if you had the money, and the Three Wise Men had it, no question, might as well spend it on a fine piano as anything else. Especially if the kid didn't mind practicing, enjoyed playing and was good at what she did. As for "go far," however, stuff that one where it ought to go. How far? The best symphony orchestra in the country, maybe in the world, paid its musicians just about enough to survive in a glum hole and eat grilled rodent tails on dry toast. Do better in a damned jazz band.

"Hi, it's Jimmy. Is Savannah handy?"

"Hi, Uncle Jimmy. Yes, she's here. If you don't mind hanging on half a minute, I'll go get her. Maybe you'd like to talk to Alfie while I'm getting Mom? Alfie's decided talking on the phone is the most fun he's had in his whole entire life."

"Sure." Jimmy raised his eyebrows even though there was nobody to see him do it. Savannah's kids were so damned polite it made you wonder how they got that way.

"H'lo? Zat you Unca Jimmy?"

"Hi, Alfie. You being a good boy?"

"I think so. You know what?"

"What?"

"Edward goes to school. And Martine goes to school. But not me. And not Bictorier."

"Victoria, Alfie. Sort of like Victor, but with a different ending to it. Victor-ee-ah. Can you say that?"

"Mommy's here. I got to say bye-bye now, Unca Jimmy."

"Hi, Jimmy. Is it an emergency or just a mild panic?"

"It's kinda halfways in between," and he grinned because Savannah was right, he didn't phone just to talk. Savannah did, she said she didn't give a shit how high the phone bill was, some things were important, and anyway it was cheaper than taking a plane with all those kids tagging along. He told her what Lucy had told him.

"Christ, I wish she'd get a job running a cash machine in a supermarket or maybe selling tickets at the movie house. What are we supposed to do now?"

"Nothin'. Lucy said it was mostly bruises and scrapes once they got the blood clot out and brought her back from wherever in hell it was she went while they were doing that. Said she was fine, no paralysis or anything."

"Oh, Jesus, isn't that great news? Just a bit of brain damage, maybe."

Savannah, he knew, would pack the tribe in the station wagon and head out inside of about half an hour, no longer than it took to grab some clothes and stuff for the kids, and kiss the Three Wise Men. (Did she go by age, alphabetical order or size, and if the latter did she start with the shortest and work up to the tallest or vice versa?)

"Savannah, there's no use you racing off to be with her, she'll be out of hospital before you get there."

There was a pause while Savannah thought about that. Then a sigh. "Yeah," she agreed. But that doesn't mean I have to stay here and worry myself sick. Get the backhoe into the hovel and clean out your mess, we'll be there in the morning."

"This place isn't a mess," he laughed.

And it wasn't. Jimmy kept everything so neat you'd think he had a degree in Home Economics. Or that nobody really *lived* in the house! Down in his work room it was less tidy. He didn't go there to clean up, he went there to work, and you don't do that without bending a few edges and rounding off some corners. But there were still things to do to prepare for the onslaught.

He phoned Seely and told her about Kitty and about Savannah coming. Seely said hang on, she'd go to the grocery store right away and get a whack of stuff and bring it over with her.

While he was waiting for Seely, Jimmy scrubbed potatoes and put them to boil in the biggest pot he could find, then put two dozen eggs on to hard-boil and brought the last two free-range roasting chickens out of the freezer to thaw. When that was done, he finally phoned Glen.

"He's asleep right now," the gorp said. Fred the Friendly Faggot, Jimmy called him. Still, you had to hand it to him, lots of others would have just hit the old road. Well, how far would the poor fucker get anyway, it was a one-way street no matter how you looked at it. For sure, if Glen had the goddamn thing, Fred would have it.

"How is he?"

"Not good. But at least he cried tonight. It's the first time he's done that since they told him."

"Fuck, eh? Listen, when he wakes up, can you tell him Savannah's heading up here with the kids?" Then he told Fred about Kitty bashing her face to hell on the front shoulder of some huge animal that ought to be turned into hot dogs or something.

Fred made all the right noises. Well, if you could get yourself past the fact the guy was a bumlover, you'd have to admit he wasn't a bad sort, considering the sort he was, of course. How in hell he'd put up with Glen Goofball, even before he got sick, was one of the mysteries of the known universe, but each to his own poison.

Jimmy had told Glen he was in line for the jackpot as soon as they heard about Greg. But hell, that was five years ago anyway, and Glen had laughed and said no way, not me, as if he was made out of stainless steel. Hell, he'd said, I haven't even *seen* the man for six years. Nothing, he said, can fester for that long. As it turned out, it could. Or maybe it hadn't been Greg after all. God knows Glen hadn't had a quiet life!

Jimmy himself held to the theory the whole thing was the result of a CIA experiment gone wrong. Like that fuckin' headshrinker in

Montreal who did all those grim things with nutbars, giving the dis-
turbed some kind of stuff that wiped their minds, sent them all the way
around the bend or turned them into zombies, take your pick.

Jimmy figured Cuba was involved in it too. Can't have some little
floating rock of a place that actually thinks it's a country giving the
one-finger salute to the great Amerikan eagle. Can't let a bunch of
greasers, spics and niggers get away with a thing like that. So they
looked around, found some kind of fuckin' germ and headed off with
it, planning to wipe out all the pigs in the country because pig meat
was what those revolutionary bastards ate. Wipe out the pigs and
starve'em to death. Except the swine flu changed the way feline
wotzit changed and became Parvo virus and nearly wiped out the
dogs. Only instead of dogs it was people got it.

The fucking experts yammered on about green monkeys in
Africa. Well, think about it. Monkeys. Nobody *ate* them. So who was
fucking the monkeys? Not a very likely story. Although if there'd
been some around to fuck Glen would probably have been the one to
do it, he'd had a go at damn near everything else you could think of
except maybe Wilkinson Sword razor blades.

There was some guy who sounded as if he knew what he was talking about who said the whole awful thing was because in 1902 or
1920, or some time way back then, they'd done experiments on
malaria or yellow fever or something you caught from mosquito bites
and they'd wound up injecting people with what they thought were
blood antibodies from people who'd been bit, god knows what all
they did when you come to think of it, look at Pavlov and his dogs or
Banting and *his* poor bloody dogs, they'd do anything at all, that
bunch, and get away with it in the name of scientific research. But
they had guys in Manchester, England, dead in 1938 of symptoms
almost anybody today would recognize. So the blood bank did nothing. Why warn the people? After all, in Amerika you paid big money
for a pint of blood, it was a stock market commodity, not something
you got because you needed it, something you got if they could pull
money out of you as fast as they dripped the stuff into you. Why warn
people and maybe lose a million dollars or so?

Well, Glen hadn't got it from contaminated blood and he didn't
get it because he was Haitian either. Might have got it from a dirty
needle, but that was choice number two.

God, it was awful. Sometimes all Jimmy wanted to do was cry. He'd done a lot of that. Now even Glen had been able to cry. He'd maybe get Savannah to go over with him, take a plate of food, though Glen wouldn't eat more than two mouthfuls. No sense asking if Glen would like to come over here, Seely would have a fucking great fit, tuck her kids under her arm, storm out the house slamming the door—probably take Savannah's kids with her—no need for a big hoo-rah, just make Glen feel even worse. Savannah wouldn't take her kids over, but she'd go herself. Last time she even sat on the edge of Glen's bed and held his hand and said she loved him and if he needed anything she wanted Fred to call on her. Put a big picture of the kids on the bedside table. Glen didn't so much as really look at it, but the idea was nice.

"Whole fuckin' family is nuts," Jimmy muttered.

"Pardon?"

"Oh, it's okay, Fred, I was nittering to myself is all. How you doing?"

"I'm fine, Jim."

"How you guys doing for money?"

"Not too good." Fred tried to laugh and failed. "Nobody seems to have any jobs. Not around here, not for me. And Glen, well, there's no use trying to move him to the city, it would cost a fortune for an apartment and even then they'd evict us as soon as they saw him, and the hospices are full, so here we sit on welfare."

"You got a bank account? Gimme the number."

"I wasn't putting the arm on you...."

"Oh shut up, fuck's sake, he's my brother, okay? Gimme the number!"

Which didn't mean that he loved Glen. Didn't even like him, if the truth be known. It shall set ye free. Bullshit. More apt to tie you up in knots. You ought to be able to give your brother something more than just money. What was money, anyway? All money was, really, was an agreement none of us had made but all of us had to honor, an agreement that certain things were worth so many certain other things. Diamonds. Diamonds are forever, diamonds are precious, diamonds are rare. Bullshit. Diamonds aren't so much. Only the agreement says diamonds are scarce and wonderful. You want scarce, find hummingbird eggs. You want wonderful, take those flower rocks on the beach on Texada Island, big or little ones, white with a pattern of little black flowers imbedded through them. But no, it's not flower rocks from the beach at Texada, it's diamonds, because the guys with the armies made the rules and they said diamonds because they were too fuckin' stupid to know about flower rocks. Maybe he'd take some from his collection and go over to see Glen and give him some. Glen would understand. You had to be able to give your brother something more than just money.

He checked the potatoes, turned the heat down under the eggs, went out to the greenhouse for a handful of green onions, then phoned Linda. Get that over with before Seely arrived. Even if she didn't say one single solitary word, Seely could bloody well nag you to death with looks.

So Linda was a hooker. So what? "One in the family is enough," Seely had yelled. When you were talking about terminal viruses, Jimmy would have said one in the family was one too many; but he had absolutely nothing to worry about as far as that was concerned. Of course Seely could only envision one kind of encounter. "Jimmy, if rubber was safe nobody would ever have a flat tire!"

"Seel, how did you get your kids?" he asked. That shut her up. Mean way to do it, but if you didn't shut her up, Seely could go on for more time than a person could endure. Just pray to god when she came over she left the frigging Legatee at home.

You wouldn't think a goddamned rat could live six or seven years, but PatsyRatsy did. And just before she finally croaked she had Patsy Two. Why she hadn't been dropping litters every six weeks like normal rats was a mystery. Seely claimed it was because Patsy got a few grains of birth control pill every day, but Seely said a lot more than her prayers and that was too ridiculous for anyone to take seriously. In any event PatsyRatsy Two wasn't her mother's daughter in every way. Nasty bitch of a rat, that one, even Seely had trouble putting up with her antics. And more damn baby rats than you'd want to even think about, and what do you do with them. Jimmy knew damn well that very often the Graingers just got there before Seely did, flushed the damned things down the toilet, bye-bye baby. The children of a pet seem to be pets, even if they aren't.

But all you have to do is stop thinking "pet" and think "rat" and the solution presents itself. "Hey, Seely," Jimmy put forth, "I have a contact at a pet store. You give me Patsy Two's babies as soon as they're weaned and I'll see to it they get to the pet store."

"Pet store?" The hope in her face made him feel cheap.

"Yeah. In the city."

She didn't ask any questions at all. Just brought him the litters as soon as they were weaned. And they went to the pet store all right. Got put on the bus in a metal box with a metal grille in it to allow air to enter. The guy from the pet store met the bus and took the rats, as many as a dozen per litter. Got to feed the exotic snakes *something!* Of course, at two dollars a rat and seven dollars on the bus each way for the cage, there wasn't a whole helluva lot of profit in it. You weren't going to cruise town in a BMW with a set of rat's ears for a hood ornament on that kind of money.

But the kids, predictably enough, wanted to keep one of the babies. Then it was a baby each. Then you had two or three litters every six weeks or so going over to Uncle Jimmy's place, so the metal cage got more crowded and the freight down was by the pound so sometimes it was more than seven dollars. Only the empty cage coming back didn't change.

Seemed to work out to one rat providing food for one snake. Make you wonder why the people with snakes didn't have a cage of rats, too. But how do you feed a pet to a pet? Some people puked when they saw what guppies did to baby guppies, yum yum yum.

Then on TV there was this thing about the woman just ten or twelve miles away who found an injured baby barn owl and took it home to look after it, and when it had grown and was healed she had to teach it to hunt. When it could hunt she turned it loose, and felt so good about it all she took in a couple of hawks who had run into some power lines. Next thing you know she has to build bigger pens and people are taking her all kinds of injured birds. All of whom need to be fed. So they had this thing on TV about how it was costing her more money than she had, could people please contribute something. Each mouse cost a dollar, each owl ate at least one mouse a day, hawks even more, and what is a mouse, really, but a small rat? No need for the damned freight on the bus!

Jimmy went over and talked to her. She stared at him. He showed her the diagrams he'd made, the dimensions, how he could get most of the stuff from the dump. "Not wood," he told her, "they'll gnaw through wood. But there's all these old metal hot water tanks, right? Take a welding torch and cut the top off the tank, put heavy mesh over top, they can't eat through that."

She thought he was nuts. Nodded her head and said she'd think about it, but he knew she was only interested in her birds. So he built the damned thing at home. Next time Seely brought over a litter he put it in the affair he'd built. Left them alone, made sure they had food and water, was all. They didn't seem to mind they were living in their own shit, why should he mind if they didn't? Every week now, he took half-grown rats over to the Owl Lady and she paid him for their feed. Six dollars something a fifty pound sack for Buckerfield's eighteen-percent protein rabbit food, and the rats thrived on it.

Of course Patsy Two, nasty as she was, came to a bad end. She bit Lizzy. Grabbed the kid by the finger and hung on, and that was her undoing. Lizzy was so much like Kitty it made a person laugh. "Fuckin' WHORE!" Lizzy yelped. Bent over, put her hand on the floor with the spoiled-brat rat still chomping her finger, ugly yellow teeth clenched right through the ball on the end of it. Then Lizzy stepped on Patsy Two. Cruncheroo.

But Patsy Two had babies at the time, and nothing would do but one of them had to replace the dead bitch. And no blaming the kids for that one, it was Seely all the way. "Oh, she looks just like her grandma," she crooned.

"Rats don't have grandmas!" he yelled, but of course they do if you're Seely the Psychotic. Who, for reasons known only to her—reasons of total uninterest to Jimmy—had called the damned thing the Legatee. "It means she has inherited it all," she said.

"Oh shut up, Seely, for god's sake."

"God has nothing to do with this."

"No, I'm damn sure he doesn't."

Pray God she didn't bring it with her, because it was too creepy for words the way that rat, no sooner than she'd arrived, would find a way out of the house and into the back yard, where she'd get herself up on top of the holding pens and if you didn't know better you'd think she had herself a visit with *that* friggin' family while Seely visited with Jimmy. It didn't bear thinking about; it made you feel weird as hell, the damned rat up there chittering and squeaking away and all the rats in the half hot-water tank squeaking back, nitter natter did you hear what ScalyTail did last week, it was so cute, I can't tell you how I laughed.

The white ones didn't go to the owls, though. They went down to the city, and not for the snakes' suppers, either. Ten bucks each he got for them. Plus the drip at the pet store paid the freight. Well, Jimmy knew what made them white. Inbreeding was what did it. He figured if he could get some of them to grow tumors on the outside of their skulls, like those goddamned fancy goldfish with the big orange bulbs of stuff—looked like clusters of grapes or something, only smaller and a different color—if he could get the rats to grow something like that on their skulls, say, or their noses, he could probably get rich. After all, there's always the fainting goats.

Of course, if the wolves left any scraps of evidence the wildlife guy would put a trap there, and when the wolves came back to finish up the leftovers, *bang* on the old leg, usually one of the alphas, *snap* and *crunch* and you're not going anywhere. Bang bang in the head.

He mashed the potatoes, added the chopped onion, peeled and put in the hard-boiled eggs, mixed up some mayonnaise, put in some horseradish, added three carrots; grated fine, stirred it all up and left it to cool. That was a start. Only two roasters. Jesus, hardly more than a hors d'oeuvre, horace do-over, whore's ovaries. Better get a couple of salmon out and thaw them too. Slow those kids down a bit.

And there were people out there in what they called the real world who said Jimmy was crazy. Did you see any fainting goats on the place? See any fish with big tumor things on their heads?

Seely got the girls to help her load the station wagon with groceries. They were so excited about Savannah and the kids coming for a visit that you'd think it didn't matter Kitty had just about had her head knocked off her shoulders. Some days you didn't know who to worry about first. Aunt Lucy with whatever it was she had in her leg: said the doctor had told her it was osteoarthritis but not to worry because there was no bone involvement or damage. Well Jesus, didn't the word "osteo" mean bone? So how could you have osteoarthritis without having bone arthritis? No, he said, just the lining of the hip joint. Just. Just the lining of the hip joint and, of course, the sciatic nerve.

Some days Aunt Lucy limped so bad she lurched. Other days it wasn't so much a limp as it was that she took a longer step with her good leg than she could take with her bad one.

And then there was Jimmy: most of the time he was just a bit odd, some of the time he was weird and a bit of the time he was loonytoons number one of all time.

The smartasses had finally found out that he wasn't an Indian, and you'd think that would mean nobody wanted to buy his stuff any more. He'd never put any tribe or band or whatever on his stuff, he'd never really said he *was* an Indian, he just hadn't said he wasn't—it was the smart farts in the city decided he was. Then all of a sudden they found out he wasn't. And the prices doubled. Now wasn't that something? Of course his work had changed, he didn't do poles or anything any more, mostly he did figures. The one he had going now was just about enough to make you suck in air until your lungs burst. He'd done a drawing first and stared at it for weeks, changed it around, grumbled to himself; then he did one about the size of a cereal bowl, and it was nice, but he ruined it cutting things out of it and fitting other things into it until he had what he thought he wanted. Then he did another one, bigger than a cereal bowl—about the size, maybe, of a big mixing bowl. He said she could have that when he finished the big one. And was it big? Savannah's piano would probably have fitted in there. Couldn't work on it in the basement, couldn't get the bloody great blocks of wood through the doorway. Got some guys to come and build this big roof, he called it his giant gazebo. Even had a stove in the middle, where he sat, to keep his butt from freezing.

How in the world would Jimmy find out that the old stories said it was the people on the Isle of Man who gave the gift of speech to all the people of the world? That's what this was all about, the giving of the gift of speech. All these people gathered around this fire. Made you wonder—well, made *Seely* wonder—how he'd done that. You could figure out the part about using arbutus wood because of its color, but damn, the way the flames curled like long skinny serpents' tongues or elongated bird beaks or something. And around the fire these people, shoulders hunched, most of them with their mouths closed and their faces not quite sad but certainly glum. And this woman, looked so much like Savannah that it made Seely's eyes flood with tears every time she saw it, until she quit thinking of it as "a woman" and just thought of Savannah herself, naked as a jaybird, hair blowing and wild, arms up, fingers spread, mouth open—and even if it wasn't there, even if there was absolutely nothing to suggest sound or words or noise or singing, you just knew, the way you know your toes are on the end of your feet, you knew Savannah was making a wonderful noise. And some of the people starting to straighten up, their mouths partway open, and some people almost fully erect, and a sort of happy smile trying to happen.

He had to make it in pieces so it could be shipped off in crates, chunk by chunk, to some place where they were going to cast it in bronze. Now *that* would be something to learn about! How you take a dead tree and cut it in blocks and then do this and that and the next thing and there it is in bronze, standing in the middle of the lawn in front of, if you don't mind, the Legislative Goddamn Assembly, with good old Queen Victoria just down the way there, gone green and covered with seagull shit.

That's maybe why Savannah called the latest baby Victoria. But maybe not. How could a woman have so many kids and still look so fine?

"No arguing, now," she warned.

"You always say that," Lizzy laughed, "and we don't even argue. Well, hardly at all."

"I know. But *we* always did and I hate it."

4

It made Savannah feel good to see the amount of work they'd done for her and the kids, made her feel special to know they'd gone so far out of their way to make her and the kids welcome. It wasn't easy for them. A lot of people in the old home town were fascinated with the number of kids she brought with her. More each time, they said. Well, maybe not each time, but it was true there was a heap and a stack of them. Sometimes she called them her pancakes, other times her waffles, made jokes about how PatsyRatsy's relatives were the ones at fault, they were the ones had set the example. And boy, didn't *that* just about rot the socks of the voting public, comparing the kids to litters of rats.

Who was that guy, the writer with all the white hair—was it Mitchell?—who wrote that thing about how we all tried to pretend childhood was the golden time, "best years of our lives", and really for most people it was a time of horror, fear and brutality? And still people pretended that what was usual wasn't, and what was rare was ordinary and everyday. Someone had made a car sign "Brat on board" with a doll for the window, an ugly little squalling doll, and the uproar was incredible, what an insult to children, how degrading, how dreadful, ban the doll, ban the sign, such a dreadful thing to say, to do, to demonstrate, to display. They're angels and we all love them so much, and don't look for one minute at how society ignores them.

Well, not her kids. Spoiled. Pampered. This was to them what going camping was to some others. Roughing it in the great wilderness. With roast beast and clean sheets.

They'd never asked, not any of them, why all the kids called her Mom, even the ones obviously not hers. Probably told the neighbors she was taking in fosters. Well, after all, they had to live here. Fine for her to drop in for a week, then go home leaving questions unanswered, but hard, maybe, on Seely and Jimmy.

Well, maybe not Jimmy, god only knew what Jimmy found ordinary, normal, acceptable, and what he found *not* any of that. "Hey," he said to the interviewer in that half-hour thing the National Film Board had done on him, "butt out, why don't you? You ever stop to think there's a reason they call it a *private* life?" Ask about his work and he'd talk, demonstrate, talk some more. Ask about any of the other and he'd clam up and give them the old lowered-eyebrows glare. Enigmatic, they called him. Well, why should they expect to know things his own family didn't know?

"Jason, if you don't sit down and behave yourself, I'm pulling over to the side of the road, the door will open, I'll get out, then YOUR door will open and the other kids will push you outside. I'll get back in, but you won't. And when I drive off you'll be standing here with your thumb out, trying to get some ignorant soul who doesn't know you to stop and give you a ride. You understand?"

"Yes, Mom."

"All right then. Fuckin' *sit*, will you?"

The Three Wise Men were pretty good in most ways, but useless as tits on a boar when it came to discipline. And their friends were no better. Kids ran wild from the time they could tuck their feet under them until they were maybe ten. Jesus, for awful! And then all of a sudden, almost overnight, you had people you could tolerate. Well, that might be how they did it—who knew, it might even work in some cases—but Savannah would go to hell if she was told what to do and how to do it by someone unable to look after themselves.

"Caroline, if you're going to cry I can always give you a good reason to do it. Would you like a broken arm?"

"He pushed me!"

"Who pushed you?"

"Alan pushed me!"

"I did not. You're squishing me! You're too fat anyway."

"Here, here, look who's talking about bulk. There was lots of room back there when we started out, why's it so crowded now?"

"Bobby's asleep and he's taking up half the seat."

"Well, for crying out loud, if he's asleep why's he even *on* the seat?"

She pulled over to the side of the road, got out, went to the back of the station wagon, got the rear door unlocked and open, half climbed in and hauled Bobby from the seat to the platform at the back. He grumbled but she told him gently to shut the hell up and go back to sleep, and put a small pillow under his head. Then she got out, locked the back door and got back behind the wheel.

"How's that? Better?"

"Yes," they chorused.

Victor was holding Victoria, who was almost asleep, sucking on her dummy-tit noisily. "Old slurp and gurgle doing all right?" Savannah checked her mirrors; the road was clear but she put on her signal anyway and pulled onto the road again. Her own little joke. Start with victory, end with victory. Go in a winner, come out a winner. The Three Wise Men might not know it, but Savannah had decided she'd had her last kid, thank you. Enough is, after all, enough, and usually you don't know it until you've got too much or too many. Well, she didn't have more than she could handle or more than she could tolerate, she'd just had enough of it.

Seely, now, she quit a lot sooner. Scandalized the whole friggin' town in the process. Savannah had never asked who the father was, or fathers were, as the case might be. They'd have to look farther afield than Savannah for someone who gave two hoots in hell. Probably Grainger but maybe not. But probably, otherwise why did he sign everything over to his wife, lock, stock and barrel, and then off himself like that? The story around town was that he had inoperable cancer and didn't want to put up with the pain. Who would? And if it was so, well, poor bugger, it should have been his choice.

"You okay, Elaine?"

"Fine, Momma. You?"

"Never better. Do you think that's the lights of Peepeeville up ahead?"

"I hope so!" Elaine laughed. "Boy, do I *ever* hope so!"

"Probably Popsville," Bobby hinted. "Maybe Chipsville."

"I thought you were asleep. Why did I stop the car, get out and move you if you're awake? I'm damn sure it's not Chipsville," Savannah pretended to grumble. "Chipsville was back an hour or two. This must be Comicbooksville."

"No, it's Peepeeville. It has to be or we're in real trouble."

The sleepers slept through the pit stop. That could only mean they'd have to pull over one more time before they got there. Well, it wasn't going to bend anyone out of shape to do that.

By the time the bladders were drained, the pop was opened and the chips were being passed around and munched up, Victoria was asleep, drooling the last bit of her formula. Savannah took her and laid her in the car bed beside herself on the front seat. The car bed was held firmly by not one, folks, but two seatbelts, and there was a harness built into it to keep the kid tethered just in case she woke up and made a lunge for something on the dashboard. Well, she was a bit young to try that one yet, but all the same Savannah did up the chest harness before she pulled back onto the highway. "You start fighting over those chips and I'm going to tell Victor and Elaine to pound you flat as pancakes, you hear?"

"Ah, lemme do it even if they don't fuss up," Victor asked. "Please, Mom? Can I hit'em, Mom, please?"

"He has all the fun," Elaine pretended to bicker. "He got to beat them up last time. I *never* get to beat them up all by myself."

"Then beat'em up, darlin'. No blood, though, the welfare takes a dim view."

And didn't it just. Didn't come around any more, though. Gave up on that when Carol moved in with them. Made it look as if there was a more, you should excuse the expression, normal setup. "You might have explained," the snoop said.

"None of your business," Savannah told her. "Why'n't you go out and do somethin' about the kids living in abandoned cars? Pull yourself out of my life. It's not *normal* to fixate on someone."

She'd thought for a while she'd open a restaurant. God knows she'd taken enough cooking courses to qualify. But you're more tied down than if you had puppies to train or cows to milk. At least with a kid you could tuck it under your arm and peel off. Try doing that with a restaurant.

They didn't mind that she just kept going to school. Seemed to think it was funny. Once they'd satisfied themselves she really *was* going to school, and not going off to meet a lover. As if she had the time, interest or inclination for crap like that. She knew when she had a good thing! And once Carol moved in, all that education came in handy, because Savannah could run the construction company for them. Put herself on the payroll. Start bringing order out of chaos. Now they had rental houses, too. Well, the kids would need something!

Silly, in a way, to be driving north and west to clutch with Jimmy and Seely when the reason behind it all was in a hospital to the south and east. Like the time Lucy was sick and someone had to phone Kitty and none of them wanted to so they all got together to do it. Except that time they all met at Lucy and Debbie's place. God, poor Debbie! She hadn't quite expected the entire tribe. Well, not the *entire* tribe, Glen didn't go—just as well, Seely would have had a big hairy bird if he had. And Debbie's son, Chad, had nearly had a bird anyway when he saw all the shortasses coming up the front stairs. "What is this?" he'd blurted, "a daycare center?"

If she had a daycare center maybe she'd enroll Chad, let him take another try at growing up. Nice enough guy, but when you've been brought up middle class you can't be anything but middle class. And God, but that's boring. He'd decided he needed to get in touch with himself as a male. You'd think all he had to do was take a look at what it was he used to pee. But no; he paid five hundred dollars for a weekend workshop so he could go out in the bush—not too far from civilization, however—and beat on a drum he made himself. Probably a garbage-can lid would have done the same thing. Took off his shirt. Oh, wow, now *there* is a real daring move. Why, they got so in touch with themselves that for a few minutes they draped their arms around each others' shoulders and danced in a circle around a little bonfire. Overcoming isolation, he called it. Talked so much about it she began to wish he'd fork out another five hundred and go take a course to overcome his run-off-at-the-mouth-itis. Jimmy just gaped. Poor Jimboh. Chad turned to him and said, "I need to tell you how much your work means to me. I went to the gallery and saw your retrospective and was almost overwhelmed. Your work speaks to my soul. You put in front of the world the things I feel." Poor Jimboh just nodded and said thank you as if he knew what the guy was rattling on about. Speaks to my soul, my ass.

Good job Glen hadn't come. The last time they'd all got together was beyond belief. Seely so quiet you'd have thought her pet rat had stolen her tongue, and suddenly Glen, in front of everybody, saying, Seely, I'm sorry, I did a bad thing and I'm sorry, it was cruel, it was unforgivable, it was awful, and I'm not asking you to forgive me, I'm just telling you I know what I did and I'm sorry. And Seely on her feet screaming, God, screaming like someone had lit a fire and put her feet in it. "You did *not!* You stop saying that. You lie, Glen, you *lie*, you hear me? Lie, lie, lie!"

And what was that all about? Whatever, it was enough to make your mind tuck its skirts under itself and run for a corner to hide.

But Seely was like that. Said and did the most unusual things. If it *was* Grainger, and if he *did* off himself because of it, why did Seely continue living in the house with Sandra and the kids? And why, when Sandra could no longer run the store, did Seely find someone to be full-time manager? And why, when Sandra couldn't get around any more, did Seely just matter-of-factly set about looking after her? And Sandra being Gran to those two ghastly brats, as if it was all normal. Well, maybe Savannah shouldn't worry too much about normal, not with the Three Musketeers in the picture. The Three Wise Men. The duck triplets, Huey, Dewey and Louie. The Three Stooges. Fucking trinity showing up all over the damned place. Groucho, Harpo, and Chico. Eenie, Meenie, Miney and we don't want no Moe!

Jesus. Seely. "You kids okay back there?"

"Fine, Momma."

"That's good, kids. We won't be much longer. I don't know, maybe this trip isn't worth it, maybe we should make this the last one, it must be boring for you."

"No! I don't mind! It's okay, really. We get to see Uncle Jimmy and...and everybody, Mom. It's worth it! Please?"

"Well, if you're sure you don't mind. Missing school and all...." She hid her grin.

"Oh." Victor stared at the rearview, knowing Savannah was watching. "Well, that part of it is hard"—he looked as if he meant every word—"but we know it's not possible to have everything. Dad says there's price tags on everything in the world and I guess missing school is the price we pay for the chance to visit Uncle Jimmy." He pulled it off. The grin didn't even start to show, let alone break through. He was getting good at it.

"Atta boy," she nodded, and Victor finally smiled.

Kitty dreamed she was in the living room of the old house and they were all sitting on the sofa, side-by-each, except for Jimmy, who kept coming in and out and in and out and in and out bringing popcorn. Glen was healthy and by himself, that's how she knew it was a dream, because when Glen was healthy he was *never* by himself. But in the dream he was just fine and all alone and looking gorgeous and they were sitting like when they were kids, except no pinching or fighting, but they were adults, and Glen was eating popcorn, which he basically hated, and saying yes to every damned one of them, from the first to the last, all those years' worth.

And in the dream he had them. From first to last, although how you'd know that for sure was hard to say. "...not as well known as 'Star Trek,'" Glen was laughing, "but established all the same, and a computer network and everything. And you can either buy or rent the episodes. And if you rent them people copy them, but that seemed like too friggin' much trouble, I mean who needs that, right? So I just bought them."

Could have bought a brand-new car with what it must have cost him. How many years? How many episodes per year? Jesus. But they were all stacked in a box, a yellow plastic box with Dairyland on it, and in the dream they were all firmly decided, they were going to sit there in a group and watch the whole damned thing from start to finish.

Except in the dream there was another dream, like she was watching more than one show at the same time. She could see them sitting on the sofa, she could see them watching TV, she could even see what they were watching on TV, but she could also see another TV in another place, and a kid maybe four years old sitting with a box of cereal, Alpha-Bits maybe, all by himself, and he'd been bawling his eyes out for a long long time, he was still sort of hiccuping, so hungry he was eating dry cereal, and watching TV because it was watch TV or know he was all alone in the dark.

And then the *bat*, Jesus, the bat was flying for her head, no sound at all, just this big black bastard of a thing, and Gran was at the softball game. Kitty was going back, back, back, trying for the flyball, and she knew, she knew and it made her want to cry, that she wasn't going to get far enough back, it was going to go over her by at least a foot, no matter how far up she stretched her arm it was going to be too high, and she jumped, no thought about it, she just jumped up, off balance, knew she would fall, and Gran yelling, *Hang onto it Kit!* Silly because Gran didn't usually go to softball games, and why would anyone try to grab and hang onto a great big black bat like that?

"Hey." The voice was real and soft, and she would know it anywhere. "Hey, Kit?"

"Christie?"

"Easy there, darlin', you're going to pull something loose if you thrash around like that."

"Chris...."

"Sssssh now, you just rest. Sssssh."

Kitty couldn't go to sleep but she couldn't wake up either. Her face was sore. Jesus, but it was sore! Maybe the old farts who'd tried to put a stop to women's rodeo were right, maybe it was too dangerous, Christ, a person could get hurt! Of course, people got hurt every day. Taxi drivers mugged. Bank clerks shot. Loggers crushed. Miners buried. Housewives beaten. Why only ban rodeo? Life hurt! Roseanne Barr Arnold said, If anyone asks you if you were abused as a child the only two answers, the only two honest answers, are yes, or I don't remember. It might be nice to not remember.

Not remember Christie sobbing and shouting, "...just make me *sick* at times, Kitty. Your way or no way. Queen Kate! I won't *live* like this, you hear me? I won't live like this because it's driving me *crazy*. You're a cold, cruel person! Everybody thinks you're so great, so much fun, joke joke joke, har har har, but *I'm* the one has to try to live with you and *I'm* the one knows what a pain in the ass you are!"

Until you felt as if someone had been beating you on the head with a brick. And even when it was over and the yelling stopped, the crying stopped and the other part started, the cups of coffee in bed, the unexpected dried-apple pie, the quick cuddle from behind, even then the feeling of having been beat up was there, only layered on top of it was total confusion, which was which and which was real and what was it, Jesus fucking Christ, what was it Kitty was *doing* that kicked it off, anyway?

No sense asking. When Christie wasn't upset, Christie wasn't the least little bit upset, and anyway, upset or not, Christie didn't talk about things. Waste of time, she said. Who has the luxury of all that time, picking over everything, talking, talking, sharing, talking, who can sit still that long?

If it's important, you make yourself sit still. But it wasn't important enough until it was so pressing and urgent that there wasn't any talking done, just the accusations, you said this in the wrong tone of voice, you looked this way in an unguarded moment, you did, you looked, you said, you thought, you moved, you you you you are making me unhappy.

"Then fuckin' check OUT!" she had yelled. "It's not *me* making you unhappy, you're just fuckin' unhappy. You and the goddamned PMS we both have to put up with! If I'm so fucking awful what are you *doing* here? *Move!*"

She didn't want to yell any more. This other thing, it wasn't working any better than yelling had, but Kitty herself just didn't have it in her to yell or fight or do whatever it was they'd done for so many years. Mostly she sat and said things in a cold and probably insulting voice, like, Oh sure, Chris, blame it all on me. It must be *me*, because *you* are perfect. Big help. Well, yes, on some level it was a help. You still came out of it feeling beat up but at least you didn't feel beaten to a pulp.

Rather tangle with a wild bull. Well, she'd done that too, and it felt just about the same. At least when you tangled with the bull you got some kind of shit squirted up your nose that made you feel like nothing in the whole wide world mattered. Maybe ask the doctor for some to take home with her. If not the spray, something similar.

Antidepressant, she figured. The depression had lasted too long this time, it was becoming a way of life. God in heaven, she was tired. Not body tired or hard-work tired, just tired. Crawl-in-a-hole-and-pull-it-in-after-you tired. Find-a-log-and-hide-behind-it tired. They didn't even sleep in the same bed any more. That about told the whole story. Difficult enough to keep the old flame burning when one of you is a morning person and the other is an evening person, but when you aren't even in the same bed, morning or evening, it gets too cut and dried. Wake up on your day off and stretch, yawn, get a coffee and take it back to bed, and know that if you drink it and get up and go outside you're in for hurt feelings because it's supposed to be our day. But it's hardly fun or exciting to know you'll be waiting through two or three cups of coffee, and then it'll be time for the other to climb into bed with a coffee and for you to get ready to have sex. On schedule. And what do you do when you're absolutely not into it? When nothing happens? What do you do when your god-damned mind is full of other things, because it's morning and you're a morning person and there's chores even if it is the day off, and how do you talk about that even if you live with someone who will *talk*, which Christie wouldn't do anyway? How do you say that the moods and up-and-down emotions and feeling beaten up and depression and separate beds and morning-evening disparity and who knows what else all lead to a great big feeling of Excuse me, I think I'll sit down and cry, which soon becomes yawn? Maybe that's what Gran was yelling *Hang on Kitty* about, maybe Gran was trying to tell her this too would pass.

She was sitting up and trying to get Cream of Wheat into herself when Janice and Colleen came to visit before heading off to the next cow flop on the side of the highway.

"Jesus, you're in great shape for the shape you're in, eh?"

"Tell me about it."

"Well, if it's any consolation, the buzzer sounded before the sky started to show between your arse and what you were supposed to be sitting on."

"Why is it that doesn't seem like such a big deal today?"

"You don't like money?"

"I won't make total aggregate now."

"Greedy bitch," Colleen grinned.

They didn't stay long, they had to hit the road. But it was nice of them to come to see her, even for only five or ten minutes. Lucy and Debbie came up for an hour in the afternoon, then left for the airport and their flight home. "Next time you want us to come for a visit," Lucy tried for a weak joke, "you might try phoning instead."

"Yeah, it's something to think about," she agreed. Lucy looked so tired. Not just old, but tired. "How's the bum leg?"

"You know how it is, when you've got a bad hip you've got a constant pain in the ass, right?"

"New pills working okay?"

"Sure," Lucy said, and Kitty knew she lied. "Be leading the corpse de ballet by the end of the week."

"Look for the corpse in the pink tutu?"

"Three three."

"Four four."

"Shut up," Debbie said clearly. "You're going to make me sick with your silliness."

"It ain't funny, McGee," they all chimed.

The doctor came in and examined her carefully—she'd have said painstakingly if there'd been anybody around to pick up on the weak joke. She had to go down for another X-ray of her face, then he came back and told her that if she wanted she could check out the next afternoon. "Why not now?" she asked.

"It's too soon," he answered, and she knew he was going to be stubborn about it.

"How soon tomorrow?"

"Probably after lunch."

"Why after lunch?"

"Well, if you'd rather wait until after supper...." She didn't get out immediately, but she did talk him down to after morning rounds.

"I didn't know women did rodeo," he blurted.

"Hey." She tried to wink, and couldn't. "Don't be piggy. We can do just about anything. There's even women stand up to pee!"

"All I've ever seen is barrel racing."

"Yeah, well, either you're showing your age or you don't get out much." She gave him a shortened version of the rap she had to give just about everybody she met, the same one Lucy had to give Kitty herself, those years ago in the basement, when they opened the old trunk. "We had our own circuit for years, but when the guys came back from shooting at each other, they found most of the rodeo stock had either been turned into bully beef or died of old age, so there wasn't enough trained stock—and anyway, all those guys needed the jobs, right? Same as any other good job, the women got aced out. Let us keep barrel racing and Rodeo Queen. So if you don't remember, maybe you're a post double-you double-you two kid. But you know what we're like, we don't know our place and won't stick to it even if it's pointed out to us, we're butting in again. We've almost got back to the point where you can make a living doing it. Almost."

"Hard way to make a living."

"Yours is easy?"

It got boring, really. Telling people the same thing over and over, and each of them so surprised. How had so many people been so quickly forgotten? Had their photos been taken down in living rooms and parlors all over the continent? Where did the silver cups go when Aunt Jane had gone to a nursing home, or to the crematorium? What happened to the incredible belt buckles, the solid silver spurs, the conchos engraved with the titles and the dates they were won? Did the nephews and great-nephews whose educations had been paid for by bruises and broken bones look at the framed photo and feel anything at all? Did the nieces who had gone to good schools, learned to play the violin, even headed off to college (where they met and married a damned dentist), ever stop to think that if batty old Aunt Jane had stayed in the rut she'd been born in, they themselves would still be pulling tits on a dairy farm? How could so much be erased so quickly?

Christie went home for the afternoon, probably just walked toward her bed and fell on it. She'd been with Kitty almost every minute since the lights went out and the brightly colored stars began to shine. Loyal. Whatever else, Chris was loyal. Barely taken the time to bop back and have the stock sent on with the broker's truck. Except for the dog, she'd be sitting in the back of the pickup, waiting. Might not be good for much else, but that dog could wait with the best!

Kitty watched some television and had supper. Ground this and pureed that. Then Christie came up with a milkshake from the Dairy Queen, and that probably saved Kitty's life. Christie looked a lot better, less strained and yet somehow more sleepy. "You look like someone who should head home and crawl into bed for some solid hours."

"I didn't feel tired until I had a nap, and now I can barely keep from yawning."

"G'wan home and catch up. And Christie...thanks."

"I love you, Kitty."

And she did. No doubt about that. With or without the yelling, there was no doubt Christie loved her.

Kitty wakened and knew it was the middle of the night. Her hand was so goddamned sore she thought maybe she ought to just have them cut it off at the elbow. Except they said phantom pain was even worse than real pain, and who needed to be hurting in something you didn't even have any more?

Jimmy's spook was prowling around the room, on edge and irritable. Or maybe it wasn't the same one. The other one had been wearing a face like a wooden mask; this one looked more like someone with shoe polish on his face. Or soot. And white lines on the backs of his fingers, a white line up his arms and legs, as if he wanted to look like a skeleton or something. He glared at her and pointed his carved stick and it was like being smashed in the chest. She couldn't breathe. Not in, not out.

She could hear a guy's voice, as plain as if he was right in the room with her, some guy drunk and saying, Listen, I'm tough, see, I can just pick you up as easy as easy can be, see? She heard a kid's voice—no, two kids, both of them with that ingratiating tone she remembered from her own childhood, the one where you flatter and suckhole to keep the drunk in a good mood, gee mister, you sure *are* strong. And then a yelp of surprise from one of the kids, and the drunk saying, See? Then another yelp followed by a deep grunt, another breathless grunt.

Savannah had scooped Victor up from behind, her forearm across his pot belly, and she'd kissed his neck and said, You ready? And Victor had grinned and nodded eagerly, and Savannah had tightened her arm, forcing some of the air out of Vic's lungs, and when he giggled she jiggled him, and the huh-huh mixed with his laughter...

but this kid wasn't laughing, this kid was just huh, followed by oh, oh no, then huh again, and the rhythm was unmistakeable. Kitty tried to yell protest. No sound. No sound because she couldn't breathe. As helpless as the second kid, who was trying to be charming and distracting, Hey mister, why don't we do that other thing, you liked that when I did it, mister, and the first kid huh, oh, oh ow, oh don't, huh-oh-oh. Never a phone when you need one, never a cop when you need one, never a sound when you need one, and oh hungh! You okay, hey, you okay? I think so. Oh, oh-ow. You sure you're okay? And the man laughing and saying, So you think I liked it, huh? You want to do it again? Good.

and the spook hit her again, not hit, just pointed and *whap*, she could breathe again. Some kind of agreement had been made and she wasn't sure she understood it, she just knew some kind of agreement had been made and it had to do with whether she was going to do something or the spook was going to point at her and never let her breathe again. You either try to stop it or you're part of what allows it to happen. And if you're part of what allows it to happen you aren't going to breathe. No two ways about it. Do something or die damn you die

and the nurse was shining a small light on her face, looking concerned. "Are you having pain?" she asked.

"My hand," Kitty managed. She sounded like she was bleating. She *hated* it when she sounded like that! Wimp.

"You really shouldn't leave tomorrow, you know."

"I'll be okay," she promised. "I'll get some pills or something."

"You can't look after yourself yet."

"I don't have to." She smiled. "I've got friends, eh?"

5

Kitty got used to doing things one-handed, she got used to breathing through her mouth instead of her nose, she even got used to seeing Jimmy's spook-things moving through life as if they were as real as she was. What she didn't get used to was the dream of the river road, the big bridge, the steep incline to her right, the river to her left, the city off beyond the river and the big black horror swooping down at her. She tried to train herself so that when the dream began she could pre-pare herself, flail up at it, grab a stick and swing it, jump to one side so it missed, roll with it, punch at it, anything except be smothered in it and destroyed. She even started practicing when she was awake, stepping to one side and kicking like a karate instructor.

"Sweetheart, wake up. Come on, Kit, it's me, you're safe, you're in your own bed, it's all right. Wake up."

"Christie?"

"It's okay. It's fine. Come on, take a pill, then lie down and go back to sleep and I'll curl up around your bum and keep your back warm and safe. It's okay, darling, it's fine."

She couldn't ride anything, not even in the barrel races, but she could haul on the clown suit and stand poised and tense, ready to distract the bull if the rider hit the dirt. Thank god there'd been clowns handy when she was hung up in her own rigging, bouncing around out there like a sheet flapping on the line in a high wind!

And she could help with the stock. She liked that part of it. It was almost like being home again, helping Lucy with the chores, feeling as if all that other stuff had been put on hold and she'd never again have to think about it or do anything about it or be affected by it, never again have to grab Victor and go out the window with Seely coming behind her and peeing on her head.

Christie had an arrangement with Shari Farkis, the teenaged daughter of Tom and Mabel, to run the souvenir stand part-time. Shari was about as dependable as a golden-winged shit fly, but Kitty couldn't always get away to cover so that Christie could leave her portable store and ride in her events.

Kitty privately thought Christie could do better if she got rid of the damned silly thing and concentrated on riding, but when someone sets things up in such a way she *can't* concentrate on doing something else full time, you have to wonder if maybe she doesn't *want* to do it full time. Anyway, it was Christie's business. She'd been doing it that way since before Kitty met her, so maybe that was how she wanted it done.

Kitty'd been rattling around for a year or two, doing fine but not really ready to aim at the big time, learning to put into steady practice what she'd learned at the school and from Lucy and on her own. As she drove onto the grounds and looked for the registration booth, she saw all the bright feathers fluttering in the wind and a dark-haired, dark-eyed, dark-skinned, tight-bodied woman setting up displays. And just like that, Kitty got the idea she should get some stuff for Savannah's and Seely's kids.

The little portable booth was festooned with hair clips—hair clips that could be used as roach clips, which was actually what they were, of course, but you can't advertise them as such. Pink, yellow, teal blue, they hung, the clip end fastened to a piece of wire. On the back wall were pennants with painted pictures of bucking broncs, and in little glass-fronted cases all along the counter were earrings, bracelets, even silver rings with irregularly shaped turquoise stones set in them.

Kitty got braided leather friendship bracelets for the boys and feathered hair clips for the girls. She even got a tooled leather belt for Savannah, and another for Seely. She doubted Savannah would wear hers, but you never knew; she might take it into her head to do damn near anything.

Kitty hadn't intended to follow the show and become next best thing to a regular. It was just a stopover, she thought, on her way to someplace else. But hell, she figured, one outfit's as good as another. And here they were traveling together, sharing expenses, with Christie's souvenir stand folded up on itself and stored in the bed of Kitty's pickup, the trailer they lived in riding along behind them. Their stock rode in the big Farnsworth Rodeo Brokers truck convoy, it cost less that way—you paid so much a season, it worked out to no more, really, than your share, less than it would cost for your own rig, the gas, oil, tires, insurance, repairs. And if they had their own stock truck they wouldn't be able to ride together taking turns with the driving; there'd be one of them in each vehicle. Unless of course Luck shit on their heads and they could get one of those two-hundred-thousand-dollar rigs with the animals below and the living quarters above, like a cross between a bus and a motor home. All that money to sleep in air scented by the stockshit on the bottom floor!

When the day came she could afford a mobile castle like that, Kitty figured, she'd quit what she was doing and buy her own place, raise competition stock and sell it to Farnsworth. Good money to be made in that. Not just bloodlines—there's good money to be made training competition stock. You just find yourself an animal that's naturally frisky, then encourage her. She likes to buck, fine—instead of doing all the things to train her not to buck, you make a big deal out of her bucking, yell and shout and encourage her, and when she does a damn fine job of it you give her carrots. Never, not ever, ride her to a standstill. Spoil the hell out of her. Let her get away with all the stuff she's not supposed to get away with in the ordinary scheme of things. Pour the food to her. Corn, lots of corn, makes them nervy and jumpy and hot as all get out.

Bucking stock is usually the best you can find. Get a good appie stud, maybe. Take damn near any ap gelding and feed him grain and you've got something could pass itself off as a bloody stud. So you wait to have him cut. Let him get his full dose of testosterone, let him prance around thinking he's the yearling king of the world. Wait till he's as close to two years old as is safe, then—about the time you begin to wonder if you're going to live through the next go-round— have him done. Crunch. The joke was they'd spelled the name wrong, ought to call it the BirdSeizer. Fit it over the cords and tubes and *crunch.* "Jesus Christ, doesn't that *hurt?*" the onlooker asked. "Only if you get your finger caught," the knacking wench replied. The nuts wither. Less chance of infection. And yes it hurts, and you've got one helluva pissed-off critter to contend with, but that's what you want for bucking stock.

Christie hated it. Said every time the animal-rights people started sounding off, she three-quarters agreed with them. Well, maybe so. Tight cinches, clanging bells, yeah, it all encouraged the animal to go nuts, and don't forget the spurring and yelling and slapping and hoorahing. On the other hand, you either take good care of them or they don't do a good job, and if your stock doesn't fight like hell the rider doesn't get good points, and a rider who doesn't get good points will go to where the good points are, and without riders you don't have a rodeo and without stock you don't have riders OR a rodeo so no, dammit, they aren't starved or mistreated or deliberately hurt. Although it's true a calf doesn't hit the end of a rope going full-tilt boogie and get flipped in the air, dropped on its side and jumped on very many times before it learns to stop as soon as the noose settles. That's when the calf finds out what's *really* cruel in this world, and leaves the dust, noise and crowding and shows up on your platter at Sizzle King, flanked by fries and a slice of pretend tomato. You want to see cruel? Look in the eyes of the nine-tenths of the world's population that's never even going to smell, let alone see or taste, that calf at Sizzle King. Save your fucking demonstration for that.

Get a good cross going, maybe a thoroughbred-quarterhorse mare and an ap stud, or the other way round. Try for a mom that isn't too calm, or the baby will come out calm too. Touch of thoroughbred ought to just about guarantee a nervy, jumpy thing.

For calves you'd need something with horns. Pinzgauer'd be good, long as it didn't come out polled. Small calves, easy birthing, fast growing, good weight gain. Mind you, if you want a narrow-minded, cranky bitch of a stubborn fighter, put in some Highland, then stand back and watch'em go. And that's when you're feeding them; god knows how nasty they'd be if they thought you meant them harm.

Horses, well, you wait eleven months to see what you've even got, and then wind up practicing absolute bloody restraint because your impulse is to be sweet to it. Then it's got to have solid bone mass before you start doing much with it—that's two years minimum, three if you want it to hang in—and then if it turns out not to have the nasties, well, you're up the creek and not a paddle to be seen, because by then the bugger is *too* nasty for your average purchaser—who, whatever else they say, really only wants a horse that *looks* spirited, not one that actually *is!* That's a lot of time, a lot of hay, a lot of CornOatsBarley and a fair bit of acreage invested.

Still, it was that or table beef, and who wants to put all that time and work into something that winds up as a washtub full of guts? Why raise'em the right way, feed'em the right way and then ship them off to a feed lot where they'll pump'em full of god in heaven knows what kind of chemical shit to double their size as fast as possible? Or if you don't ship them off, you have to do'em in yourself, and how can you do that after you've been out there putting disinfectant on their raw navels and watching them bleat after their mammies? Might as well feed your dog to McBurgers, too.

The thing was riding on the hood of the pickup this time. There was no doubt in her mind it was there. And no doubt, either, that Christie didn't see a thing. But there it was on the hood, as if it wanted to keep its arse end warm with the heat from the engine. Black all over, but not black-skinned; it had rubbed something black on itself. Big white circles around the eyes and mouth, chalk, white shoe polish, crushed clamshells, white clay. Bits of stuff in its hair, cedar tips, shells off a beach somewhere. Bit of string or something tied like a bracelet around one ankle. How could it be a bracelet if it was around the damn ankle, it'd have to be an anklet. Whatever. Big ugly callused bare feet, wider at the front than at the heel, splay-footed, never get *that* in a pair of shoes. Sitting comfortable as hell, and if she watched it too long she'd be off the highway and into the dingleberries.

They'd taken the packing out of her nose at the emergency ward of the hospital in some shit town two days ago. Had to phone the guy who'd stuffed it all in, have a long chat about things, then gave her a shot in the bum and waited for it to take effect. Yards of stuff were pulled out again. Yards of it. But it felt better, that awful, hurting pressure was gone. More X-rays, of course. It's part of a plan to sterilize the population and increase the number of people with pernicious anemia or leukemia or something. There's probably a multi-million-dollar industry in treating radiation sickness from casual use of X-rays.

With the packing out, the swelling was hardly noticeable. Still a bit of discoloration, but not enough to be noticed, really, unless you were eyeball to eyeball. The hand would take longer. But at least, once the thing with the nose was finished, they'd jabbed her a second time and taken those friggin' pins out of her fingers. The downside was that with the pins out the cast was bigger. And taking them out had kicked off all the little worms that lived in there and gnawed away determinedly, munch munch munch bite bite bite hurt hurt.

And that JimmySpook, not content to stay on the hood of the truck. She could see it peekin' around in the stock pens, sitting at times on the fence watching the show. Catch a flicker-glimpse of it out of the corner of her eye. Losing your grip, old thing, one bang on the bean too many is what it is. They didn't get all that blood clot, you'll wind up on your back, paralyzed, like the Old Biddy.

"Want me to drive?" Christie asked.

"Next stop'll be fine."

"We need gas."

"Yeah, and something to eat, too. I'm hungry."

"That's a nice change." Christie smiled. "You must be getting better."

"Yeah. Getting all that packing stuff out of my beak is what did it. I can smell what I'm eating. When you can't smell stuff, you can't taste it. Except for the dried old blood. Jesus!" she laughed, "and you'd keep shoving rice pudding in front of me, yum yum, every spoonful of it tasted like a nosebleed."

"You should have said something."

"Didn't know what it was until the packing was gone and it wasn't there any more."

They stopped at a PetroCan and filled the tank, checked and topped the oil, then pulled in beside the grill and went in for burgers and fries. Kitty would have liked a milkshake too, but the places that make them get farther and farther apart every day. So she had Seven-Up instead.

Christie moved behind the wheel and Kitty sat over by the passenger's door, her head resting against the window. When she turned her head to look out at the scenery, the JimmySpook sitting on the roof of the pickup cab looked down at her and grinned horribly. "Don't look any better upside down than you do rightside up," she muttered.

"Pardon?"

"Oh, just muttering to myself, I guess."

"You know what they say, you aren't in trouble until you start answering back."

Kitty opened the glove box and brought out the pink pills, took one out of the bottle, then grabbed a lukewarm juice and washed it down.

"Face sore?"

"Hand."

"We should get smart." Christie sounded casual but Kitty knew she was about to hear something that had been mentally rehearsed a dozen times. "We should park the trailer at my cousin's place, rent a stock truck, go get the animals, take them to Lucy's, turn them loose with hers, then go for the trailer and take *it* to Lucy's too."

"You won't sell much parked in Lucy's driveway."

"T'hell with it. Sell the damned stand, feathers and all. I'm sick of it. It's not as if selling souvenirs was a career."

"What about your barrel racing?"

"What's so great about fourth place? Winning may not be everything, but anything else sucks. I barely make expenses."

"Got it all figured out, don't you?"

"Think on it."

"Okay. No promises, though."

The pink pill was starting to work. The JimmySpook wasn't as intrusive, the throbbing was fading, she could even take Christie's suggestion and put it in that place where she didn't have to actively think about it, she could just let it simmer until either yes or no surfaced. Lucy would go for it. Lucy would love it. And if Lucy loved it, Debbie would be all for it, all for anything that meant Lucy wouldn't have to do so much work. Lucy wouldn't be stiff-necked about Kitty doing the chores, it wouldn't even bother her if Christie did the chores. It was just when Chad tried to do them that Lucy got prickly. "He presumes," Lucy grumbled, "acts as if all he has to do is waste the rest of his life the way he's wasted it so far and sooner or later his mom will croak and he'll inherit. Then he thinks he can pop me in the old ladies' chronic care ward and sell the place to a developer. I *told*'im it wouldn't work that way, I *told*'im you inherited my half. He just nodded like he'd known it all along, but I know him, he'll try to buy you out, he's got no feel for animals or farming or anything except his own self." And no use trying to tell Lucy anything, no use trying to say Chad wasn't that bad, the plain and simple truth was that they didn't understand each other and couldn't accept what they didn't understand.

Christie muttered, pushed the brake pedal. The pickup slowed and a fat old sheepdog waddled across the highway, unconcerned. "It's a miracle the old fart lasted this long," Christie said. "You'd think he owned the road. Well, who knows, maybe he does. They keep saying the country's going to the dogs...."

Seely'd had a dog like that, only smaller. White with black markings, like a mini old English bobtail. Not as big as a spaniel but all spunk. Grainger's house had its garage stuck onto the garage of the house next door and the two places shared a common driveway. So Spunky's lying in his driveway, sleeping on the hot tarmac, and Venutti comes home from work. His wife's brother's car is parked in front of Venutti's garage, so Venutti pulls in alongside and parks in front of Grainger's garage. And runs over Spunky in the process.

Seely flips out, the Graingers flip out, Spunky doesn't do much except lie there and die. Grainger races over, pounds on the door, tells Venutti to get his goddamn car out from in front of the goddamn garage so Grainger can goddamn well get his goddamn car out and take the goddamn dog to the goddamn vet.

The vet says it's good-night nurse, Spunky was already gone before they got there. Seely pitches a fit, convinced that if Venutti hadn't parked his car in front of the garage they'd have made it in time. Venutti says he's sorry but why was the damn dog sleeping there in the first place? Grainger vows he's going to put a fence down the middle of the driveway, Venutti says if you do I'll sue, so they paint a line and Venutti is supposed to stay on his side, the Graingers stay on theirs. Things are tense.

Then Jimmy shows up with a replacement. Good old Jimmy, somehow he came up with the right dog, a cross between a cocker spaniel, a poodle and a pekingese. Milly. Milly is one of those dogs, you show her something twice in a row and she has it aced for life. Not only "sit" and "sit pretty", she'd sit pretty and wave her front feet, then cross them under her chin. Get up on her back legs and dance in a circle. Put a dog biscuit on her nose and say, "Wait," and she'd sit there, cross-eyed as hell, watching her biscuit, until Seely said, "Go for it"; then Milly'd toss her head, send the biscuit up in the air and catch it.

They had some kind of fund-raiser at school and decided on a talent show: kids took their guitars, their accordions, their kazoos, the glee club sang, the music teacher did her thing, and then out comes Seely with Milly. Ended the show with Milly standing on her hind legs, "clapping" back at the audience with her front paws.

Two nights later Venutti goes outside in the dark, gets in his car and backs up quickly. Somehow winds up over the fading painted line. Slam, he gets Milly with the rear wheel.

Milly screams, ki-yi-yi's, tries to get back to the Graingers' house. Seely comes out screeching bloody murder, Grainger racing for the garage, the Mrs. yelling she's going to call the police this time, she's had enough, by God. Off to the vet. Milly nearly dies. The vet has to amputate one of her back legs; this dog is never going to sit pretty again.

They come home from the vet's and Grainger heads for Venutti's place, Seely right behind him, still snotting and sobbing. Venutti answers the door. Grainger looks at him and shakes his head gently. "You get your driver's license out of the catalogue or do you just like running over dogs? And is it any dog, or just *our* dog?"

"You don't talk to me like that," Venutti blusters.

"You wop bastard!" Seely screeches, her low-rent origins surfacing. "Just because they called your city Rome don't mean you gotta roam all over our lawn killing our dogs!"

"Brat!" Venutti says, and gives her a shove that sends her down the stairs on her ass. Grainger smokes him a good one. Venutti falls back into the living room and his flailing arm knocks over the classic trilight lamp, smashes the milk-glass shade to ratshit. Cops arrive. Assault charges. Lawyers. Counter-charges. Small-claims court for the vet bill. Fading line replaced by a picket fence. Fence enrages Venutti so much he takes it out with his car. More lawyers. Milly finally comes home from the vet. Every time Seely takes the dog out of the house, Mrs. Venutti starts to cry. She enjoyed watching Milly sit pretty, too.

Kitty closed her eyes and drifted off, the drone of the pickup soothing her. She roused briefly when the rainstorm hit. "Monsoon time," she grumbled. "It was a dark and stormy night. The damn ring'll be a sea of mud."

"Maybe we'll all be lucky and they'll cancel it."

Christie turned on the heater and put the wipers on full. It was like driving through the spray from a garden hose, or trying to steer through a carwash. The highway was awash, a half-inch of muddy water spraying from the tires of the car in front, sluicing her windshield. She slowed the truck, widening the gap between her windshield and the spray, checked her mirrors. The rodeo convoy stretched behind her, the stock truck three vehicles back. She braked several times, briefly, flashing her taillights, and the convoy headlights flashed answer. She slowed some more, the first gusts of gale-force winds hammering the pickup, slewing the trailer they were dragging. "Shit," she grumbled. At this rate they'd crawl in barely ahead of the first of the spectators—if indeed there were any.

Kitty jerked awake, her arm freezing cold, her sore hand banging and pounding like fury. The JimmySpook had her by her bad arm, shaking it and pointing repeatedly, almost frantically.

"Pull over!" Kitty said. "Pull over *now*, Chris!"

Christie hit her flashers, pulled to the side of the road, hoping Kitty wasn't going to puke. Behind her the convoy slowed, not sure what was going on or why, whether they should all pull over or pass.

The taillights of the car in front vanished. Just vanished. The sound hit them at the very second the red circles disappeared. The road shook, the pickup shuddered and the high beams illuminated a wall of mud, rock and fractured trees coursing down the steep slope, over the highway and beyond, to where the hillside fell down to pastureland.

"Jesus freakin' old baldy!" Christie gasped.

PART
FIVE

1

Brian Farnsworth, the old man's eldest grandson, had a CB in his truck, so the first of the emergency response vehicles was on the scene in less than ten minutes.

No traffic was coming from the other direction; the entire roadway was blocked by thousands of tons of mess and debris. Clumps of mud and muck still slithered and oozed down the deep cut in the face of the cliff, and the shattered trunks of trees gleamed raw and yellow in the headlights cutting through the downpour.

Christie and Kitty walked the two hundred feet to the edge of the slide but saw no hint of the vehicle which only a short time before had been in front of them. They looked at each other, shook their heads and moved back to the pickup.

The police were trying to clear the snarl of traffic and still keep the northbound lane clear to allow the Highways crews access. Already an enormous backhoe with a bucket just about big enough to hold the average barn was scooping mud from the road and trundling it to the embankment, sending it down to where the railway lines vanished into the overflow from the slide.

"That was more than luck," Christie said quietly. Kitty looked at her, then looked away, feeling almost guilty. "What's going on?"

"Nothing."

"Come on, Kit. We've got an agreement, remember? You shit your friends and I'll shit my friends, but we won't shit each other."

"You'll think I'm crazy," Kitty pleaded, feeling she was about to sit down and bawl like a two-year-old.

"I've thought that for years and it hasn't got in our way. What gives?"

"The JimmySpook warned me."

"The *who?*"

"I told you you'd think I was nuts."

"The *who?*"

"The JimmySpook. I've been seeing them for weeks." She got into the pickup and sat behind the wheel, and when the cop waved his arm she turned into the other lane and headed back the way they'd so recently come. Christie sat in the passenger's seat, waiting patiently.

"You've seen those things my brother used to carve, when he was pretending to be an Indian and making lots of money at it? Well"— she took a deep breath and blurted it out.

When she finally finished, she was afraid to look in case Christie was getting set to either scream or bust a gut laughing.

"Squeyanx." Christie sounded as if she'd been hit on the back of the neck.

"Huh?"

"Squeyanx."

"Skwee Yanks?"

"Close. Close as you'll get, probably. Stick people. Bone people."

"You mean the JimmySpooks?"

"Yeah. You say it touched you?"

"Yeah. Once on the chest, with his stick. Felt like I'd been frozen. Then just before the mud came down, he grabbed me by the arm."

"Jesus." Christie reached over, put her hand on Kitty's knee and rubbed gently. "Usually when they touch you, that's it. People just stiffen and stay that way until they smother because their lungs can't work. People have been sent flying backwards as much as twenty feet because a Squeyanx pointed the power stick at them, never mind touched them."

"Yeah, well...there's some other weird shit, too." She was so scared to tell about the kids' voices, the uh-uh-uh gasping sounds and what she knew it all meant, that her own voice shook. She even told about the big bat-shape coming at her from somewhere up near the bridge, and Gran's voice railing at her to grab and hang on. "I don't *want* to hang on to the bugger, I want to shove it away before it gnaws out my throat or something."

"Yeah. Well. Jeez, eh?" Christie drew a deep ragged breath and Kitty felt the hand on her knee tremble. "I think we need to go see someone who might know something about this, because all I know is that it's heavy stuff. And I mean *real* heavy, Kitty."

The next four hours were so much like being half awake, half asleep that Kitty paid no attention to anything except the mechanics of keeping the pickup on her own side of the road and out of everyone else's vehicle. Most of the traffic seemed to be emergency vehicles of one sort or another, heading to or from one mudslide or another. Seventeen miles west of Hope, the JimmySpook appeared on the hood, his fright-face split by what Kitty supposed was an encouraging grin. He moved his fists in circles, like a kid playing see-the-shoemaker, and she stepped on the gas, suddenly certain she was safer in his care than she had been in her own mother's arms.

"Jesus, Kitty!" Christie gasped.

"We're okay," Kitty answered calmly. She took the pickup around the hairpin turn and felt the trailer shift only slightly. "We're fine," she repeated, and pointed. "See, it straightens out up ahead."

They got to the village in time for breakfast. Christie's great-aunt sat over a mug of coffee, staring at Kitty as if she wished she'd never had to see her face. Christie did the talking, and Kitty was glad to let her do it; the great-aunt looked like someone you wouldn't want to tangle with. With some people, the choice of one wrong word was tantamount to an insult or a challenge.

"That's not Squeyanx," the old woman snapped.

"It sounds like it to me," Christie insisted.

"*You* ever seen it?"

"No."

"Just look at her. Not a drop of blood in her veins. How could *she* see Squeyanx?"

"Then...what?"

"How would I know? I don't know what those people have." The old woman refilled her coffee cup, as if that signaled the end of the conversation. Christie just sat. Kitty sat and wished she was almost anywhere else, while the great-auntie stared holes in her head.

The JimmySpook cavorted around the small house, playing with the hawk wings fastened to the windowframe, outlined against the windowpanes, put there not only as magic catchers but to keep songbirds from slamming their frail bodies against the glass and killing themselves. He picked up a wooden flute and played a tune, put the flute aside and fingered some crystals, then turned, frowning, his playful mood gone. He pointed at Kitty and she felt her body stiffen, felt the color draining from her face. "Hiche'ca keum," she blurted. "Kleco. Hiche'ca keum."

The great-aunt put her coffee mug on the table, folded her hands and spoke briefly. Kitty felt her mouth move, felt her throat quiver, but not one sound she uttered made any sense to her. She heard Christie sobbing; then the JimmySpook laughed silently and walked through the wall, was gone.

Feeling returned slowly, and by the time Kitty was able to drink some coffee and collect her wits, Christie had stopped weeping. The auntie glowered as if she was past angry to something else, and didn't really care who knew it.

"The stick people," she said grudgingly, "are as many and various as we are in this life. Some of them make themselves known to us, some don't. We do not know why. We don't have to know why. That's just how it is. Some of us are chosen to be bridges, to be the connection between those others and ourselves; and those who are chosen become dancers. They study, they learn the old language most of us have forgotten, they learn the stories, they learn the songs. When it is time, they give theirSelves over and allow the stick people to enter their bodies and dance." She looked as if, somewhere in this room, there was a pile of fish, rotten and stinking. "I do not know why *you* have been visited."

It was obvious she didn't approve. Given her own way in things, she would have done it all very differently. "You people!" she shouted, slamming her hand on the tabletop. "You take everything! Now you even take this!"

"I didn't," Kitty answered, almost as angry as the old woman. "I didn't ask for this. I didn't do a thing to invite this. I was minding my own business, living my own life, and bang! You think I *like* this? You think I want to feel *crazy* all the time?"

"Don't yell at me," the great-aunt said coldly. "I am not the one visited you. I wouldn't walk across the street to say hello to you!"

"And if you did I wouldn't answer." Kitty stood up, so angry she wanted to slap the old fart alongside the face. "Thank you for absolutely fuck-all, madam. Your help has been no use whatsoever." And she headed for the door.

The old woman laughed. Kitty whirled, all set to tell the old bitch to take a flying leap at her own arsehole. Then she felt her anger draining away, leaving her light and empty. The room was full of JimmySpooks of every size and shape, dancing, pointing, mocking. Some wore wooden fright-masks similar to the ones Jimmy carved and sold to the art galleries, others looked like ordinary people except that their faces were smeared with black and they walked through tables and chairs as easily as through thin air. Some had white markings to indicate arm bones, leg bones, ribs, some were decked with feathers and bits of rag, some were naked. She felt as if her strength was being sucked from her, and she reached out for the wall to support herself.

"You already know everything you need to know," Christie's great-aunt said quietly. "You know where to go, you know what to do, you know as much as anyone is ever going to be able to tell you. Now it's up to you. Either do it or don't do it. You people"—she laughed again, but not harshly, and when she spoke there was no trace of anger or bitterness in her voice. "You are always going from one person to another asking why, asking how, asking, asking, asking. You *know* what you must do. Stop talking, either do it or don't."

"I'm scared," Kitty blurted.

"Who isn't?" The great-aunt shrugged. "I don't understand it," she admitted. "All I know is our Squeyanx visit us. Yours are called other things and visit you. I once heard of a woman near Seattle who saw little Irish people in funny hats, and she was not Irish. Maybe...." She shrugged again. "I do not understand it. Not all the ones who are called to you are your own. Some of them"— she didn't want to say this, and obviously didn't want to believe it—"some of them are indeed our Squeyanx. The others, I don't know. Not who, not how and not why. And"—she laughed softly—"those who tell you they *do* know are probably lying."

2

Jimmy faded after supper, taking the leftovers and scraps with him. He checked the rat cages, refilled the feeders with eighteen percent rabbit feed and shared the remains of their meal with his chosen charges. Sometimes it almost seemed as if the rats understood more than anyone would believe possible. It even seemed, at times, as if they were laughing at him.

The kids came trooping into the shed, and of course they all wanted a chance to hold a baby rat. Darlene and Lizzy took the opportunity to lord it over the others. "They came from *our* rat," Darlene bragged. "We had Patsy, and these are her children and her children's children, and *their* children's children, and we could have them back if we wanted, couldn't we, Uncle Jimmy?"

"No." He gave her a light shove on the shoulder. "No, you're not getting these back. You didn't want them, remember? And anyway, you never even saw PatsyRatsy's whiskers twitch. She was dead and gone before you were ever born."

"Well, we could too have our rats back!"

"Why don't you fall on your head? Might shake some sense into it."

They went back to the house whining about how Uncle Jimmy wouldn't let them have their own rats. "And he said we should fall on our heads," Darlene grizzled.

"Rather you fell on your mouth." Seely yawned. "With any luck you'd bite your tongue and not be able to talk."

"She doesn't talk *now*," Savannah agreed, "she just whines. Shut up, Darlene, will you?"

"I don't like you," Darlene said coldly. "I never have."

"That's okay. You don't have to like me. No more'n I have to like you. Which I sometimes do, when you aren't working overtime to be a pain in the ass. You don't really want those rats. You'd have to feed them, fill their water, clean their cages, all kinds of stuff. You wouldn't do it before, when they were at your place, why would you do it now? If it wasn't the friggin' rats it'd be something else, anything to whine about, to get attention. If you want attention that bad, find some fun way to get it. Learn to sing or clatter spoons or tap dance or something. Just stop all this whine whine whining."

"It's *boring* here." Darlene switched from one reason to complain to another. "There's nothing to *do!*"

"Go do the dishes."

"Oh really!" The tone of voice was supposed to wither Savannah. All it did was make her grin.

"Yeah, really. Make yourself useful for a change."

"Do the dishes," Seely agreed. Darlene burst into tears. Seely looked at Savannah and shrugged. "See? She's always crying."

"I don't care if she cries the whole time she's doing them, but she'd better do the dishes or she'll have a reason to cry. I'll beat the shit out of her."

Darlene had no doubt at all about Savannah being able, and willing, to beat the crap out of her. Savannah was big, and Savannah was strong. And Savannah had no objections to thumping her own kids, so she wouldn't hesitate to thump someone else's. She went to the kitchen and started doing dishes, her bitter sobs loud and phlegmy.

"That was a good supper," Seely sighed. "I wish I could cook like that."

"You don't cook at all, let alone cook like that." Lizzy sat on the floor, her back resting against the sofa Savannah was lying on, her head propped by an old pillow with Souvenir of Spuzzum written across a background of sky and snow-capped mountains. "We eat take-out," Lizzy told Savannah. "One night pizza, one night Chinese, one night fish and chips...some nights I make supper. Mostly ham-

burger patties, mashed potatoes, frozen mixed vegetables and gravy. I
used to use the gravy in a can but it all tastes the same, not chicken
tasting or beef or anything except itself, so I got the Home Ec teacher
to tell me how. But mine's lumpy."

"You eat take-out?" Savannah sat up, glaring. "Seely, get real, will
you?"

"Well, I can't cook!"

"What do you mean, you can't cook? Jesus Christ, there's people
on the face of the earth can't even read a cookbook and *they* manage
to cook. What's wrong with you?"

"Nobody ever showed me how," Seely said sullenly.

"Nobody showed you how to make cakes, either, and you managed to learn."

"Somebody did so show me how!" and she went off on a long song
and dance about the Graingers and mixing bowls and licking clean the
beaters. Savannah listened and then laughed. "So I'll show you how to
cook." She lay back down on the Spuzzum pillow. "You just decide
what it is you're going to eat, then open the cookbook to the index."

"Easy for *you!*" Seely yelped. "You've had cooking lessons for years."

"So take some yourself. But Jesus, to eat take-out?"

"I hate cooking," Seely grumbled. "I just hate it!"

"See. I knew it wasn't because you didn't know how. You just
won't *do* it."

"You knew, did you? You know everything, *you* think!"

"No wonder that friggin' kid whines and cries."

"You shut *up!*" Seely grabbed the Souvenir of Cloverdale pillow
from behind her in the big chair and threw it at Savannah, who
caught it, tucked it under her head and laughed.

"Give me back my pillow," Seely wheedled. "Come on, Savannah, you're supposed to throw it back. Then I catch it and put it
behind my back again."

"I'm not playing that game. I'm playing the game where you throw
ALL the pillows, one after the other, and I keep them. ALL of them."

"Oh, you! Honestly. You're too much. Really, I mean it." And
Seely giggled happily, then launched into a detailed account of her
go-round with the woman who wanted sponge cake instead of fruitcake. Savannah howled with laughter and wound up tossing the
Cloverdale pillow back across the room, Seely's prize for standing her

ground. "Jesus, eh?" Savannah gasped. "Sometimes it's enough to make you bloody well wonder, right?"

Seely fluffed the Cloverdale pillow, then lobbed it gently, so gently it didn't quite make it to the sofa. Savannah leaned to catch it, leaned further, then lost her balance and toppled. Hooting with laughter at her own clumsiness, she put out her right hand to brace herself. There were two clear and distinct snaps. Savannah paled, her eyes wide and round as a seal's. "Holy God," she blurted, "I think I just broke the bugger!"

Seely started screeching. Jimmy came whipping up from the basement, where he had been hiding in his carving room, safe from the questions and bickerings of the kids. "It's my fault!" Seely sobbed. "It's all my fault."

"What's your fault?"

"I broke Savannah's wrist. I did it."

"Lemme see." But Savannah wouldn't let Jimmy anywhere near her wrist, and just kept yelling at Seely to shut the hell up and start the damn car.

It was Jimmy went out and started the car, and Jimmy who promised to bang heads together if the kids didn't stop pitching fits about who was going and who wasn't, who was riding in front, who in back and why. "None of you are coming," he roared. "Chrissake, nobody gets clear of the emergency ward in less than four hours, if you think I'm putting up with the lot of yous, you're even crazier than I thought. Shut up or I'll slap you. Hard."

They didn't seem to believe Jimmy would slap. The noise kept up. So Jimmy took aim at the closest two and managed to get in four or five good whacks, sharp enough to cause real tears. That shut them all up. "Take a goddam telling, will you? I said I'd slap and I meant it. Now get the hell outta the way so's Savannah can get to the car. And you two"—he pointed at Darlene and Lizzy—"get in there and finish the dishes, because if that kitchen isn't tickety-boo by the time I get home I'm going to get *really* nasty."

Savannah got in the front seat beside Jimmy. Seely climbed into the back seat and leaned forward, holding Savannah's head against the back of the front seat. "Take the corners easy," she lectured, "the swaying around might make her feel pukey."

"Don't tell me how to drive, Seely. I never took no car through the garage, I only ever drove inside one, not into and then beyond like you did."

"For God's sake, that was eleven years ago, when I was only just learning how to drive. And anyway it wasn't a garage, it was just a carport, and I didn't take out the wall, just one two-by-four. You make it sound like I demolished the entire friggin' house."

"Probably would have done if you'd'a had a big enough car instead of that little japcrap peepot."

"It isn't the corners are going to make me hork," Savannah warned, "but I'll ralph for sure if you two don't stop nattering. I guess we'll be there half the bloody night. Maybe we should go see Glennie while we're waiting for the X-rays to dry or whatever it is takes so long."

"You go see him," Seely said promptly. "I've seen too much of that bastard already in my life."

"Last time I went to see him"—Jimmy spoke softly, a slight smile on his lips—"he said to tell you he won't die until he makes everything right with you."

"Then he'll live one helluva long time," Seely retorted. "Be the oldest human skeleton in the history of civilization."

"Jesus, Seely, you're some pissed off at him. What did he *do?*"

"*Nothing!*" Seely slammed her fist on the back of the front seat, mere inches from Savannah's ear. "Shut up, why don't you? He did *nothing!*"

"Ah, Seely," Savannah sighed. "If you want it to stop eating holes in you, then you'll have to give it a name."

"You want a name?" Seely calmed immediately, her face set and hard, her eyes glittering in the light from the dashboard. "Hate. That's the name of what he did. He hated me."

Jimmy opened his mouth to say something and Savannah dug him sharply in the ribs with her left elbow. Jimmy shut his mouth. Savannah's injured right arm lay across her chest, hand elevated. She stroked the back of her swelling wrist with her left hand and nodded. "Oh, Seel," she almost whispered, "you should have said something."

"To whom? The old lady? Been a fine excuse for her to get drunk again. I told Gran. She called him over and talked to him and I don't know what she said or did, but he didn't get out of hand after that. Should have told her sooner, I guess. I just"—she laughed shortly, harshly—"didn't know what to *call* it. It started when I was that little."

"You mean...?" Jimmy woke up suddenly. "Glen? I'd'a broken his fuckin' neck!"

"Great, Jimmy, then you'd have gone to reform school. You were halfways there anyway."

"Well, no wonder he turned into a pervert." Jimmy sounded so matter-of-fact Savannah burst into loud laughter. Even Seely snickered.

"What's so funny?"

"You are, Jimboh. Funny as hell. But nice." Savannah leaned back, feeling Seely's small hand stroking her forehead. It felt good, broken wrist and all, to be inside a little metal world, moving down a rain-slick highway, the car heater warming them, safe with people they didn't have to pretend with, didn't have to try to appear to be sane or reasonable or acceptable with, on their way to a place where one very small and insignificant hurt could be fixed.

3

The storm hammered the roof of the pickup, the wind buffeting against the trailer until the job of keeping everything hanging together and on the road started to seem like a horror story. Even the JimmySpook on the hood was starting to look as if he had his work cut out for him. He turned, looked at Kitty, then waved ahead of them and pointed to something off the side of the road. "Maybe there's a parking spot or something up ahead," she muttered. Christie just looked at her, then nodded, her face pale.

Not three minutes later a small Parks Department sign indicated a road leading to a picnic site. The pickup left the highway carefully and picked its way along the unpaved road, splashing through puddles big enough to qualify as Olympic swimming pools. The road curved gently around a clump of small fir trees and there was a clearing, and around the clearing a number of heavy split-log picnic tables with attached benches. The table-and-bench affairs probably weighed at least half a ton, and were set into wide blocks of cement. Just to be sure nobody chainsawed the legs off where the cement ended, the Parks Department had run boom chain around the center strut of each table and down into the concrete.

"Must be a market for hot picnic tables," Christie suggested. "Must be people lined up five deep for the chance to buy a stolen Parks Department picnic rig."

"Maybe they were afraid my brother Jimmy would take it into his

head to come and get them and carve them into soup spoons or something. For a while there I thought Jimmy was going to swipe every
frigging thing in the country that wasn't either nailed down or fastened in place. Christ, he stole everything! Stole a Siamese cat,
brought it home, and when it had a litter of kittens not five days after
he swiped it, he put an ad up in the laundromat and sold one of them
to the very people who'd owned the damn cat before he stole it!"

The JimmySpook shook with silent laughter and nodded agreement, then slid off the hood of the pickup and walked into the wind-
whipped brush. Kitty put on the emergency brake, turned off the
wipers, switched off the engine and sat listening to the rain and wind.
After a while she opened her door and went out into the storm. The
dog jumped from under the tarp and looked up at her pleadingly.
Kitty held open the pickup door and the dog jumped inside, leaving
wet paw prints on the plastic seatcovers.

Kitty unlocked the trailer door, went inside and lit a match. By its
feeble glimmer she made out the propane lantern and got that lit,
bathing the interior in a clear white light more like something you'd
expect from the moon than from the sun.

She lit the propane heater and found sandwich fixings. She had
the sandwiches half made when Christie came into the trailer with
the dog skulking along behind her. "She'll make the place smell like
wet dog," Kitty warned.

"There's worse things than wet dog." Christie put the thermos on
the counter and unscrewed the cap. "You want some? It's still hot
enough to blister your lips."

"Sure. Nothing could keep me awake tonight, not even your thermos coffee. You want onion on this sandwich? It's cold cuts, tomato
and cheese."

"Thin slices or I won't get it in my mouth."

"You okay?"

"What in hell is 'okay'? What does 'okay' mean any more? Yeah,
I'm okay. I'm chilled to the damned bone and the heater doesn't do
me any good and I'm so scared I have cramps in my guts and I want to
sit down and cry but other than that I'm just peachy-keen, Kitty."

"You and me going to have a fight or something?"

"No. It's just that sometimes you ask the dumbest damned questions.
Of course I'm not all right, Kitty! You're seeing ghosts or something!

And what's more, I'm crazy enough to believe what you see is real, and we're both nuts enough that when your ghosts tell us to park the bloody trailer, we do it and think we're being intelligent!" She almost started to cry, then shook her head and forced a grin. "If the goddam spook had any sense we'd have been told to park a half-hour ago. All *hell* is breaking loose out there."

They were just sitting down at the small table when the trailer door opened and a woman walked in, rain dripping from her plastic raincoat.

"Oh, Jesus, do come in." Kitty got to her feet, not knowing what to think or do. The woman nodded and smiled, then slipped her plastic poncho-type raincoat over her head. She stood holding it and looking around the trailer. "Here." Kitty reached for the coat. "I'll hang that from the showerhead over the bathtub, then it can drip where we won't all drown." The woman nodded again and rubbed her hands together, grateful for the warmth.

"Would you like a cup of coffee?" Christie got up and went to the cupboard for another mug. "And I could make you a sandwich if you'd like one."

"I'd like one." The woman nodded again, moved to the table. "It's awful out there. Can't hardly see your hand in front of your face, and the rain! It hits like someone's throwing rocks at you or something."

"I guess you had to pull off the highway too," Christie probed. But the woman just looked around the trailer, nodding satisfaction.

"This is nice," she decided. "It's like a little house. You got good stuff, too, I see." She pointed at the hawk wing above the small bench that could pull out into a bed. "You shoot that yourself?"

"No. We were parked by the highway having lunch and a transport truck went past and the hawk, I don't know, must have got caught in the draft or something, it clipped the top of the transport and got tossed into the ditch. She went and got it." Christie pointed at Kitty, busy making more sandwiches.

"It was dead when she got it?"

"Not quite," Kitty said. "Died soon after, though. Didn't seem right to just leave her to rot. Skinned her and packed the wings and legs in salt, then later on, month or two I guess, unpacked them. What was left I buried with some cigarettes."

"Why cigarettes?"

"Christie said to give tobacco and so I did."

"Why tobacco?" The woman stared at Christie, who shrugged, half smiled and then sat back at the table, putting the mug of coffee in front of the nosy stranger.

"It's what my cousins say you should do."

"Always do what you're told?" the woman teased, sipping the coffee, then nodding approval.

"Never do what I'm told," Christie laughed.

Kitty slid the sandwich in front of the woman, then sat down and lifted her own, took a big bite and sighed. "Fuck, another night like the past few and I'll be old enough to collect my pension."

"Someone did a job on your face. You win the fight?"

"Lost. I always lose. Don't think I've won a fight in my entire life. But I haven't lost many by that wide a margin." She held up her hand, still bandaged, and laughed. "Haven't been able to scratch my head or pick my nose since it happened."

"Oh, Kit, that's gross!" Christie laughed.

The strange woman finished her sandwich, drained her coffee, then looked meaningfully at Kitty. "You got makings?" she asked. Kitty just nodded and pulled her pouch and papers from her shirt pocket. She handed them across the table and suddenly Christie's appetite faded. She looked over at Kitty, who just nodded, in either agreement or reassurance, Christie wasn't sure which. The dog sighed, her eyes closed, her paws twitching slightly. "Must have caught that rabbit she was dreaming about," said the woman with a smile.

"Who are you?" Christie dared.

"Ask no questions," Kitty chanted like a half-mad child, "and hear no lies."

The strange woman rolled and smoked two cigarettes, one after the other, and said nothing. Christie wasn't about to break the silence; she knew she was afraid of what she might be told if she asked any more questions. And finally the strange woman smiled and stubbed out the short butt of her second smoke. "You going to find that place?" she asked Kitty.

"I think so. Going to look, anyway. I think it must be the city because of all the lights and the big river."

"Well, you gotta go with nothing, you know. No truck, no trailer, no dog, no sidekick, nothing. Was a time you had to go naked but not any more." The stranger laughed softly. "Take a dim view of that now. Was a time you went naked and lived off the land."

"This thing. In my dream it's awful, it's scary, and I fight it off. But *is* it?"

"You gotta hang on. Scary or not."

"Will it hurt me?"

"Course it will. Anything hurts." And the JimmySpook pointed at Christie. "She's hurt you, more than one time, and you're still with her. You've hurt her lots of times, she's still with you. Goddam dog would hurt you if it had to."

And she was gone. Just like that. Christie almost screamed. Instead she went into the bathroom and stared at the showerhead. No raincoat. Just a puddle of rainwater in the bottom of the bathtub.

That's when Christie started to cry.

4

Savannah and Jimmy braced themselves before they walked into Glen's hospital room. They thought they were ready for anything. Four steps into the room, they knew they weren't even half ready.

Savannah had never seen anyone or anything look so dead without actually having quit breathing. And yet Glennie smiled at them, and reached out with a hand that was nothing but skin over bone. "Hey, darling," he managed. "Hey, good to see you."

"Oh, Glennie...." She swallowed, then shook her head, her eyes bright with tears. "Are they taking good care of you?"

"Sure. Doing everything that can be done, I guess." His voice was thin and thready, each breath an effort. His scrawny chest heaved and the cords in his throat stood out plainly. There was a smell coming from him, a smell that reminded Savannah of wintertime and wet wool, of gumboots draining onto newspaper, of blue mildew forming in the corners of the room.

"You need anything?" Jimmy took Glen's hand and held it gently, stroking his scarred fingers over the parchment-thin jaundiced skin. "I can get you ginger ale or something. Maybe some nice peaches."

"Maybe later. I'd rather see you." Glen tried to squeeze Jimmy's hand, and didn't have the strength. "Seel wouldn't come, huh?"

"No. You knew she wouldn't." Jimmy shook his head sadly. "You shouldn't'a done to her what you done, Glennie. I mean..."—he licked his lips—"that was just downright *mean*, is what that was. Ugly mean."

"Yeah." Glen blinked rapidly. "Mean and ugly and hateful. And even at the time I felt bad about it. I just felt worse about goddam near everything else! And I'd like to make it up to her, or at least tell her I'm real sorry for what I did."

"Well, that might make you feel better." Savannah sat on the chair by the bed, her wrist in a wet cast, the sling holding her hand up near her collarbone. "Might not do *her* any damned good, though."

Glen nodded and closed his eyes. They watched him struggle for each breath, and Savannah knew she was supposed to feel willing to do anything to save him, knew she was supposed to say she would even rather switch places with her brother than have to watch him suffer. But she didn't feel that way. She wouldn't have traded places with him for anything, except maybe to save the life of one of her own children, and she wasn't even sure she'd do it for that, unless it was for the lives of all of them.

"If it was a movie," Glen whispered, "Seel would walk in now. And she'd come to the side of the bed and she'd say something that made everyone in the theater feel all weepy. Maybe she'd say, You can die now, Glennie, or something like that. But I guess it's not a movie."

"No." Jimmy laid Glen's hand back on the counterpane, and patted it. "No, it's not a movie. And Seel isn't going to walk in and give you forgiveness. She's not going to lift any load off you. But you can die any time, Glen. I told her what you'd said, and she said if you were waiting for her forgiveness you'd live longer'n old Methuselah. So you might's well give up on that one."

"Fuck." Glen smiled as if smiling was easy for him. "We sure done a number on each other, huh?"

"Yeah, well, that's all they taught us to do, I guess. Except for the old lady. She was okay."

"Yeah?" Glen laughed softly, the fluid in his chest gurgling thickly. "If she was so okay, how come her own kids had no fuckin' use for her?" He looked over at Savannah. "What were you doin'?"

"Pickin' m'nose." She grinned.

"Are you happy, Van? I mean, really happy?"

"Hell no," she said easily. "I figure all things considered my life is better than it was and better than it might have been, but it's still a pile'a shit anyway you look at it. Were *you* happy?"

"For a while I thought I was. Busy, anyhow. Had what I thought were lots of friends. Lots of good friends. Then I got sick. Found out who my friends really were, I guess. You still livin' with the Three Wise Men?"

"Three Stooges, more like it." She shifted the weight of her injured arm, and smiled with practiced seeming ease. "I might not go back this visit. Might do something outrageous like move in with Jimmy."

Jimmy's head swung; he stared, surprised. Savannah just grinned at him, then shrugged. "Why not? It's not *your* house," she teased. "Gran left it to all of us."

"You want to move in," Jimmy growled, "I can't stop you, but I'm tellin' you, them damn kids'll have to smarten up some if they're gonna be around full time, because I can't stand noise. And if those black-assed rag-head bastards come around raisin' hell and yellin' about how they want their kids, I'll throw the kids to'em the way you throw bones to a mean dog."

"Ah, hell." She tried her pretend-smile again, and it almost fit. "You think they want'em? They'll send money, because they made an agreement to do that, but their families want'em married up proper, to women the families choose for'em. They don't like what they consider mongrels, you see." And the pain she felt about that was something only Jimmy and Glen would know. "They got some dumb-shit ideas, believe me. Somethin' about how babies inherit the souls of people already dead, and the souls won't go into bodies with mixed blood. Or some dumb damn thing like that. Won't be anybody turning up with rifles in the middle of the night," she added bitterly.

"Wouldn't make any difference to me," Glen whispered. "Shoot all they want, won't bother me. Know what I'd really like, Jimmy? I'd like it if you'd bring the player down with some of the rerun tapes. We could pretend Seel was here. Pretend Kitty was here. You heard from her? She okay?"

"She's fine," Jimmy lied. "Everybody's tickety-boo except you, you dumb bugger. Just because it's a *new* thing to get, you hadda go get'er, I guess. You always did follow too many trends, Glennie."

"Yeah?" Glen managed a wink. "But at least, whatever ugly things I might'a done, you got to admit I never joined the RCMP. You workin' hard?"

"No." Jimmy shook his head, gnawed at his lower lip. "No, I go down in the hellhole and I look at the wood and...all's I see is wood.

Usually I stare at it a while and I start to see what's hidden in it...then all's I have to do is take away what's too much and there it is...but...." He shrugged. "I guess it's what they call writer's block, only in my case it's like a chopping block or something. It's as if they all went somewheres else. All the faces, all the...faces," he finished weakly. Glen reached out and patted Jimmy's hand.

"Maybe they're all busy with something else. Or someone else...."

"Wish they'd get busy with Seel," Savannah blurted. She told Glen about the fast food, the take-out. "Says she doesn't know how. Fuck, anyone can read a book! Boil a spud or two. Sizzle some hamburg and throw on a can of cream a' mystery soup...."

"She's had a hard time," Glen wheezed. "And she's doin' okay, in her own way. I mean, she looks after Sandra most of the time, how easy can that be? And she does better by her kids than was done by us."

"Christ, they run all over her!" Jimmy snapped. "Whine whine whine, and if you tell them to shut up it's a mouthful a' cheek'n'lip from'em. There's times, so help me god, I wish Bobby Grainger had'a put them in the car too."

"Why would he do that? He might'a had to spend eternity with'em then." Savannah tried to do something with her arm to take the weight of it off her neck. "I always figured they were his, though."

"Naw." Jimmy shook his head. "Christ, if he didn't have kids with Sandra, he wouldn't'a had'em with Seel. I always figured it was an accident."

"Oh sure, he just happened to accidentally put the vacuum hose over the exhaust pipe and just happened to run it up into the car and just happened to close off the doors'n'windows with tape and just happened to sit in the car and...get real."

"I dreamed about it one time." Jimmy had that stubborn look on his face, the one that said you could shove dynamite up his bum, light a fuse and blow him to hell but you couldn't change his mind. "I figure he was going to check Sandra out...I dreamed she cried and asked him to do it and he tried and...he couldn't do it...couldn't kill her...he thought the world of her, for chrissakes, and how could he? Helluva thing to ask a person to do...and he got drinking...tryin' to get up the courage...only he wasn't a drinking man...and before he got round to goin' back for her...and settin' her in the front seat with 'im...he...passed out drunk and didn't come back again...that's what I dreamed, anyway."

"Oh yeah, sure. Meanwhile, back at the Longbranch, Mz Kitty, not knowing Matt Dillon had disguised himself as a door, pulled out a gun and shot his knob off," Savannah jeered. "Jesus, Jimmy, you and your fuckin' dreams."

"Yeh." Glen tried to laugh and nearly choked. Savannah sat him upright, hit him between the shoulder blades until he nodded, then lowered him back to his pillows. "Remember that time you dreamed we was all of us dead but didn't know it? Scared me so bad I had the willies for months."

"How do you know we *ain't?*" Jimmy laughed. "For all you know we've all been dead for years, we're just too stupid to lie down and rot."

"Yeah, sure, Jim, and me, I'm even stupider than that because I keep havin' kids. Dead people ain't fertile, okay?"

"Wasn't a dream," he said stubbornly. "I was wide awake in the hellhole workin' on a piece. And clear as clear can be I saw it. And we were all of us in the house...and he come in the bottom door...and wasn't any of us made it safe...he got Glen'n'me as we ran across the field to Gran's place...bang bang bang bang...."

"Glen wasn't even *there*, Jimmy!"

"In my dream he was! I'm tellin' you...."

Savannah reached over and pinched his face. Hard. He yelped and glared at her. She waved her good hand. "See? If you were dead you'd'a never felt it."

"How do you know?" He started to sing, "Merrily merrily merrily merrily, life is but a dream."

"Broken by the occasional fuckin' nightmare," Glen yawned.

"So maybe we're still dreamin'. Or maybe"—he shrugged—"maybe we were such awful little fucks even the ghosts and spooks and haunts didn't want us...or maybe...they decided there was something else we were supposed to do...."

"Know what I think?" Savannah tucked the bed covers around Glen, and stroked his face. "I think you've worked with cedar wood too long, Jimboh. You got cedar poisoning and it's gone to what in some people would be called the brain." She kissed Glen's forehead. "You go to sleep, okay? And don't wait for Seely to forgive you before you die. She's so goddam mean-minded about some things, she'll keep you lyin' here in agony for a hundred years, and then she'll spit in your eye."

"Tell her I'm sorry."

"Oh, shit, man, she *knows* you're sorry. She's enjoyin' that part of it so much she'll make it last forever! You didn't give a shit what she thought before you got sick, why give a shit what she thinks now?"

"If I had my life to live over...." He looked up at her and smiled as if he had every reason in the world to be happy. "I'd live it over a cappuccino bar."

"Not the Longbranch?"

"Nah." He winked. "Chester fucked sheep, Doc did opium, Mz Kitty was a dyke and Matt, he was a cross-dresser, spent his days off pretendin' to be one a' the girls. What would a nice guy like me be doing in a tacky story like that?"

They left him and went to where Seely was sitting patiently waiting in a chair in the hallway of the emergency ward. She heard them coming, put down the magazine she'd been reading and stood, stretching easily. She didn't ask how Glen was, they didn't offer the information. They might have been returning from the washrooms for all the interest Seely showed.

Glen lay in bed, listening to the sound of their receding footsteps. He yawned, his jaundiced hand tugged the covers under his chin. He wanted to tell them the Longbranch was the *Enterprise*, Matt was really Jean-Luc Picard and Mz Kitty was Dr. Crusher, but he didn't have the energy. He could either hang on and tell them or he could drift into his dream, the one where he was trying to help Gran with something and he wasn't sure what it was but the old girl had told him she needed help otherwise Kit-Cat was going to spend the rest of her life looking for a way to get herself killed for not having stopped and thought before scoopin' Vic. Jesus, the things we scour ourselves with, the ways we set up no-win situations, the numbers we do on ourselves, like holocaust survivors feeling guilty because they wound up in the minority instead of the ovens. Well, he didn't know what it was he was needed for, but he owed Kit-Cat at least that much. And it would give him something to do until Jimmy could get the player and the tapes. Be nice to do that again. And if he couldn't eat the popcorn, he could maybe smell it. Sit with them and pretend Seel was there too, and watch the escape. Jean-Luc was probably just Mickey Mouse without his fuckin' ears. And why had they killed off Tasha?

PART
SIX

1

Kitty spent four hours in the anthropological museum at the university, peering at the remnants of a civilization trapped under glass. She saw small totem poles, she saw large totem poles, she saw mortuary poles, house poles and memorial poles. She saw dance masks and shaman masks, she saw feast bowls and intricately carved and decorated spoons—and the JimmySpook moved with her, staring, staring, staring at the artifacts in hermetically sealed glass cases, better cared for and more respected than the people who had given birth to the culture and done the art work. There was no way of telling what, if anything, the JimmySpook thought or felt about what he-she-or-it was seeing.

Some of the masks looked like the ones Jimmy had carved. One or two of them actually were the result of her brother's crazy impersonation, and she grinned to herself when she thought of going up to the museum attendants and asking if they knew the carvings had been done by a non-native who didn't even consider himself an artist, just a glorified whittler. She might have done it except for the deep conviction nobody in the place would have believed her.

There were other carvings, too. Masks from just about any corner of the earth you'd care to name. And some of them even looked like work Jimmy had done. Some of the New Zealand Maori masks were so similar to things Jimmy had carved that she half expected to find his name displayed there, too.

She stood for almost twenty minutes looking at a wooden flute. Not much by way of design carved into it, and if anyone had asked she wouldn't have been able to say what it was about it held her attention. The JimmySpook pranced up and down the aisles, lifting his bone-legs until his knees were level with his chest, his bone-hands held near his mouth, pretending to play the instrument. She wished she knew what the fuck he was going on about, if only half the time.

She thought, then, of Aunt Lucy, and the solid haybarn-horsesoap smell of her, how her arms had been strong, the muscles like ropes, and yet gentle, as she held Kitty and just let her sob. "It wasn't as if I *did* any-thing, Auntie Lucy, it wasn't as if I *thought* about it. I didn't even know I'd done it until we were almost over at Gran's place! I could'a just as easy left him there. It wasn't *me* did it! I ran, that's all I did, I just up and ran like hell and I don't even remember Victor or that part of it."

"What counts, darling, is that you did it. Whether you thought about it or not, you did it."

"I didn't help Seely or Savannah and I didn't even *think* about...the others...the boys...I just *ran* is all."

"Damned good job you did. Would'a been a helluva note if you'd stopped to consider all possible options. Okay, you ran. But you grabbed Vic on your way past, and for me that's what counts. Nobody expects you to be Wonder Woman, Kitty. And you should give your-self a break, okay?"

"If they'd been depending on me they'd *all* be dead!"

"Well, they didn't depend on anybody but their own selves. Nobody should ever depend on someone else! And I'll tell you again, give yourself a break."

She hadn't had time to think then, but she had plenty of time to think this time. She could tell the JimmySpook to take a hike and chances were he'd take it. Even if he didn't go the first time, if she just kept telling him to go away, leave her alone, take a long walk on a short pier, buzz off, shoo, scat, beat it, sooner or later he'd find someone else to drive crazy.

She'd thought about that, but couldn't bring herself to do it. Well, even Seely, who'd thought the sun came up in the morning only because Kitty told it to, had said more than once, Curiosity not only killed the cat, it's going to kill Kitty, too.

She knew it was more than curiosity, but she was so used to shrugging off the kind of things which can make you go nutbar if you brood
on them that, even to herself, she couldn't quite manage to confess
there was a rightness to this, a kind of inevitability, and if she didn't
go along with it she'd be damned good and sorry. And there was too
much in her life already to be damned good and sorry about, too
many unsaid things, too many of everything it was too late to fix. If
nothing else, she could have been a little nicer to those two horrible
rugrats; and would have been if she'd known they were going to get
shot in the head. But you don't know these things beforehand, and
she hadn't been nicer, and they'd been blown to mush, and that, as
they said, was that.

She walked from the museum to a bus stop and rode back almost to
the city. When she saw the outline of a bridge against the sky she
stood and peered through the rain-slick window. It might be the
bridge in her dream. But it might not. Who was to say? A bridge is a
bridge, for god's sake, long or short, wide or narrow, high or low, a
bridge is a bridge is a bridge. But there was a bus stop not far from
where the bridge started, and she got off, then stood in the drizzle,
watching the red taillights of the bus until they were lost in the hundreds of others heading across the span to the city.
    She crossed the street and walked slowly toward the bridge. She
could see the river, dark brown with mud and the mess of every town
between here and the headwaters, mile after mile after mile of high-
tech sewer pipes laid street by street, all of them culminating in a big
outfall that dropped the waste into the current. Next to the bridge,
running down from the roadway, a beaten footpath, littered on either
side with pop cans, paper and garbage of every description, twisted
and angled down to an unpaved commercial access road along the
bank. Kitty was willing to bet anything, even her pacing horse, that
they called that muddy collection of potholes "River Road".
    She slid, slipped and slithered her way down the unplanned path,
nearly losing her balance in the goo. She grabbed for a bush and managed to save herself a filthy fall, then let go of the wiry branch and
jumped the last few feet.
    On the other side of the road the bank dropped steeply to the filthy
water. Nothing grew there, and the foul-smelling mud was littered with

everything from plastic bread wrappers to bits of what had once been abandoned cars. Kitty picked up a large rock and dropped it gently. It landed in the mud with a sinister "glup", then sank beneath the oily black goo. She was willing to bet there were more unwanted dogs, cats, puppies and kittens under that mess than had been incinerated at the SPCA, and she wondered how many unwanted newborn humans were down there with them.

She didn't like that river. It might be beautiful, it might even be glorious, miles upstream. But here, something had gone very seriously wrong; the river had become the use to which it was put, a huge, flowing, festering sewer, ripe with poison, rampant with death.

If you fell into that gumbo, even if you didn't get sucked under, even if you didn't drown, the corruption and filth would be sure to cause, at the very least, gangrene.

2

He could hear them arguing. She was shouting and crying, and he knew he'd be scared if Thingy wasn't sitting on the bed with him. Thingy smiled, then pushed his fingers in his ears and pulled a funny face. Noel nodded, and though he didn't stuff his own ears, he tried hard not to pay any attention to them. They were always shouting. She was always crying. And she always wound up doing what Jerry told her to do. For all the good it did to argue and shout she might as well not bother. But each time she argued, and each time it ended up the same. Once she had blown up about the cupboard doors. Gotta keep'em closed. An open cupboard door means you'll lose your fortune. Jerry laughed and said for all the fortune you'll ever have you might just as well not bother puttin' a door anywhere. Your best days are done, he said. She really cried then.

He pushed his car back and forth, back and forth, on the rumpled blankets. Thingy reached over and did something with his hands, turned all the rumples and crumples into roadways so the car could move easily in big loops and turns.

He heard the sound of slaps, and her crying increased. But the arguing stopped, and that meant Jerry had won again. Jerry always won. Jerry was the one with money, and Jerry was the one could hit the hardest, and that meant Jerry won and Noel did what Jerry told him to, because Noel didn't want any more of the belt.

He didn't know what he'd done that made Jerry mad yesterday, but something had done it and Jerry had used the belt. Noel still hurt. His bum hurt and his legs hurt and right up his back to his shoulders hurt, and anything Jerry said, Noel knew he was going to do, toot sweet was what Jerry said, toot sweet. Just grabbed Noel by the throat and held him at arm's length, slashing with the belt, squeezing with his hand, choking and hitting, strapping and squishing and yelling, You're gonna *die*, you little bastard, you keep this up and you're dead meat!

Then got even madder because Noel couldn't help it, he peed. So then Jerry *really* gave it to him. Let go of his throat and that was good, but then he punched.

He looked up and Jerry was standing in the doorway, waggling with his fingers for Noel to go to him. Thingy nodded and walked with him, one hand on Noel's shoulder for comfort. Jerry couldn't see Thingy, good job or he'd probably tell him to go and stay gone forever, and Noel didn't know what he'd do without Thingy. His shoulder felt cold where Thingy's hand rested, but the cold was a good cold, it took away the ouch where Jerry had landed the punch that knocked Noel to the floor. Then the belt had started landing on him again and it was Thingy rolled Noel to his belly so the slaps didn't get him on the face or the dingus.

"Get into the shower." Jerry pointed. Noel nodded, walked past the broken-down sofa where his mother was sitting, still sobbing. Jerry followed and turned on the taps, ran his fingers under the water, nodded and waited while Noel stepped out of his underpants and pulled his dirty teeshirt over his head. When Noel stepped under the water, Jerry left the bathroom.

The water was too hot but you didn't argue with Jerry. Noel stood under the outer rim of the spray, where it wasn't so hot, and he soaped as best he could—even his hair, because when Jerry wanted you clean, you better get yourself clean. He felt like crying, but that would only make Jerry mad, and you didn't want to get Jerry mad. His legs were shaking and he couldn't make them stop, his hands were trembling and he couldn't stop that either, he wanted to pee so he did, he could do that much, at least. He aimed for the drain, because even if it was his own pee he didn't want to stand in it. He knew his lips were trembling, his body shaking, and he knew something awful was going to happen, something awful always happened when Jerry made him get showered up like this.

And then Thingy turned the hot water tap and the too-hot was gone, the water cooled enough Noel could step right under the spray and get himself rinsed all off. Thingy put his bone-hand over Noel's eyes so none of the soap would go in and sting him, and the touch calmed the boy. His hands still trembled, his legs still shook, he still wanted to cry and cry and yell, but not as bad because at least he wasn't alone. Thingy was going to help him just as soon as he could find a way to do it, he had promised, and Thingy always kept his promises, because he was a friend. There were lots of things Thingy couldn't do, and lots of things he couldn't stop from happening, but Noel knew if Thingy could do it, he would. Thingy was a friend.

Then Jerry was there, turning off the taps, grabbing Noel by the arm and pulling him from the stall. He tossed a towel in Noel's face. "Hurry up," he said coldly, "we don't have all night."

"Yes, Jerry," Noel managed. "I'm hurrying."

Oh no, bad luck for you, kid, the clothes were there again. New shorts, new undershirt, nice clean white shirt with long sleeves, new socks, the shiny shoes, the clip-on tie, the gray pants, the blue blazer. And Jerry even combed Noel's hair and nodded. "C'mon, for Jesus' sake!" he yelled. She jumped off the sofa and hurried into the bathroom to wash her face, fix her hair and make herself at least halfways presentable.

Noel stood by the door, so scared he wanted to go to sleep. She came from the bathroom, even more scared than he was, and Jerry tossed her coat at her. Then he grabbed her little silly purse and stuffed it in the side pocket of his jacket. "C'mon, for chrissakes!" he yelled, "do I gotta do everything around here? Christ, you'll need someone to breathe in and out for you at the rate you're losin' it."

Noel hurried outside, not wanting Jerry to decide there was more than one person moving too slowly around here. He scuttled along the cement walkway that passed beside the big old house. The landlady was snooping again, some of the slats on the venetian blind were lifted. Noel made sure he didn't look up at her; if he did, Jerry might get mad all over again about how some people couldn't mind their own business and other people were all the time showing off for the snoops, calling attention to things other people had no business knowing.

Jerry opened the door of the fancy little car, did something with the passenger seat so it slid forward and the back folded down, making enough room for Noel to scurry into the back seat and sit right in the middle, stiff as a board. Jerry was really in an awful mood tonight. You'd better be good when he started to be like this, moving jerky and talking rapidly, you'd better be good, and good and careful, too, because if Jerry got mad when he was like this, it was just awful. Bad enough when he got mad, but when he was like this and then got mad, it was awful.

The cold hole in where his stomach was kept was starting to cramp up again. There was always a cold empty feeling there, a scared hollow feeling, but sometimes, like now, it got deeper and colder and then started to crunch, not quite like when you've got the trots, but close enough. Sometimes it got so bad all Noel could do was lie on his side, curled in a ball, with tears leaking from his eyes. If it got that bad now, with the good clothes and all that meant, Jerry would probably just beat him until he died.

Maybe died wouldn't be so bad. Maybe died would stop the hitting and being scared.

Thingy sat beside him, leaned back, crossed his stick-legs and winked. Noel tried to relax, but even with Thingy sitting with him he didn't feel safe.

She was talking, her voice thin and shaky. Jerry gave her a shove and told her to shut the fuck up, he was sick of the sound of it all. She looked sick. When she looked like this it meant she needed medicine, and only Jerry had the medicine, and as long as he was mad like this he wouldn't give it to her. Him being mad like this sometimes meant he was feeling a little sick too, but Jerry never got real sick, like she did, because Jerry always had lots of money for medicine, it was just sometimes he couldn't find the man he bought it from and then he got like this.

She was saying things like, But he's just a little boy, he doesn't even know what it's all about, and Noel wished she'd stop that. If she kept it up and Jerry got mad he'd blame it on Noel. But Jerry said he was going to give her a good one if she didn't shut up, and she must have believed him because she shut up fast.

Jerry drove to a motel. Noel could hardly breathe, but then Thingy patted him and the coolness of his touch was like magic.

Everything moved away and nothing much mattered—it was like watching TV, only better, because watching TV didn't make you feel all dreamy and safe. The cramps in his belly stopped, he could even breathe without feeling as if he had to use his breath to shove down a thing in his chest, a brick maybe. Thingy smiled again, and stroked Noel's face, just light and soft down the side, from above his ear, along his cheek, to the place on the side of his throat where sometimes he could feel his blood trying to force its way out of his skin.

He felt as good as he had the first time he saw Thingy. That had been in a hotel room. Such a nice place. The things that happened weren't nice, though. It wasn't the first time Jerry had made him get all dressed up, but Noel never got to keep the nice clothes, Jerry always took them away afterward, and only brought them back when it was time for them to go someplace like this. It got to where all Noel had to see was the bag with the clothes in and he knew what was going to happen. He was going to get hurt. Jerry told him he was nothing but a big sucky baby, and Jerry said it didn't hurt at all, it was just Noel being a chickenshit, but Noel was the one got hurt and Noel was the one who knew what hurt was. Hell, Jerry said, we've all had to do it, but Noel didn't think that was true at all. If Jerry'd had to be hurt he'd know it hurt and he wouldn't make someone else get hurt.

And he'd been getting hurt real bad, right up until it felt as if he was being hurt all the way to his bellybutton, and he was screaming and crying and the man just pushed him harder down on the mattress, with his legs sticking over the edge, and he hurt him and hurt him and hurt him and hurt him and suddenly Thingy was there and he was so scary-faced Noel would have screamed if he'd had anything left to scream with. And Thingy reached out and touched him between the shoulder blades. Like a piece of ice. Touch, and it felt as if Noel went all the way through the mattress to the floor below, and then it didn't matter at all because Noel was up near the ceiling, the same as flying, looking down at the man with no clothes and the little boy lying face-down on the mattress and the Thingy dancing and screeching soundlessly, whirling and spinning and Noel knew the Thingy was madder than Jerry could ever be. And the Thingy took a carved stick, it had a snake or something on it, and other things too, and he touched the humping man, touched him light, light, like a butterfly light, and the man just zoomed off the boy, off the bed, across the room, slam!

Slam! up against the wall, his back hammering into the gyproc, *Slam!* stiff as a board, and then he took two steps, stiffer than the sticks that made Thingy what he was, two stiff steps and *bop*, like a board, onto his face.

And Noel drifted down from the ceiling to the ice-cold boy and didn't know anything at all until Jerry was carrying him, running for the car, so scared he was almost sobbing, Jesus kid we're in for it now, Jesus kid how was I to know, god damn, who'd'a guessed, but Noel just went to sleep again and then he was home and in bed, and she was flipping out and Jerry was saying over and over, How'n hell was I to know he had a bad heart, and saying, If you don't stop your damn noise you'll be as dead as he is, you hear me?

Every time Jerry made him go to some place where the men gave money to Jerry and took Noel's clothes off, Thingy showed up, and every time he touched Noel's face the dream time happened. And the men no more than touched him and they were slumping, and no more of them died, and some of them seemed to think the slumping was what they'd paid for, but how could that be, and one time a guy only wanted to lie next to him and hold him and stroke him and talk soft to him, and Noel went to sleep and so did the guy. Thingy didn't whap *that* guy.

Jerry parked the car and got out, then tipped his seat so Noel could climb out, too. "You stay put," Jerry told her, and she just nodded, shaking and trying hard to please him. "Come on." Jerry grabbed Noel's hand and yanked. He held too tight, he always held too tight, squishing the hand and making the bones crunch against each other, but you didn't dare say so or he'd hit and that hurt even worse.

Thingy capered like a chocolate-bar wrapper caught in the wind, pointing at Jerry and then doing a thing like playing guns, pow pow, gonna get you yet, pow pow. Why didn't Thingy just hit Jerry with the carved stick and send him sailing? That'd be a good thing. Touch him with the stick and *slam* against the wall, face looking as if he would never ever believe what was happening, eyes fixed and round, seeing Thingy and somehow knowing. *Slam*, Jerry, *slam*. Gonna get you Jerry. *Slam!* The thing was, she'd find some other Jerry and he might be even worse than this one.

And couldn't hope Thingy would slam her. No. She was all he had.

3

Kitty sat on the dry ground under the bridge, rolled and lit a cigarette and smoked it staring at the oily water and the bright lights on the other side. So many lights were still on the city had a glow over it, like some reverse kind of halo, one put there not by holiness but by something else, stupidity maybe, or selfishness, ignorance perhaps, or basic assholiness. Entire office towers where surely nobody was working at this hour of the night, and all the lights burning. She could see the Hydro office, and grinned sourly—all that money spent on TV advertisements haranguing the public to save on electricity, be sure to turn the light out when you leave the room, and the place glowed from bottom to top as if the ones in charge thought it was up to them to burn up every kilowatt the huge dams produced.

She was hungry. She could probably get her butt in gear and walk to a fast-food—there was sure to be one close by, they were everywhere, estrogen-flooded chicken and steroid-soaked beef by the burger, the hunk and the chunk, and enough stray and random antibiotics left in the meat to either cure or give you anything from infected hangnail to ulcerated bowel. But the nightmare kept her where she was. In the nightmare it was dark and she was near a bridge and a bat-thing flew at her head. Well, it was dark, she was near a bridge and if she left to get something to eat she might miss whatever the bat was supposed to show her, or bring with it, or do, or whatever in hell it was all going to be.

A shadowy form scuttled from deeper under the abutment; she couldn't tell if it was male or female, but it was two-legged and human-shaped and nothing for her to fear because it was more scared of her than it had any reason to be.

She turned slightly and watched it panic away from her, down River Road. It moved as if it was fairly young, no more than thirtyish. Hard to tell the age or the shape, impossible to tell gender, the army overcoat obscured everything except the jean-clad legs from below the knee down to the ratty sneakers splashing through the mud. Couldn't even tell if it had hair or not, there was a wool hat or cap or toque on the head. Jesus Christ, it moved the way PatsyRatsy moved when she was upset. But it wasn't as healthy as PatsyRatsy had been, it wasn't fat and sleek and shiny and well coordinated. If there's some big cosmic plan, you'd think there'd be a place in it for everyone. What part of the plan needed people living under bridge abutments, kept barely alive by the scraps of other peoples' lives? Damned dogs probably ate better.

Well, hardly any doubt about that. Some of the finest bloodlines in the world wound up in dogfood cans. There was this ad in the paper and she'd been in bad need of a job, so she'd answered it and wound up with a nice enough little apartment in part of the haybarn, everything you'd want, little gas stove, little gas fridge, made by the same good folks as had supplied gas fixtures to the extermination camps, so you could be sure the design had been tested thoroughly. All the comforts of home plus a little bit of change every month, not much until you remembered what it cost to rent shelter. Every morning she put on her work clothes and went down to start working with the horses, hours and hours and hours of it, and sometimes it just blew her mind to look at the registration papers. Names like you'd only read about before, Man o'War, Northern Dancer, Native Dancer, Secretariat and their granddaughters and grandsons walking on the end of a rope, doing what she asked of them. One young gelding in particular, although why anyone could claim to have a working brain after making the decision to geld a colt whose great-great-grandfather was Man o'War was a question she didn't ask. Manny, she called him. Totally typey, classic head, and a disposition so kind and so affectionate you could have let a little kid lead him around and not have worried the kid would get hurt.

Except not every horse wins the race. And if they didn't do well enough, that was pretty well it, especially for the geldings. The mares might luck out and be used to breed yet another generation of spindly-legged babies who would go to auction and be sold to the ones who thought they were experts. But the geldings for the most part went to the slaughterhouse, and the great-great-grandson of Man o'War wound up supper for cairn terriers and mini-schnauzers.

If she'd known ahead of time she'd have phoned home for a loan and bought him herself. God knows he'd have been cheap enough, they were only getting about fifty cents a pound for them. Twelve to fourteen hundred pounds of bloodline, then figure another, oh, hundred, hundred and fifty to get him shipped home. Tie a big blue ribbon in his mane with a card wishing Aunt Lucy a happy birthday.

But she hadn't known ahead of time. Didn't know until the stall was empty.

She didn't like the way they trained race horses, anyway. Young horses are afraid of small spaces, and the starting gates are small. So they put clips on their ears, almost exactly the same as the ones on jumper cables, and then they just *hauled* them into the gate. Nobody seemed to care that the pain probably convinced the leggy yearling she'd been right to try to get away from that strange metal riggins. Then, to get her to come out of that place at top speed, they had a setup so when the gate in front of her opened, the one behind her zapped her ass with a hurting jolt of electricity.

Off she went and they all grinned, lookit'er go, she's a good one. Except of course the next morning, when she saw the starting gate, she was ten times as terrified as she had been the first time. Same thing, clips on her ears, zap in the ass, over and over and over until she knew in her heart there was no use fighting. If the ear clips didn't work there was the dealy-bob they clipped into her nostrils and used to twist her lip, she had to go with it or get even more hurt. She went into the starting gate expecting to be hurt, and they encouraged her fear so she got the idea if she could get out past the front gate fast enough she'd get away from whatever was biting her ass, lookit'er go, we got us a real contender this time, they said, got the heart of a champion, they said, blood will tell, they said, and all it was in the final analysis was terror. But at least her ovaries could extend her life, she might last, oh hell, all of fifteen years. Longer if her babies won money. Blood will tell.

Got to where she couldn't stand it. And the morning she went down to start working with the dark bay gelding and found his stall empty, she knew he'd had it and so had she. She'd argued with the trainer, she'd said he wasn't a sprinter, give him a break, sell him to someone willing to train him as a jumper or a sport horse, hell, there's more to a horse than racing, give him a chance to show what he can do. But no, none of that, Dr. Ballard was paying fifty cents a pound and the stall was empty. She went out back and there they were, eleven of them, already dead. Eleven of them being lifted into the back of a big truck by a front end loader. Eleven registered thoroughbred geldings who were fractions of a second away from a winning time.

She was gone before lunchtime. Gone with her stuff in a backpack, and so angry she couldn't see straight. Hopped into the pickup truck and headed for the slaughterhouse to give the guy a piece of her mind.

Got there about the same time as the stock truck, got there in time to recognize what she was looking at when the pacer was brought out of the truck and turned loose in the corral. Oh Jesus, there are things a person just cannot let happen. She wanted to go up like a hot air balloon, but she knew if she did the driver would be so pissed off at her he'd kill the pacer himself just to teach Kitty a lesson. So she bit it all back, after all, it wasn't his decision, he wasn't in on any of the decisions, he just drove the friggin' truck was all. She rolled a cigarette and handed the makings to the driver. Half an hour later the pacer was back in the stock truck, the driver had two hundred bucks in his jeans pocket and Kit was hurrying back to the slaughterhouse with a borrowed horse trailer attached to the pickup. She was tempted to call the pacer "Patsy" after Seely's bloody rat, but resisted. Because it was no joke. She'd managed to keep one distinguished bloodline from the petfood can, she'd managed to save one pacing mare, but there was nothing she could do for the others. Fifty to a hundred every day at every slaughterhouse, more when they rounded up the wild ones and brought them in. Brought them in with broken legs because wild horses don't know you can't break out of a stock truck, brought them in with broken pelvises because they slipped in the shit on the floor, fell with their front legs spread and another terrified herdmate fell on top of them.

Up in the northern interior the cattle ranchers wanted the Crown rangeland for themselves. The politicians either didn't know or didn't care about anything except votes. And up on that rangeland, since about the time the ice began to retreat, there'd been a herd of horses. Others of the same kind in other countries had been declared national treasures. Others of the same rare sort had been given protected status. But the last prehistoric horses in this country weren't given much chance; the government signed permission for the ranchers to hunt them down, shoot them, do with their thirty-ought-six what centuries of nature hadn't done.

Food for dachshunds, beagles, boxers, and Maltese terriers. But she got at least one pacing mare out of it. Took her home and turned her into the pasture at Lucy's place. Lucy took one look and grinned, then looked over to where the big buckskin stud was already trumpeting his invitation. Well, why not? A pregnant mare could prance and show off her paces at the head of the parade just as well as any other.

She looked back, under the abutment. The slope rose, bare dirt, up to where the decking of the bridge passed like a ceiling. No grass grew here, no bushes, but there was surprisingly little in the way of garbage or trash. Just sleeping bags and bundles of cloth supposed to serve as blankets. She tried to count, then gave up; it was too dark, the forms too shapeless, some of them bunched together as if couples or even, god forbid, families lived here, protected, at least, from the endless winter rain. Maybe a dozen, maybe twenty places where poor souls huddled. Probably the most the police ever did was show up and hassle them, throw their few miserable possessions into the shit-choked river, leave them more bereft than ever, then head off, without making a move to improve the situation for anyone.

Jesus, where does all the fucking tax money go, and for what purpose? Turn on a TV and they're flying here, flying there, flying somewhere else—and you know they fly first class, with champagne and probably glorified fish eggs on something only a low-rent workie would call a cracker.

She'd helped Aunt Lucy and Debbie with the receipts and the cash-in cash-out books often enough to know there wasn't a thing you could buy, sell, produce, have or hide that you didn't pay tax on, and she'd paid enough of her own prize money in taxes to know she was breaking her bones to profit the federals. Someone had told her the average person worked seven months of the year to pay federal tax, two months to pay other taxes, and had a whole three months of the year for their own pocket. Whoopy-ding, joy supreme, then we take gas cans out to burn what we call "surplus" food while people live under bridges and eat out of garbage cans and other people pretend god's in his heaven, all's right with the world.

Should have brought more sandwiches with her. But she'd been afraid she was fudging on the rules as it was. She figured she had probably forty dollars in her jeans. The JimmySpook had said go with nothing—well, you could easily argue the fifty she'd left with was as good as nothing. What was it the old song said, a dollar isn't worth a dime today? Not worth a plugged nickel. Not worth a red cent. Something like that. Fifty dollars was about five times the square root of sweet fuck-all, all things considered. She'd bought week-old foals for fifty cents, though. Gave the stock-truck driver the address of Lucy and Debbie's farm, the good old L/D, got so's he knew when it would be worth his while to detour past. Got four up-country wild ones that way. God damn but it's crazy, people will drive three hundred miles to the damned zoo to see a real live specimen of a kind of horse once thought to be made extinct by the ice age, and do nothing at all while an entire herd of probably prehistoric horses is systematically wiped out in the north central interior of B.C. Oh, they'll say, what a shame, they didn't tell us until it was all done, and another genetic pool is gone. Except for the lucky and crafty ones who moved even deeper into ever-rougher country and the four captives the driver didn't want to see turned into poodleburgers. Big-headed, wheat-colored, barrel-bodied, placid fillies with strong dorsal stripes and tiger markings on their legs, they had been too young to keep up when the survivors of the herd had raced from the high-powered rifles and the portable corrals placed where none had been before; they tried to keep up, but ran out of strength and luck. When their mothers tried to defend them, the rifles spat. After that it was just a matter of some ropes and the terrified babies were dragged to the waiting stock truck. Foals raised on goat's milk have a good chance of survival, if you luck out and have on hand an older "auntie" mare who'll accept them and give them love and attention. She wondered if the kids raised under the bridge even knew what an auntie was. Debbie, who didn't even particularly care for horses, had fallen head over heels for the orphans and immediately named them Faith, Hope, Grace and Patience.

She'd started out with fifty dollars. Next best thing to nothing. And she'd spent some of it. Lucky if it was forty. Probably more like thirty-five. Was this why you weren't supposed to bring anything with you? Was this why you were supposed to walk into whatever it was naked and defenseless? Were you almost guaranteed to get yourself distracted and sidetracked by dithering over how much you had left in your pocket? Surely to fuck, if you really wanted to know, you'd haul'er out and count!

Defenseless and naked. Well, defenseless was open to interpretation. Most of her life Kitty had known how to fight. And known, without anyone ever having taught her, that she might not win the fight, there was a good chance she wouldn't win, but whoever the mad bastard was who got into it with her would go away knowing there'd been a real doozy. If she could do nothing else, she'd make noise. Someone might wind up doing whatever it was they'd had in mind, but they'd sure know she hadn't gone along with it. Naked. You could have on more clothes than the Sears catalogue advertised and still feel as naked as a newborn baby, with all your life spread out for others to pick over, judge, find lacking and scorn you for it. There weren't enough clothes in the whole wide world to protect you from the stares and glares of those who considered themselves better than you.

She rolled another cigarette, lit it, broke the paper match into two pieces and pushed them into the bare dirt. Bring this city to a quick halt if you rolled a couple of plastic bags of nitrogen fertilizer and some diesel up there where the decking almost met the hillside. Look maw, the BMWs and Corvettes, the Buicks and Caddies, are all learning how to fly! Maybe she'd tell Jimmy about it. He had the hand-eye co-ordination. Well, Seely had it too, probably could have been just as famous, just as rich, just as respected as Jimboh if she'd ever got past her cakes and icings. Be a real something to hang on your wall. Make the tall buildings of the city look as if they're leaning away from it all, pulling up their tattered skirts, recoiling from the narsties.

That's what Gran had called them, the narsties. The narsties of civilization, which were, after all, epitomized by themselves. Maybe make the windows extra wide so they'd be like googly eyes. Or extra long, whichever worked best, sometimes you had to do one to see. And the bridges could be like the strands of a spiderweb. And coming off them, like sowbugs fleeing when you turned over a bit of punky wood, all the shiny cars. Leaping into absolutely zip-all, at that moment just before gravity caught them and yarded them down out of what looked like it might be freedom but was going to wind up as the toxic river and all that smothering gooball mud. Do it right and it would take a second look for people to realize the bridges were exploding. Jimmy'd know how to do that. False perspective or whatever it was he called it. Ker-thunderin'-pow!

What was the thing with fire, anyway? What was it about fire that drew the thoughts and imaginings of troubled people? How many trash fires, how many blazes in Smithrites, how many brush piles in vacant lots had gone up in sparks and everyone in town convinced it was Glen, and all the time it was Seely creeping around with little cubes of solidified napalm, the kind you bought anywhere, supposedly for starting your charcoal on the barbecue when you had the folks over on Sunday. The cops had even put a twenty-four-hour stakeout on Glen. How much had *that* cost? Two guys per shift, three shifts per day for how long? Even so it took four or five more cars going up in flames in driveways or carports before they reluctantly admitted it couldn't possibly have been him, it's against all known scientific principles for a person to be in two places at one time, especially time and time again.

And then bang, bang, bang, dead, dead, dead, and the fires stopped. And what was *that*? And what did it mean? Had Seel decided just being alive was great? Not likely. Probably decided there was no use fighting back or protesting. Sometimes it seemed as if the supply of spunk, or something, in them had diminished one by one. Nobody, by God, was going to shove Savannah around, just dare to try and see what it got you, and Jimboh, well, only the ones without brains were going to get snarky with him. But by the time you got past Kit and Glen to Seel, whatever it was that started pumping the old fight-not-flight adrenaline had slowed. Sometimes it seemed as if Seely was a bit...what? Not retarded, because she had all her marbles.

They just didn't seem to roll right when you tried to shoot them. Maybe Mom took one drink too many, maybe she didn't drink any more than usual but she just wasn't eating properly one day. Or one week! It was almost as if Seely saw what other people saw but didn't know how to sort it out, as if she heard what other people heard but had no place to put it; you could explain something to her and she'd look blank, she understood every damned word one by one but put together it made no sense. Maybe she was just scared stiff, scared so much entire parts of her were paralyzed.

Naked and defenseless. Well, some were. Some weren't. A few just refused to be. With or without fifty dollars in their pocket, or thirty-five, or twenty for that matter.

Crazy? Of course. Who wasn't? Anyone who claimed to be sane in a world as mad as this one probably needed to be lugged off to a rubber room.

Or as the Old Biddy had put it, "Anyone who wastes time and money going to a psychiatrist needs their damned head examined."

4

Jerry drove back to the motel and parked in the shadows beside the unit where he'd delivered the brat. She sat quietly in the passenger seat, her eyes dreamy, a small smile on her lips. He was sick and tired of the sight of her. It was all turning into more bother than it was worth. She wasn't bringing in half what she used to, and the amount of bullshit, pony puckies and heifer dust she caused was double what it used to be. Maybe he'd just fix her up with some near-pure and let her white-light it out of his fuckin' life. He could take the kid, someone would babysit, make some good money with him if he didn't have to put up with her whining and nagging and sniveling about it.

Make ya fuckin' sick is what it would do. Oh he's just a little boy, hunga hunga hunga weep weep weep. The world was swarming with them, for God's sake. People shooting at them, dropping bombs on them, spraying them with chemicals of some kind or other, what did he have to complain about, he ate, he had a roof over him. What was the use of having his kind of looks if you didn't make something from it? And of *course* you have to make it when they're young, the career life expectancy, as they say, is abbreviated. Oh sure, there were some who liked the knobby-kneed early-teen types, but the real money was in the near-rugrats. Jerry himself knew about it from first-hand experience. Brains are one thing, but without the money for education brains can be a pain in the ass, just make you discontent with everything. Even with education, brains aren't all that much. You can buy all the fuckin' brains you want for a few bucks an hour. Looks. You make more per hour with looks than you're gonna make with brains. So if your looks get outgrown and you start to sprout whiskers or something, you'd best develop a few of the other, someone with looks needs someone with a clue or two to handle the damn details so the looks can make the bucks while the looks are still the kind the bumwhackers will pay big to have. Law of supply and demand. I'll supply what you demand, and fuck the law.

God, it felt good. You never miss the water till the old pump looks like it's gonna start suckin' dust. For a while there it looked as if it was going to be panic city. Well, Jerry didn't have a habit, not him, no big hook goin' in through *his* belly button, but the bitch, well, if she was even five minutes late she got ridiculous. Just down and out ridiculous. And where had the bastard *been?* On the friggin' nod, if you please. On the friggin' nod, no less. Well, it was all water under the old bridge, the deal was done, the commerce successfully completed, and by God it felt good. Shine up the old glow and drape it over the world at large.

Something caught his eye and he stiffened. Too many cars for this time of night. Too many cars parked not in front of the motel, but on the street. Another one drove by slowly, then pulled to the curb and turned out the lights. The driver didn't get out. That was bad news. It was, in fact, very bad news.

There now, see, if ever anyone needed proof that a person had to stay tip-top alert while working, here was the proof. If he was as dippy as the bitch, he'd have indulged his damn self and been as dreamy as she was. But he knew better. He'd learned better. Hell, he hadn't learned better, he'd always *known* better! Just enough to sharpen the old edge. Just enough to put things in proper perspective. Just enough to notice that the street was filling up with parked cars, as if this was some residential area where every house had two or three or four of the buggers. But it wasn't residential, and there shouldn't be that many cars, no place for the drivers to be, christ, it was a route march from here to any place a person would want to go at this hour. They were in the cars. And who ever expected so many damned *vans* parked alongside the road? Oh no, mister cat, you don't fool this craphouse rat.

He wasn't afraid to open his door. He'd fixed the light the first day he had it, one little snip and we don't ever worry about that problem again, or about the seatbelt sound, either. He stepped out and very gently closed the car door. Even the bitch-on-the-nod wouldn't know he was moving.

Probably the goddamn desk clerk. Probably saw him delivering the kid. Damned snoops. World full of snoops. The desk clerk or maybe the damn pump jockey over at the gas station. Now *there* was a bunch if ever there was one. Gas jockeys probably make a fortune dialing TIPS. Guaranteed anonymity, they say. How do you collect your reward anonymously? Do they give you a number? Pay to the order of number umptydump the sum of whatever pittance it was they paid the squealers?

He wished he could get into the unit without being seen, but there was no way around that one. Nothing but blank wall at the back, only one door in and it was in front, with a lightbulb shining over it. Maybe they'd think he belonged there. Maybe they'd think he'd been out here for a smoke, or giving someone else some privacy time, or why did he give a shit what they thought, he'd already been paid and he was getting that damn flapjawed kid out of there because otherwise names were going to get said and who needed the heat? Little bugger could probably even give them street directions. And he would, oh, you could bet he would. Kid hated him. Jerry knew that. The kid hated him so much you'd almost believe the slopes were right about past lives, because the kid hated him back probably to the time of the friggin' pharaohs. Well well, we'll see, little boy. Maybe this is going to be the very last time Uncle Jerry bothers with you. Maybe this is going to be the very last time anybody bothers with you, except maybe the undertaker.

He was shocked the fool hadn't locked the door. Some people just bloody well deserve to get caught! He moved quickly, crossing the few steps to the bed, shrugging off his jacket, grabbing the half-limp kid, Jesus, more rough trade, what's a person supposed to do when they leave the kid in this kind of shape? The skinner looked as if he was paralyzed, be just the kind of luck that had no end if this one was popping coronary arteries too. And hadn't *that* been a kick in the throat? Christ. Ought to be a damned law, nobody about to cop a heart attack is allowed to get a stiffer. But if you have to go that might be as good a way as there is, halfway between Christmas and New Year's when *pop* and it's finished.

He wrapped his jacket around the naked child and hurried back out of the motel. A car door opened across the street; some bozo stepped out, peering at them. Jerry opened his own car door, tossed Noel onto his mother's lap, then rammed his key in the ignition and backed out of the parking space, knowing the cars across the road were exactly what he'd thought they were and those were cops running his way, some of them already reaching under their jackets.

Well, he wasn't going to halt just because they yelled for him to. He floored the gas pedal and to hell with it, there was nothing else mattered except getting away, if he had to open the goddamn car door and shove'em both out into the traffic, he'd do it. That'd sure slow down the ones coming behind him!

Great. Just great. Now they had the sirens going and the lights flashing. They'd be yammering on the radio, bringing other cars to try to cut him off. Well, we'll just see what we'll see, if he could get across the bridge to the damn freeway he'd be fine, get lost in a string of headlights, then off at a bottleneck, near Burnette maybe, get into a maze of streets, sidestreets, alleys and driveways, turn off the lights, do a yewey and be headin' back, speed limit respectable, before the boys in blue had it even halfways figured out.

The expensive sportscar was a hair'sbreadth away from destruction at least five times before it spun to the right and headed onto the bridge.

Kitty heard sirens and stood up, looking across the river. There must have been cops coming from every street, lights flashing. Red lights, mostly, but blue ones too, and she could even hear brakes screeching. She was so cold she felt as if she'd never stop shivering. If only the JimmySpook would show up and give her some kind of sign of what she was supposed to be doing.

She came out from under the bridge and started up the slippery footpath. Maybe she'd get to see what all the sirens, lights and hulla-baloo was about, and when she'd seen that, well, piss on it, she was half frozen and had been sitting waiting long enough, she'd just take herself to a fast-food and get something to eat.

All Noel wanted to do was sleep, but she was screaming and yelling, and Jerry was hollering. It was cold in the car and Noel pulled Jerry's jacket tighter, slipped his arms into the sleeves. The car was rocking

and buffeting, other cars were blowing their horns, and then Thingy
was pitching a fit, swinging his whistle, tap tap tap bap bap bap, and
Jerry was as stiff as a board, his eyes wide. That'll show you, old poop,
you're the one said I was 'mag'nin' things, you're the one said Thingy
wasn't real, and you've seen him now, you've *seen* him! Oh, boy, have
you ever seen him!

And Thingy was outside the car, how could he do that, how could
he ride outside like that? Waving his hands, come to me, come to me,
come. Noel hit the door handle.

The sportscar hit an oncoming car side to side, careered off,
slammed the side of the bridge and went into a spin. Noel went out
the door, screaming with terror, Thingy nodding, nodding as if everything was okay, but it wasn't the least bit okay, because Noel was
falling, over the side of the bridge and down, down, down.

There was no time to think, no more than there had been when
she'd leaped out of bed and headed for the window. The bat was coming at her, coming out of the noise of rending metal, coming over the
guardrail of the bridge, slamming down toward the steep slope not
two feet behind her, and she knew, knew right up her spine, the bat
would hit, would bounce, would roll and fall into the ghastly goo of
the riverbank.

She wanted to duck, she wanted to jump out of the way, she
wanted anything but what was happening. She whirled, leaped up and
back, and the bat was all over her, wings flapping and Gran yelling
hang on hang on hang on so she did, she hung on, so scared she almost
pulled a Seely and peed herself, and then her feet were on the slippery
path and she was sliding, it was like coming off the back of a speeding
horse and heading for the calf at the end of the taut line, her roper's
boots skidding but not out of control, the heels not breaking off like
rider's heels would, the smooth leather soles giving just enough trac-
tion to help her keep her balance, and then her arm reached out and
grabbed that goddamn bush and she had the bat tight against her
body, pinned with one arm, held solid with one hand, the bush with
the other, and her feet were digging in while the old woman screeched
and screeched *hangonhangonhangon* and every JimmySpook in the
world was dancing, leaping, bouncing, mouth open, screeching soundlessly. Fright-masks she'd seen come out of a block of wood under
Jimmy's chisel, masks from the museum, masks from here, from there,

from everywhere, skeleton bodies, stick bodies, some with no bodies, some identifiably male, some undoubtedly female, black spooks, white spooks, every-shade-of-brown-in-between spooks, celebrating, darting in and among the growing crowd on the bridge, jumping on the roofs of police cars, clambering over the firetruck, swarming up and down the bridge and the JimmySpook leading the mad pack.

It wasn't a bat. Those weren't bat wings had flapped, they were the overlong sleeves of an adult jacket, and what was clutched to her, shaking with cold and terror, eyes rolled back so the whites showed, mouth almost purple with panic, was a kid no more than five, a kid who in no way looked like either of the dead rugrats and yet was so totally the two of them that she knew second chances were being handed out all over the damned place, but not necessarily to her. It still wasn't as if she'd made any real decision about anything. All she'd done was what she'd done, and there was no use wishing that just one of the JimmySpooks would, even for a second, change shape and be recognizably Gran.

Or even, god forbid, Aunt Phyllis. Or Mom. No matter how old we think we are, we always want our mother. Our mother which art in heaven, small chance of that, all things considered.

Well, okay. Good enough. Caught him and hung on, and he wasn't a cinder in whatever in hell was burning up there, nor was he under the oily glup where the River Road ended and the septic mess began.

She pulled the jacket around his bruised body, set him on her hip and started up the slippery pathway. The traffic was choked solid for blocks, cars every which way on the approaches, both directions blocked. A crumpled heap was blazing furiously, squeezed between a large truck and the solid cement guardrail. The driver of the truck was trying to talk to some police, but suddenly he turned away, gagging and choking, losing it all in the face of such ugliness.

"Easy on, Bubba." She stroked the fright-stiff back of the child clinging to her. "Easy on, it's all over now," but she knew it wasn't even half over, wouldn't be over until she herself made a decision about how things would happen from here on in. You can only play it by ear for so long, and then it's head-outta-the-ass time.

There was a whole bunch of stuff she could make happen. She could make sure some authority type knew the kid had been in the burned-out car and been thrown clear. That would set something in motion; foster homes, probably. Or she could decide control was best left in the hands of the JimmySpooks. They might take one goddamn weird and convoluted way to get things how they wanted them, but they probably had their reasons. She shifted the kid's weight and tightened her arm around him. She'd find out what the JimmySpook wanted. If he wanted this kid turned over to the guys in uniform, that's what would happen. If he didn't, it wouldn't happen unless she made it happen, and she knew she wasn't ever again going out of her way to contradict the Squeyanx. Was there a damned decision in any of that? Probably no more than in heading for the window and mindlessly scooping Vic. The Old Biddy had grabbed her by the shoulders and shaken her, once, then squeezed her hard and tight. "Och, Kitty, m'bairn, don't be sae damned *hard* on yourself, you *did* it."

The kid sat on Kitty's hip, his legs locked around her body, his arms clutching tight around her neck. The jacket covered him from the neck down; it kept the winter rain from soaking him, and it ought to have kept him warm, but he was shivering so hard she wondered if the gristle in his joints would come loose and he'd collapse like a little bag of sticks. Maybe he wasn't a boy at all, maybe he was a stick-kid, a mini-version of the JimmySpook. Maybe the slam that broke her nose had addled her wits too. The whole thing might be nothing more than a concussion. Or a fractured skull, who knows? Toto, I don't think we are anywhere *near* fuckin' Kansas!

She moved toward a cop who stood in an ankle-length slicker, waving traffic past with the help of a flashlight. The slicker was glittery with rain, bright with the reflection of the headlights. She saw pale faces like balloons staring from car windows, the mouths round Os, the eyes wide, eating up the sight of the burning gasoline, the flaming, melting plastic.

The cop turned his head, barely glanced at her. "Move along, lady," he said, sounding bored.

"Officer...," she started.

"Come on, lady, gimme a break here, will you?" His boredom was replaced with impatience.

"This little guy...."

"Lady! This is no place for a kid! Come on, please, don't push me on this. Get him away from here, please."